JEFF GLARED AT CHUCKIE AS HE WALKED IN.

"Why are you still here?"

"Because we have a problem," Chuckie said. He wasn't looking at Jeff or me, and he was still pacing.

Jeff somehow reined in the jealousy all on his own. Either he wanted to impress me, or Chuckie's stress levels were particularly high. I figured on the latter. He shot a worried glance at Chuckie, then looked at me. "With the C.I.A.?"

"In a way. More with what you were doing in Paris."

Jeff nodded. "Whatever we were fighting, they weren't superbeings."

I felt all proud. "See, Chuckie? Someone other than us was monitoring the weird."

Chuckie heaved a sigh. "And that makes it better how?"

"Pardon me, Mister Glass Half Empty."

"It doesn't," Jeff agreed. "We have nothing left to study."

"You weren't able to contain them any other way?" Chuckie asked.

"No. We weren't the ones who destroyed them."

"This delightful romp has many interesting twists and turns as it glances at racism, politics, and religion en route. It will have fanciers of cinematic sf parodies referencing *Men in Black*, *Ghost Busters*, and *X-Men*."

—*Booklist* (starred review)

DAW Books Presents GINI KOCH's
Alien Novels:

TOUCHED BY AN ALIEN

ALIEN TANGO

ALIEN IN THE FAMILY

ALIEN PROLIFERATION

ALIEN DIPLOMACY
(*coming in April 2012*)

ALIEN PROLIFERATION

GINI KOCH

DAW BOOKS, INC.
DONALD A. WOLLHEIM, FOUNDER
375 Hudson Street, New York, NY 10014
ELIZABETH R. WOLLHEIM
SHEILA E. GILBERT
PUBLISHERS
http://www.dawbooks.com

Cover art by Daniel Dos Santos.

DAW Book Collectors No. 1569.

DAW Books are distributed by Penguin Group (USA) Inc.

First Printing, December 2011
3 4 5 6 7 8 9

DAW TRADEMARK REGISTERED
U.S. PAT. AND TM. OFF. AND FOREIGN COUNTRIES
—MARCA REGISTRADA
HECHO EN U.S.A.

PRINTED IN THE U.S.A.

To Veronica, Michelle, Zachary, Hunter and Preston
—for being here.

ACKNOWLEDGMENTS

I'm running out of creative ways to thank Sheila Gilbert and Cherry Weiner, my editor and agent, or Lisa Dovichi and Mary Fiore, my crit partner and main beta reader. So this time around, the simple "you're the best in the world" will have to suffice.

Thanks again to everyone I thanked the last times, anyone I might have missed at any time, and everyone else added onto my own Alpha Team along the way, for all you do and keep on doing—you know who you are and why I love and appreciate you.

Love and thanks again and always to Team Gini, all those on Hook Me Up!, and all Alien Collective Members in Very Good Standing around the globe—you remain the best fans in the world and each and every one of you continue to totally rock my world. Extra love again and always to the legion of book review bloggers who continue to support books in general and my books in particular. *Smootchies* to all my Twitter peeps and Facebook folks, just 'cause.

Extra shout outs to: Nicole Snyder for being my consistent entourage and cheering section at what seems like every con; Terese Simpson for always being ready to meet me at Brent's (and stay for hours) whenever I'm in L.A.; Adrian and Lisa Payne for always showing up at my signings, with smiling faces and books in hand; everyone who came out to see me when I was in NYC, both at Posman Books (waves madly to Stacey Agdern) and other less exciting locations, particularly those who came from far, far away and through all kinds of wet and windy weather (love you ALL), just to see me; authors Marsheila Rockwell, Seanan McGuire, Amber Scott, Erin Kellison, and Erin Quinn for writing awesome books I love as well as making me laugh and feel like a much bigger author than I probably am every time I talk to or see them; everyone at DAW

Books, but most especially Joshua Starr, Marsha Jones, and Debra Euler who manage to handle every frantic email or call from me with aplomb, speed, and efficiency; and my Sanity Buddies—Helen King, Colette Vernon, Linda Artac, Tina Barker, and Dixie McMullan—the gals who drag me off and out of the house for the occasional reminder that there's life away from my computer.

Last, but in no way least, the biggest thanks and all my love to the two people who make this all worthwhile, my husband, Steve, and daughter, Veronica. I continue to be the luckiest wife, mother, and author because you're in my life.

YOU'D THINK AFTER FIGHTING parasitic jellyfish things from space that turn humans into fugly monsters, fending off some killer alligators while dodging mystery explosives, and warding off an alien invasion, I'd be able to handle anything, right?

Right!

Um, well, let's define "handle."

From what I've read and every single freaking person on the planet I've talked to has told me, pregnancy is a wonderful time in a woman's life. None of them mentioned the nausea, hypersensitivity, headaches, blurry vision, or exhaustion. Nope, it's all ducks and bunnies and blue bears and purple dinosaurs.

Of course, the few people whose information actually counts don't quite agree. There are only a few of them, because there are only a few of us, so far—those who've gone where no other women have gone before—interspecies procreation. What can I say? I like to be cutting edge.

When you're married to an alien from Alpha Four of the Alpha Centauri system, there are benefits. Jeff's smart, funny, and drop dead gorgeous. He also has two hearts, which gives him hyperspeed, superhuman strength, and amazing regenerative powers that are particularly pleasant in the bedroom. He's also the strongest empath on Earth and, most likely, the galaxy. Which means I never have to whine for the tummy and foot rubs, and he knows my odd food cravings before I do.

The downside is that human-alien hybrid babies have human genetics dominant for the outside and A-C genetics dominant for the inside. You try being kicked by a hyper-speeding supermule for five months straight and then tell me it's the most wonderful time of the year.

But no worries! Plenty of women continue in their careers while they're preggers. Oh, sure, I'm dealing with end of the world as we know it stuff, but hey, I take on megalomaniacs and psychopaths for breakfast! Got an entire extended team who're all at the top of their respective games. What could they possibly throw at us that we haven't seen before?

I mean, you know, besides what we haven't seen before? Something tells me I should be worried about this, but pressing duty calls—it's time for my nap.

CHAPTER 1

THE DAY STARTED OUT like all the days had in recent memory—I was confined to my bed while everyone else got to do fun things like fly jets, kill the random parasitic superbeing that might have passed up the Alpha Centaurion system for a vacation out Earth's way, or just walk around. Interspecies pregnancy, it was a joy.

Jeff came out of our walk-in closet like always, in his perfectly fitted black Armani suit and white shirt, tightening his tie. This meant nothing, other than he was dressed and ready for action. A-Cs love their Armani and formality.

He hypersped our breakfast trays to the living room area of our living quarters—what I called his Human Lair—zoomed back, leaned down, gave me a kiss, and rubbed my tummy. "How're you feeling, baby?"

"Bored, frustrated, tired, and, oh, did I mention bored?"

I got the standard "good husband chuckle" that I'd gotten really used to these past couple of months. "It won't be for too much longer."

The com came to life. "Commander Martini, situation in Paris. Euro Base is requesting you and Commander White, and I quote, immediately if not sooner."

Jeff went from relaxed to all business immediately. "Got it, Gladys. I'll meet Commander White at the launch area." He gave me the hairy eyeball. "And you'll be staying in bed."

"Commander Martini, reminder that you have a meeting scheduled in less than an hour," Gladys shared.

"Cancel it," Jeff snapped.

"Sorry, Commander Martini, I assumed you were already at the launch site, since Euro Base has an emergency." Gladys could get a lot of sarcasm into what, in other mouths, would be mere statements of fact. "I'm talking to Commander Mother-to-Be Martini."

"Huh? Oh, me." Right. Married name. You'd think I'd be used to it. Still wasn't, almost nine months in. Barely used to thinking of Jeff as Jeff versus Martini, let alone thinking of myself as Kitty Martini versus Kitty Katt. And Gladys knew it, which was why I knew she enjoyed moments like this. "What are we talking about?"

"You have a meeting." I couldn't see her, but I felt sure Gladys was rolling her eyes.

"I do? Oh! Right, I do."

I got a hairier eyeball from Jeff. "Just whom do you have a meeting with?"

"The C.I.A. Discussing what we're going to do while I'm out for maternity leave."

Jeff growled. "You mean Reynolds is going to be here, in our bedroom, with you, while I'm in Paris?" Jeff had disliked Charles Reynolds even before he'd found out that we'd known each other since ninth grade.

"No. I mean my oldest friend, one of my two best guy friends, and someone I've known since I was thirteen is going to be here, discussing work." The growling continued. I heaved a sigh. "The jealousy chat. It's been working so well with everyone else. Why do you persist in the Chuckie-jealousy?"

"Because I'm an empath, and I can feel exactly how he feels about you."

"I'm sure he's past it."

"I'm sure he's not."

"Jeff, really, the jealousy is so hard to take right now."

"It's not jealousy. It's fact. He's still waiting. Patiently." The way he said it, I realized he wasn't kidding.

"Well, I don't know why. I'm in love with you and have been pretty much since we met."

"He's not waiting for you to get tired of me. He's waiting for me to make another mistake, where it makes more sense for you to leave me and go to him." His expression made it clear he was reliving old guilt.

"Jeff, you were drugged out of your mind by our enemies. It was well over a year ago. And I was heartbroken, and all I wanted was to have it all have been a bad dream and you still love me. Which is what happened. Now, I'd love to continue to have this fight, again, but apparently Paris is calling you. I, on the other hand, get to have a video conference with people at the C.I.A. because, and this time I quote, your husband isn't being at all cooperative."

Jeff ran his hand through his hair. "They want things we can't and shouldn't give them."

"No argument. Chuckie agrees with you. He's trying to keep us from becoming the War Division. Isn't it nice that the head of the C.I.A.'s Extraterrestrial Division is on our side?"

"He's on *your* side, I'll give you that." Great, we were going to have the Chuckie Argument anyway. "He's always ready to take care of you, isn't he?"

"It wasn't my idea to faint at C.I.A. headquarters." In the middle of a really high-level discussion about Centaurion Division's future, where I was representing Centaurion's interests. Right into Chuckie's arms, as it turned out. And right in front of the people I was supposed to be meeting with today. The fun never stopped.

"Yeah. Reynolds was all over the save on that one."

"Chuckie caught me just in time, Jeff, and you know it. I'd have cracked my head open if he hadn't been there."

"There's nothing like seeing the man you know still wants to take your wife away from you carrying her unconscious body in his arms to really make you feel good."

Chuckie had proposed when Jeff and I were in the middle of a bizarre breakup that lasted a few hours but almost caused me to be killed, several times. That event still seemed easier than all the pregnancy stuff I'd been going through in the last few months.

"He was taking me to medical at the Science Center instead of letting a bunch of human doctors get me and take me away to perform horrible tests on me and our baby. Tito said he did the right thing medically, too, bringing me to Dulce."

Tito Hernandez had been a medical student working three jobs in between cage fights when he'd helped me out in a big way during the fun interplanetary invasion that

Jeff's proposing to me had accidentally started. He was part of both Alpha and Airborne Teams now and, since he no longer had to work three jobs, had his medical degree. He was functioning as my personal OB/GYN for a variety of reasons.

Jeff grunted, and I was sure we were headed for the next level of the Chuckie Argument, when the com crackled. I was fairly sure Gladys made it do that when she was annoyed. "Commander Martini? Will you ever be joining Commander White, or will he be handling the situation in Paris alone?"

"Fine, fine, be right there," Jeff snapped. He gave me a good, long kiss. "I love you, baby. You behave."

"Always. I love you, too. You be careful."

"Always."

He disappeared out of the room. Almost two years with Centaurion Division and the hyperspeed was still rather amazing. I took a deep breath, let it out slowly, and forced myself to relax.

"Gladys?" Many times I'd found that Gladys hadn't actually turned the com off.

"Yes, Commander Martini?"

"Could you send the nice A-Cs with the video conferencing equipment down, and please ask someone, anyone, to help me finish getting dressed?" Yeah, I was *that* pregnant.

"Crew on the way, Doctor Hernandez alerted."

"Great," I grumbled. Tito was a wonderful doctor, but he really walked on the strict side of the medical house. "I'd like to know what's going on in Paris, too, you know."

"All of Alpha Team, other than yourself, Doctor Hernandez, and Pontifex White, are in Paris, Commander."

"As mentioned earlier, Charles Reynolds is going to be here shortly, and I can promise you he's going to want to know what's going on. I want to know, too. Save me the time and energy and yourself the whining and get someone down here who can share all the details with me before Chuckie gets here."

"Commanders Martini and White have asked that we not share situations with Sometime Supreme Commander Reynolds unless absolutely necessary." Chuckie had had to take over Centaurion Division at the start of Operation Invasion, just before my wedding. Gladys loved reminding everyone of that. I wasn't sure if it was because she secretly liked Chuckie or just liked to have everyone on edge.

"Gladys, have you ever heard the human term, 'put a cap in yo ass'?"

"You open new avenues for all of Centaurion Division regularly, Commander. Am sending briefing materials down to you now."

Great. The so-called light reading. There were many times I wondered if Gladys hated me for some reason, though everyone insisted that she just liked having fun with her job. Since she was the Head of Security, you'd think that would entail being helpful to the Head of Airborne, but that seemed to be mood-based, hers and mine.

A knock sounded, and several competent-looking A-Cs whose names I should have known by now but didn't came in and started setting up the mobile video conferencing equipment I'd become familiar with these past few months. Jeff wouldn't allow the equipment to remain in our rooms, under the impression that either Chuckie or the C.I.A. would be spying on us. Chuckie wouldn't do so, but I couldn't say the same for the rest of the C.I.A., so I didn't argue.

One of them handed me a nice, thick file. I put it on my nightstand. "You guys going to stay here while we do the conferencing?"

Two of them, who looked related, nodded. "Yes, ma'am, Commander," the one who looked older replied. He was also the one who'd given me the file I was now ignoring. "Per how Commander Martini and Mister Reynolds prefer it, we'll have additional equipment set up in your living area. We'll be there to maintain it, and in case anything goes wrong." He indicated who I was now pretty sure was his younger brother in the "we."

The rest of the A-Cs did a sound and video check, then zipped out of the room. This left me with the two brothers. I decided pretending I knew their names would be both stupid and useless, since, if they were staying, it meant one was an imageer and one was an empath, and the empath would undoubtedly pick up my confusion. Jeff said I broadcast my emotions.

The younger one grinned at me. "I'm Wayne, Commander. This is my older brother, William."

I looked at him. He was a little bigger than his brother, and per Chuckie's comments based on keen and alert observation, and my sometime awareness, the empaths tended to run larger in body size than the imageers.

Before I could say anything, Wayne winked at me. "Yes, I'm an empath. William's an imageer."

"Nice to meet you two. Officially, I mean. I'm sure I've met you many times I don't remember." I was sure I had. But every A-C I'd ever met, other than a couple of psychotic megalomaniacs, had been drop-dead gorgeous, and these two were no exception. I wouldn't have thought it possible, but after a while, all that beauty tended to look alike.

They both laughed. "It's okay, Commander," William said. "We understand and don't mind."

Wayne grinned. "Our younger brother works gate security. I know you've seen him. Even though I'm sure you wouldn't remember him." Seeing as it was me, this was a safe bet.

William snorted. "We know this because he's always mentioning it at family dinners. 'I sent the Commanders to New York today, and they said thank you.'" He shook his head. "Kid's ready to burst with pride every time he spins the dial."

I found this somewhat endearing. Gladys certainly wasn't ready to burst with pride any time I asked her for help. It was nice to know someone in Security thought my needs were paramount and appreciated that we were polite. "That's very sweet."

Both brothers made gagging noises. I found myself liking them a lot. "Commander White asked us to make sure that we're recording everything the C.I.A. says in this meeting," William said. "Are you alright with that, Commander?"

"Let's see what Mister Reynolds has to say about that."

"Let's see if I allow you to have this meeting first." The tone was almost as annoyed as Jeff managed when speaking about Chuckie, but for a different reason. And it wasn't coming from my husband. Ah, yes, my Doctor From Hell had arrived.

CHAPTER 2

TITO JOINED US, looking as annoyed as he'd sounded. "I'm not happy about this meeting, Kitty."

"Join Jeff's club, then. It's necessary."

Tito grunted while Wayne and William did a fast fade into the living room side of the Lair. Chickens.

The Lair was the only "human" set of rooms in the entire Dulce Science Center, which in its turn was home to the majority of A-Cs on the planet. The Center went fifteen stories down into the earth, and I still wasn't sure how wide it was, it was that huge. The fifteenth floor was used for high-threat incarcerations, morgue, and some other niceties, including top-secret meetings, and, these days, our living quarters, since both Jeff and I preferred the Lair to other options.

Two younger, female A-Cs joined us. To myself I called all the female A-Cs Dazzlers, because if the men were gorgeous, the women were more so. And they were all brilliant, too. The ones considered dumb as posts by your average A-C were all Mensa material for humans. It really wasn't fair.

They were also all, for the most part, extremely nice, which made hating them close to impossible. These two were standard Dazzler beautiful, both obviously up on the medical expertise or Tito wouldn't have had them with him, and, sadly, just as nice as all the other Dazzlers around. No hating allowed. Always the way.

They fussed over me and thankfully helped me get

dressed while Tito did his horrible array of tests I did my best to ignore. They looked as though they were in their early twenties, but it was hard to tell. As with the other A-Cs, I was fairly sure I'd seen them around before, probably down at the Isolation Level, which was where empaths had to go to regenerate, my personal empath in particular. The less said, or thought, about the isolation chambers the better, at least as far as I was concerned. They'd creeped me out from my first days with Centaurion Division and hadn't stopped yet.

Medical horrors were still going on as the com sprang to life. "Sometime Supreme Commander Reynolds is headed down to you, Commander Martini."

"Thanks, Gladys. Com off," I added, just in case. "Tito, really, could you and the girls stop now?"

"Take your time, Doctor Hernandez," Chuckie said as he joined us. "I'd rather you approve Kitty for this than cause another issue for her."

At the sound of Chuckie's voice, two small bundles of adorable fur made their presence known. The Poofs had been our parting gifts from the Royal Family of Alpha Four—where all our Earth A-Cs were originally from—at the end of Operation Invasion. They looked like fluffy kittens with no ears, no tails, and black button eyes. They could go Jeff-sized at a moment's notice.

They also had hyperspeed or something like it, and they used it to get to Chuckie. Poofikins was mine and Harlie was Jeff's, though he didn't like to admit to the ownership. They were on Chuckie's shoulders, purring up a storm, in an instant.

Another ball of cuteness appeared out of Chuckie's pocket and leaped onto my shoulder. Poofs were supposed to be owned by members of the Royal Family only, which, as it so happens, I'd married into. But in the Poofs' world, if you named it, you owned it, and during Operation Invasion, Chuckie had named his. "Hi, Fluffy. How's a Poofything doing?" I cooed. I couldn't help it. I loved the Poofs.

Chuckie petted Harlie and Poofikins, which made all the purring get louder. "Okay," he said finally. "Kitty and I need to work." They all mewled at us, and then, Poof greetings over, all three of them headed back to their Poof Condo, which was really an extra-luxurious cat tree with a whole lot of levels. I wasn't kidding; I *loved* the Poofs. They curled up and promptly went to sleep.

Chuckie turned back to Tito. "Is Kitty okayed to have this meeting?"

Tito nodded. "She's fine, just don't get her riled up."

I noted the two Dazzlers eyeing Chuckie, which wasn't a surprise. Dazzlers preferred brains above all other traits, and the brainier and, therefore, by human standards, geekier and nerdier a guy was, the more they wanted him. Barring him hanging out with Stephen Hawking, Bill Gates, Steve Jobs, and their ilk, Chuckie was always going to be the smartest guy in any room. That he was tall, had dirty blond hair, blue eyes, was the rangy and muscled type, and was, frankly, quite handsome for a human, should have made him the Dazzler dude of choice. That he was a multimillionaire twice over should have been a mere cherry on top.

And yet, I'd never seen one of them throw herself at him, or even hint around that he might be able to get lucky if he even considered the possibility. It was as if there were some sort of Dazzler Free Zone around Chuckie, which I didn't understand.

These two looked almost willing to go for it anyway, but then one of them noticed me watching them, nudged the other, and they both busied themselves with repacking Tito's medical supplies.

I would have questioned this, but Wayne and William had rejoined us and were discussing video setups and recording with Chuckie, so I figured I'd better take an interest. "Should Tito stay for this?"

Chuckie shook his head. "No need."

Tito shrugged. "You want me to stay anyway, Kitty?"

Part of me did. Most of me didn't. The part that did knew Jeff would prefer Tito being around. The part that didn't wanted some time with Chuckie where I could say, think, and feel whatever I wanted. "No, it's okay. Wayne and William will be here."

Tito nodded his good-byes to me and Chuckie, then he and his Dazzler assistants left. "I'd like a few minutes in private with the Commander," Chuckie said to the brothers.

They both shrugged and left the room, closing the door behind them. I raised my eyebrow at Chuckie. "What's up?"

He took off his overcoat, and I noted that he was dressed

as if he were an A-C—black Armani suit and tie, crisp white shirt. Chuckie was amazingly good at adaptation, which was undoubtedly a reason he was in the position he was in.

He pulled out a wrapped package from the inner coat pocket. "I wanted to give you your Christmas present in private."

Guilt, always on standby when Chuckie and I were alone, leaped to the forefront of my brain. I had no gift for Chuckie. As I thought of it, I had no gift for anyone. As the daughter of a Jewish father and a former-Catholic and also former-Mossad mother, we didn't really celebrate the December holidays so much as sort of wave as they went by. But my friends celebrated.

Chuckie had always given me something at Christmas, usually something small and extremely thoughtful. I'd always given him something, too, at least when we were in school. As we'd gotten older, I was more sporadic. He wasn't.

"I—"

"Don't have anything for me," he said with a grin. "I know. You're very pregnant, and it's not as if your husband would want to shop for you in this case." He kissed my forehead. "I don't care. Please, open it."

This package was rectangular and felt like a book of some kind. I kicked Guilt away for a while and did as requested. It was a leather photo album, well worn. I opened it up—there were pictures of me in it, pretty much exclusively. From ninth grade up through just a couple of years ago. In fact, right up until I'd met the gang from Alpha Centauri.

"I don't get it." My brain and mouth so rarely worked together. One day, I'd do something about that, but pregnancy had, among its other joys, made me an almost complete space cadet, and not the kind with genius-level IQ.

Chuckie sat down on the bed next to me. "I know. I took all of these shots of you over the years."

"I figured. Still have no clue why you're giving me this."

"It's also a baby present."

"Um, excuse me? My impression is that you give babies diapers and cute little outfits, not pictures they can't comprehend." Dread over impending, as-yet un-registered-for baby showers loomed. I kicked Dread over with Guilt and went back to paying attention to Chuckie.

He sighed. "Your child will want to know what your life was like before you met his or her father. I have pictures your parents and other friends don't. So, these are my memories of you. I doubt your husband's going to allow me to share them with your child. But if I give this to you, then I can, even if I'm not doing it personally."

My throat felt very tight. "Oh." I looked at the pictures more carefully. Yes, there I was, in all my awkward teen-aged and young adult glory. Chuckie had been a great photographer, though he'd rarely allowed his picture to be taken. "You're not in any of these."

"Can't put anything past you."

"When did you know there were aliens who could read people through their pictures?"

"Not as long as my aversion to being photographed would lead you to believe." He sighed again. "I wasn't an attractive kid, Kitty. Why have extra photographic proof?"

"You were better than you want to give yourself credit for. And you were hot from college on."

Chuckie laughed. "Nice to know. Anyway, this is for you and your child. Martini will, I'm sure, not appreciate this."

"There's nothing illicit in here, so I'm sure he'll be fine with it." I actually wasn't, and I knew Chuckie was probably right, but why stress myself out? I leaned up and kissed his cheek. "Thank you."

He hugged me gently. "You're welcome. Where is your husband, by the way? I expected to have a fight about getting a minute alone with you."

"Called to Paris for some sort of emergency. All of Alpha Team is there other than me, Tito, and Richard."

Chuckie's eyes narrowed. "That's interesting." He looked at the screens. "Good, there are enough. I'll want to see if we can connect with Euro Base after we talk to my people."

"Fine and dandy. I get why we're doing this meeting—I fainted as my introduction to these people last time, and that was the entire agenda. But I don't understand why you wanted to do this now."

"These people need a diplomatic touch your husband seems unable or unwilling to muster. I can't blame him for not wanting to, but we don't have a lot of choice in who we have to deal with. They want reassurances no one from

Centaurion Division has seen fit to give them. The Agency is about to go to a skeleton crew for the holidays. I want this settled and these people off my back before everyone disappears. And then I want my own questions answered privately."

"Like what is Alpha Team doing in Paris?" I put the photo album into the nightstand drawer, thought about it, then put the big stack of briefing materials over it. Why upset Jeff if I could avoid it?

"Maybe." He looked at his watch, then around the room. "I'm actually more concerned about other issues."

"Like what?"

"Things that have been bothering me. And should have been bothering you, your husband, and the rest of Alpha Team for a good long while."

I pondered and came up with nothing. "I have no idea what you're talking about."

Chuckie sighed, stood up, and wandered the room. "I'd like to know how it is that the traitors in the A-Cs' midst haven't been detected. By, say, the strongest empath and the strongest imageer on the planet. Otherwise known as your husband and his cousin."

CHAPTER 3

A-CS HAD VARIOUS TALENTS that, to humans, were amazingly impressive. Not every A-C got them, but those who did had to learn how to handle them. Empaths, imageers, and troubadours were normally male, with scientific and medical aptitudes and talents falling to the females in general.

Dream readers, like Paul Gower, who was the Head of Recruitment, aka the Pontifex's right-hand man, and also Jeff's cousin, were rare, and could be either sex. The cousin Chuckie was referring to, however, was Christopher White, who was the strongest imageer on the planet, just as Jeff was the strongest empath. While empaths felt emotions, imageers were able to manipulate any image, and also know all about a person by touching the image. Christopher's explanation for this was that pictures copied the soul and mind as well as the body.

Due to the drugs a fun group of megalomaniacs had given him during what I not so fondly called Operation Drug Addict, Jeff's empathic talents were greatly expanded. He could feel more emotions from farther away and interpret their meanings more accurately. He could also read my mind. Just mine, so far. That I knew of or he'd told me, anyway. Meaning Chuckie's question carried even more weight and probably a lot more suspicion on his part.

"I have no idea. I mean, they can't lie."

Chuckie shook his head. "No. *Most* of them can't lie. Clearly, some of them can. The woman who was working with the Yates-Mephistopheles in-control superbeing certainly was lying."

"Good old Beverly. I hit her with a baseball bat." Ah, memories. Operation Fugly never seemed all that long ago.

"In the head. Yes, your mother told me. My point is that she'd managed to lie to everyone for years. And if she had accomplices, your mother hasn't found them, and that means they know how to lie to both other A-Cs *and* humans. Per your husband, he doesn't think any A-C can lie to him, based on emotional responses. Clearly, he's wrong."

I considered this. "Is he? I mean, they're great at avoiding the question. And, if no one went up to Beverly and said, 'Hey, are you a traitor?' then she'd never have had a reason to lie."

"Maybe. It's something we need to work on. Something, I might add, your husband is resistant to."

"You think there are more A-C traitors lurking about?"

"Yes." The way he said it, I didn't question. Chuckie's nickname all through school had been Conspiracy Chuck. I hated it, but it was accurate. I preferred to call him the Conspiracy King. It was not only a more positive spin, but, as my new life among the A-Cs had proved, daily, Chuckie was always on target. Experience showed if Chuckie was positive, Chuckie was right—and he sounded positive. How depressing.

"I was sort of hoping Beverly was an anomaly."

"I'm sure you were. From now on, I want you looking for the liars, not assuming there aren't any."

I heaved a sigh. "No problem. I'm sure I'll have time once I'm on maternity leave."

He laughed. "No, you won't. You're going to be busy with the baby. But I know you'll still be able to think and observe. Just be aware—at least one A-C's fooled both your husband and his cousin, and if one can do it, so can others."

I got the impression Chuckie wasn't done, but it didn't matter because we were interrupted by Wayne. "I'm sorry, but we have incoming transmissions from Langley."

Chuckie nodded. "Keep some of the screens free and blocked from them, will you?"

Wayne looked at me. "Commander?"

"Do what he says." Wayne shrugged and went out of the room. "Why do you want some screens free?"

"I want to be able to speak to your husband and White, if necessary." Chuckie's jaw was tensed.

"You don't like whoever's coming on, do you?"

"They don't like me, either, so it's fair." Chuckie didn't sit. Of course, there was only the bed, and maybe he didn't want to give the impression we were having an affair. Then again, maybe he just wanted to feel that he was in a position of strength.

"Are they clear on what we do over here?"

"Yes. They all have top-level security clearances." Chuckie didn't sound happy about this. The main screen in the room came to life. There were three men and one woman in the room. I vaguely remembered them—fainting tended to wipe out the little details for me.

"Reynolds," one of them said. He was sitting—they all were—but he looked as if he'd be about Chuckie's height, though he was built more like Jeff, on the brawny side. Otherwise he was fairly average in looks, with dark hair and eyes. "Missus Martini."

"That's Commander Martini, Cooper," Chuckie snapped, eyes flashing. I got a little more alert. Chuckie was normally hard to rile and harder to read. That he was betraying this much emotion toward Cooper was proof positive he hated this guy.

Cooper smirked. "My apologies. *Commander* Martini. When are you due?"

"In a couple of weeks." Tito hadn't given me too clear a due date, but he felt the baby wouldn't come until sometime in January.

"Really? You look ready to pop." Cooper said this with what I assumed was supposed to be a friendly, joking tone and expression. But our video equipment was top of the line, and his smile didn't reach his eyes. I decided to show solidarity with Chuckie and hate this guy, too.

"Thanks so much."

The woman with them rolled her eyes. She was older, dressed severely, with short hair and cat's-eye glasses. "Men. Commander Martini, congratulations on your upcoming happy event. I didn't get a chance to congratulate you when we met before."

"Yeah, sorry about that. And thank you, I'm looking forward to it." I had no idea who this woman was. I felt well within my rights to blame my pregnancy for this, even though I proved every day that I didn't remember names unless I felt I had a real need to. And, with this crew, I clearly hadn't felt the need.

"This is Missus Madeline Cartwright," Chuckie said. "She's a liaison to the Pentagon. This is Esteban Cantu," he pointed to a rather handsome Latin man. "He's the head of our Antiterrorism unit."

"Reporting to my mother?"

"Separate," Cantu said quickly, but with a charming smile. "Your mother controls a very separate agency." This was somewhat true. My mother, as I'd found out during my introduction to the A-Cs, aka Operation Fugly, was actually the head of the P.T.C.U. No ever told me anything until they absolutely had to. This news hadn't reached me until I was twenty-seven. In some ways, I dreaded what my family would share with me when I hit thirty.

"Vincent Armstrong," the last man said with a little wave. "Head of the Senate's subcommittee on anti-American activities." He was older and had the Senior Senator from Wherever look going.

"What state are you from?" I asked.

"Florida," he replied with a charming smile. I faked a return smile. My last experience with a politician from Florida had resulted in Jeff getting drugged, us breaking up, and me almost getting run over in the middle of the Arizona desert. I didn't have too many fond memories from most of Operation Drug Addict, and the worst ones were of Leventhal Reid. I managed not to ask if Armstrong knew him, because, of course he would have. Whether he liked him, was an intimate crony, or was one with Reid's plan to turn the A-Cs into the War Division were probably not the right questions for a pre-Christmas chat.

"Our time's limited," Chuckie said, saving me from having to make any comment. "Let's please get things settled so Commander Martini can rest and prepare for the birth of her child."

Cooper nodded. "We'd like to know what Centaurion Division is putting in place to cover while you and your husband are on maternity leave, Commander."

"The rest of Alpha Team will be stepping in. Commander White will be in charge."

Cartwright looked mildly concerned, but the three men looked pleased, Cooper in particular. Cartwright opened her mouth, but Cooper spoke before she could. "Excellent. I'm sure you're fine with that, Reynolds?"

"Yes," Chuckie said slowly. "But I believe Missus Cartwright had a question?"

She nodded. "I'd like to know what the protocols will be in case of an emergency, Commander Martini."

"Define emergency. We have all sorts that crop up."

"An emergency that threatens Centaurion Division, such as clustered superbeing activity, like what's going on in Paris right now."

CHAPTER 4

CHUCKIE AND I BOTH managed to control our reactions. I couldn't speak for him, but it took effort on my part. "How is it you're aware of that?" My father had always told me that if I didn't want to answer a question or didn't know how to reply to one, asking another question in return was a great way to handle the situation.

Everyone other than Cooper looked a little uncomfortable. Cooper's eyes narrowed, just a bit. "We're concerned about Centaurion's ability to handle things while you and your husband are ... incapacitated."

"Yes, so you said earlier. But you didn't answer my question." I hadn't answered theirs, either, but that wasn't important now.

"Yes, I'd like to know that as well," Chuckie said. "Since nothing in Europe affects any of your main day-to-days."

"What are their main focuses?" I asked him quietly.

"South America mostly."

"Paraguay in particular?" I asked, watching them, not Chuckie. All four of them looked as though they were reading my lips, and none of them looked happy with what they saw. It figured. Paraguay had been cropping up in one way or another for the past year and a half. I still had no idea why it was seemingly so important, but I had a feeling I was going to have to find out.

"Not more than any other country," Chuckie said, but I could tell he was saying this because he, too, realized they were reading our lips. I knew him better than anyone, and what his tone said was I was right on and he wanted me to shut up about it.

"Okay." I smiled brightly at everyone on-screen. "So, why is it you're aware of what's going on in Europe right now?"

Cartwright shrugged. "Our people keep us apprised. We're clear that the situation was dire enough that all of Alpha Team was called out. We're concerned that if something similar happens, your husband, the leader of the A-C military, will be unavailable."

"If he's needed, Jeff will be there, baby or no baby."

Cooper shook his head. "I'm sure Commander White can handle anything while the Commanders Martini are enjoying maternity leave."

Cartwright glared at the back of his head. "John, you're the one who wanted this meeting. I'd prefer to get all our questions on the table, both ours and theirs, before we power down for the holidays."

Cooper shrugged. "They have a plan in place. That's good enough for me."

Cantu smiled at me. "I'm sure there are other protocols in place when Centaurion Division feels threatened?"

"The usual. Lockdown, strike teams. You know, what the rest of the government does." I didn't know why they were asking this. None of the questions seemed to warrant either a meeting or a diplomatic touch. I wasn't sharing anything new, and they weren't asking anything remotely newsworthy. We had a personal paparazzo who asked better questions than these in-the-know people were. "What about my having a baby—which I have to add the majority of women do—is causing such concerns within the C.I.A.?"

"Interspecies birth is quite an event," Armstrong said. He made it sound like a campaign slogan.

"It's happened already," I reminded them. "We have living, healthy hybrids. You've met at least one of them, I'm sure."

"Mister Gower," Armstrong said with a nod. "Yes. However, at the time of his and his siblings' births, his parents weren't among the most influential members of Centaurion Division."

"We've had sitting presidents with little kids. I really don't see what you think is going to happen, other than a lot of diaper changes and feedings. Both sets of our parents are alive, healthy, and practically banging down our doors to be first in line to take baby duty."

Chuckie turned around and gave me the "are you crazy, is that your problem?" look. Sure enough, Cantu jumped on it. "So the head of the Presidential Terrorism Control Unit will also be indisposed."

"Dude, my mother probably wasn't indisposed when I was born, let alone now." By now, if someone shared that Mom had taken down a contingent of terrorists in between contractions, it wouldn't have surprised me. "I'm really not feeling what it is you're all going for." An idea dawned. "Do you want Ch-, ah, Mister Reynolds, to take over or something?"

Armstrong shook his head. "We're . . . aware of your close friendship. I'm sure Mister Reynolds, like the rest of those closely associated with Centaurion Division, will be distracted by your baby's arrival."

This was getting ludicrous. Chuckie could multitask better than anyone. And I knew they knew it. They wanted something. But I had no idea what, and I didn't really get the impression Chuckie did, either.

"Standard protocols will be in place," he said firmly. "Commander White will be assuming control of all Field and Imageering if necessary. There are plenty of people to step in if, for some reason, the new parents aren't available. Either tell us what it is you're hoping to hear, or stop wasting my time."

Cooper smirked. "Got it. I'm satisfied. Everyone else?" There were general nods and assents. "Then we'll let you get back to whatever it is you do, Reynolds. Enjoy the holidays." He made a kill gesture and the screen went blank.

Chuckie went to the door. "Make sure they're really cut off," he told Wayne and William. The all clear was given. "Get Commanders Martini and White on-screen as fast as possible, please. Presuming they're not in the middle of a parasitic attack."

He turned back to me. "That was interesting. Any guess as to what they were trying for?"

"None. That's your bailiwick."

He grimaced. "Yeah. I have no clue. Which makes me very, very nervous."

William stuck his head in. "Mister Reynolds, have an issue with getting the Commanders on-screen for you."

CHAPTER 5

THE SCREENS LIT UP. There were a lot of explosions going on. Half the screens showed some nasty-looking monsters. The other half showed some really impressive fireworks. I didn't see any humans or A-Cs I could identify. From what I could tell, though, the monsters were being herded into the Seine.

"Left side's real, right side's the imageering fake, right?" Hey, I liked to be sure.

"Yes, Commander," William said. He and Wayne both came into the room, the four of us watching The Creatures That Claimed Paris.

"There's something wrong with the superbeings." I said this because I was thinking of them as monsters. They were, but that wasn't the normal reaction I had to them. I saw a superbeing as something to kill, not something almost familiar.

"I agree," Chuckie said slowly. "Not sure what, though."

"They don't seem as . . . real . . . as the superbeings I've seen." I studied them. "They look a lot alike. Not as alike as the dozen we dealt with in Paraguay, right before Operation Invasion started. Differently alike."

Chuckie was used to me, so he didn't comment on this. "Can you get us close-ups on the superbeings?" he asked William.

"May I, Commander?" Wayne asked, while his brother complied with Chuckie's request.

"May you what?"

He went to the drawer, pulled out the briefing papers,

and handed them to Chuckie. He grinned at my expression. "It was an easy guess where they'd disappeared to."

Chuckie thumbed through the papers, a lot faster than I would have. I knew he was reading them. Like everything else, he was top of the class in speed-reading. He grunted after a minute or so. "Interesting. Euro Base had no prior warning of the attack. There were no rage indicators . . . no emotional indicators at all."

"Are they real?"

William put his hands onto the screen. He pulled them away quickly. "Yes. They're . . . distasteful." This was the standard imageering reaction to touching a superbeing via their talents.

Wayne handed him a wipe, which was the standard reaction from any A-C standing by an imageer who had to touch the superbeing images. "You're sure?" he asked, and it was clear he wasn't being funny.

William looked at him. "Why do you ask?"

"Your reaction time. You were slower than normal."

Chuckie's eyes narrowed. "I hate to have to ask this, but can you touch the screens again and give us everything you can on what you get from them?"

"Do the go-team move," I suggested. I was greeted by blank stares from the brothers and a snort of laughter from Chuckie. "I know Wayne can feel whatever it is through William." Jeff and Christopher had done this during Operation Fugly.

"Ah," Wayne said. "Sure. You up for it?" he asked his brother.

William grimaced. "Yes." He put his hands back on the screen. "They're repugnant, evil, mindless—"

"No," Wayne said. "There's a mind there. It's not . . . normal."

"Do we consider superbeing minds to be normal?" Maybe they did. What I knew about the inner superbeing workings could fit onto a fingernail. I was all over how to kill them. I hadn't found a real need to dig deeper—that's what the Dazzlers were for.

"I mean not normal for a superbeing." Wayne looked at us over his shoulder. "There's absolutely no rage emotion coming from them. There's no emotion other than the desire to be obedient."

"*Aliens*," I said instantly.

"I don't think so," William said slowly.

"No, I mean the movie *Aliens*. The bad people tried to make supersoldiers out of the horrible alien monsters."

"You're sure you're getting no emotional reading?" Chuckie asked Wayne.

"Positive, sir."

"Me as well, sir," William added.

No sooner were the words out of his mouth than there were a series of explosions. The superbeings blew up. From what we could see, there were no traces left.

Chuckie cursed while William and Wayne used their hand wipes. "Now we've got nothing to examine."

"Just like in Paraguay?"

He turned to me. "I have no way of knowing if it was just like in Paraguay. Because there was nothing left to study. Your husband ensured that. And since he was on the scene here, I'm sure he's ensuring all traces are gone in this instance, too."

"Well, it's what we do," I reminded him.

"And they know that," he muttered. He rubbed his forehead. "You two are probably the only proof we have that these weren't normal superbeings. I'm sure no one else was monitoring like we did."

The brothers nodded. "Unlikely, sir," William said. "Ah, what do you want us to do?"

"Record your impressions, all of them," Chuckie said briskly. "Leave nothing out. And then get that information to me as well as to Alpha Team. I want to be sure we have more than one copy of the data."

"Leave the equipment and take care of that now." They nodded to me and zipped off. Chuckie started pacing. I knew he was thinking—I could see the conspiracy wheels turning. I could also tell he wasn't getting anywhere. After five minutes of this, I couldn't take it any more. "Dude, relax."

He shook his head. "Can't. This is bad, and we have nothing to go on."

"Fine." I patted the bed. "Sit while the wheels turn. You look seriously stressed."

I heard a step and a growl. "He sits and he'll be seriously dead."

CHAPTER 6

JEFF GLARED AT CHUCKIE as he walked in. "Why are you still here?"

"Because we have a problem," Chuckie said. He wasn't looking at Jeff or me, and he was still pacing.

Jeff somehow reined in the jealousy all on his own. Either he wanted to impress me, or Chuckie's stress levels were particularly high. I figured on the latter. He shot a worried glance at Chuckie, then looked at me. "With the C.I.A.?"

"In a way. More with what you were doing in Paris."

Jeff nodded. "Whatever we were fighting, they weren't superbeings."

I felt all proud. "See, Chuckie? Someone other than us was monitoring the weird."

Chuckie heaved a sigh. "And that makes it better how?"

"Pardon me, Mister Glass Half Empty."

"It doesn't," Jeff agreed. "We have nothing left to study."

"You weren't able to contain them any other way?" Chuckie asked.

"No. We weren't the ones who destroyed them."

Chuckie spun so fast I was worried he'd fall over. "Explain that, please."

Jeff sighed. "It looked like normal clustered activity, only there were no emotional warnings whatsoever. There were a dozen of them. We were barely able to contain them, but they destroyed no significant property, and, as far as we can tell, no one was killed."

"That's not normal at all." Every superbeing was a destruction machine, and their overriding desire was to kill any humanity in their vicinity.

"Right, baby, it's not. We herded them to the Seine—we were going to use self-contained nukes to destroy them. Right before I could give the order, they all blew up. At the same time."

"I monitor for supersoldier projects all the time," Chuckie said. "So does your mother. Nothing like this has come up on either of our radars."

"If the lie is good enough, and the support is high enough . . ."

"Yeah, that's what's really worrying me."

"How trustworthy are your superiors?"

He chuckled. "They're top in the C.I.A. How trustworthy do you think that would make them?"

Jeff snorted. "Not at all." Chuckie shrugged and managed a grin.

"I meant for you, for us, for the safety of the U.S. and the world. That kind of thing?"

"They seem reliable. Your mother doesn't trust them overly much, but she trusts them more than some." He looked thoughtful. "There was a shake-up right before I became head of the ET division."

"Any of our four friends involved in that?"

He nodded. "Cooper and Cantu for certain. Cooper wasn't promoted, Cantu was." He shook his head. "I'll need to discuss this with your mother."

"She's on alert, just waiting for the baby. You should be able to get a hold of her easily enough. But I'm kind of curious why and how the people we met with today, who shouldn't have known anything about this, knew all about the attack when none of us did."

Jeff's eyes narrowed. "Who shouldn't have known?"

"A senator, a Pentagon liaison, the head of one of our terrorist units, and John Cooper," Chuckie replied. "Cooper's angling for my job."

"He's a prick," I added. "Not that I liked any of them much."

Chuckie nodded. "I'd really hoped to have both of you at this meeting, and White, too, if possible. I need these people read."

"Sorry, busy trying to stop an international incident. Christopher's still there—the imageering alterations necessary are unreal."

"Why are you back already?" I asked. "Normally you'd be taking care of the cleanup portions."

Jeff shot me a "duh" look. "I knew who you were with."

Chuckie rolled his eyes. "Just the two of us and four people we can't trust at all."

"Am I right that all four hate you and want Centaurion turned into the War Division?" It was such a safe bet—most people were intimidated by Chuckie's brains, drive, and success and channeled that into hating him. And there was a much longer list of those who wanted us to be the War Division than those who didn't. Every day it seemed as though the ones who didn't got fewer and fewer.

"In a nutshell." Chuckie sounded like he always did when talking about people who didn't like him—resigned. I knew there was hurt under there, too, but he hid it well.

Jeff looked like he was going to say something nasty to Chuckie, but I glared at him, and he stopped himself. Possibly he'd picked up the hurt, too, but I wasn't sure if he cared about it. "But are they in any position to be in on whatever the hell is going on?" he asked instead.

Chuckie nodded slowly. "It's possible. I wouldn't put anything past Cooper. He wants my job and every job above mine, too. Cantu's a slippery bastard. And Armstrong's your typical politician on the rise. Cartwright I'm not sure of, but she works closely with the three of them."

There was a knock at the door, and Wayne and William came in. "We have what you wanted, Mister Reynolds," William said, handing him a file. Wayne handed one to Jeff.

"That was fast."

The brothers grinned at me as Jeff and Chuckie both sighed and shook their heads. "Hyperspeed," Wayne said.

"Oh." Okay, had to give Jeff and Chuckie the "duh" on that one. I chalked it up to another space cadet moment and called the Poofs over to make myself feel better. I petted the cuteness bundles while Chuckie and Jeff both read through the files.

"Good work," Chuckie said finally. "I wish I could get field reports from my operatives this well-detailed."

Wayne and William looked pleased, but then they both

looked at Jeff. He nodded. "Lots of good information here, thank you." Both brothers visibly relaxed. "I appreciate the notes from the C.I.A. meeting, too."

"We recorded it as well, Commander," William said, "per Mister Reynolds' request."

Jeff raised his eyebrow at Chuckie. "You tape everyone?"

"Just everyone I don't trust. I'd like a copy of the recording." Jeff nodded and William pulled out his phone.

"Coming down to you now, sir," he said, hanging up.

Chuckie heaved a sigh. "I don't think we have enough to go on definitively yet, but I'll work on it."

"It's the holidays. You're allowed time off. The rest of your agency's taking their two weeks, why not you?"

Chuckie shook his head. "You know the saying—evil never sleeps."

"Yeah, too true." I yawned. Wow. Nap time already. In addition to the other joys, I got tired out much more quickly these days.

Jeff opened his mouth, but Chuckie beat him to it. "I'm going to get back to my office. I'll be in touch on this, and I expect the same from you if you hit on anything. You get some rest Kitty. Gentlemen, Martini," he said with a nod. He whistled softly, and Fluffy jumped up onto my shoulder, purred, rubbed, and then leaped onto Chuckie's shoulder, did the purr and rub thing, then snuggled into his pocket. I managed to refrain from saying how adorable this was, but it took real effort.

Before Chuckie could leave, William's phone rang. He put up his hand. "Yes, got it." He hung up. "Commander Martini, we have an issue with the recorded copy Mister Reynolds requested."

"And that is?" Jeff asked.

William looked grim. "All the recordings have been destroyed."

That sat on the air for a moment. "How?" I asked finally.

He shook his head. "We don't know. All recordings for the past week have been corrupted, the ones from today are completely gone."

"Internal sabotage," Chuckie said, and from his tone, he was certain. "Not good. Any clues as to who did it?"

"No, sir," William said. "Imageering contacted Commander White already. He's ordered a full investigation."

"It'll have to do." Chuckie didn't look happy, and I couldn't blame him. I also couldn't control another yawn. "I'll add this to the pile of things we need to know about. Please guard those reports—you two are the only proof we have now that something was wrong with those superbeings."

"Yes, sir," Wayne said with a small smile. "We'll guard them with our lives."

Chuckie managed a short laugh. "Good job."

Jeff seemed to be struggling with something. "I'll walk you out," he said finally. "You two, take down the equipment."

They left while William and Wayne did as instructed. "You didn't give me a file," I mentioned.

Wayne laughed. "We're already clear you wouldn't read it." He grinned and put a folder into my nightstand. "Here's a copy for later, though. You know, when you get around to it. In about a year."

"Wow, you *are* good. So, what's the CliffsNotes version?"

They both looked at me blankly for a moment. A-Cs were capable of reading at hyperspeed, too, so why read an abbreviated version? William recovered first. "You want the highlights, Commander?"

"Please and thank you."

"We think they're genetically engineered," Wayne said. "But there's no human in there."

"That we can tell," William added. "Didn't feel like there's parasite in there, either."

"That we can tell," Wayne said. "They didn't feel . . . right."

"Robotic?"

"Could be," Wayne allowed. "But if so, it's a more natural robot."

"Like an android?"

William shrugged. "Could be. We don't really work with this side of things. Kill 'em, get the folks to safety, that's our normal assignment."

"Why are you doing live at the exciting scene of my bedroom, then?"

They exchanged a quick glance. "Ah, special assignment," William said.

That meant either they were being punished or they were specially selected. "Assigned by whom?"

"Commander White," William answered.

So, handpicked. Unless Christopher was really interested in seeing how my space cadet ways messed with their minds. I voted for the former. "Why you two?"

Wayne's turn to shrug. "We're really good. Commander White doesn't trust the C.I.A. any more than any of the rest of us do."

"So, what did he have you read on Chuckie?"

They both busied themselves with the screens. I doubted these two were going to fall into the "able to lie to us" category.

"Dudes, don't make me pull rank. What were you monitoring Chuckie for?"

"Whatever he might be hiding," Wayne said.

"Chuckie's not hiding something from us."

"Everybody's hiding something, Commander," Wayne said as Jeff came back in, accompanied by several other A-Cs who were clearly along to help with clearing out the video stuff. "Everybody. But not always for the same reasons."

CHAPTER 7

ON THAT CRYPTIC NOTE, the brothers left, equipment and extra A-Cs in tow. "You want to explain that?" Jeff asked me.

"No. You want to explain what you were talking about with Chuckie?"

He grinned. "No, other than to say we're not going to panic or spend undue amounts of time on the supersoldier theory just yet. Christopher's handling the loss of our recordings, so you can stop worrying about that. You want to nap or are you hungry?"

"Both."

Jeff laughed and hypersped out of the room, returning shortly with a couple of laden food trays. The rest of the day shifted back into the normal, dull routine of me being really pregnant and him being really great about it. In between, I napped and he did the paperwork part of his job. It was an unexciting schedule, but it currently worked for us.

After dinner and a variety of reruns of old, cheesy shows Jeff couldn't stop loving if his life depended on it, we went to bed. Well, I got back under the covers again, and Jeff did, too. After some fun cuddling that was interrupted by the baby kicking the crap out of me, we snuggled up and went to sleep.

Slept for a few hours, then I woke up. For no reason, other than possibly the baby being frisky. Jeff was still asleep. I was wide awake. This was not fun. I didn't want to wake him up, so reading or watching TV were out. So I went for thinking, which meant I tossed and turned the issues of the day over in my mind.

If there was a secret supersoldier conspiracy afoot, who was behind it? The people from today's meeting? Someone else? The President or one of his nearest and dearest advisers?

And if there was one supersoldier project Chuckie and my mom knew nothing about, did that mean there could be more? There was so much going on at any time, and Chuckie always felt that there were a huge number of active conspiracies going all the time. So, competing clandestine groups could be creating supersoldiers. In fact, the ones in Paraguay from last year could be run by a completely different set of megalomaniacs than the ones from Paris earlier today.

After an hour or so of this, I accepted that I couldn't sleep. I also knew Jeff wouldn't want me to wake him up merely to fret about things we had no info for and I had less than no idea of how to solve. So I had to come up with something else to do to pass the time in the wee hours.

No problem. We still had to register for baby things. No time like the present, right? Of course, I couldn't be expected to make these decisions alone, since Jeff was as picky about this stuff as I was.

I nudged him. "You awake?"

He heaved a sigh. "I am now."

"Great! I can't sleep. Let's look at baby product catalogs."

Jeff groaned. "I can remember a time when, if you were waking me up in the middle of the night, it wasn't to thumb through catalogs."

"Yes, the result of which is why we need to look at baby catalogs now."

Jeff rolled out of bed, turned on the lights, grabbed a handful of catalogs, and came back to bed. "Maybe we should just open pages at random and pick whatever's on them." We weren't having much success with the registry—if one of us loved it, the other hated it.

"Worth a shot." We tried it. I opened my catalog to the pages with bath toys. Jeff opened his to the pages with car seats. "I don't want twelve car seats." I wanted one really awesome one, but Jeff felt it wasn't safe enough. I wasn't sure if he was going to think an armored tank was safe enough.

"What child needs that many bath toys?" Jeff felt that too many toys was a bad thing. I felt there was a lot of cute out there, and our baby should have as much of it as possible.

We closed the catalogs. "Well, we still have time. The big baby party thingy isn't until after the baby arrives. So we have at least a couple of weeks."

Jeff sighed. "It's an induction ceremony. It's traditional."

"Right. That." The positive was that the A-Cs waited for the baby to arrive and then showered child and parents with gifts. When I'd first heard about it, it had sounded great. One big party, lots of goodies, what's not to love? Then I realized everyone would be staring at me, expecting me to squeal with delight over every single item, and my anticipation had gone downhill.

"Lorraine, Claudia, and Serene are all looking forward to theirs," Jeff reminded me, with more than a little chide in his tone.

This was true, because they were right behind us in the baby race. They were also all A-Cs, so to them, the whole massive group baby shower ceremony thing was normal.

But this was why Tito was covering most of Alpha's and Airborne's medical—our three other female members had all gotten married shortly after Jeff and I had and were, just like us, immediately pregnant. We were at the head of what was about to become a baby boom of epic proportions, and we were all scared as hell about it.

Which was the main reason Jeff and I were stalling out on the baby stuff. We were both frightened, and not just for us. If something was wrong with our baby, that meant there was a likelihood something was going to be wrong with a lot of babies.

Precedent said they'd be fine. But we'd become used to nothing working out like we planned—story of my life, really—so we'd become apprehensive. Tito's insistence on bed rest for me after the fainting incident hadn't made us any calmer.

"I know they're all excited about their induction ceremonies. I am, too," I lied.

"I know you're not." Jeff sighed and hugged me. "I think I understand. You're afraid. And," he said in a low voice, "I can't blame you."

I knew where this was heading. "Jeff, let's not rehash it. You weren't responsible for what happened to you." I nuzzled his chest. "Besides, the drug made your powers stronger, so it all worked out."

"What if—" He snapped his mouth shut.

"What if what?" He wouldn't answer, so I thought about what he could be worried about. "I'm sure it won't have hurt the baby. Tito and every medical A-C you've dragged by to check me out all say everything's fine."

"How the hell would they know?"

I managed to sit up to look right at him. "Uh, 'cause they're doctors?"

"The last hybrid birth was Abigail Gower, and she's twenty-four now. No one working medical was around for her birth."

"Her parents were. And Ericka and Stanley both have said that the pregnancies were hard but nothing life-threatening." I looked at his expression. "Jeff, just because your parents had a hard time with you, it doesn't mean we will. You and Christopher put blocks into all your nieces and nephews. If our baby isn't an empath, Christopher will put in an imageering implant, and it'll be fine."

He nodded but didn't look convinced. Point of fact, he looked worried, though I knew he was trying to hide it.

"Besides, Serene is younger than Abigail." Yep. I could see his worry spike.

"And we know nothing about her human father, and her mother's been dead for almost two decades."

I sighed. "I know we're not supposed to find out the sex early by A-C tradition. And I swear Tito hasn't told me. But you've been worried since June, so I have to guess we're having a girl, right?" We'd figured out that male hybrids had no power issues—they got standard A-C talents or they got no talents. But the female hybrids, of which there were very few, all had advanced, mutated talents.

"Doesn't it seem odd that in all the original hybrid tests, there were only two girls born? Naomi and Abigail?"

"Yeah. It seems odd that you have two hearts and can run fifty miles in the blink of an eye, too. I stopped worrying about it, oh, about an hour after I met you." I hugged him. "Baby, you worry too much."

He hugged me back, so tightly I almost couldn't breathe. "I don't want anything to happen to you, or to our baby."

"Nothing will. We'll be fine."

Before I could try to reassure him any more, a voice came over the intercom. "Commander Martini, we have a situation."

CHAPTER 8

"WHAT IS IT, GLADYS?" Jeff asked, as he moved me gently so he could get up. "It's the middle of the night."

"Situation is not here, sir. And, apologies, I was speaking to the other Commander Martini, former Commander Katt, now Missus Commander Martini." Gladys had sarcasm available at any time of the day or night.

"Oh. What's up?"

"Long distance call from Paris." Paris was the hot epicenter for us today, apparently. Oh, well, at least it wasn't Paraguay.

"What's wrong with cell phones or landlines?"

"No idea, Commander. Shall I patch it through?"

"Sure."

There was a lot of static on the line. "Kitty?" The voice was faint, but I'd known it a long time.

"Ames? Amy, is that you?" Amy was one of my two best girlfriends from high school. She was a corporate lawyer living in Paris and working for a huge company. She also came from money. Charmed life was the phrase that leaped to mind when people talked about Amy. Cool, loyal friend was the phrase that leaped to mine.

"Kitty." She was crying. Amy never cried. She also was never dramatic, never sarcastic, never exaggerated, never impetuous, and never held a grudge. We were friends because, I guess, opposites attract. "Kitty, I need help."

Jeff pulled his clothes on. They were exactly like the

clothes he'd had on this morning—black Armani suit, white shirt. In deference to the time and urgency, he passed on the tie. For any A-C, this represented that he was going *casual.*

"Where are you?"

"The Metro, Gare du Nord, near the trains. I have to get out of here. They're going to kill me."

Well, that was dramatic.

"Stay there," Jeff barked. "I'll be there in a minute."

"Is that Jeff?" Amy asked, sniffling. I waited for sarcasm or exaggeration, figuring we might get the trifecta tonight.

"Yeah. He's going to get you. Go to the women's restroom near the main information desk and wait there, inside it."

"I'm sorry, I don't think I heard you right. Where do you want me to go?"

Jeff was on his cell. "Christopher, emergency. Need a gate to the Paris Metro, Gare du Nord, five minutes ago, need you, too. No, near our usual entry point, but closer to the main information desk." He kissed me, and hypersped out of the room.

"You heard right. Are you on a cell?"

"No, payphone." She was still crying. "Kitty, where do I go?" I repeated the directions, loudly and slowly. "Um . . . I know you do something weird now, but are you kidding me?"

"No. Look, hurry, they'll be there in a minute, maybe less." The phone went dead. "Gladys?"

"Believe the caller hung up, Commander. I've alerted Euro Base. They're sending two teams to assist Commanders Martini and White."

"Thanks, Gladys. How did she get through to you?"

"She called using an international emergency number."

"Huh. Um, I didn't know we had such a number."

"*We* don't, Commander."

"Who does, Gladys? Tired, cranky, being kicked to death. Make it easy on me."

"United States agencies, Commander. Covert United States agencies."

"Ah. Okey-dokey. Thanks."

So, what the hell was Amy doing with a covert ops emergency number? And, point of concern, had she left the phone to run to the bathroom as instructed, or had she been snuffed?

I tried not to think about that possibility. I also tried not to think about the fact that Jeff and I had had some wild sex in the same place he was going to be with Amy. He wasn't the only one who had a few jealousy or confidence issues.

Not that he had any real reason. He was the classic—tall, dark, wavy hair, light brown eyes, great features, killer smile—so handsome. And then there was his body. Broad shoulders, totally built, ripped, but not overly muscled like a bodybuilder, six-pack abs, awesome pecs and biceps, great legs, fabulous butt, hung like a horse. I hoped he'd get home soon. According to all the medical data, it was still safe to do the dirty deed. And, by now, I was ready. Of course, I was always ready. Any time I wasn't, I just had to look at him and, presto, ready.

Of course, I was still sort of surprised he was interested in sex with me at all any more. I looked like I'd stuck a tube up and inflated my stomach to clown-level proportions. The rest of me wasn't totally porked out, but you sure couldn't tell that I'd run track all through high school and college, nor that I could do any form of kung fu other than Cow Wallows in the Mud.

Supposedly my skin was glowing, my hair was more luxurious, and my eyes were sparkling. I guess. I looked blotchy, scraggly, and tired, at least whenever I risked a look in the mirror these days.

Between worrying about Amy, listing how crappy I looked, wondering if Jeff and Christopher were going to be okay, and hoping Jeff didn't think about our time in the Metro bathroom with the wrong kind of nostalgia, I was crying in short order. This was guaranteed to make me look worse than like crap, but I hadn't been able to control any emotion for the last six months, especially when I was tired.

There was a knock at the door. I almost shouted for them to come in, then I stopped and considered.

Jeff wouldn't knock. Neither would Christopher, come to think of it. As Jeff's cousin and best friend, he had certain leeway with the niceties. As the head of Imageering, he also had the right to enter if he felt there was a risk. Plus, we were all almost totally past the time he'd ravaged me in the elevator. Jeff hadn't brought it up for months, and Christopher and I had gotten to where we didn't feel like we had to act like opposing magnets if we were near each other. I was pretty sure he was over me. I knew I was over him—I had been for a long time. Besides, for me, in the choice between Jeff and Christopher, my decision had been made even before the ravaging moment. The aftermath of that incident had merely confirmed who I was in love with.

The knocking continued. I realized I'd wandered off into my own little dreamland there, which was happening more and more. Of course, the idea of getting up and walking through two rooms to get the door seemed like a lot of work. I got a weird feeling.

"Com on." Jeff had installed the A-C version of "the Clapper" for me the day after Tito had insisted on bed rest.

"Yes, Commander Martini?"

"Gladys, someone's knocking at my door."

"Politeness is, as you may recall, an A-C trait."

"Yes, great. But here's the thing—everyone knows I'm on bed rest. And Jeff isn't here. Even if he were back, he wouldn't be knocking. None of Alpha or Airborne knock, or at least, they don't knock and then keep on knocking when I don't come to the door." Earlier today, as an example, everyone knocked and then came right on in, because everyone knew I wasn't coming to the door in anything resembling a hurry.

"Security on the way."

"Good. 'Cause that big old unused for anything but sneaking in drainage pipe is right by my door."

"Security is on the way, Commander. And, let me remind you, again, that we secured said pipe during your introductory mission, and it's been secured ever since. Your mother confirms this every month, which you, somehow, forget."

"And I'm alone. And very pregnant. And extremely freaked out right now."

"Yes, Commander, I'm picking that up. Security is on the way."

"Are they hyperspeeding?"

"Yes."

"I ask because the knocking is still going on." I was full on freaked now. Well, I did have a defense that I didn't have to get up to get. "Harlie, Poofikins, come to Kitty."

Our royal pets purred and leaped from their Poof Condo onto my lap. No one was more shocked to discover he was in line for a throne than Jeff. He'd given it up to stay with me on Earth. I got all misty thinking about it.

The knocking got louder. Wow, off on that daydream tangent again. But back to reality and a higher level of being totally freaked out. The Poofs picked up my fear, because they went huge. They weren't growling, but they were ready.

I heard noises, and the knocking stopped. Then there was silence. And then the knocking started again.

"Com on."

"Yes, Commander?"

"Gladys? Have your Security guys checked in?"

"No. Are they with you?" I heard concern in her voice, faint, but there.

"No. I just heard scuffling and then silence and now the knocking again. I'm thinking there's something really beyond horrible outside my door, and I'm also afraid that Jeff's going to walk into it, or worse. And God alone knows what's happened to the Security guys. Bottom line—I'm about to have total horror movie hysterics in here."

"Sending a larger complement of Security. Com line will remain open."

"Great." The knocking continued. It was louder and more insistent. "Maybe it's a vampire. They can't come in unless they're invited."

"Vampires don't exist, Commander."

"Neither do aliens, if you ask the general public." I cuddled next to Poofikins. I hated feeling helpless. But Jeff had taken my Glock away, because I always forgot to set the safety for one, and because I'd gone into one of those daydream things when I'd been putting a clip in for the other. So, no gun. Couldn't do the most basic of kung fu moves. Couldn't run. Could barely walk. Could cry and freak out. Not exactly "stop the psycho killer" options.

My cell was on the nightstand. When in terror, my motto was to share the fun. And, when sharing the fun, if my husband's unavailable, my other motto was to pick one of your best friends first. My other motto was to pick the friend who wouldn't cause my husband to have a conniption fit.

Dialed, got a very sleepy James Reader on the other

end. "Girlfriend, what's up and why are you calling me at this unreal time?"

"James, um, I don't want you to come down here."

"No worries, babe. I'll just go back to sleep, okay?"

"No, um, I'm really scared."

"Isn't Jeff the one who should have to deal with your nightmares?"

"If he were here, yeah." I filled him in on what had transpired.

"Gladys is on the com?"

"Yes."

"But you called me."

"Yes."

"I feel special."

"You are."

"Is the knocking still going on?"

"Yes." I looked at the wall where the com was located. "Gladys? What's the Security status?"

There was no response.

CHAPTER 9

"JAMES? I THINK WE ARE in extreme, terrifying danger. Please activate your Poof."

"I wish you were kidding."

"I'm not, I'm really and truly not. Gladys isn't answering on the com, and she'd left it open."

Reader cursed. "Okay, hang on." I heard him waking someone else up. The someone else was Gower. "Okay, Paul's awake. And this is fun—something's knocking at our door, too."

"Don't answer it!"

"Yeah, clear." He was quiet for a moment. "You think it's a vampire?"

"I suggested that to Gladys! She said they didn't exist."

"Yeah, well, they probably don't."

"I'm really beyond scared. Oh, God, what if Jeff comes back and whatever it is eats him?"

"Hang on." I could hear Reader telling Gower to call Jeff or Christopher. "Okay, Paul got hold of Christopher. They have your friend. She didn't make it to the bathroom, but they got to her before the thugs after her dragged her off. But they have to get to another gate."

"Gladys said she called in Euro teams."

"Really? Trading phones, tell Paul."

"Kitty? This is surreal. You still okay?"

"Yeah, just freaked. The knocking isn't stopping. Did Christopher say there were other teams with them?"

"No. It's just him and Jeff with your friend." I told him what Gladys had said. "Okay, got it, trading phones back."

"James? The Pontifex is in danger."

"Yeah, great, but we can't leave our rooms, and Security's been breached."

"Okay . . . I'll be a big girl and call Richard."

"No, I want you staying on the phone with me."

"But I want Paul staying on with Christopher."

I heard Reader talking to Gower. "Okay, fixed. Jeff's calling Richard. And . . . he's got him. He's in his room, he called Security first, got no response, so didn't go to the door. He's got the knocking, too."

The realization that we were all in some sort of cell phone round robin would have been funny if I weren't scared out of my mind. The baby picked it up, of course, and she was kicking and moving like crazy. I rubbed my stomach. "It's okay, Jamie," I said quietly.

"Um, Kitty? We're not pretending to be lovers, are we?" Reader sounded confused. Jamie was the pet name Gower had for him, and I only used it if we were doing something covert to save our lives, as a clue that things were off.

Thing was, I'd figured we were having a girl the moment Jeff started showing his worry, and Reader had become my best friend in my new life. That I was best friends with the former top international male supermodel never failed to amaze me, but we had a tremendous amount in common, however odd that seemed. Our joke was that if he were straight, we'd have gotten married and left all the alien stuff behind us.

He'd almost died right before Jeff and I got married, had recovered miraculously, and pretty much created our dream wedding in two days, out of nothing. Next to Jeff, my parents, and Chuckie, there was no one I loved more than Reader. And Reader, being gay, didn't really make Jeff's jealousy meter go off the scales.

Once Jeff had told me I was pregnant, I'd wanted to name the baby after Reader—James Jeffrey if it was a boy, Jamie . . . something . . . if it was a girl. I hadn't mentioned this to Jeff yet, for a variety of reasons, keeping the jealousy meter on low in regard to Reader being one of them.

"Uh, I was talking to the baby."

"You're naming it Jamie?" He sounded funny.

"I want to, yeah. I think I'm having a girl, so Jamie."

"Oh." He still sounded funny.

"Is that okay?" It hadn't occurred to me that he might not like the idea.

"Yeah." I heard a sniff. "That's great. Jeff know?"

"Not so much."

He laughed. "Okay, well, then I won't count on it."

"No, as long as you don't mind, I mean, really don't mind, I'm naming the baby Jamie. I call her that all the time when Jeff's not around."

"I don't mind at all. I . . ." His voice trailed off, and I heard what sounded like a nose being blown. "I'm really flattered. Just kind of a shock to find out at three in the morning when we're under siege by God knows what."

"Yeah. It was kind of lucky Jeff and I were awake when Amy called."

"What *were* you doing up?"

"Couldn't sleep. Well, could, woke up around midnight, and couldn't get back to sleep. So, you know, I woke Jeff up to share the fun."

"And here I was wishing I was straight a few seconds ago."

"I wish you were here right now. I'm really scared." The knocking wasn't stopping at all.

"You want me to give it a shot?"

"No!" The baby did an all-limb assault at this. I couldn't help it, I shouted in pain. I heard Reader curse. And I could tell he was moving. "James, stay in your room." I heard him say something to Gower, then the phone went dead.

I sat on the bed and tried not to cry. Failed. I hadn't meant to do something that would cause him to think I was in more danger than he was. My husband and his cousin were off across the world with one of my oldest girlfriends, in mortal peril from what I could tell, and now one of my other best friends was in horror movie peril. And I was incapable of doing anything to help any of them.

Just as I was thinking it couldn't get worse, the door opened.

CHAPTER 10

I DREW IN A DEEP BREATH, all the better to scream at the top of my lungs with, when Reader ran into the room, wearing the standard issue A-C nightclothes—blue pajama bottoms, white T-shirt. I was in the same thing, only the maternity version.

He was still the most gorgeous human male I'd ever seen in the flesh, one of the few humans who could pass as an A-C. However, I wasn't checking him out for hotness, I was checking to make sure he wasn't injured. No blood on him, no limbs missing, so far, so very good.

The Poofs knew and loved him, so they merely shifted so he could get to me. He wrapped his arms around me, and I started to calm down. "Kitty, you okay?"

I nodded. "How did you get in here safely? What was outside?" I was shuddering, and the baby was going nuts.

Reader rocked me. "Nothing. There's nothing outside. Not outside our room or your room. I have no idea where the Security guys are, but they weren't there." I gasped and jerked from the baby's kicking. He started to stroke my stomach, and she calmed down.

Once the baby calmed, he kept one arm around me and started making calls. "Richard's fine. Paul's checked every floor—everyone heard the knocking, everyone was scared by it, no one answered the door."

"What about Security?"

"They're fine. Asleep, but fine. All of them. Paul brought

Serene over, they are who they're supposed to be. Gladys, too."

I kept my head on Reader's shoulder. It was always a comfortable place to be. I closed my eyes and worked to relax. "Okay, so I guess we just have to worry about Jeff and Christopher and whatever's going on with Amy, and then figure out how we attracted ghosts or something."

He chuckled. "Yeah. It could still be vampires, of course. They can go invisible or to mist."

"Did you look up? Maybe they're clinging to the ceiling."

We both looked up. "I feel like an idiot for doing that," Reader said after a moment's silence.

"Me too, but at least we know there isn't some horrible monster hanging up there waiting to pounce."

"I'm not looking under the bed," Reader said with a laugh.

We were both humans. We both lifted our feet up. "Let's scoot into the middle of the bed."

He scooted without argument and helped me move. The Poofs got on either side of us. "Jeff's going to love this when he gets home. Hope he doesn't kill me."

I shook my head. "He'll understand." I hoped. Because I wasn't letting Reader leave me now that he was here.

He knew it, too. He shifted so I could lean my back against his side. "Better?" He kissed the back of my head. Poofikins cuddled next to us so we could both lean into it. Harlie remained on guard. Neither Poof had growled at all, which was unusual in a danger situation.

"Yeah. Still freaked out, just not as freaked since you're here."

"That's my job, at least until Jeff gets back." He made a few more phone calls while I went in and out of dreamland. I heard him confirm that everyone was all right in Dulce, run checks of all our other U.S. Bases, then call the Euro team. "Well," he said as he hung up, "I don't think the teams not meeting up with Jeff is related to this. They're there and they're fine, and they did get the orders from Gladys. But since Amy wasn't where she was supposed to be, neither were Jeff and Christopher, so the Euro teams had to find them. They're heading back soon."

"Good. You won't leave until they're back, right?"

"Right." He moved his arm and wrapped it around my

shoulders, so I could lean my chin on his arm. We'd gotten used to this position since my stomach had gotten huge. It let him hold me in a nonsexual way, support my back, and comfort me all at the same time. Jeff occasionally had to be reminded that Reader was gay, but otherwise he was okay with it.

Leaned my chin, felt sleepy, closed eyes. "Everything's okay then?"

"Yeah. Well, as far as we can tell. If we don't count mysterious knocking that freaked out the entire population."

I opened my eyes. "James? Doesn't that seem . . . odd?"

"We passed odd a while ago."

"No, I mean that everyone was freaked out? Me, I can understand. You and Paul because I was on the phone with you, sure. But Richard? Everyone else? You said no one answered their doors, right?"

"Right." I could tell by the way he said it he was on the same wavelength I was now. "Everyone Paul talked to said the knocking frightened them, or similar, and they wouldn't answer the door."

"That's beyond unusual. I mean, there are plenty of people who would open the door. All of Airborne, for starters. My flyboys wouldn't be thrown by someone knocking in the middle of the night."

"But they were. Paul checked with high-level personnel first. All of them felt the same as us: It's creepy, it's scary, it's wrong, don't open the door."

"But you did."

"Babe, you were either in agony or being attacked. Yeah, I opened the door."

Something was tickling in my mind. "Security was down here. At least the first contingent. I heard something, scuffling, and the knocking stopped for a little bit, then started up, stronger."

"Security, all of them, are back at the main command center, Level Three."

"So whatever knocked them out put them back there. Why?"

"No idea."

"More to the point, why weren't you knocked out and put back, either into your room or into the Security command center?"

"Maybe it was a group hallucination?"

"I point you back to the sleeping Security team." A thought occurred. Decided to test it. "Which, I have to say, puts us all in terrible danger. And means that Jeff could have trouble getting back."

The com went live. "Commander Martini, are you all right?"

"Yeah, Gladys, I'm okay."

"Is Captain Reader with you?"

"Yes." It always cracked me up to hear someone use Reader's official A-C title. He never used it unless he had to, and no one on Alpha ever referred to him that way, but because we were a military unit, in that sense, we all needed military-type titles. And he was our best pilot, even better than my flyboys, which, considering they were Top Gun trained, was saying a lot.

"Security is back up and live, running complete facility scans."

"Thanks, Gladys. Glad you and the rest of the team are okay." One more test. "James, maybe you should leave." The baby kicked, hard. I gasped.

Reader reacted instantly and massaged my stomach. "I'm not going anywhere until Jeff's back, girlfriend." Calmed right down.

"Okay, I don't actually want you to leave anyway." I looked down at my stomach. "There are better ways."

"Better ways to do what?"

I leaned my head back against Reader. "I'll tell you when Jeff's back. But, I think I've seen the future. And, boy, do I hope we're ready for it."

CHAPTER 11

READER WAS QUIET, though he was still rocking me. "I have a funny feeling I know where you're going with this."

"Figure you're right."

"Why me?"

"Because, realistically, you're the one I always turn to if Jeff's not here. Not Christopher, not Chuckie, not Paul or any of the others. You. And if Jeff and I are fighting, who is the person I call or run or, for the last few months, waddle to?"

"Me."

"Bingo."

"Commanders Martini and White are back on premises, Commander."

"Thanks, Gladys." I patted the Poofs. "Back to bed, you two." They purred at us, went back to small, and then trotted to the Poof Condo.

In about five seconds, I heard the sound of running feet. Jeff burst into the room and stopped dead. "What the hell is going on?" His expression and tone of voice said that he suspected Reader was only pretending to be gay whenever Jeff was around.

The baby went nuts, and I shouted in pain. Jeff was next to me before I could finish my first shriek. He started to rub my stomach, sat on the bed, and moved me into his lap.

I was too busy whimpering and shuddering to talk, so Reader brought Jeff up to speed on what had gone on. Jeff held me and rocked me. The baby didn't stop. "Jeff, stop being jealous, please." I sobbed this out. "Jamie doesn't understand it."

"Why are you calling him Jamie?" Jeff didn't sound any less jealous.

"The baby, you idiot. I'm talking about the baby." She kicked and hit, and it was so painful I started to black out.

"Jeff, for God's sake, calm down." Reader sounded furious. "You're killing her." He took my hand and held it. "It's okay, girlfriend. Just try to relax."

Something got through to Jeff. He kissed my head. "Baby, it's okay. I'm sorry. Relax, I'm not upset. I was just worried about you and didn't realize James was in here." I sobbed from pain, but at least I was seeing more than a pinpoint of light. "Shhh, baby, shhh. It's okay, I'm here, it's all right." His voice was soothing now, and I could tell he wasn't angry any more. The baby calmed down.

Managed to take in a deep breath without it hurting. "I wanted to name the baby James Jeffrey if it was a boy and Jamie pick-a-middle-name if it was a girl. It's a girl, clearly. And I've known it since you started showing you were worried, so I call her Jamie when you're not here."

He was quiet for a few moments, and I wondered if we were going to have a fight, which, from how the baby was reacting, could kill me. But he nuzzled my head. "Jamie Katherine."

Reader and I both relaxed. I could tell because the baby went very calm and I could feel her being happy. Jeff reached out and pulled James into a group hug, which was a common A-C thing. "Sorry, James. Just been a stressful night after a stressful day."

"No problem. About to get more stressful. Just try to keep your cool." Reader kissed my cheek. "Go for it, girlfriend."

Group hug over, I took another breath. "She's your daughter, let's just say that. When you left I was worried, and then I got the usual hormonal overload."

"You mean you started panicking that I didn't love you any more, no longer found you sexually attractive, might consider having sex with Amy just because she was there, and might decide being chased by goons in the middle of Paris was more fun than being up with you at three a.m. looking at baby strollers?"

"Wow, I didn't think your sarcasm knob went past eleven, but I think you were at twelve there."

He sighed. "Not only could I pick all that up, I could also pick up when you started to get terrified. I'll do the reassurance drill later. What do you two think caused the knocking and unnatural fear? And why was James not as affected by it?"

"I think the baby picked up that I was frightened and that her daddy wasn't here. So she did her best to get the most acceptable surrogate over." I cringed, waiting for his reaction.

"That makes sense."

Reader and I looked at each other. "Personal growth is a great thing, babe."

Jeff sighed. "Look, all jealousy aside, if the person you run to when I'm not here is your best friend who happens to both be gay and married to one of my closer cousins? I'm great with that. The baby wasn't trying to get Reynolds in here. I can't even say how grateful I am for that."

"Maybe you could stop dwelling on Chuckie and his supposed still-romantic interests in me, Jeff. Since, for the past nine months at least, I only think about him as a romantic alternative when *you* bring it up."

"Huh. Fine. So, why knocking? And why did she knock out and move the Security team? I get that she wanted James with you, not them, but I don't understand the rest of it."

"I have no idea. She's a baby in the womb. I don't have a good idea of how babies in the womb think, Jeff."

Reader looked thoughtful. "She's reacting to you, though, isn't she, Kitty?"

I thought about it. "I suppose. The knocking stopped my crying. But it scared the crap out of me, too."

"Yeah, you're not kidding." Jeff hugged me. "I wasn't joking—I could feel your terror in Paris. If we hadn't been running for our lives, I'd have gotten home a lot faster."

"I probably don't want to know." Of course, I knew I'd find out. And soon.

Reader cocked his head. "That's it."

"What's it?"

He shrugged. "The baby wanted Jeff back, right? To calm you down and make her feel safe and secure. Mommy started crying, but Daddy wasn't there to do the reassurance drill. Jeff, I'll bet you wanted to get home when you felt Kitty start to go hormonal, but it was still something that was a lower priority than your assignment."

"Right," Jeff said slowly. "But, to finish where I think you're going with this, the moment I could feel how terrified Kitty was, I almost left Christopher to handle the situation so I could get back here."

"But you couldn't. And Jamie must have realized that. But, by then, I was scared out of my mind, and that meant that . . . what? James had knocking on his door, too."

"Testing," Jeff said. "Who's going to come when Daddy can't?"

"Uncle James to the rescue." Reader grinned as Jeff snorted. "What? You're naming her after me but I don't get the uncle title?"

"Of course you do. Uncle Christopher would have come, too," I added. "But she already knows that . . . ."

"What do you mean?" Jeff sounded like he was heading back to Jealousy Land. And he'd been doing so well for the past few months.

"Jeff . . . for God's sake, I cannot physically handle Jamie's reactions to your jealousy, okay? Can you just curb it? If you go all wiggy on me right now, she's going to freak out, and if the last bout was any indication, I'm going to be in ICU."

"Sorry." He rubbed my stomach. "I haven't heard this story."

"It wasn't that big a deal. You were somewhere else, Christopher wasn't. I fell, he came and helped me."

"First of all, why do I know nothing about this, what were you doing that you fell, and how did Christopher know to come to you?" Jeff sounded like he was just holding the jealousy in.

Reader shook his head. "Jeff, I don't know about it, either. Christopher got to save the day instead of me. Maybe I should stomp around the room a bit, whaddaya say?"

"Okay, fine. I've been up since midnight, and we're heading toward dawn, and I had to dodge bullets and thugs on the Parisian streets with a moment's notice and less sleep, after a day from hell, but, you know, don't cut me any slack."

I managed to laugh. "Oh, poor baby." I leaned against him and snuggled closer. "I didn't tell you because it wasn't a big deal. I tripped over something and fell in the bathroom. It scared me a lot, though, because I just missed hitting my head, again, and I wasn't sure if I'd done something to the baby."

"So, again, how did Christopher get the call?"

"He told me that our wedding picture he has on his nightstand fell over. He put it back up; it fell over again. Did that a couple more times, he got freaked out, came down to check on me while he called in to check on you."

"Oh. I remember that call. I thought it was weird." He looked at Reader. "When we were at Top Gun, for the flyboys' ceremony thing."

"Right, Kitty couldn't go and Christopher had something planned with his father. Explains why I wasn't here to save the day." He flashed the cover-boy grin. Even at four in the morning it was awesome.

"So Christopher found me, got me up, did the broken-bones check, did the is-the-baby-okay check, called Tito, who did the whole freaking check, they put me back into bed, and that was about it."

"I don't remember getting a feeling of terror from you then." Jeff sounded thoughtful. "You must have been frightened, though."

"Sort of. I was more embarrassed. I tripped on nothing and couldn't get up. I honestly didn't want you to see me like that. I just couldn't figure out if I should crawl up or lie there or what."

"Confusion versus fear." Reader shook his head. "Kitty was scared about the baby but not scared for anything else, like does my husband still love me. So Surrogate Daddy White was a fine option because he was close by and also wouldn't cause Mommy more embarrassment."

"Look, I'm the size of a freaking hippo. If we were at the zoo, the tourists would take pictures of the hippo in black and white Armani maternity wear and toss their popcorn to me and, sadly, I would eat it. I, personally, cannot wait to see Amy's reaction when she gets a look at me, particularly since the last time she saw me I looked fairly decent and not like I'd swallowed an entire supermarket whole. So, yeah, I have a lot of confidence issues right now. So sue me."

Reader kissed my cheek. "Surrogate Daddy Reader is going to bed. Surrogate Daddy White sounds busy, but I'm sure he'll be able to help if necessary." He winked at Jeff. "I'll let the real Daddy handle this issue. 'Night, babe. Really, you look a lot better than you think you do. Fertility's sexy in every culture, even this one." He yawned a goodbye to Jeff and then left, shutting both the bedroom and main doors behind him.

Jeff sighed and lifted me off his lap, put me gently back onto the bed, and then started to get undressed. "Amy's installed in a room on the transient floor. She's fine, long story that we have little of, but we'll make sure you hear at the same time we do, since I guess they taught confusion-speak at your high school."

"What is that supposed to mean?" He had his jacket off and was halfway with the shirt. I was losing interest in the conversation.

"We couldn't figure out what the hell she was talking about. However, the twenty goons after her were convincing in their desire to kill her and anyone trying to help her."

Statements like that could bring me back even from staring at Jeff's pecs. "Are you hurt? Are you okay?" The baby started to get edgy and shifted around.

Jeff was out of his shirt now, and he knelt next to the bed. He kissed my stomach. "It's okay, baby. Both babies," he added with a grin. "I'm fine. Christopher and Amy are fine, too. It was just a situation I couldn't leave, not even to get home to you two." He got up and sat next to me. "But I wanted to."

"I'm sorry, Jeff." I felt guilty for being so needy.

He hugged me. "Oh, baby, stop. I don't mind that you need me so much right now." He chuckled. "You know I love it."

"No, I don't." The hormones were doing their thing. I started to cry. Again.

He cuddled me close. "Baby, I love to take care of you. You're mine, mine to cherish and protect and love. You could have picked so many other men, and you chose me. And you're carrying my baby." His voice was soothing, and he stroked my stomach, tracing the infinity symbol against my skin. "You think you look fat. I think you look even more beautiful."

I sniffled. "I think you're lying."

He laughed. "As you love to point out, A-Cs can't lie. Therefore, when I tell you how beautiful and sexy I think you are, you're going to have to accept that it's true."

"I guess."

He nuzzled my neck. "I want a better response than that."

I moaned. As he well knew, my neck was one of my main erogenous zones. I hadn't thought my neck could get any more sexually sensitive, but pregnancy had shown that it could.

Jeff continued to nuzzle and kiss my neck. I started moaning in earnest. He got me relaxed, helped me lie down in the bed, and then took his pants off, pulled the A-C nightclothes on, and joined me. "I want to make love to you, but I think you need to rest from the baby's kicking earlier."

I couldn't argue, because he was right. I wanted to make love to him, too, but I was suddenly so tired. "Okay."

He shifted me to my side, put the extra pillows all around me, then slid his arm under my neck, put his chest against my back, and stroked my stomach with his other hand. This had been our standard sleeping position for the last few months. It was comfortable and made me feel safe and secure.

I started to fall asleep, when I felt something funny. I considered ignoring it. Felt another something funny. Thought about all the movies Tito had forced us to watch and all the private chats he'd had with us. "Jeff?"

"Yeah, baby." He sounded like he'd almost been asleep. "You okay?"

"I think I know why Jamie woke everyone up and wanted James here."

"You were scared."

"Yeah, but, um . . ."

"Um?" He sounded wide awake now.

I felt the funny again. "I think I'm going into labor."

CHAPTER 12

"COM ON!" JEFF WASN'T BELLOWING, but he was close.

"Yes, Commanders?" I found myself wondering if and when Gladys ever slept.

"Need a gurney down here immediately, as well as Doctor Hernandez. And whoever else. And her parents. And my parents. And her grandparents."

"No! Not my grandparents!" I didn't need them betting on this.

"Yes, Commander Martini. Noted, no grandparents. Medical will be there immediately. I suggest you two be clothed."

"Hilarious, Gladys." Our sex life was somewhat legendary, due mostly to the fact I hadn't found a way to be quiet when Jeff was making love to me and spent most of my time yowling like a happy cat in heat. He didn't mind at all, but we'd made a lot of people happy when we'd chosen to sleep in the bowels of the earth, several levels away from the other living floors.

"Now isn't the time for jokes." Jeff was snarling. He was still holding me. Clutching, really. I got the impression he'd forgotten every chat we'd had with Tito.

"Now's the best time. I'll handle Jeff, Gladys. If you could . . . oww . . . please call my parents . . . ooowww . . . that would be great. . . . OW!"

"Yes, Commander. Deep breaths, relax, on a four count."

"Gotcha." I did the breathing. Jeff clutched me. "Baby, you need to get up."

"What if I jostle you? What if I hurt you, or the baby?" He sounded panicked.

It was interesting. I'd figured I'd be freaked out of my mind when labor showed up, probably a total mess, only hold it together because Jeff would be a tower of strength. I mean, the man handled huge military operations against scary outer space beings trying to destroy the Earth all the time. I'd assumed he'd be in full on Commander-mode when the baby was coming. Turned out, I was cool, calm, and collected, and he was terrified.

I threaded my fingers with his. "Baby, it's okay. This is the part where I scream in pain, and you tell me to push, and you hold my hand and tell me how brave I am, and I tell you I hate you because you did this to me, and you don't let it hurt your feelings, and then we get the baby, and you tell me how amazing I am, and I tell you I couldn't have made it through the ordeal without you, and we both say how much we love each other and how wonderful the baby is."

"Deep breaths, Commander."

"I am, Gladys."

"I meant Commander Father-to-Be. You know, the one I can hear hyperventilating. Do I need to send two gurneys?"

"No!" Jeff sounded insulted and still freaked out. "I'm fine. She's just in labor. Women can die in labor! Where the hell is the gurney?"

"Jeff? Can we not focus on the 'die' part?"

"You think you're going to die?" He sounded horrified and terrified.

I started to laugh, in between contractions. "I wish I was recording this."

"No worries, Commander. We like to have a good laugh in Security, too, you know."

Tito arrived, along with a gurney, in medical scrubs. I got the impression he'd changed into them, as opposed to been sleeping in them. "Jeff, why are you still in bed?"

"She's in labor!"

Tito and I looked at each other. "It's sweet, endearing, and funny. But no one's getting through to him."

"Jeff, I need you out of bed. I have to get Kitty onto the gurney, and I was thinking you'd help me with that."

"She can't move!"

"I could if you'd let go." I was still laughing in between contractions.

Reader, Gower, and Christopher all arrived. They were, to a man, in the nighttime fatigues. A-Cs lived for clothing conformity. Reader and I had no idea why; we'd just learned to accept it, sometimes unwillingly.

"Hi, guys. Someone want to explain to Jeff that I don't want to have the baby on the bed, as charmingly old-fashioned as that might sound?"

"Jeff, get off the bed so we can get Kitty onto the gurney." Christopher sounded tired. He looked tired, too. He was smaller than Jeff, wiry and muscled versus ripped, though he had the great abs, which I assumed ran in the family. His hair was light brown and straight, though right now it was pretty messy. Normally his eyes were green, but they were so bloodshot I'd have gone with red if I didn't know him. I would have worried, but another contraction hit, and I had to focus on that as opposed to why Christopher looked so much more exhausted than Jeff.

"She's in labor!"

"Yes, we've picked that up. Gladys alerting us was also a tip-off." Reader shook his head. "Let her go, man."

"No, and I don't want anyone talking about her dying in labor again!"

"Jeff, you're the one who brought it up." I shot a "help me" look to Gower. He was Jeff's size, ebony skin, bald, and, just like every other A-C on Earth, gorgeous. He was also normally pretty calm, and usually a calming influence on Jeff.

Gower walked over, shook his head, moved Jeff's arm off me, picked me up and put me on the gurney. "How're you doing, Kitty?"

"So much better now. OW! Well, other than that contractions hurt."

Tito had been looking at his watch. "If I use when you were shouting, your contractions aren't regular yet. Let's get her upstairs. Oh, and someone help Jeff, he looks like he's going to pass out, and I need to pay attention to Kitty."

Reader took one end of the gurney, Tito took the other, and they pushed me through the Lair and to the elevators. "I knew I should have taken over the baby prep planning like I did your wedding," Reader said as we waited for the elevator.

"The baby wasn't due for another couple of weeks."

"They come when they want to," Tito said, as he checked my pulse.

"Yeah, picking that up, oh Sage One."

Reader sighed. "You don't have a crib. You don't have a stroller. You don't have a room for the baby."

"James, enough stress going on right now."

"Bassinet for the first couple of months, anyway," Tito said. "I want the baby right by her mother." He closed his eyes. "I mean its mother."

"We already figured it was a girl, Tito, no worries."

"Oh, good. I thought that was some huge A-C thing."

"It is," Reader said as we all got into the elevator, Jeff being held up by Christopher and Gower. "But certain things have become obvious, including the baby's sex."

Tito looked at me. "That weird knocking was the baby?"

"Damn, you hire well, Kitty," Gower said. "Seriously, I think you hire better than I do, without any dream or memory reading talent."

"Flattered. I'd take your job if you'd take the labor pains."

"Passing on that offer."

"Baby, are you okay?" Jeff sounded freaked.

I put my hand out, and he grabbed it. "I'm okay. Just stay with me, do what Tito says, when he says it, and stop being so scared. Women have been having babies for a long time—that's how we're all here."

"Jeff, can you handle the gurney?" Tito asked. I wondered if he'd lost his mind. Jeff didn't look like he could handle a fork right now.

But the request helped. He took a deep breath, nodded. "Yeah." His voice sounded normal again. Tito had been by my head, so Jeff moved there. "I have to let go of your hand, baby."

"That's okay. I can still see you." Out of the elevator, off to a medical bay. There were three Dazzlers there. I took the gorgeous for granted on them, since they were in the full scrubs, hairnets and surgical masks. Tito started to consult with one while the other two moved me to the bed and hooked me up to a variety of things I didn't want to pay attention to.

The men weren't leaving, and I got the impression they planned to stay. No sooner thought than Tim Crawford ran into the room. Tim was Airborne's driver and the last member of Alpha Team not represented in the delivery bay. "Is Kitty okay?"

Nods all around. I heard more thundering feet. Three more guys showed up—Jerry Tucker, Matt Hughes, and Chip Walker, three of my five flyboys. We were missing the female members of Airborne and their mates, I assumed because the girls had the brains to keep their men in their damn beds.

My wellness was assured for the new arrivals, and now I had a stag party in the delivery room with me. None of them looked like they planned to leave. "Uh, guys? I love you all very much, and I'm really touched that you want to be in here to see the miracle of birth and all, but other than Jeff, if James wants to be here to give me someone else to scream at, that's fine. But the rest of you? Clear the hell out before I go all *Exorcist* on you."

They stared at me. "But . . . you might need help," Tim said finally.

Tito looked around and seemed to notice the team in here for the first time. "What the hell are you all doing in here? Out! Now! Jeff stays. Period."

Reader shook his head. "Me too."

"Yeah, that's fine." Jeff stroked my hair. "But, everyone else, wait outside, handle the parents and family members."

"I don't want any of them in here, not even my mother," I added quickly. "Christopher, you'll be the only one who can keep her out."

"Why don't you want her?" He sounded confused.

"Because I don't want anyone jollying me up, telling me to be a big girl, sharing how it's not as bad as their labor, or anything else." Another labor pain hit and I yelled. All the guys backed up a step.

"Out!" Jeff wasn't bellowing, but his Commander voice was on full. The rest of the guys nodded and left.

One of the Dazzlers dragged Jeff and Reader off to get washed up and into the scrubs and masks while another closed all the curtains in the room so I was no longer in a fishbowl. Tito was watching a machine near my stomach. "Contractions are about three minutes apart. That's really fast to go from zero to this in less than thirty minutes." He and the last Dazzler moved me into the stirrups and Tito took a look. "Jeff, James! Hurry up!" He looked up at me, from between my legs, which was a surreal moment for me. "You're dilated to nine already. The baby's coming fast."

"A-C babies do," one of the Dazzlers said. I recognized her voice.

"Emily?"

"Yeah, Melanie's getting the boys washed up."

"What are you two doing here? You're science side."

She chuckled. "We're doctors, too. We just like the science stuff more. But, under the circumstances, we wanted to be here with you."

The Dazzler on drapes duty came over. "I'm Camilla. I don't think we've met officially, Commander."

I tried to say something polite back, but another labor pain hit, and I shrieked instead. Jeff and Reader were back and were installed at either side of me. I grabbed their hands and squeezed.

"It's okay, baby." Jeff kissed my forehead. "I love you."

I usually did this same thing right before I slammed an adrenaline harpoon into his hearts, which I had to do often because when his empathic blocks were shot, or he was too past overexertion, he needed adrenaline or he'd die. It was horrible and agonizing for him. "I don't need adrenaline, do I?"

"No," the third Dazzler said, and I recognized Melanie's voice. "Just relax as much as you can, Kitty." She and Emily were both massaging my legs. "Our babies come fast, because of the hyperspeed. It can be very hard on a human woman."

"Will it be hard on Lorraine and Claudia?" Melanie and Emily's daughters, who were both due to deliver a few months from now.

"No, they're A-C. It'll feel like normal delivery to them. Serene, too." Speaking of our last Airborne member, who was right behind Lorraine and Claudia in our own Baby Olympics.

Jeff's hand tightened on mine. "How hard is it going to be on Kitty?"

There was a pregnant pause, which I tried to find funny but could only manage ironic. "Ericka Gower did just fine," Melanie said finally.

"That you know of." Jeff's voice was crisp.

"She had four kids," I gasped out. "Clearly, she survived it."

"Contractions two minutes apart," Tito said, sounding calm. "Dilated to nine and a half."

"At least it won't be long and drawn out."

No one laughed. I got really nervous.

Jeff stroked my head. "Try not to worry, baby." Of course, he looked and sounded beyond worried, so I had a little trouble with the do-as-I-say-not-as-I-do mind-set.

Reader had my hand and was massaging my shoulder. Jeff followed suit. I had four people rubbing me, and yet I didn't feel relaxed at all. I heard Camilla talking quietly into the com. She was requesting a variety of extras, blood foremost among them. I went from nervous to frightened, fast.

"One minute apart, dilated to ten." Tito's hand was on my stomach. "Baby's still moving around."

The way he said it made one of his lectures come to mind. "Is her head down?" Thudding silence. Okay, that meant no and that meant dangerous for her and for me. I closed my eyes and tried to send some sort of message to the baby to let her know she had to turn around again.

I felt someone else helping talk without speaking to Jamie, and she shifted. "Head's down." Tito sounded incredibly relieved.

Pain hit, bad, hard, and fast. I screamed, couldn't stop myself. The room went nuts, with a lot of fast medical talking and a lot of movement. I felt myself detaching from it. I didn't think this was a good thing.

I heard some scary beeping and saw Jeff's face drain of color. "Kitty!" I could hear Reader calling to me. "Focus, Kitty. Stay with us. Come on, babe, stay with us."

I looked at him, and I tried to stay, but something dragged me off.

The last thing I heard was Jeff, speaking softly. "No, please. Please don't take her away from me. Please."

CHAPTER 13

I WAS FLOATING, and I had perfect clarity. All of a sudden, I remembered that nine months ago Reader had told me he'd died, seen all sort of things, then been sent back. To take care of me.

I didn't have a body, which I verified by looking around. All I could see was a thin golden line, like a string, attached to me and something else. I got a very possessive feeling about that string.

The nice part of this was that there was no pain at all. I kind of liked that. Sadly, it was quiet and somewhat dull, which meant my mind was wandering. Well, I was only my mind or soul or whatever, but it was bored and wanted some stimulation.

I saw what looked like an old-fashioned wheel for a slide projector, only the wheel was huger than I could really comprehend, and the slides were thinner than my string. They sat next to each other. I realized I was seeing the universes just like Reader had. It was pretty weird and awesome at the same time.

They flipped through, and I saw myself in a lot of them. Like Reader had told me, we were together in most of them, married in at least half. The ones where we weren't married we were still each other's best friend. We were never enemies or indifferent to each other. The universes were moving quickly past me, but I got full information from them as they went by. I understood what the term "soul mate" meant now, and why he and I had gotten so close so fast.

Saw a ton where I was married to Chuckie, almost as many as where I was married to Reader. They were interesting, too. I knew Reader in most of them, for a variety of reasons, but there were a few of the Chuckie-worlds where Reader and I didn't cross. There were almost no worlds where I didn't know Chuckie, however, and it was the same as with Reader—we were always best friends, married or not. So I had two soul mates, which was nice.

Seemed pretty happy with Chuckie. Or Reader. Very happy, actually. Good marriages with both Reader and Chuckie. Interesting.

Of the few worlds where I wasn't married to Reader or Chuckie, there were a variety where I was married to men I didn't know and a few where I was married to girls I didn't know. But even so, Reader and Chuckie were there in almost all of these as well.

There was another sampling where I wasn't there at all—most of these seemed to have been those where anti-Semitism had won the day so definitively that my father had never been born. Me not being in them aside, I found those worlds horrible—dark and cruel and joyless for far too many of the people in them. There were so many races missing from Earth in those, I had to figure genocide truly did equal misery for all, not just the races being wiped out.

There were some where dinosaurs still existed and some where the Earth was so odd I couldn't comprehend what was going on. It was fascinating to see, but I found myself wondering how anyone, God or not, could keep all this stuff straight. Remembered that ACE had said God gave us free will for just this reason.

ACE was a superconsciousness I'd funneled into Paul Gower about a year and a half ago. ACE had told me a lot about God and other things, and I found myself wondering where it was and whether it was watching me. Maybe ACE was the string. I checked; the string was still there.

The universe wheel was still spinning. In fact, as far as I could tell, it was going around again. I realized something scary—there was only one universe where Earth had A-Cs on it, at least, only one where I knew they existed. I hadn't seen Jeff, or any of the other A-Cs on Earth, in any other universe. So there was only one where I was with him.

I felt cheated. I knew if I died, I'd be with Reader and

Chuckie and my parents, and so many others, in other universes. It would be hard for them in the one I was from, but I was there, elsewhere. But Jeff wouldn't have that. He and I had one chance in what seemed like a zillion, and it was being taken away.

Surprises abounded. If someone had asked, I would have said a disembodied soul or mind couldn't cry. Would have been wrong. I was sobbing. I wouldn't see my baby, my husband would be alone, and I wouldn't see them in any other world, either. This was it, and I was going to miss it all. I didn't want to miss any of it, not even the pain, if it meant I would never hold my baby, never see Jeff's smile again.

I want to go home! I shouted it, but no vocal cords meant no sound.

I felt a tug. The string jerked me. But it was frayed, I could see it. I chose not to panic and started to move along it, as best I could. I was able to move, and I found myself wondering if this was what the superbeing parasites felt like—lost, alone, held to life by a fraying string. If they didn't turn mammals into horrifying, murderous creatures, I'd never kill one again. Then again, maybe I was going to turn into one, fly into some world I didn't belong in, or even into my own, and attach to some poor unsuspecting sap and make him or her an evil superbeing. I didn't like where my mind was going with this.

I want to go home to Jeff and our baby. I was begging. *It's not fair.*

I waited to hear some big voice in the ether tell me that life wasn't fair. Got the silence of the uninterested instead. I'd have called God a jerk, but remembered He'd sent Reader back for me nine months ago. Guessed that was a short-term loan.

Kept moving along the string. Got past some frayed portions but had no confidence I'd be able to hold on if something snapped. Had to figure I needed to speed this up. The universe wheel was spinning, and I had no guess as to how I was going to fling myself back into the right one, string or no string.

Started to focus. My kung fu instructors had spent a long time working with me on learning how to meditate. I still sucked at it, but one thing I'd gotten was that slavish devotion to one idea was good. I tried to figure out which one thing I should focus on. Ran through my options, then reminded myself that Jeff was only in one place, at least for me, and if I ever wanted to see him again, perhaps he was the right focus object.

Problem was, any time I thought of him, I had trouble doing much other than thinking about how great he was, and this tended to shift my focus onto our sex life. Even disembodied with nothing to enjoy sex with, I was right back to thinking about making love to him.

I was more than resentful that I was apparently going to die without getting to make love to him again. In fact, the more I thought about that, the more pissed off I got. Bad enough to die in childbirth and saddle my poor baby girl with that kind of unwarranted but hard to ignore guilt, but I wasn't even getting good-bye sex? I'd kind of planned on going via death by orgasm, since sex with Jeff was always a good bet for that kind of end. I'd also planned on going when we were like ninety or something, not when I wasn't even twenty-nine yet.

In fact, the baby was supposed to have come on or around my birthday. As I thought about it, we hadn't even made it to Christmas. Couldn't remember when Christmas was right now, but it was close. And I'd been denied. Sure, my family had pretty much avoided the December holidays my entire life, and Jeff, as an A-C, had no Christmas at all, since their religion wasn't from our world. So it wasn't like we'd planned anything big. But it was the idea of the thing.

Denied good-bye sex. Denied death by orgasm. Denied my baby. Denied years of marital bliss with the alien sex god. Denied a Christmas I didn't care about. Denied baby showers I didn't want. Denied getting to be a mother. Denied getting to see my friends have their kids. Denied what I did want and what I didn't, indiscriminately. And for no good reason that I could see. I was not a happy girl.

Fascinatingly, anger seemed to speed me along that string. I was sailing toward something. I hoped it was the right something, between my righteous wrath about denial and why I didn't like it.

Do not ask me how, but I managed, disembodied and pissed off, to trip over my own string. This was—as I thought about it and watched my perspective go end over end while the string wrapped around whatever was functioning as "me" for this experience—the story of my life. Figured I was at least going out in my own personal style, whatever that was. Decided again that I really didn't want to go.

I know I'll forget all this. I'll forget it all right away if you let me go back and live out the life I'm supposed to with Jeff. Bargaining—could not remember where that was on the Death and Dying steps. Refused to leave it. I was not getting to Acceptance, at least not without a fight. *Oh, and I'm not kidding. If I get back there and then you kill Jeff, I'll figure out a way to come and kick your butt for it.*

Did some more disembodied tumbling. It was less nauseating than going through a gate, the alien transference system that still looked more like an airport metal detector than anything else, but this was damning with faint praise.

I had to ask why I could feel all this stuff if I was on this side of dying. Added resentment to my anger about being denied. I got to do the whole "see the other side" thing while totally sick to my stomach.

Had another thought. *Oh, and you're not trading me for Jamie, either. I want my whole family—me, Jeff, and Jamie—all together. And any other kids we might have. None of this family tragedy stuff. Jeff's had enough of that already, and, for that matter, so has Christopher. Losing Terry was more than they deserved, and then they lost Lissa, and they don't deserve this, either.*

Terry was Christopher's mother, who'd pretty much been murdered by the head in-control superbeing when the boys were ten. Lissa was the A-C girl they'd both wanted to marry, who'd been murdered by a different in-control superbeing. I was the human girl they'd both wanted to marry. I couldn't imagine how Jeff would recover from losing me in childbirth. Not at all leaped to mind. Christopher might not, either. And they needed to reproduce. I'd known that since Operation Fugly, when I'd taken out the two in-control superbeings who had killed Terry and Lissa.

You don't want Mephistopheles to win, now, do you? I mean, all that work, just to wipe out the chances of Jeff and Christopher having kids and doing whatever your master plan here is? I don't think so, Big Guy. Really, it's a bad choice for you.

Yeah, focus the greater power on the suffering of others

and the master plan, whatever the heck it was. Still figured that was Bargaining. I was great with Bargaining. And Anger. That was a step. Ah, college—how it all came back to me at odd moments.

Kept tumbling while the universe wheel spun. Wondered if the other Kittys in the other universes were feeling dizzy or nauseated right now. Kind of hoped they weren't. Didn't seem fair. Of course, none of this was fair. Back to Resentment.

Tried to focus on Jeff again. Heard something now. It was being repeated over and over again. Recognized it—Mi Sh-beirach, the Jewish prayer for healing. Figured my father was handling the asking nicely portion of this event and was glad someone was.

Realizing my parents must know I was floating around in the ether made me angrier. They'd been looking forward to being grandparents, in part because they could then say all the things I'd done the same and differently as my own child. Added this "denied" to my long list.

Heard something else, also being repeated over and over. It was fast—I couldn't make out the words—but I recognized who was making the sounds. Richard White was the Sovereign Pontifex of the Earth A-Cs, their religious leader. I guessed he was praying, too, but all the beings from the Alpha-Centauri system naturally talked faster than humans could comprehend—they learned how to slow down to deal with humans. Apparently they prayed that fast, too. Richard was Christopher's father and Jeff's uncle, and I added him onto the list of people who didn't need to go through the tragedy of losing me.

This was starting to sound totally self-centered. Didn't care. Figured if there was ever a time to be self-centered, it was when I was hanging between life and death.

A voice came through. I recognized it as Christopher's. *Come on, Kitty. Don't give up. Jeff'll never recover, and I can't keep him going alone. Where the hell's the fight in you when we need it?* He'd said that to me once before, in a dream.

I'm not letting her go. You take her, you take me, too. We're supposed to be together, forever. Jeff's voice. He sounded awful, ready and willing to die.

Fight, Kitty. Reader's voice. Not scared, urgent. *Come*

on, I know you're still there. Fight to come back. You can do it.

Heard something else now. It was music. Not soft, not funereal, not religious in any way, so to speak. It was rock and roll. Rock and roll I happened to love. Point of fact, it was "Nine Lives" by Aerosmith.

I started to laugh.

CHAPTER 14

"KITTY! FOCUS, COME ON, babe, you're still here, I can feel it. Come on, fight, dammit!" Reader wasn't shouting but his voice was pretty strong.

"Tim, really, stop blasting that music." This was from Tito. "James, she can't hear you. Jeff, you have to let go." He said this gently. "We need to hurry to get the baby out."

"No." I realized someone was holding me and rocking. Recognized the arms and the body as Jeff's. "I'm not letting her go." I could tell he was crying.

"Tim, the music," Tito snapped. "Turn it off."

"I like the music." Dead silence, other than Screamin' Steven Tyler singing. Loved Aerosmith. Nice to hear my boys in between bouts of agony. Felt a contraction. "Am I supposed to be pushing? Or something?"

Bedlam. Always interesting, especially since the A-Cs only went for it when they were both really freaked and not thinking. Of course, from what I could tell, I had a huge crowd of humans in here. Most of whom were male.

"Is every guy I work with staring at my crotch, or am I just imagining that?"

"Out!" Tito sounded pissed again. "Leave the stupid music, fine, but get out of here, all of you, parents included."

"Hey Mom, Dad?" I called before they left the room. I hadn't realized they were in the room, probably because the place was so crowded. My father was holding my mother, and they both looked like they'd been sobbing. "Can you get a bassinet? Like fast?"

"Uh, sure, kitten," Dad managed to say. My mother just started bawling.

"Geez, Mom, they aren't that expensive." Heard more sobbing, realized Alfred and Lucinda were there. Martini's parents were now holding my parents up as they left the room. "One request for a bassinet and everyone goes to pieces. Fine, she can sleep in a Poof bed until I can get to the baby store."

Jeff started to laugh. "Push, baby. We got a little delayed."

I pushed. "Why?"

"Uh, you died on the table," Reader said. I looked over at him. He had a funny look on his face.

"No, I didn't. I mean, I'm right here."

"Yeah." Reader took a deep breath. "Good." I looked right into his eyes and saw a lot of things, but they all flashed by too fast to remember. He was still holding my hand. "I'm glad you're back, girlfriend."

Jeff was kissing my head. He was also close to hysterics, which I'd never seen him get remotely near to before. "Jeff? What's wrong? Is the baby okay?"

"I think so, yeah." He clung to me. "Push again, baby. We need to get Jamie out."

I pushed.

"You're not pushing hard enough, Kitty," Tito said. "You have to push, hard, or we go caesarean right now."

Pushed harder. Did not want the surgery, especially since it was a longer recovery before you could have sex. Jeff laughed again. "I love how you think." He took my other hand. "Hold onto me and James and really push, baby, hard."

I did. "I can see her head," Melanie called.

Did the pushing and straining thing. It wasn't great but I wasn't very tired for some reason. "Did anyone give me that thing where the pain gets muted?"

"Epidural, and no." Tito's voice was crisp. "Trust me, we don't have time. Push . . . push . . . Kitty, really, *push*."

Did, hard. "By the way, Jeff, this hurts, and to keep the tradition, I'm forced to say that it's all your fault. *You* did this to me." It didn't hurt as bad as it had before, but, you know, I didn't want him to miss out on the full Daddy Experience.

Jeff started to laugh hysterically.

"Calm down, Jeff," Christopher said soothingly. "Kitty, push."

Pushed harder. "Why is Christopher still in here? I thought only Jeff, Tito, and James were going to see me like this."

"Let him stay," Reader said. "Trust me."

I moved my head to take a look. Christopher was holding Jeff. It looked like he was keeping Jeff upright. They both looked like they were just this side of breaking down. "It's just childbirth, guys."

Jeff started back toward breaking down. "Push, Kitty," Christopher said, snark suddenly on full. "Where's the fight in you when we need it?"

"Geez, do you ever stop saying that to me?"

"It's the first time I've ever actually said it to you," Christopher snapped.

"Now isn't the time," Reader said. "Kitty, push."

I did, hard. "I thought only Jeff or Tito were going to say push."

The room rang out. "PUSH!" Apparently, everyone was going to tell me what to do right now. Fine. Pushed, harder than hard.

"More Kitty, she's almost here." Tito was doing something to help, I couldn't tell what. At least I assumed he was down there doing something helpful.

"Come on, baby," Jeff said quietly. "One more big push and we get a prize."

I pushed and felt the baby move out. "Got her." Tito looked up. "Does Daddy want to cut the cord?"

Jeff clutched me. "Uh, no. Daddy doesn't want to risk doing anything wrong that could hurt Mommy or Baby."

Tito shrugged. "Not a problem here." He did whatever. "Jeff, really, these days, we let the father help with this. It's fine."

"Go on. That way you can tell me about it."

He let me go, slowly, but then hypersped over to Tito. They went off with Melanie to the sink. Reader still had my hand, and Christopher was stroking my forehead while Camilla and Emily did something down in my personal regions I didn't want to know about. "Good job. Knew you could do it if you tried." Christopher sounded relaxed, finally.

"My girl can do anything," Reader said, flashing the cover-boy smile. He kissed my hand. "I'm really glad you're back, babe."

Wanted to say I hadn't gone anywhere, but I was tired all of a sudden. "Yeah."

Jeff was back, carrying a bundle. A-C hospital beds were nice and large. He sat down next to me. "She's beautiful. She looks just like her mommy." He was looking at her and smiling and making all sorts of goo-goo faces.

"Uh, Jeff? Can I see her?"

"Oh! Yeah." He turned her so I could look at her. Big blue eyes stared back at me out of a little red face. I couldn't see me in her. I couldn't see Jeff in her, either. It didn't matter. I reached for her and Jeff put her in my arms.

"Do I feed her now?"

"Not quite yet," Emily said, mask off. She looked as though she'd been crying. "What are you naming her?"

"Jamie Katherine." I thought about it. "She should have A-C and human godparents, wouldn't you think?" A-C traditions were different from human, but the result was the same in terms of godparents.

Jeff nodded. "Fine with me. You okay with me asking?"

"Unless I've missed something, the male side's still in the room with us."

"Yeah." He grinned and looked at Christopher. "You good with covering godfather duties for the A-C side?"

"Yeah." Christopher sounded like he was going to lose it.

"James?" Jeff looked over. "You up for it?"

"Happy to. More than happy to."

"We'll pick the girls later." I was really tired. "When do we nap?"

"Now." Tito shook his head. "I know telling Jeff to leave the room will be a complete waste of breath. James, Christopher, you two, however, need to go for now. I don't want anyone coming in and upsetting Kitty, either. I want her to sleep."

"You're all acting like I died or something."

Jeff's eyes closed. "You did."

"You just worry too much." I yawned. "Can we go to sleep? Unless I'm supposed to feed her now."

Melanie was over, mask off, also looking as though she'd been crying. "Let's get James and Christopher out, then I'll show you how to feed her. She probably won't want much."

"Works for me. By the way, Tito? How soon can we have sex again?"

Jeff started the hysterical laughing I assumed was what all new fathers did. I didn't have a lot of experience with it, after all. Tito just chuckled. "You didn't tear, so reasonably soon. But not too soon."

"Jeff, pull it together," Christopher said quietly. "Everything's okay now and heading back to normal."

Jeff nodded. "Only my girl." He looked like he was contemplating laughing again. Or possibly crying. I wasn't totally sure. I was tired enough, though, that I decided not to worry about it.

Extra males removed and Tito happy with the results, he and Camilla left. I had a monitor on my wrist, and Jamie had one on hers. Tito and Camilla had the receptors. Melanie and Emily helped us get situated a little better on the bed, did the breastfeeding thing, which was pretty awesome. They left once we got going, leaving the three of us alone.

Jeff stroked the baby's head. His touch was gentle, but the movements looked deliberate to me.

"Did you implant the blocks for her?" Jamie looked so peaceful I had to assume he had.

"Yeah, just now. I don't know how effective they'll be. She's more powerful than my sisters' kids. There's more than empathic in her, too."

"How can you tell?"

"I just . . . can."

I yawned. I was even more tired all of a sudden. "Something you learned from that glowing cube thing?"

Jeff stiffened and I remembered something. He didn't know that I knew about the glowing cube thing. Whoops.

CHAPTER 15

"WHAT ARE YOU TALKING ABOUT?" Jeff's voice sounded strained.

I considered lying, but didn't have the energy for it. Besides, now this affected our child, so it was probably the time to get the pertinent details. "Terry showed it to me. In the implanted memory you put in way back when."

"Oh." He sounded no less strained. "What . . . what did you see?"

I contemplated how to safely answer this while I desperately focused on flowers in the hopes that he wouldn't see or feel what I was thinking. I was pretty sure Terry had shown me her last acts before she died, when Jeff and Christopher were both ten. I didn't think, based on the complications everyone seemed to insist I'd had, that Jeff would be able to handle seeing and essentially reliving those moments.

"Oh, God. You saw her dying?" He clutched me. "Baby, I'm so sorry."

So much for my ability to multithink just after having given birth. Oh, well, nothing for it. "Jeff, it's okay. She showed me so I'd understand, when the time came. So I'd know how and why she'd programmed you to find me. It wasn't a bad thing for me to see—it was like seeing someone else's dream." And it had helped me to save the day during Operation Fugly, so, in my opinion, it was all good.

"Is the implant still . . . in you?"

This wasn't really the conversation I'd planned to have

to welcome our new arrival, but under the circumstances, I just went for it and hoped Jeff wouldn't freak out. "No. There was a trace of Terry's consciousness in me for a while, but ACE removed it. That part of Terry is a part of ACE's collective consciousness now."

"Does Christopher know?"

"No, and neither does Richard. Paul knows, and me, and now you. And that's all. And I think that should stay all. I really don't think Christopher could handle it." I wasn't sure that Jeff could handle it, and it was only his beloved aunt, not his beloved mother.

"No, you're right. And you were right not to tell anyone else."

"Are you sorry I told you now?"

He hugged me. "No. In some ways, I wish you'd told me earlier, but I can understand why you didn't." He sounded guilty, as he always did in regard to the implanted memory.

I sighed. "Baby, you need to stop with the guilt. It's silly, especially after all this time. You didn't do anything wrong." I snuggled nearer to him. "I think the benefits received have far outweighed the fainting spell when we first met."

Jeff's body relaxed a tiny bit. I noted that Jamie wasn't reacting to any of this. In fact, she was asleep. We hadn't burped her. My first hour as a mother, and I had a feeling I was already a failure. It figured. But pressing matters being what they were, I decided to merely start a list of my motherhood screw-ups to save everyone time and get back to the issues at hand. "The blocks you put into Jamie are really strong, aren't they?"

"Yes." He took a deep breath. "You want to know about the cube, don't you?"

"Yes. And how the blocks do and will work for Jamie. But if it's too upsetting for you, we could wait." Even though I wasn't sleepy any more. Stressful conversations with my husband tended to wake me up for some reason.

"No, it's not upsetting. When I was born and had . . . so many problems, Aunt Terry realized someone was going to have to find a way to protect our stronger empaths, beyond isolation chambers and what we did typically, because she figured if there was one who manifested early, there could be more. When Christopher was born and turned out to be as strong an imageer as I was an empath, she realized stronger talents could be cropping up all over."

Considering most A-C talents showed up in the teenage years and Jeff's and Christopher's talents had appeared at birth, Terry being the only one worried about the potential for stronger, earlier talent manifestations seemed odder than the fact that she'd figured out what to do about it. But my experience with the A-Cs had shown that most of them really didn't like to rock the boat or question the status quo or those in authority, even if they weren't happy with the rules they were living under. That Terry had and Jeff did regularly identified them as mavericks, not trendsetters, of the AC community.

"Makes sense. What did she do?"

"She created a program, almost like a computer program, that could be implanted into someone's mind."

"Sounds pretty advanced."

"She had help, I'd guess. Not sure from whom, but she was good with science and medicine, as well as being our Head Diplomat and a strong empath."

Female empaths were rare, so Terry being unusual in other ways wasn't too surprising. "But you don't know who helped her?"

"No idea. She never said, and I could be wrong. No one has ever asked me or Christopher about the cube, so maybe she did it alone."

I thought about it. "It could have been some older A-Cs who helped her, too. They might have passed away before you were old enough for them to ask."

"That makes sense." He sighed. "The cube was the transference system to get the programming into us. I don't know that I can explain how it worked. We opened the cube, looked at it, and the information downloaded."

"What happened to the cube?"

Jeff was silent. I shifted so I could look at his face. He was looking at Jamie, not at me, but his expression was one I was used to—he was trying to lie.

Chuckie's undoubtedly accurate belief that there were some A-Cs who could lie notwithstanding, I surely wasn't married to one of them. "Jeff, it's me. Look at me, and tell me the truth, because whatever you're thinking of saying right now is an utter fabrication, and I already know it."

He sighed again and met my gaze. "Fine. The information was programmed specifically for me and Christopher. I think it was attached to our DNA in some way. The information went in, we both passed out, when we woke up, the cube was gone."

Interesting. "Did you look for it?"

He shot me a dirty look. "Of course we looked for it. We couldn't find it."

"Where were you, when this happened? The Embassy, with Richard, or with your parents?"

"My parents."

"Ah."

"Ah?"

I sighed. "One of your family found it, Jeff. And if they didn't understand it, they took it to figure out what was going on with the cube. However, since we don't have this process as an open, admitted function, I'm betting whoever found the cube knew exactly what it was for and took it, either to hide it away forever or to use it against your people."

Jeff looked worried. "I don't know."

Before we could discuss this any further, there was a knock at the door and my mother put her head in. "Kitten, Jeff, can I disturb you for a minute?"

Mom sounded strange. She kind of looked strange, too. "Sure, Mom. What's wrong?" I asked as she came in and shut the door.

She gave me the "are you crazy, is that your problem?" look. I was garnering that one a lot these days. "Jeff, you all look very cozy, but could I have some time alone with Kitty, please?"

"Sure." Jeff got out of bed quickly. "I'll just, uh . . ."

"Jeff, find your mom and dad and ask them about what we were talking about. Really monitor for emotions. I'm praying one of them found it, but we need to know, either way."

He nodded, kissed Jamie on her head, kissed me full on the mouth, hugged my mom tightly, then zipped out of the room.

Mom came over and sat where Jeff had been. "How are you doing?"

"Fine. A little tired. Breastfeeding is pretty cool. Oh, and Jeff implanted blocks into the baby."

"Good, good." Mom stroked my hair. She also seemed really distracted.

"Mom? What's going on?" She wasn't looking at Jamie; she wasn't asking what we'd named her, nothing. Something was off.

She pulled me into her arms and gave me her by-now-legendary breath-stopping bear hug. "I thought we'd lost you forever." I realized my mother was crying.

This knowledge instantly freaked me out. I'd been too busy earlier to have the fact that my parents and Jeff's parents had been crying in the delivery room register as anything other than a part of the general confusion. But I hadn't seen my mother cry much in my life. Mom was always the one taking care of problems, handling emergencies, holding other people while they cried. "Mom, what's wrong? Is Dad okay?"

She gave a strangled laugh. "Well, yes, we're both okay now that our only child has come back from the dead."

"I don't remember the dying thing."

"You did. You flatlined. We saw it. Christopher was hysterical when he came to get us and Alfred and Lucinda. I don't know how he managed to be calm for Jeff while he was in the room with you, but thank God he did."

I managed to get an arm around her and hugged her back. "Mom, you're kind of scaring me right now. I'm fine, you can relax."

She hugged me tighter. "I am relaxing."

"Air . . . need air . . . relax the hug . . ."

Mom let go, though she kept her arm around me. "Well, you certainly sound like there was no harm done," she said dryly.

"There wasn't. Tito said I didn't even tear. Down there, I mean."

"I know what it means. How nice for your sex life. At any rate, I just wanted to tell you that I'm so thankful you're still with us, kitten." She hugged me one-armed and kissed my forehead. "I love you so much and I'm so proud of you, and I really thought I'd never get to tell you that ever again."

I decided arguing that I hadn't died was stupid. I'd almost never seen my mother this emotional and, as sluggish memory finally served, she was only like this when the people she loved most were in a danger she couldn't prevent or protect them from. "I'm fine now, Mom. Not leaving you and Dad for a long time. I promise."

"Good." She kissed my head again. "I'm going to go home."

"Why? You haven't even really seen the baby yet."

Mom sighed. "Your father and I went home after you . . . gave birth. We just . . . needed to be in your room, see your things, be alone without having to try to be brave or supportive or any other emotion for anyone else. Your father's still there—he didn't feel that he could see you right now and not break down in front of you and potentially upset you and the baby, let alone Jeff."

Wow. My parents were wrecks. I felt hugely guilty for no good reason, but guilty nonetheless. "I'm so sorry, Mom. I didn't mean to upset you and Dad like this."

She gave a strangled laugh. "Kitten, there's no woman in the world who wants to die in childbirth. It happens, even to the healthiest and those with the best medical care. I'm just thankful God gave you back to all of us."

There was something about that, what she'd said, that I felt I really and truly ought to remember. But nothing came. "Well, me too. You want some grandma time while you're here?"

She stroked Jamie's head. "No, not right now. I want to get home and reassure your father that you're really okay. I want both of us to calm down, so that when we see you again, we're the parents you're used to."

"I'm all for everyone getting back to normal as soon as humanly possible." I thought about it. "And alienly possible."

Mom chuckled. "You certainly seem like you're back to normal." She hugged me again. "Love you, kitten. Try to relax and enjoy this next phase of your life."

"Especially since I'm here to have it."

Mom sighed. "Yes. And thank you for proving that it was a good thing I left your father at home." Mom's sarcasm knob was turning. She wasn't at eleven, or even close to it yet, but it was clear that eleven would again be a likely happening. Strangely enough, this comforted me much more than her crying had. I decided to table the mental and psychological ramifications of this for another time.

"I love you, Mom."

I got the bear hug again, then Mom got off the bed. "We'll be back later, once you've had some more family alone time."

Jeff came back in as she said this. I wasn't sure if he'd been lurking outside the door or the timing had just worked out. He gave Mom another big hug and she left.

"Is my mom still freaked out?"

He shook his head. "No, she's normalizing." He ran his hand through his hair. "I've never felt her that upset. Not that I can blame her."

"Enough talk of me going to the other side and coming back and all the emotions stirred up therefore. What did you find out from your parents?"

"Not much. I can't be certain, but I don't think either one of them found the cube."

"Why can't you be sure?"

He shrugged as he got back into bed. "They're as upset about what happened, and as relieved, as your parents. There's not an emotion in the Science Center that's not off the charts in some way." He looked tired all of a sudden.

"You need to keep your blocks up. I'm sorry, I didn't think." The last thing I wanted was Jeff having to go into isolation right now.

He kissed my head. "Relax, baby. I'm fine. I kept my blocks up. But it's why I can't be sure with my parents. I'll ask again when things are calmer. But I want *you* staying calm."

"I know, I broadcast my emotions."

"You just gave birth to our daughter. I want you to relax and enjoy this time."

On cue, Jamie woke up and made some baby noises. She wasn't crying, but my breasts were right there, and I gave feeding her again another shot. She went for it.

"So, how are all these emotions affecting Jamie, implanted blocks or not? You said she was stronger than your sisters' children—do we need to worry?"

"Probably. But not right now. Now's for just being together." Jeff was watching me breastfeed as though this was the most fascinating thing he'd ever seen. He was wrapped around me, kissing my head. I could feel his hearts, and they were pounding. Jamie finished up, and Jeff helped me move her to the other side. "I never thought it'd be possible, but those are even more spectacular right now than they've ever been before." He sounded awed.

"It's just a pair of breasts, when you get down to it, Jeff."

"Your breasts have always been more than just a pair to me. Perfect breasts are a rarity, something to be treasured, held, enjoyed, and pleasured."

"Hold that thought. For, I guess a couple of weeks. You get to burp her, they told me not to sit up." He took the baby and did the against the shoulder thing. "She looks so tiny in your hands. I can't believe how much she pumped my stomach up."

Jeff gave a strangled laugh. "She's eight and a half pounds. Thank God she came early. Any later and—" His eyes closed and he looked like he was going to break down again. Jamie burped, rather discreetly, and Jeff put her back into my arms.

"Are we supposed to sleep with her?"

"No, but we're going to anyway." He pulled the railing up on the side Jamie was on and then got back into bed on my other side. He wrapped around me again, and I shifted to have my head lean on his body so he could wrap both arms around me and the baby. Emily had brought in a blanket, and he pulled it over us. "You comfy, baby?"

"Yes. This feels nice. Labor was less horrible than I'd thought it would be."

"That's a matter of perspective." His voice was shaky. "If you only want one, that's okay."

This was against everything he'd ever said. Jeff wanted lots of kids and had never made any comments to the contrary. With this and my mother's reactions, whether or not I remembered it, clearly I'd had some real trouble during labor.

"You really don't remember?" He sounded shocked.

"No, I don't. Maybe the equipment was faulty."

"Hardly. The only one who still had any belief you were really still hanging by a thread was James. Thank God. He wouldn't let Tito take you off the machines."

Thread. Hmmm. Why did that sound familiar? Couldn't come up with it. Decided not to care. "Well, whatever. I'm fine, the baby seems fine, and once you calm down, you'll be fine, too."

"You're still alive, you and Jamie are both okay, I'm better than fine."

"You're always better than fine."

Jeff laughed. "I love how you think. Even right after a hard delivery, your mind is laser-focused."

I snuggled closer and hugged the baby. She was already asleep. "It's a gift."

CHAPTER 16

THE BABY WOKE UP a few hours later, this time really wanting to eat. Which was good. I didn't have breasts any more—I had torpedoes filled with milk.

Jeff was amazing. Changed her diaper, put her on one breast, took her off, helped me switch sides, put her on the other side, took her off, burped her, checked the diaper, back in the bed. He did most of this at hyperspeed, exhibiting yet another reason why A-Cs were superior mates.

"So, the blocks," I asked as he snuggled next to me. "They work how? And will Christopher need to put some in?"

"Probably. I can't really tell what talents she has, but with what she did in the womb, empathic's in there for sure."

"They work how?" I asked again. I'd never badgered Jeff for this info before, but that was because I already knew what to do to take care of him. I didn't want to have to slam a huge needle filled with adrenaline into my tiny baby's hearts unless I absolutely had to. Prevention seemed like a smart plan, therefore.

"I don't know that I can explain it, but I'll try. The ones I put in—I . . . rearranged things in her brain. Just a little. As she gets older, she'll need some medically implanted blocks and to have regular injections of serums that all empaths use to control their talent. Imageers need less of this, but if she's strong like the other hybrid women, I imagine she'll need some. The implants and injections are slightly different for imageers, but the process is the same. As we get older, we learn to move the implants and blocks around in our minds on our own. The serums allow us to do this."

"So you and everyone else are going to be fiddling with our daughter's brain? And this doesn't sound like a bad idea to anyone?"

"It's similar to the implants we use to manipulate the gases on this planet, and it's not fiddling like a human would do it," he said, patience clearly forced. "We've been doing this for centuries. It works. No one dies from the implants or the injections. We can and will die without them. You've never had an issue with any of this before."

"No need to get testy. I just want to be sure we're not doing something that would hurt the baby."

Jeff made the snorting exasperation sound. I looked at him. I was getting a dirty look. "I'm not going to do anything to hurt our baby. The blocks will protect her. She won't be able to feel any emotions, other than her own."

"What about mine? Or yours?" Jeff said I broadcast my emotions, and when his blocks were down, I had to assume he broadcast his.

"As far as I can tell, she won't feel either one of us. Unless she's in life-threatening danger."

"In general or from us?"

I got another dirty look. "She'd better not be in life-threatening danger from one of us. But if the person whose emotions she's blocked from is a danger to her, she'll feel their emotions."

"How?"

"I can't explain it to anyone who's not an empath. It works, that's all I can tell you." Or at least all he was willing to. I decided I had another question that was more important. "And," Jeff went on, "because I know you and know the next question you want to ask, when she has to go into isolation, I'm going with her, at least until she's old enough to understand what it is."

"Not that I mind that you want to, but if two empaths are in isolation together, doesn't that mean neither one is actually isolated?"

"It would if I were a normal empath. Since I'm not . . ." Jeff looked upset, affronted, and a little hurt.

"I know, you're Superempath. I just want to be sure that—"

"That we avoid having to give her the adrenaline shot," he finished for me. "I know. I don't want to do that to her if we don't have to, either." Jeff ran his hand through his hair. "Why are we fighting? I mean, really, why? And why right now?"

I considered this question. "Hormones?"

"I'll take it. Look, can we just rest until the baby needs to eat again? I'm almost as exhausted from this conversation as I was when I thought I'd lost you forever."

"I'm sorry." I was. I hadn't really meant to upset him.

Jeff heaved a sigh. "No more guilt. No more stress." He hugged me. "Let's just relax and enjoy that we're all here together."

"I can do that." I snuggled closer to him, cuddled Jamie while Jeff wrapped around us again, closed my eyes, and went back to sleep.

I was glad Jeff had gotten me to shut up and rest because we were up again in a few hours, to do the feeding, burping, and diaper changing all over again. I dreaded when he was going to have to go back on duty.

Third time for the drill; now it was sometime in the afternoon. I had no idea any more. Heard a knock on the door. Jeff got it, and Amy was standing there. "Kitty, how are you?" She saw the baby and squealed. I didn't remember Amy as a squealer, but then again, I didn't remember Amy around babies, either.

She raced over and hugged me. "Christopher told me you'd had a horrible time. I'm so sorry I pulled Jeff away from you when you needed him."

"It was okay. I'm fine." I hugged her one-armed.

Amy stepped back and took a critical look at me and Jeff. "Right. Jeff, you want to go take a shower and I'll guard Kitty?"

He looked like he was going to argue. He also looked like he was going to drop. "Jeff, go ahead. One of us should take the opportunity, and it's not going to be me."

He struggled with it, but finally he nodded. "Okay, baby. I'll be back in a flash." He kissed Jamie on her head, me full on the mouth, which reminded me that I wanted to ask Tito for the exact moment we'd be allowed to have sex again. Jeff pulled away with a grin. "Truly, I love how you think. Be right back, baby."

"Take your time, it'll be fine."

Jeff left and Amy relaxed. I found this interesting and took a good look at her. She looked pretty much as she had when I'd seen her in Paris—taller than me, willowy, long auburn hair, green eyes, great skin. She looked the way you expected someone from money to look, honestly—poised, confident, happy. Well, she was happy looking at me and the baby. The moment she looked away, I saw fear and worry.

"You want to tell me what's going on? Jeff said you were garbled last night. I don't buy it. You didn't want to tell him and Christopher what's up."

She nodded and pulled a chair over. "I am in so much trouble."

"Twenty guys trying to kill you usually indicates trouble, yeah." She nodded but didn't speak. "Ames, you're seeing me and the baby, really, before my parents." I found Mom's visit from earlier hard to count in the "seeing the baby" category, after all. "Make the whining I'll hear for the rest of my life worth it and share the news, okay?"

"I discovered a government conspiracy."

CHAPTER 17

I LET THAT ONE HANG on the air. "And you called me instead of Chuckie, why?"

"Why would I call Conspiracy Chuck?" Amy seemed genuinely shocked.

"Gladys said you called using a covert ops emergency number."

"I have no idea what number I used. I met this guy; he was helping me get the information on the conspiracy. He gave me the number, said to use it if I was in life-threatening danger."

"What happened to him?"

She started to cry. "They slit his throat in front of me."

"Were you in love with him?"

I got the "are you crazy, is that your problem?" look. They must have taught it at our high school. Maybe it was a Pueblo Caliente specialty, since Mom was a pro at it, too. No matter, I now had the hat trick and could congratulate myself later. "He was like sixty years old, Kitty."

"Was he really handsome, like Jeff and Christopher handsome?"

"What is with you? No, he was a normal guy for sixty. Not too much of a gut, since I guess he was an agent, but I thought he was just a businessman."

A-C agent out. Well, it was worth checking. "So, what's the conspiracy?"

She took a deep breath. "Elimination of some heads of

some businesses. I've never heard of them. The P.T.C.U. and the ETD. I don't know what the letters stand for. "

"I do. Com on!" I was bellowing. Jamie didn't wake up. What a good baby.

"Yes, Commander Martini? And congratulations. Is this baby-related?"

"Thanks. No. I want Charles Reynolds and my parents, Kevin Lewis and his family, and any other key P.T.C.U. or ETD personnel taken into full protective custody, like yesterday. My mom and dad are at our house for sure, no idea where the others are. Bring them to Dulce. Be prepared to have to bring in a lot more human personnel as well, just don't know yet. I need Chuckie here, with me, also like yesterday."

"Handling, Commander. Anything else?"

"I want Alpha, including Richard, and whatever portion of Airborne can move, in here. Jeff's taking a shower, so don't panic him, but need him, too."

"Done, Commander."

"Thanks, Gladys." I took a deep breath. "Amy? Why didn't you contact me before now?"

"Uh, why should I have? I mean, you and Jeff told me you did something vague that sounded like you worked in some level of antiterrorism."

"Ah. Well. Um." She had a point. Then again, Jeff and Christopher appearing out of nowhere must have been a clue. "Why did you think Jeff and Christopher were able to get to you so fast?"

She looked at me blankly. "You know, I was so scared, I didn't think about it. How did they?" She looked around the room. "Where, exactly, are we?"

"Dulce Science Center. Otherwise known as the heart of the U.F.O. rumors. Hi, Amy, nice to see you." Chuckie sauntered in. "Kitty, you look great for just giving birth." He came over and kissed my forehead. "From the little I heard, we almost lost you."

"I'm fine."

"Good." He kissed my forehead again, then looked at the baby. "She's beautiful. Looks just like you."

"That's what Jeff said. I don't see it."

"Human genetics are dominant, but regardless, trust me, I see you."

"Human? Why wouldn't the baby look human?" Amy started to sound freaked.

Chuckie and I exchanged looks. "You handle it. I just popped out a kid. With, from what everyone tells me, complications."

He nodded. "Amy, you know all those conspiracy theories of mine that you and everyone else in school other than Kitty teased me about?"

Amy blinked. "Chuck? You're Conspiracy Chuck?"

Chuckie and I exchanged another look. "Dude, I'm telling you, you really matured well. Your timing sucked, but, trust me, you look great."

"Thanks." He turned back to Amy. "I'm Charles Reynolds, yeah. I'm also the head of the C.I.A.'s Extraterrestrial Division."

"Or the ETD. Which means, according to Amy, you've been marked for death."

"Oh? Interesting." Only Chuckie would find this interesting as opposed to scary. "Who else?"

"My mother."

"Kitty, why would your mother be marked for death?" Amy was bordering on hysteria. There was a lot of that going around. Maybe it was the room.

"My mother is the head of the Presidential Terrorism Control Unit, or the P.T.C.U. Welcome to my world. I only entered it less than two years ago, so you're not that far behind. Oh, almost forgot. Jeff, Christopher, and most of the people you're going to meet shortly are all space aliens from the Alpha Centauri system. We call them A-Cs. We have a lot of them living on Earth. Positive point? They're all totally gorgeous."

"Thanks. What the hell is going on?" Jeff was back, in the standard Armani fatigues. No tie—again, he was a new daddy, so going *casual*. Jeans. Was it too much to ask to see his butt in denim? I didn't think so, but had only won that battle twice. In just under two years. "Why is *he* here?" The way he hissed the word "he" I knew he wasn't emotionally able to block any jealousy.

"Marked for death, like my mom, Amy's stumbled onto her own *Pelican Brief* and we're at DEFCON Worse, without benefit of DEFCON One or anything. Oh, and, Chuckie, the baby's name is Jamie Katherine." Mom hadn't seemed interested before, Amy hadn't asked—I decided to offer so I could pretend one of my nearest and dearest cared about what I'd named my child.

"Nice. Reader must be flattered."

"He is." Jeff had the sarcasm knob up to full. "Note that your name is nowhere connected to *my* baby."

"Boys."

Chuckie gave him a look I could only think of as snide. "Yeah. Noted, Martini. Kitty had me brought in, wasn't my idea to come this early after she delivered. Though she looks amazing. As always."

"Boys, really."

"I'm sure. I'm sort of surprised you weren't here while she was in labor."

"Guys. Boys. Menfolk."

"I would have been if I'd known. But, unsurprisingly, no one advised me."

"Boys, really, do I have to bring out the big guns again?"

"No one advised you because what happens with Kitty is none of your damn business." Jeff was growling.

"They're not in a bra this time, guys."

"Oh, please. Everything Centaurion Division does is my business, including what the head of Airborne for Centaurion is doing. Especially when we almost lost said head of Airborne in labor." Chuckie was right in Jeff's face.

"About to lose her to disgust, boys."

"She doesn't need you to take care of her." Jeff was growling *and* snarling.

"I'm okay with the taking care of. Not so much with the stag fighting."

"True, she's an independent woman. She's now on official maternity leave, but some women manage to work while having babies. Kitty's one of them. But, sorry, I keep on forgetting—you're old-fashioned. Where's her gingham dress, her stove and her washing machine?" Chuckie had a sarcasm knob, too. His was turned to eleven. I also thought I was about to watch him lose his cool, which was more rare than sighting Halley's Comet.

"Boys, really. I don't want to flash you. What example will that set for Jamie?"

"She's also *my* wife and what she does or doesn't do isn't any of *your* business."

They were nose-to-nose. Physical fighting was bound to be an issue.

"Kitty, go for it. All the guys are here, waiting to get a load of the maternity rack." Reader was in the doorway, cover-boy grin on full. He wasn't kidding—all the rest of Alpha and Airborne were behind him. All of them were watching my chest, not Jeff and Chuckie.

Amazingly, the two of them were still glaring and snarling at each other. I looked at Amy. Her mouth was hanging open. I caught her eye. "Sometimes they don't fight and just glare at each other from across the room. Occasionally they work together. Chuckie was at our wedding, too. Helped pick out my dress. They still fought then, just not as much, in deference to the solemnity that wasn't really our wedding."

"I'm really confused." Amy sounded confused. And scared.

My mother shoved into the room. "What the hell is going on here?" She sounded normal, and, as she looked around, I confirmed that she looked normal, too. Good. My world was no longer teetering more oddly than usual. "Hi, Amy, nice to see you. Charles, Jeff, is this the right time or place for this?"

They both ignored her. "Mom, could you take the baby?"

"Oooh, yes." Mom hustled over. "Christopher told us her name. Love it." I refrained from mentioning that I'd have been glad to tell her the baby's name earlier. I got the feeling she wanted and possibly needed for us to not discuss our private mother and daughter moment. No worries, I didn't like to show weakness in front of others if I could help it, either.

Mom picked up Jamie and rocked her. "She's such an angel, sleeping while her daddy and Uncle Charles fight over her mommy."

"He's not her uncle anything," Jeff snarled.

"That's as much up to Kitty as you, Martini." Chuckie wasn't snarling, but he was close.

I sighed and got to the edge of the bed. Felt pretty good. Looked down. Wasn't a hippo anymore. Wasn't in great shape, but at least I only looked as if I had a watermelon in there now. Stood up. Moved. Felt fine. Turned my back to the door. Looked to make sure there were no mirrors or reflective surfaces about. Check.

"Jeff? I'm about to pull up my top. Either the two of you stop it, or Chuckie gets a good view of the torpedoes."

They both spun toward me.

"Don't even think about it," Jeff hissed.

"Torpedoes?" Chuckie was now staring at my chest. "Oh. Wow. I honestly hadn't looked. Damn." A-C sleepwear T-shirts were white, after all. Thick, but not *that* thick.

"Take your eyes off my wife's chest or I kill you." Jeff sounded ready to follow through.

"I could just shoot them both," Mom offered.

"True, but I kind of like them."

"Why?" Reader asked this one. "I mean, it's sort of flattering, I'm sure. But the timing is always so bad."

"It's only when they're both frightened and don't want to admit it." Hit with that one. I got two big men staring at me with a mixture of hurt, guilt, and embarrassment on their faces. Decided to be nice. "But we do sort of have a situation here. It would be kind of nifty if we could, and I'm just spitballing here, get the full details out of Amy, before we lose her to Oh-My-God overload. Then, you know, you two can go back to the manly posturing and grunting."

They both had the grace to look sheepish. "Love you both. Touched by the display, as always. Tired, cranky, worried about my girlfriend, who's sitting there in total freaking shock since we have just turned her world upside down, worried about my mother and, realistically, everyone else, too."

"Why?" This was from Amy. "They're after, I guess, Chuck and your mother. Who else would be in danger?"

I sighed. "Ames, in the world as I now know it, everything's an elaborate ruse to gain power. And you're sitting at the heart of much of that power everyone's trying to get their grubby mitts on."

"But we're in a high-class medical center-hotel combo for pregnant celebrities." She looked around. "That's what they said."

"Who said?" Jeff and Christopher couldn't lie, and there was no way they'd come up with that one on their own.

Tim whistled softly while looking at the ceiling.

"Spill it."

He looked at me and grinned. "You know, her room is right by mine and all. Not my fault I ran into her in the hallway. She was freaked out and confused. Seemed the best way to keep her calm."

"Lying to me?" Amy sounded outraged.

"Tim's a human. You can spot them, normally, because they will be average to good-looking but not quite as good-looking as the A-Cs. My boys are, needless to say, hotter than most humans. I hire based on looks."

This earned me a lot of laughs and "we love you" looks from Tim and the flyboys. Tito, who had arrived now, just grinned and moved me back into bed. Funny thing was, I wasn't lying. Tim was the most average of all our guys and he was pretty darned cute. For a human.

"Humans can also lie. A-Cs cannot. At least not believably. At all. It's a great trait, believe me."

Reader laughed. "Yeah, it's great during fights, too."

Amy looked more closely. "Oh, my God. I recognize you! You're that guy who did the Calvin Klein ad a few years ago that had all that controversy over it. Kitty and I both had that spread up in our rooms for months."

Didn't look at Jeff for that reveal. Hey, Reader was gorgeous. Sue me for lusting after him in his Calvin's. Me and every straight woman and gay man in America.

Reader flashed the cover-boy smile. "Yep, that's me." He walked into the room and over to my mother. "My turn." She laughed and passed him the baby. He cuddled her. "Where's Sol?"

"Getting the pets," Mom said with a sigh. "He has a contingent of four agent teams with him," she added to my mouth opening. "The Lewises are here, too, just getting settled in. Kevin's pulling in the rest of our team. As always, threat to one is likely to mean threat to all."

"This sounds so much like Operation Fugly. I'm getting all nostalgic."

Reader laughed and moved next to me. He bent down and whispered in my ear. "Then place your bets for the love connection, girlfriend."

CHAPTER 18

I LOOKED AROUND. Amy was our new girl. Had no guess as to whom she could potentially hook up with out of this group. Tim was spoken for and pretty darned happy with his girlfriend Alicia, who was a human. It was almost exotic for our group, two humans dating.

Joe Billings and Randy Muir were married, to Lorraine and Claudia, respectively. They came into the room and insisted on baby holding. Jeff started to get antsy, but at least it took his attention off of Chuckie.

The single guys started to make baby-holding noises, and Jeff lost it. "No, that's enough. She's not even a day old yet, enough with the handling." He snatched her out of Randy's hands.

Mom laughed. "Jeff, the baby will be fine."

"Huh." He was cuddling her and had a very possessive look on his face.

"Jeff, come here." I patted the bed. "Sit down so we can try to get the story out of Amy." He did, making sure to sit on the side that blocked Chuckie from me. I just laughed and took Jamie from him. Reader sat down behind me, and I leaned against him. "Ames, really, try to give us all the details."

"Hang on," Christopher said. "My father's not here yet."

"I asked Gladys to call him." Hated the funny feeling this gave me.

"Com on!" Jeff was in Commander-mode.

"Here, Commander Martini."

"Gladys, where is the Pontifex?"

"He said he had a meeting he had to attend, Commander."

"At any of our Bases?"

"No, Commander. Off-site."

"Why did you let him leave?"

"Commander Katt didn't say the Pontifex was in danger."

She was right, I hadn't. Jeff looked at me. I shrugged. "I always consider it self-evident."

"What?"

"That everyone's always trying to get Richard, in some way, shape, or form."

Mom had already dug her phone out of her purse and was talking urgently to someone. Chuckie was doing the same. Both of them looked supremely worried. Christopher had his phone, but he wasn't talking to anyone. He looked at me. "My father's not answering."

"Security has expanded the search to all locations, all active agents notified, Commanders." Gladys sounded upset. Richard was the head of our A-Cs' religion, but he was also her half brother.

"Gladys, please make sure Jeff's parents are okay, too, just in case. Amy, details, all of them, now. No more playing around. I don't care that you're confused, scared, whatever. You're safe here. Someone of extreme importance isn't."

She nodded. "Gotcha. Okay. I was on leave from my company, at the request of a business partner of ours. I was supposed to be helping them with an environmental issue. I handled it fast, then they had another business they partnered with, but my company didn't, that had the same issue, so they asked me to help them, under the auspices of my leave arrangement. I figured it was good for relations, so I said yes. But then I got moved again, to another company, one not connected with my real employer or even our business partner at all, at least, I'd never heard of them before this."

"Is that common?"

"Not in legitimate business." Chuckie answered over his shoulder. "Note that the employing company has no idea of what's going on. I promise you, if we investigate, they will think Amy's still working for their business partner. It's a typical plan, though. Use a network to get a smart, young, single, preferably one who's not native to your country, who can do the work you need, kill them off when they finish the work; no one notices until it's too late."

"Jeez, Chuckie, how often does that happen?"

"A lot more than you want to know. Sorry, Amy, carry on." He went back to his call.

She gave me a look that said she was one word away from losing it. "He's right? He's always been right?"

"Yes. Figure any bizarre theory Chuckie ever had is true. You'll be better off. He might have been wrong on one of them, but not most."

"I was wrong about where Hoffa was buried."

"See? One. Anyway, go on. Wait, where *is* Hoffa buried?"

"This is my father's life we're dealing with here!" Christopher barked.

"Sorry, right. Ames, continue." Jamie woke up and gave a contented gurgle. I kissed her head and did the baby-jiggle. Jeff tickled her tummy, while still paying full attention to Amy. He was going to be the best daddy ever. All my worry from earlier sort of dissipated in a warm, happy little glow.

"The environmental issue was no big deal. I solved it at each company by identifying the governmental jurisdictions for the parent company."

"Were they all the same parent?" Jeff asked, as he played with Jamie's toes.

"I didn't think so at first. But when I was working at the last company, I hit a weird name I'd hit before. I did a little digging and found out there was a parent connection."

"Name? And the relevant company names?"

"Ronaldo Al Dejahl, Al Dejahl Shipping. It's a weird spelling for the name."

"No worries. We know how to spell it." Mom and I looked at each other. "He's dead. I killed him. Personally."

"Kitty? You killed someone?" Amy sounded freaked.

"Um, at least, uh, five someones. More, really. Starting to lose count. They were all bad guys. Some of them weren't human, either." This sounded as lame said aloud as I'd feared. "So, you know, bad guys beware and all that."

"Got him." Chuckie turned around. "We need to have a

long talk with the Pontifex about humans and why they should not be trusted."

"Where is he?"

"Paris. I know, what an amazing coincidence." Chuckie's sarcasm was up to eleven again. He didn't believe in coincidence. "He's been picked up by C.I.A. operatives. They're in touch with the Euro Centaurion team. He should be back here shortly."

"Gladys, make sure that happens." Jeff looked at Christopher. "You want to go back to Paris?"

"Not with you. You need to stay here with Kitty." Christopher looked ready to leave.

"Not at all." Chuckie rolled his eyes as Christopher hit him with patented Glare #3. "If ETD and P.T.C.U. personnel are targeted, it stands to reason we are so targeted in order to, once again, attempt to destabilize Centaurion Division. I want Alpha Team here, right here, until we have the Pontifex safely back."

"Reynolds, you don't control Centaurion any more." Jeff was ready to go again, I could tell.

"Oh, Jeff, stop. And, Chuckie, don't start. I'm just too freaking tired, and the baby's going to need to eat soon, at least if my inflatable chest is any indication. Jeff, Chuckie's right, let's get Richard back and not risk someone else to do it. If he's already safe, there's no reason for us to go racing off to help finish the save."

"I'm going to get my father, sorry," Christopher snapped. "I'm not going to be in danger."

"Sure you are." Mom sighed. "Remember when you first met Kitty? They were trying to kill her to get to me. It's an age-old plan—put the people the target loves in danger—and it always works."

"I foiled that one." Just wanted it on record. Besides, Amy hadn't heard about it.

"Yes, yes, kitten, well done." Mom shook her head. "You'd have thought she didn't need constant praise still, but you'd be wrong."

"Humph."

"*Anyway*," Mom went on, "Christopher, stay here. We're pulling everyone in for safety. If you go running off, that means you could indeed get into trouble, and then more of us would have to run after you, and soon the entire facility's running around out and unprotected."

Jamie started to cry. "Okay, everyone out. Conspiracy theories later. Jeff and I need a few minutes alone here." Mom and Reader weren't budging. I looked at them. They looked back. "Oh, fine. You two can stay." I handed Jamie to my mother. "Enjoy the diaper check."

She smiled and took the baby over to the changing area. This room was, as all A-C facilities were, set up really nicely.

Everyone else filed out, Chuckie staying right by Christopher. Amy looked lost. "Ames, you can stay, too."

"Okay, thanks."

Jeff sighed. "So much for that special bonding time between parents and baby."

I kissed him as he helped me lie down. "We'll have plenty of time. But, Jeff?" I wanted to ask him to stay with me unless it was dire, but I felt that was being sort of needy and potentially risky.

He kissed me. "I'm not leaving you and Jamie unless that's the best way I can protect you two. Okay?" I nodded and felt much safer. He grinned. "More than anything else, you feeling that way makes me feel good."

Fed Jamie while Mom, Reader, and Amy all watched. It was kind of like being on my own reality TV show. Thought about something. "Gladys, you there?"

"Yes, Commander Martini. What happened to the 'com on' shout?"

"Figured it was still on. Could you please ask Serene to come in here?"

"Okay." Gladys sounded confused, but she didn't argue.

Serene arrived a minute or so later. She was only a few months pregnant, just barely showing. Lucky thing. She walked in the room and looked at Amy. "Oh, wow. You're Kitty's friend from high school, aren't you?"

Amy looked shocked. "Yes. Uh, have we met?"

"No. I've seen your picture. Brian showed it to me."

"Brian?" Amy looked at me. "Your ex Brian?"

"Yep. He's married to Serene now. They're good together."

Serene nodded. "I was going to convert to Catholicism, but Brian said he didn't need me to, but he's going to convert to our religion. He says he thinks it's the right thing for the baby." She looked around the room. "Hi, Angela. I'm so glad Kitty didn't die."

That was Serene, sweet and blunt. "Me too," Mom said dryly.

"Serene, you've already covered one of my concerns. Do me a favor—I need you to be sure Christopher is who we think he is, and Richard, too, when he returns."

"Okay." She concentrated. "Christopher's in the hall. He looks really upset. What's up with his eyes? He looks like he hasn't slept in days."

"Yeah, that's why I was worried. But it's him, right?"

"Right." She was quiet. "Everyone here is who they should be, Kitty. But Richard isn't here."

"He should be coming, soon. At least, I hope it's him."

"Why?" Jeff asked. He didn't need to elaborate.

"Robotics. Yates was going to switch me for a robot to get to Mom. Could have done the same thing with others. And after the shapeshifting and image overlaying from the invasion, I just like to be sure we are who we think we are."

Jeff got up and touched Amy's shoulder. "Human. No superbeing."

"I figured you'd have noticed while you were in Paris."

He shrugged as he came back to the bed. "Christopher had her, not me. I was handling the rough stuff."

"Do you need adrenaline?" Worry, as always, crashed over me. Along with guilt because I hadn't even thought to ask him this before.

He kissed my forehead. "No, baby. It wasn't that bad."

"Define not that bad."

He grinned. "Didn't get overtired, didn't get hurt. Hurt a lot of them. Enjoyed it."

"Okay, that's fine then."

"The Pontifex is back on premises," Gladys' voice came through the com.

Serene concentrated. She heaved a relieved sigh. "It's him. He seems fine. A little shook up, though."

"Good. Someone let Christopher know." Serene nodded and trotted out of the room. "Jeff, do you have any idea why Christopher looks so awful?"

"No. I thought it was because we were dragged up in the middle of the night after a busy day handling suspicious superbeings in Paris."

"I don't think so." I thought about why someone's eyes would be bloodshot. No sleep. Drinking, but since A-Cs were deadly allergic to alcohol, he'd be dead not bleary-eyed. Crying. Hmmmm. If that was it, what was he crying about? It wasn't as if he was normally out of control, so it would have to be something really huge. Tabled for later, had to save the world right now. "So, Mom, there's no way Ronald Yates is still alive."

"The media mogul? He died almost two years ago, didn't he?" Amy sounded almost normal. Anticipated my next statements. Couldn't be helped.

"Ronald Yates was, in addition to being the creepiest man around, an exiled A-C, the former head of their religion, Christopher and Jeff's grandfather, the actual head of the Al Dejahl terrorist organization, and an in-control superbeing called Mephistopheles. He was a total Renaissance Man for evil."

"Mephistopheles? You mean like Faust's devil?"

"Honors English was great, wasn't it? Yes, exactly like Faust's devil. Only bigger and uglier. And with the worst breath imaginable."

I saw realization dawn. "You killed him? You killed Ronald Yates?" She sounded horrified.

"No. Mephistopheles let Yates die. I killed Mephistopheles. Took out the Devil, yay me. And all that."

Jeff took the baby and burped her. "Mommy kicks evil alien butt. You're gonna be just like her when you grow up, aren't you, Jamie-Kat?"

"Jamie-Kat?"

He grinned. "Sticking with your Nono Dom's theme and all." My mother's father had made cat jokes from the moment my mother had introduced him to my father. He'd shared that he expected Jeff to be a big tomcat and take care of me. Jeff was all over the big tomcat idea. I didn't mind it, either. He always reminded me of a big cat, in all the positive ways.

Mom laughed. "I think it's cute. Your father will love it, kitten."

"You killed Ronald Yates?" Amy wasn't letting this one go.

"Ames, was he a close family friend?"

"Well, no. But my parents knew him."

"Mom, get Chuckie in here, pronto. Jeff, no snarling. Seriously, need him to hear this." Mom trotted to the hallway, and Jeff grunted. I thought about his naked body.

"Okay, fine, I'll behave. Just keep your mind where it's at."

I tried to move, and then Jeff and Reader helped me. Got situated so I was leaning against Jeff's chest. Reader sat next to me and took Jamie. He leaned her against his shoulder and rocked her. She went right to sleep. Yeah, I found his shoulder totally a great place to be, too.

Mom came back with Chuckie. "Ames, you want to expand on your last statement? Your parents were friends with Ronald Yates?" Chuckie's eyebrow went up.

"Not friends, but acquaintances. They knew him. I think my dad might have done some business with him, but not a lot."

I looked at Mom. "What is Mister Gaultier's business? Not the one he told Amy about, the real one. I ask," I explained to Amy, "because, as I discovered, parents lie like wet rugs a lot of the time."

"Geez, get over it," Mom sighed. "He's a legitimate businessman or I'd never have let you be so close to Amy. Imports and exports. No illegal drugs, no sex trafficking, nothing unlawful."

"Why would Yates be associated with him then?"

"Always a good idea to have some legitimate businesses to run your illegitimate dealings through. Show off Gaultier International as a friend, show how clean you are."

The rest of Alpha and Airborne came back in the room. Richard White was still surrounded by C.I.A. agents, identified because they weren't in Armani and weren't drop-dead gorgeous. Chuckie had the agents leave the room but not the premises, which Jeff wasn't happy with. I mentioned being tired of the posturing, and they didn't get into it again. Brought the rest of the team up to speed. Then asked the big question. "Richard, who were you meeting and why did you go?"

He shook his head. "I'm not at liberty to say."

"Richard, no choice." Jeff had his Commander voice on full. "We're in a Field situation. I want an answer to Kitty's question."

White's eyes flashed to Chuckie, to me, to Jamie, where

his eyes stayed for several seconds, and then back to the ground. It was rare to see the Pontifex act like this, ergo, I was pretty sure it was an act. So, what did he want me to figure out? Thought about it. "This is about the Gower girls, isn't it?"

CHAPTER 19

"YES." WHITE LOOKED UP AT ME rather expectantly.

"Geez, who did you give your promise not to talk about this to? The President?"

"No."

I looked at Chuckie. He shook his head. "Wasn't me. I'm all over hearing what the Pontifex has to say about why he was in Paris and what it has to do with Naomi and Abigail. Who, just to reassure you, are being picked up, along with Michael and their parents, and brought here as well."

"You're so good with the details."

"Yeah, whatever. So, Pontifex White? Please answer Kitty's question. I'm asking as the head of the ETD now, not as your son and nephew's favorite punching bag."

He still didn't speak. I considered the possibilities of why.

Naomi and Abigail Gower were Paul Gower's younger sisters. Unlike their two older brothers—Paul, who had the A-C talents of dream and memory reading, and Michael, who had no A-C talents but was a successful astronaut—the Gower girls had expanded, mutated A-C talents. They were the product of an A-C father and human mother. Serene, the product of an unknown human father and dead A-C mother, also had expanded and mutated talents.

Christopher had identified the Gower girls' talents a couple of months before our wedding, which was when Jeff and I had been advised. The C.I.A. had been running tests on the three of them, in conjunction with Centaurion, for months now. The tests on Serene stopped the moment she got pregnant, because Jeff insisted upon it. But Naomi and Abigail had continued on, to the point where they were at C.I.A. headquarters more often than any other A-C personnel.

However, the biggest mystery was that all three women had been helped to deal with their powers—helped by an unknown source they thought was a man, but couldn't confirm. A man they'd never met but only heard in their heads. They'd been taught by this person when they were little, so their powers were kept hidden until we'd stumbled upon Serene during one of our more fun and frolicsome adventures, by which I mean most of us almost died a lot of times. In between food cravings and hormonal stress, I'd actually given this conundrum some thought. Thoughts it looked like it was time to confirm or deny.

"Paul, could I speak to ACE please?"

Gower sighed. "If you must." He twitched. "Yes, Kitty, ACE is here." Gower's voice was still his voice, just a little different—a bit stilted and unsure—which always signified ACE having control of their now-shared mind.

"What's going on?"

"Many things, Kitty." ACE sounded as evasive as White had. Great.

"ACE, first off, let me ask something no one has yet. Were you the one helping Naomi, Abigail, and Serene to handle their mutated powers?"

Dead silence. Everyone looked at me.

"ACE? Really, no one would be upset by that. You helped them stay sane and not hurt themselves or others. Just wondering why you did that, when you'd only been paying attention to those in space, from what I'd understood when we first, uh, met."

"Their powers were vast, they reached us from the Earth. And they were so young and terrified . . . ACE had to help." His voice sounded filled with dread and remorse.

"ACE, you didn't hurt them. You helped them. Why are you feeling so guilty?"

"Others do not like ACE to help."

"Who? Anyone in this room?"

"No."

"Then I don't care what they think." Another thought

occurred. "ACE . . . are there sentient nets, like you were, up in places other than around Earth and in the Alpha Centauri system?"

"Yes, Kitty. Around other star systems with intelligent life. They are not A-C made, but . . . we can speak. Occasionally. They . . . do not like what ACE has done."

"You mean help your penguins instead of hurt them?"

Reader coughed. "Girlfriend, really, the penguin analogy was confusing enough when you first put it out there. Don't stress ACE out, please. Paul's hell to deal with when you do."

"ACE understands Kitty's penguins. Kitty is right. The others do not . . . love . . . their penguins as ACE does."

"See? ACE understands me."

"At least someone does," Mom muttered.

"So, ACE, you're the one who helped the Gower girls and Serene?"

"Yes."

"Okay, thank God, and more on that later. Thanks, ACE, love you as always, carry on, give us Paul back, do not berate yourself, we adore you and all you do for us, and so forth."

Paul twitched. "God, the palsy stops when? ACE is relieved you're not upset with him, Kitty. Couldn't care less what anyone else thinks, just for the record."

"ACE is the best, Paul, just like you. Now, Richard, since ACE doesn't lie, and that means whoever contacted you was lying, it stands to reason that you need to stop protecting them and tell us what the hell's going on. Before Jamie's next feeding, please."

White sighed. "Understood, and agreed. I got a call from someone who said he'd been helping them and wanted to speak to me about their futures."

"Who?"

"He identified himself as Herbert Gaultier."

Mom, Chuckie, and I all looked at Amy. She shook her head. "My dad's in New York right now, not Paris." Mom pulled out her phone and made a call.

"Did you meet with this man?" Chuckie's eyes were narrowed.

"Yes, well, I thought I was."

"Describe him." Chuckie's voice was clipped, and I noted he was watching Amy.

"Shorter than me, small, dark hair, eyes, and skin. Not black, darker than Mister Hernandez, however."

Chuckie relaxed. "Amy's father's my height, redheaded, and fair skinned."

Amy glared at him. "You really think I, or my father, had something to do with . . . whatever this is?"

"Yeah. I think it's awfully coincidental that you're here and that your father's name was used to attempt to kidnap the religious leader of a group of exiled aliens, the control of whom is the basis for at least half of the conspiracies active at any one time."

Mom hung up. "Herbert Gaultier is in New York with his wife. I've assigned an operative team to guard them."

"Thanks, Angela," Amy said gratefully. She glared at Chuckie again. "See? She didn't think my dad was involved."

"Sure I did," Mom said with a smile. "Just not after I confirmed his whereabouts and Richard confirmed the man he met with looked nothing like your father. Stop thinking this is simple, Amy. We're dealing with the highest levels of terrorism, internal, international, and interplanetary diplomacy, and a variety of other issues. All of those issues are a lot bigger than you. Catch up fast, or get run over."

"She was just chased by twenty thugs and got to discover the world's not the way she thought it was," Christopher snapped. "Give her a break."

Mom rolled her eyes. "Kitty killed a superbeing and was dragged off to fight Mephistopheles in less time than Amy's had to get with the program. I note that never at any time, Christopher, did you suggest cutting her any kind of a break."

Wow, hadn't even thought Mom had noticed that, in between her pushing me to notice that Christopher liked me. Felt all special for a couple of seconds.

"Kitty's different." Christopher had patented Glare #1 going. He never glared at my mother. Something was really off with him.

"Hey, I'm as smart and capable as Kitty." Amy sounded really offended.

"Not saying you aren't." Christopher shot her Glare #2.

I nudged Jeff. He bent down. "I want full medical run on Christopher, right now. You and Paul are probably going to have to restrain him for it."

Jeff nodded and made eye contact with Gower, who nodded back. They both moved at hyperspeed and grabbed Christopher. "What the hell are you two doing?" He was snarling.

"Tito, need you to rally the best med team and run a full scan on Christopher, ASAP."

Tito didn't argue, just pulled out his phone and started making calls.

"Kitty, what the hell are you talking about?" Christopher was shouting.

"Jeff? I want to see his arms."

Jeff and Gower held Christopher's arms out. Tim shoved his suit jacket up, unbuttoned his sleeves and shoved them up, too. My worst fears were confirmed.

Christopher's arms were covered with needle tracks.

CHAPTER 20

"WHAT THE HELL HAVE YOU been doing to yourself?" Jeff sounded angry and horrified.

"Son, why?" White sounded shocked.

I looked at Chuckie. He shook his head. "Not C.I.A. sanctioned, encouraged, or known about."

Christopher's teeth were clenched. "Let go of me and leave me alone."

I looked right at him. "I know why you did it. It's stupid, let me mention, and totally dangerous, but I understand it." I looked around. "I want everyone out of the room but me, Richard, Jeff, Paul, and Christopher. Stay in the hall in case he makes a break for it, but otherwise, out."

"Should I take the baby?" Reader asked me quietly.

I looked into Christopher's eyes. "Should he?"

"No." Christopher shut his eyes. "I wouldn't hurt her. Or you. Any of you."

"I know, just yourself. Out, we'll call you back in a couple of minutes. Tito, knock when the med team's ready. Christopher's going to need to go into isolation, like Jeff normally does."

Mom took Jamie. "Just to be sure." She and Reader left the room. They both looked as though they didn't want to.

Chuckie left last. "You sure?" I nodded, and he went out, closing the door tightly behind him.

"Let him go." Jeff didn't look like he wanted to, but he did. Gower followed suit. I looked closely at Christopher. "You want them out, too?"

"Yeah." He was close to breaking down.

"No." Jeff and White said this in unison.

"Yes. Christopher's not going to hurt me. Please, Jeff. It's hard enough on him right now. You'll be able to get to me if I need you."

Gower put his hand on Christopher's shoulder. "You know we're here to help you, not hurt you."

Christopher nodded. The others left the room. Gower had to drag Jeff out. I patted the bed. "Come sit down."

He shook his head. "Not a good idea."

"You're not in love with me any more. Jeff knows it, I know it. Come here, Christopher." He moved stiffly and sat down at the edge of the bed. I pulled him into my arms and put his head on my chest. "I told you I understood. You're an idiot, but I can get why."

"You don't understand."

I kissed his head. "Sure I do. You can't fool the comics geek-girl. Happens in the comics all the time. Superhero sees others get more powerful than he is. There's some ego involved, sure, but usually it's motivated by wanting to stay strong, to be able to protect better. Jeff got enhanced in a scary way from that drug the Club Fifty-One people shoved into him. Serene did, too. Why not you, right?"

He started to cry. I knew there had to have been a reason for how crappy he looked. I'd sure hoped it wasn't this one, though. I rocked him and kissed his head.

"Jeff has to focus on you and the baby now. He shouldn't have had to go to Paris with me to deal with the superbeing mess or to get Amy. He shouldn't have had to leave you, ever. I should be able to take care of business now."

"Oh, honey. I know you did this out of love and to try to protect everyone. But it could kill you. It's making you nastier than normal, too."

He gave a half-laugh, half-sob. "Yeah, I suppose."

"What about the tests they did on the girls started this with you?"

"I just . . . they're the next stage, like you've always said. But they aren't ready to take over what Jeff and I do. We need to be better, to take care of our people. Every day, there's a new threat."

"I know. It scares me, too." I stroked his hair. "How'd you get the drug?"

"We have a supply, so we can identify it and counter it."

"Did it work?"

"I'm stronger, more stamina. It's easier to create a full-body image and hold it."

"Nice. Needless, but nice. Not worth the risk, however."

"I can see the people I care about, when they're in trouble, if I'm thinking about them. Sometimes, anyway."

"Okay, helpful, but still not worth it."

"Worth it to me."

"But not to anyone who loves you. You know, the easy way is just to find a girl and have babies."

"Yeah, so I can watch her die in labor?" He was clutching me the way Jeff had.

"I came back."

"Most girls aren't you."

"Maybe that means they'd do better. Paul's mother had four, and she looks fabulous. Everyone's different, honey."

"Jeff won't like you calling me honey."

"He won't mind." I kissed his head again. "Here's what he's going to mind. That his cousin, his best friend, the person he's always known loves him is slowly killing himself. Even when you hated him, he knew you loved him. Christopher, for so long, you were the only person he *knew* loved him. Don't you know what that means to an empath, and to Jeff, in particular? How in the world do you think he'd manage if he lost you to something like this?"

"He has you and Jamie, now."

"That doesn't mean he doesn't need you any more. It just means there's more of us who need you. But we need *you*, not some super-enhanced version of you. I know Jeff's glad his powers were enhanced. But, Christopher, he's been terrified for my entire pregnancy that because of the drug he was endangering me and the baby. We have no way of knowing. Maybe the drug is the reason why I, according to everyone, died and came back. Why would you risk that, risk putting yourself and the people you love, into that kind of danger by choice? Jeff didn't take that drug willingly, neither did Serene. And they got it out of their systems as fast as they could. Serene and Brian are afraid, too, of what the drug might have done to her, might do to their baby. I ask again, why risk that willingly?"

"I'm never getting married, so it won't matter."

I sighed. It was really reminiscent of Operation Fugly, only this time it was Christopher who had his fatalism set to high.

"Oh, honey, sure you will. Maybe you'll meet a nice girl in rehab."

He managed a weak laugh. "Our rehab is isolation. Not a lot of girls in there."

"You can't make me believe that in all the world, the only two possible girls for you were Lissa and me." He shifted uncomfortably, and I hugged him closer. "I love Jeff so much, as you know. But I think I could have managed to be happy with Chuckie. I'll bet I could have managed to be happy with someone else, too. Maybe even you."

"Uh, thanks. Not feeling better."

"My point is that I had more than one or two options, and so do you."

"Not seeing any."

"Well, most nice girls do try to avoid getting attached to drug addicts."

"I'm not an addict."

"Yeah, right. Needle tracks say otherwise, honey."

"Why honey, all of a sudden?"

"I'm a mother now. Comes with the territory."

"You're not my mother."

"No, I'm not. But I know she wouldn't want you doing this, more than me, even."

"We have to protect you, you have a daughter now." He sounded freaked and scared . . . and like a little boy.

Ah, there it was. "Christopher, you turning yourself into some scary super-A-C isn't going to protect Jamie or me. You being you has been pretty effective all this time."

"You save us a lot more than we save you."

"Well, I am a modern feminist, after all."

"Yeah."

"And, it doesn't matter who saves whom. It matters that we're all trying to save each other. We're not alone, like your mother was. We have each other. But Jeff and I won't have you if you continue to do this to yourself. We want Christopher, not Scary Man, the raving Imageer Lunatic, who will terrify you with his bloodshot eyes."

He managed a laugh. "I suppose."

I held him and rocked him and spent some time hating

their family. Not White or Jeff's parents, but their parents and grandparents and all the ones who'd exiled an entire race here because they believed in a different version of God. The ones who'd turned little boys into men at ten years of age. The ones who'd cared more about power than love. The ones who had helped to shove Christopher into a mind-set where he could convince himself that what he'd done was a good course of action. Sure, he'd made the decision on his own, but it was easy to connect the dots to what his motivations were and who'd caused them.

"My father's never going to forgive me." He was crying again, quietly. "Jeff won't, either. He won't understand."

The door opened and Jeff came in. He didn't say anything, just came to the bed and pulled Christopher into his arms and held him. Like me, he kissed Christopher's head and stroked his hair.

"Medical's here," he said softly to me after a few minutes.

"He needs to be with you a little more first." Christopher's shoulders were shaking, and I knew he was crying again.

"He blocked me." Jeff sounded worried. "I didn't get anything from him like this, until you exposed him." He was still holding Christopher tightly. "Because if I had, I would have kicked his butt."

"I'm sorry. Jeff, I'm so sorry." Christopher sounded close to hysterical. It had to be the room.

"Yeah, well, we all make stupid mistakes." Jeff rocked him some more. He was holding him so tightly I was surprised Christopher could breathe. "Remember when I drank the vodka? In a while, I'll get to tease you about being an idiot, too. But before then, you're going to get cleaned up, and you're never shooting that poison into yourself again."

Christopher nodded and pulled away from Jeff. "I'll understand if you don't want me to be Jamie's godfather after this."

"Are you high? I mean, yes, you are, but I'm asking more in the sense of saying you're really an idiot."

"What Kitty's so eloquently saying is that we both love you and will be hurt and insulted if you decide that your addiction is more important than being our daughter's godfather."

"We really need to get Christopher a girl."

They both managed to laugh at that, though Christopher's was still shaky. "Let's clean him up first, baby."

"Oh, I agree. So, Christopher, you still supposedly like 'em stupid?"

He shook his head. "I don't know what I like anymore."

White came in before I could ask a couple of pertinent dating questions. Oh, well, probably more important, that father-son reconciliation thing.

White shook his head as he came to us and Christopher cringed. "Son, I'm so sorry."

"For what?" Christopher was shaking. I stroked his back.

"For not seeing what you were doing, for not realizing you needed me. Can you forgive me?" White opened his arms.

Christopher was crying again, but it was probably healthy. His father grabbed him and held him, kissed his head, stroked his hair. Christopher was going to need isolation just to calm down.

"How did you know?" White asked me.

I shrugged. "It's a common theme in the comics. And real life, sadly."

"Mister Reynolds is running a check to ensure that none of his people were assisting Christopher in obtaining the drug."

"Good. Because if we have a dealer, we have a bigger problem than Christopher's overinflated fear of losing his family."

"I hate how you're always so damned blunt." Christopher sounded almost like himself.

"I'm also always right."

"Yeah, whatever." He looked up at his father. "I'm so sorry."

White shook his head. "I just want what Jeffrey and Kitty want. For you to get better and never do this to yourself again. Do you think you can do that? With our help, of course?"

Christopher nodded. "Yes, sir."

“Then we’ll be fine.” White hugged him again. “The medical team is ready and impatiently waiting. The drug replicates, if you recall. I have some very concerned doctors out there waiting for their patient.”

Christopher came over to me, and I kissed his cheek. “Be a good boy and go into isolation so we get your old, snarky self back, okay?”

He nodded and hugged me. “Thank you.”

“This is what family’s for, Christopher. And you’re my family, now and forever.”

CHAPTER 21

CHRISTOPHER HUGGED ME AGAIN, then Jeff and White helped him up and to the door. "I'm going to take him down," Jeff said to me as Mom and Reader came in with Jamie.

"Sounds fine. I'll be here."

He smiled. "Good."

Got my baby back. She opened her eyes, gurgled, and gave a little sigh. "I think she missed you," Mom said. "She was a little fussy, though she's sure happy with James."

Reader grinned. "Uncle James dances better than Grandma."

I laughed. "Good to know."

Mom sighed and sat on one side of the bed while Reader took the other. "How did you know, about Christopher?"

"Mom, I went to college. Really, 'nuff said." I shifted my back, and Reader started to massage it. "I love you, James. But what we really need to figure out is what's going on with Amy and the Al Dejahl stuff."

"Charles is very suspicious of Amy right now." Mom sounded concerned.

"You think he's wrong?"

"I don't want him to be right would be the better way of putting it."

"Well, only worry if she's his only theory. As long as he has more than one, we should be okay." I hoped.

"Do you suspect her?"

"No idea, Mom. Serene says Amy is Amy. She's acting

like Amy, only freaked out, which is understandable." I thought about it. "Chuckie!"

He popped his head in. "You shouted?"

"Gotta run a theory by you."

He came inside and shut the door. "Nice catch on White, by the way. Was he trying to kill himself or just break his father's heart?"

"Oh, stop. People make mistakes. You're just self-righteous 'cause you and I never did drugs."

"Ever. Because they're stupid."

"Yes, thank you, Mister DARE Leader. He was trying to be better, stronger, faster, the six-million dollar alien sort of thing."

"A-C steroids. Great. They're illegal in sports, they're illegal religiously for the A-Cs, and they're damaging. Should I go on?"

"Geez, dude, no. Jamie's not quite at the point where she needs the 'Just Say No' lecture, okay? I think her Uncle Christopher's going to be able to give her that all by himself, too, but nice to know you're ready with the lecture at the drop of a hat. What are you so upset about?"

"Oh, nothing. I just have the heads of Airborne, Field, and Imageering out while your mother and I are apparently marked for death, after we've discovered a potential supersoldier project we know nothing about. Can't imagine why I'm tense. Alpha Team's out of commission, and as near as I can tell, no outside influence caused it."

"As you so nicely put it to Jeff earlier, I'm capable of taking a call while I'm a new mother."

"Yeah. You're not capable of doing anything active. White's out for God knows how long, and even when he's back, Martini's going to have to watch him like a hawk, which means they'll both be focused internally, not externally. The less said about Airborne's overall status the better."

"Okay, thanks for the Doom Update. Back to why I called you in here. We need to break down the theories for what's going on, Al Dejahl-wise."

"Amy's involved, get used to the idea."

"We know she's involved. We don't know that she's a bad guy or willingly involved or anything but a pawn."

"Give me a theory that says pawn, because right now I see mole, and I don't like moles. At all."

I knew what Chuckie's people did to moles. Couldn't blame them. Just didn't want Amy to be one.

"Okay, I'm thinking back to Operation Drug Addict, partially because of Christopher, I'm sure. When we were in Florida, Serene's lunacy seemed unrelated to anything else going on, but it was a direct result of the many plans Leventhal Reid and Howard Taft had going."

Chuckie nodded. "Right."

"So follow me here. Whoever Ronaldo Al Dejahl is, figure he's got connections. They knew who I was the first time they tried to take Mom out. I've been a pretty active, obvious girl over the last couple of years, at least in certain circles. I may be hard to find now, but my past is an open book. Brian has one of those books, and he looks at it, because Serene knew Amy the moment she looked at her. How hard would it be to figure out who my friends were, the ones I still talk to?"

Mom pulled out her phone.

"Who are you calling?"

"Figured out where you're going. Getting security on Sheila and her family and Caroline and the senator and his wife. I'm just glad the rest of your close friends are in the Science Center or another solar system."

"Yeah, that's me, friendless." Sheila was my other best girlfriend from high school, and Caroline had been my sorority roommate. Sheila was a housewife; Caroline worked for Arizona's senior senator. Neither one of them really knew what I did, but I was in sporadic communication with them. Other than for my wedding, I'd become sort of invisible to most of my other sorority sisters, friends, and acquaintances since joining up with the A-Cs. For the first time, I was glad. I hoped that meant they weren't marked for death.

Chuckie nodded. "So you think they targeted Amy because she's one of your oldest friends, not because she's the bright thing they needed?"

"I think they saw it as a double win. But twenty guys after her? I know why you find that fishy. She should have been dead before Jeff and Christopher could get to her. Of course, I've beaten those odds, and I'm sure you have, too, so maybe our high school just trained well. Anyway, we need to identify the man who gave her the emergency covert ops number. If we believe her, she had no idea who she was calling."

"Why did she ask for you?"

"Jeff and I gave her some lame Homeland Security lie about what we did. She could call strangers or ask for her friend who she knew worked in some sort of antiterrorism thing. Gee, which would I do?"

"Can't imagine. Okay, we find out who the mystery agent is."

"According to Amy, he's dead. They slit his throat in front of her. Whether that's true or not may depend upon who he is and whether they had great special effects."

Chuckie took a deep breath. "You want to be with me when I question her?"

"Yes, because I know she's pissing you off."

"I wasn't that awful in high school, at least not like she's acting."

"Not to me, no."

Chuckie gave me a wistful smile. "Yeah, I know."

Reader coughed "Jeff's going to hate the way this conversation's starting to head."

Jamie opened her eyes again, yawned, and went back to sleep. "You know, what day is it? I have no idea what day she was born on."

"Christmas," Chuckie answered. "I wasn't doing anything, conveniently."

"Oh, man, that's really crappy timing."

"For you to have the baby? No. For them to start their plan rolling, whatever it is and whoever they are? Great timing."

"Where are your parents?"

He sighed. "Hanging out on the transient floor with the rest of the families. Your grandparents got moved in, too. Be prepared—we've kept them out claiming a lot of important reasons, but they're going to descend on you soon."

"Is Dad here yet?"

Mom was still on the phone, but she nodded. "You're sure the family's okay?" I didn't like how that sounded. Chuckie, Reader, and I all focused on Mom's call. "Good work. Get them here. Scan them first, just in case. Oh? Well done. I'm sure. Yes, good, see you soon. Thanks, Kevin." She hung up.

"What was Kevin doing going after Sheila?"

Mom rolled her eyes. "He's my best operative. His family's safe. He's back to work, so to speak. He went with a team of A-Cs, thank God." She shook her head. "Got to Sheila's family just in time. They were being kidnapped."

"Merry Christmas, hope we make it to the New Year."

"Pretty much." Mom's phone rang. "Yes. Are they safe? Oh, really? You're certain? Fine, well, keep the team with them. Right. If he has an issue, he can call me directly." She hung up, eyes narrowed.

"What was that about? Is Caroline okay?"

Mom nodded slowly. "Yes. She and the senator and his wife are in Paraguay, as part of a fact-finding mission. They're not the only politicians there. There is absolutely nothing out of the ordinary happening, and the senator refused to allow any of them to be taken into protective custody."

"And you allowed that?"

She shrugged. "My team sees nothing amiss. And there's a tremendous amount of security already in place. There are three A-C teams from Sao Paulo Base with them, one each assigned to Caroline, the senator, and his wife. I don't think there's anything we can or should do. It's politically unhealthy to force an entire Congressional fact-finding team to go into isolation unless you can give them a pertinent reason why."

I considered this. Paraguay kept on coming up, and no one ever told me why it mattered. My meeting from the day before, and who it was with, combined with the suspicious superbeing event, suggested a potentially large conspiracy. Or maybe more than one. I resolved to find out, but that had to go onto the back burner, since, clearly, the action wasn't happening in South America. "So they're all safe, and nothing's going on other than Christmas without snow?"

"As far as our teams there can tell, yes." Mom sounded tired and pissed off. Couldn't blame her.

"That's sort of weird, isn't it? I mean, if they're targeting my oldest friends."

Chuckie looked thoughtful. "It depends."

"On what?"

"On who's doing the targeting."

CHAPTER 22

"YOU HAVE A GUESS YET?" I didn't, not really, but then again, I wasn't the Conspiracy King.

Chuckie shook his head. "Not yet." I knew him better than anyone, and, human or not, I knew he was lying. But I also could tell he hadn't solidified on one theory, so I decided to let his wheels turn while we waited for the next disaster to strike. That I was sure something more was coming wasn't indicative of psychic skills—experience was a great teacher.

Mom sighed. "Okay, I'm going to go count noses. I know your father's here, but I want to be sure we haven't missed someone they'll think to grab as a hostage. Alfred and Lucinda already moved a huge number of our family and theirs into their compound, so we should be all right." She kissed me and Jamie, then went out.

Left me, Reader, and Chuckie in the room. Chuckie sat down in a chair. "There are times when I think we should just move everyone we know into a Centaurion base and keep them hidden. It might be easier."

"Ain't it the truth."

Reader's phone rang. "Yeah. Yeah, be right there." He sighed. "Paul's family's here, and Michael's hitting on Amy with intent to score."

"Routine."

"Yeah. Paul needs some help, though." He looked at Chuckie and then back to me. "You okay if I leave you?"

"I've known him since I was thirteen. Yeah, it's fine."

Reader didn't look as though he agreed, but he kissed my cheek, nodded to Chuckie and then left the room. He left the door open.

Chuckie shook his head, got up, and shut the door. He sat back down in the chair. "I guess it's flattering they think you're going to fling yourself at me the moment we're alone."

"Why were you alone on Christmas day?"

He rolled his eyes. "It's not exactly relevant to anything that's going on."

"It's relevant to me. You weren't with your parents, but you didn't say they were in Aruba or something."

"They were home. I was home."

Chuckie lived half the year in Australia and half in D.C. In light of our meeting from the other day, it was a safe bet he'd been in D.C., so I spared myself the potential "duh" look and didn't bother to confirm it. Besides, the where was less worrisome than the why. "Why were you home alone? On Christmas day?"

"Why are you still asking me that?"

"I may have said no and married Jeff, but that doesn't mean I don't love you. I just don't love you like I love him. But, I still love you. I just had to do the whole drug addict expose on another guy I happen to love but not love as much as Jeff. If something happens to James, we'll be batting a thousand. You sitting home alone on Christmas scares the crap out of me, Chuckie."

He shrugged. "It's just a day."

"Right. Stop lying to me, it's insulting."

"She's a beautiful baby."

"Yeah, I think so, too. You drinking a lot?"

He laughed. "No, I'm not a closet alcoholic."

"Then, why all alone? I'll just keep on asking until you give, you know."

"I just have very few people I care about enough to spend a holiday with. I didn't want to spend Christmas with my parents and have to pretend I don't care you're married to someone else, okay?"

"I see we need to find you a girl, too."

Chuckie closed his eyes. "Look, the last thing I want is you trying to fix me up with someone. Truly, the last thing. I don't want you to find a girl for me."

"Jeff thinks you're waiting for him to screw up."

He opened his eyes. "I am. I'm not looking forward to it, but, yeah, I'm waiting."

"Why? And don't say it's because you love me. I know that part. I'm curious why you think Jeff's going to screw up. Was it just that you showed up to propose during the highlight of Operation Drug Addict?"

"No."

"Then why? Badgering again, in case you weren't sure."

He sighed. "It keeps him on his toes."

"What is that supposed to mean?"

"The married-for-life mind-set's great. It's also hard. And I'm not a trusting person. I love you, I care about you, and I want to be sure he doesn't get complacent. I'm watching him, he knows it, and I'll *be* watching him. I could be married with twenty kids—I'd still be watching him."

"Something to look forward to. You two really like pissing each other off. I guess I'm lucky you're both straight, or you'd be married to each other."

Chuckie laughed. "Maybe, couldn't tell you." He sighed. "Any chance I can hold the baby before he gets back and accuses me of trying to steal both of you?"

"Sure."

He got up, and I handed Jamie to him. He held her well. "She really looks like you. Beautiful baby."

"I still don't see it, but I'll take the compliment for both of us."

He held her for a few minutes, walked around the room with her. He finally handed her back to me. "Thank you."

"For what?"

Chuckie kissed the top of my head. "For letting me pretend."

CHAPTER 23

CHUCKIE HAD JUST STEPPED AWAY from the bed when Jeff came in the door. "Out. Now. I'm not kidding."

Chuckie chuckled. "Oh, yes, sir." He looked at me. "See you in a while, Kitty." Then he sauntered out.

"What was he doing?"

"Oh, God, Jeff, not now. How's Christopher?"

He closed the door, heaved a sigh, and came to the bed. "He's a mess. I think he'll be okay. I don't know if he'll be the same or not, though. He's been shooting that poison into his system for weeks."

"Yeah, I could tell from the needle marks. Was he shooting in adrenaline, too?"

Jeff nodded. "Not too much, enough to just counter the drug. So he wasn't going to the superlevel I got to."

"He was on the Serene method, not the Incredible Hulk method, yeah." Jamie started fussing, and we fed her again. Jeff held her and rocked her when she was done. She gurgled at him. I snuggled next to him and got a kiss. "Jeff, I'm going to say something, and I really don't want you freaking out, okay?"

"Ronaldo Al Dejahl is Ronald Yates' son that no one knew about. And he's after you for killing his father." Jeff sounded matter-of-fact. I managed not to faint.

"Wow, yeah. You're so calm."

He sighed. "No, but I don't want to upset you or Jamie."

"I thought you said you didn't think she could pick up emotions with the blocks you put in."

"I don't think she can. However, she can still hear, and if we start getting upset, she'll hear it and see our body language."

"Oh. Good point. So, back to the latest bad guy du jour."

"Right. I assume we figured it out the same way—Sheila's family being targeted."

"Yeah. Mom checked them out a long time ago. So did Chuckie. Her husband's a computer programmer, she's a housewife, they are exactly what they appear to be. So the only reason to target them would be to use them as bait. And they were being kidnapped, not killed, meaning they were going to be more useful alive, at least initially."

"Yep." Jeff shook his head. "I know Reynolds suspects Amy. I hate to say it, but I can't argue with that theory, especially if you're the target."

"I hate to admit it, but with Caroline not being a target, at least as far as my mom and the Sao Paulo teams can tell, but Sheila and Amy being in danger, it does seem like someone is going far back. But I can't believe Amy would willingly do something that would endanger me. We've been friends too long."

"Maybe. But people change."

"Not that much."

"Yeah? Christopher's a drug addict. Let's discuss the idea of 'not that much.'"

"Okay, point taken. But he did it to make himself a better protector, and that's not a change at all."

"I suppose." He kissed Jamie's head. "The doctors said it'll take less time to flush the drug out of him than it did me or Serene. They've made a lot of advances over the past few months."

"That's a relief." I leaned my head on his shoulder. "I'm so worried about him."

"Me, too. I should have noticed something was wrong, and I didn't."

"I know, I feel the same way."

"You're the one who figured it out. Thank God."

"Yeah, but I've seen him every day since he started using, and it took seeing his eyes look as if he hadn't slept for weeks to make me notice anything."

"At least he didn't fight it." He was quiet for a moment.

"Is that normal? For drug addiction, I mean? We don't have a lot of experience with it."

"I don't either, at least not personally. For some, though, no. I knew some druggies in college who are probably dead now. Once hooked, forever hooked sort of thing. But I think Christopher's been scared. I don't believe his eyes are red from the drug, only. I think he's been crying a lot. And I also think he wanted someone to figure it out and make him stop."

"He's scared, I'll say that. Richard's staying near him. Isolation's hard to take—you get used to it as an empath, mostly because it's such a relief that you can have some true peace and quiet—but Christopher's only been in there a couple of times."

"We can all take turns with it."

"Yeah." Jeff sighed. "I let him down completely, didn't I?"

"No. If you'd confirmed his real fear—that you'd never forgive him, never understand, and wouldn't love him any more? Then you'd have let him down. He knows he still has you, unconditionally. And his father. That's what he needed. And what he wanted, I'd guess." I sighed. "We really, really need to get him a girl."

Jeff laughed. "I suppose. No idea who."

"Me either. Hopefully the right candidate will present herself soon."

"Thing is, his right girl was murdered. And the next right girl married me."

"Yeah, but I wasn't the right girl for him. I mean, I can imagine Christopher's reaction to how I handled the wedding parade. I don't think he'd have found it cute or endearing—I think he'd have been humiliated."

"Yeah, maybe." Jeff put his arm around me. "I still think it was great."

"I still think you did all the running around to make me feel better."

"Of course I did. But I enjoyed it, a lot more than the parade because that was just hell." He nuzzled my head. "You should be able to wear your wedding dress again soon."

"I hope so, but I'm not counting on it."

"I am." His voice was a purr.

"You still have your tux, right?" He was even more gorgeous in the tux he'd worn for our wedding. I started to drool a little as I rubbed against him.

"Yeah. I asked Tito, he said we should give it at least a week, but then as soon as you feel physically ready."

"Marking my calendar. Plan to ring in the New Year."

Jeff chuckled. "I can't wait. I can if you need me to, but otherwise, ready the moment you are."

"When can we go back to the Lair? I feel even more helpless stuck in a hospital room."

"Tito and Camilla want you in here for at least another day. Then we'll see."

"When do I get to take a shower?"

"There's one in this room. We *are* in the delivery wing."

"One day I'll keep every floor and section straight."

"I'll believe that when I see it. You need me to get your mother in here, baby? She can watch Jamie while I help you shower, or vice versa."

"I want you to help me shower." I loved showering with Jeff. Of course, we normally took a long time because we'd never taken a shower together where we didn't have a lot of great sex. Even pregnant he'd managed to make showering totally worth my while. Taking baths, too. Generally, getting cleaned up for us meant having fabulous sex. Considered that this was likely to change now. Felt depressed.

"Oh, baby, I can still make it worth your while." He kissed my neck while I moaned softly. "There are plenty of ways I know to make you happy."

"You know every way."

"Mmmm, good."

Before we could continue this discussion, Jamie started crying. Did the diaper check, it was fine. Offered a torpedo, refused. Cuddled and held her, seemed to help a bit. She wanted me more than Jeff but seemed quietest when I was holding her and Jeff was holding us both.

"I should have let James register us."

"Yeah, I know. I was thinking the same thing. We just can't make decisions on this sort of thing quickly, can we?" He sounded a little concerned.

"James says it's because we want everything to be perfect. We make fast decisions all the time when we're in danger, though."

"Yeah." He heaved a sigh. "Seriously, baby, if you want to stop with just Jamie, I'm okay with it."

"I'm not. You've wanted a lot of kids your whole life, Jeff."

"I don't want to live without you. And I just faced that possibility in the most real way since Leventhal Reid almost ran you over with that Escalade in the middle of the desert. I was less afraid of losing you when we were fighting the Alpha Four invasion force than when you were in labor."

"You know, wouldn't you think I'd remember it? At least part of it? I remember a beeping, and you going white, and James yelling at me to stay with you guys. Then, the next thing I remember is hearing Aerosmith, which was great, I have to say."

"Tim insisted it would pull you back. I guess he was right."

"But I don't remember anything else. At all. How long was I supposedly dead?"

"No supposedly, and several minutes. Brain dead first, then your body started to go."

"My brain's fine."

"Yeah. I call it a miracle. First James and then you. I'll take miraculous recoveries for the people I love, believe me."

I leaned my head back against Jeff's shoulder while he rocked me and the baby gently. Closed my eyes, and talked in my head. ACE, are you there?

ACE is here, Kitty. ACE is sorry, ACE could not warn Kitty about Christopher. It would be . . . interfering.

I know, ACE. You do a great job of helping when we really need you to and letting us be alive and make mistakes when we can probably handle it. Do you think Christopher will recover?

ACE believes so. Christopher was so afraid, but Jeff and Richard and Kitty did the right things. Christopher is still afraid, but not as much.

Speaking of afraid . . . Jeff and everyone else say I died. I don't remember.

Kitty was . . . not there . . . for a while. ACE sounded evasive. Usually meant he desperately wanted to tell me something but felt it would be wrong. Which also meant he wanted me to figure it out myself.

Did you bring me back?

No. Kitty did that herself.

Did you take me away? To protect me from the pain? I could remember that the labor pains had been fast and horrible.

No . . . ACE did not do that.

The way he said it made me really think. Jamie made some baby noises, and I cuddled her a little more while Jeff stroked her head. I looked at her and considered what it would have been like to never get to hold her.

ACE? Jamie is very powerful, isn't she?

Yes, Kitty. Jeff is right to be concerned.

Are you helping her, like you did Naomi, Abigail, and Serene? ACE was silent. ACE, really, there is no way in the world I would be upset if you are. I'm thankful you helped the other girls, why wouldn't I want you to help my baby?

ACE is not sure if that is too much interference, if ACE is disrupting God's plans by helping.

You said God gave us free will. That means you have free will, too, ACE.

ACE supposes Kitty is right.

Jamie wasn't head down when she was about to come out. I tried to tell her to turn, but I felt someone else helping, too. I thought it was Jeff, but it was you, wasn't it?

Yes, Kitty. ACE can speak to Jamie differently than Kitty can.

Thank you, for doing that. She could have died if she'd come the wrong way.

ACE knows. Jeff asked ACE to save Kitty. But ACE could not. Jeff asked ACE to kill Jeff, if Kitty died. But ACE could not have done that.

I hated hearing that, but I was extremely glad I'd recovered. I still couldn't figure out how I'd almost died, though, especially with no memory of anything.

But I'm here.

Yes. ACE, like everyone else, is happy.

Jeff was really worried about me dying in childbirth. He mentioned it a lot when I started labor.

Yes. Jeff was right.

Again, something in how ACE said that line made my mind tickle. ACE? If Jeff hadn't been worried about that . . . would I still have almost died?

Thudding silence in my mind. I looked down at my sleeping baby. Who knew how babies in the womb thought? How a superpowerful baby in the womb, who was the daughter of the galaxy's most powerful empath, thought?

Did Jamie, uh, kill me?

CHAPTER 24

NO! JAMIE DID NOT UNDERSTAND! Ace sounded freaked and ready to defend the baby. This was probably a good thing. Nice to have the superconsciousness as your real fairy godfather.

She thought she was supposed to? Jeff had been afraid of me dying, not looking forward to it.

Kitty was only in danger if Jamie had been taken from Kitty.

Connection to the baby meant still connected to life?

Yes. ACE was relieved James did not give up hope.

Did you tell him not to?

No. James will never give up on Kitty, as Kitty will never give up on James.

Good to know. So, what are the chances my next child will be like this?

ACE cannot see the future, Kitty. The future is not set. Every act changes it.

Okey-dokey. So, did Jamie bring me back?

No, Jamie could not. Only Kitty could bring Kitty back.

Power of the will and all that?

In a way. ACE believes Jamie will not do something like that again.

Well, she's already born.

Silence.

ACE? Is she capable of killing someone? Unknowingly, I mean.

Jeff implanted blocks. When Christopher is well,

Christopher should implant blocks, too. ACE will watch over Jamie.

When you say you'll be watching over her, does that mean protecting her from emotional onslaught and things like that?

ACE was silent for a few long moments. The blocks will work as Jeff and Christopher want them to.

As they want them to. I wasn't sure if this meant that ACE felt the blocks were a-okay on their own, or if ACE was going to be giving the blocks a superconsciousness assist.

Does that mean you're helping the blocks?

ACE will do for Jamie what ACE did for Naomi, Abigail, and Serene. Jamie will not lose Jamie's free will.

Sometimes children want things that aren't safe for them or for others.

Jamie will not do something like that. The way he said this, I was pretty sure this meant that ACE both wouldn't allow it and also didn't want to explain any more.

ACE, what did you mean about Jamie's free will?

ACE will not interfere if Jamie wishes to do something that is not a wrong thing for Jamie to wish to do. I'd been a marketing manager before I ran into the gang from Centaurion Division, so I knew doublespeak really well. I was almost impressed that ACE had developed the skill.

I also got the impression this was all I was going to get out of ACE for a while. Okay, thank you. Truly. I don't mind at all that you're protecting my baby. You may have a lot of other babies to worry about soon, ACE. I give you permission to help them and protect them, too, if they need it.

Thank you, Kitty. ACE appreciates Kitty's love and support.

As always, not deserting you, either, okay?

Okay, Kitty. ACE needs to help Paul now. Paul is working with Christopher.

Okay, big guy, thanks again. I opened my eyes.

"Good nap?" Jeff nuzzled the side of my head.

"Wide awake. Jeff? Why were you worried I was going to die in labor?" He didn't answer. "Was it because of the drug?"

"That, and I did a lot of research. It's hard enough when you're having a regular baby. I just never thought about it, how dangerous it would be for you." He sounded guilty and worried.

"It's okay. Women do it all the time. But, baby? Really, try not to focus on the negative, okay?"

"Why not?" He sounded suspicious. "What did ACE tell you?"

"Yeah, okay, I wasn't napping, and yes, I was asking ACE some things. Put it this way—Jamie thinks her daddy is always right."

He clutched me. "Oh, my God, so it *was* my fault?" He sounded guilty like I'd never heard before.

I leaned up and kissed his cheek. "No. I don't remember a thing, but ACE said I brought myself back. And I know if I came back, I came back for you. But she's a baby, and she doesn't understand. I couldn't get everything out of ACE, but I think she thought she was doing the right thing but couldn't fix it when it wasn't the right thing. So, just don't dwell on bad things, okay? So she doesn't. She's really in tune with both of us."

He was shaking. "Okay. I'll work on that."

I pulled his mouth down to mine and kissed him. "Stop. No guilt. ACE said you asked to die if I died. I don't want you to do that, especially now. If something does happen to me, you have to take care of Jamie. Promise me."

Jeff moved me so I was on his lap and he could hold me more tightly. I buried my face in his neck. "I promise," he said finally. "But if it's a choice, I'll die to protect you or save you, or Jamie, you know that."

"Yes, I do. I don't want to face that kind of choice. So let's stop dwelling on it. Not good for us, not good for the baby." I yawned. "I really want to be in our own bed."

Before I could whine for this, Tito and Camilla came in. Jamie and I both got a full once-over. Since they were there, I asked them to watch the baby while I showered. Neither one of them seemed to feel confident that Jeff and I wouldn't have sex in there, but we promised we'd be good.

Jeff opened a drawer, and there were clothes for me. I still had no idea how this worked. You were in a room, you needed clothes, you opened a drawer, there were the clothes, in your size. Almost always Armani, which was the A-C designer of loyal choice. You'd separate an A-C from his or her Armani only if world safety depended upon it.

It worked the same way with the refrigerators. Say what you wanted, it was in there. My Coca-Cola addiction was well served. I hadn't been able to break it, even during pregnancy, though I'd gotten down to one Coke every few days. But if I wanted something different, I just had to ask for it, and there it was.

I called whoever did this the A-C Elves. Jeff refused to explain how it worked. The Elves could get to any A-C facility or vehicle. I'd played around with the soft drink selections while thirty thousand feet in the air—never failed to work.

So I was only mildly surprised to see I had a nursing bra and nursing top, as well as leggings for my new mother wear. At least the Elves didn't want me in a slim skirt, for which I was very grateful.

Took the fastest and most boring shower with Jeff ever in our experience. But it wasn't like we were going to get remotely amorous with Tito and Camilla waiting on the other side of the door.

Well, we got a little amorous, since Jeff got into the shower with me and soaped me up, washed my hair, and did the full body rinse. He was careful not to do anything that would start me howling, but it was still nice, and I felt a lot better afterward.

"You know, I feel pretty good." He was toweling me off while I combed my hair out. "I'm sure I still look hippoish, but I feel a lot better."

"You never looked like a hippo. And you look wonderful, as always." He finished drying me and then toweled himself off. I tried not to look and drool. Failed. He grinned and kissed me, and just like every kiss of his, it was great and made me forget everything else.

I heard the baby start crying the moment we pulled away from each other. "I hope she's not doing that because we were kissing."

"She's a baby, I'm sure she just wants her mommy's breasts. I want her mommy's breasts, so I can't argue."

I nuzzled Jeff's chest. "Hurry up and put your pants on. My Mommy-Alert is screaming and I can't stay in here much longer." He grinned and did as requested. "You can just wear your pants, that's okay with me." I raced out.

Jamie was in full-on baby-shriek. Camilla handed her to me. "I think she's hungry."

"She never stops eating." I kissed her and made the comforting goo-goo noises. Seemed to help.

"Need to make sure she's getting milk then," Tito said briskly.

"The torpedoes inflate, she eats, they deflate." I didn't want to sit on the bed, but there weren't any loungers in here, which was weird because they were in every living quarter. "No lounger?"

"I'll bring you one, baby." Jeff kissed me and hypersped out of the room. Sadly, he had his shirt on. Came back in moments carrying a nice lounger. Happily, his shirt wasn't buttoned. A-Cs were strong, and Jeff, in particular, was able to do the massive heavy lifting and not have it seem like anything.

Got settled into the lounger, leaned it back, started the feeding process. Camilla and Tito both watched. Back to starring in my own reality TV show. Changed sides, Jeff burped her, diaper check, baby gurgled and went back to sleep.

"How long before it stops being this easy?"

"Couple of weeks, tops." Tito took her from me and weighed her. "Good. She's up an ounce or so. Kind of early to weigh, but I want to be sure. She could just be a big eater. Are your nipples bruised?"

"I beg your pardon?" I was shocked by the question, but the look on Jeff's face was priceless.

"You're fair skinned. More of a risk for bruising. Let me know if it starts to hurt, there are things we can do."

"Oh, good. So, basically, every guy I work with's seen my crotch, and you're going to ask me about my boobs all the time now?"

Tito grinned again. "Yep."

"The little joys of motherhood are without number."

CHAPTER 25

THE NEXT COUPLE OF DAYS were a blur of new parenthood, investigations, and doctor checks. We still had no bassinet, mostly because everyone was still restricted to the Science Center, Martini Manor, or one of the other A-C Bases.

Jeff and I were still adjusting to the demands of taking care of someone other than ourselves. It was pretty awesome, especially since Jamie was an amazingly good baby, at least if I took the comments from everyone who had kids of their own as proof. I had no arguments, of course. So far, while I was still tired and felt pretty unprepared for everything, all had gone smoothly.

We'd had a steady stream of visitors. My entire family had made the pilgrimage to my hospital room. Thankfully, most of them didn't seem to know I'd died and come back, for which I was incredibly relieved. It upset Jeff too much when I said I didn't remember it happening. Besides, my parents were with us for most of our relatives' visits, and I didn't want to risk seeing either one of them cry, Mom in particular.

In addition to all the usual friends and family suspects, it felt as if everyone I'd ever even passed in the hallway at the Science Center came by to visit, too. We'd seen Jeff's sisters and some of the older kids, all of whom were under lockdown at Martini Manor but came out to see the baby anyway. I had no idea where Jeff's brothers-in-law were for this, but I was happy they weren't with us—it meant that many fewer people handling the baby and asking me incredibly personal questions. I was getting concerned about Jamie being exposed to every disease in the world, but Tito and Camilla weren't overly worried. Neither were any of the other Dazzlers, so I tried to relax about it.

Interestingly to me, in a rather offensive way, was the fact that the Diplomatic Corps wanted a look at our child. I wasn't a fan of any of them, and the head Diplomatic couple, Robert and Barbara Coleman, I despised with a passion. Happily, Jeff had point-blank refused to allow them access to Jamie or me. When they'd protested all the way up to the Pontifex, Chuckie had stepped in and tossed around some C.I.A. muscle to share that they weren't seeing my baby until I wanted them to, which was likely to be never.

They were still complaining about this, even though Chuckie had had them sent back to the Alpha Centaurion Embassy and told them to stay there "for their safety." Considering how anti-interspecies marriage this group was, them wanting to see Jamie was odd and infuriating, since I didn't believe for one moment that any of them had changed their stances in the last week. I wasn't sure what their game was—but I *was* sure they had one. However, I didn't want to have to be around them to discover what it was, so I chose to table these concerns for later. We had plenty of other things going on to occupy my attention, including diaper changes, which were moving up on my Least Favorite Things About Being a Mommy list.

Finally back in the Lair and able to lock some of the madness out. Not as much as I would have liked, of course—we were in the middle of some kind of operation. None of us were sure what, which made getting anywhere difficult.

In between visits and fending off the Diplomatic Corps, Jeff and Chuckie had spent a lot of time questioning Amy. The three of us were in the Lair, bickering about the results.

"Look, I can't get a thing from her other than confusion, fear, and jealousy." Jeff wasn't snarling, but I knew he wanted to be. "Unless she's able to block me, she's being used, not part of the issue."

"Confusion and fear I get, but what's she jealous about?"

Jeff sighed. "She's jealous of you. And Sheila, but mostly you."

"Of me? Um, why?"

He shrugged. "You're happily married, just had a baby, have an exciting career, and an interesting life."

"She's had an exciting career and interesting life, too."

"No husband and baby. Sheila's been married for over seven years and has four kids, you're married with an immediate baby, Brian same thing. The clock is ticking and Amy's losing the race." Chuckie didn't sound surprised. "But does that mean she's happy to be working against Kitty?"

"I don't think she's working against anyone." Jeff shook his head. "I'd like you to find the agent who was supposedly helping her."

"I would, too." Chuckie shook his head. "No idea who it was at this point."

"Had to be someone involved in covert ops," I pointed out. "The number worked."

"Yeah, and it traced back to the payphone Amy said she was at. But a lot of operatives had that number. It was an older number, but still active." Chuckie didn't look or sound overly worried, but his eyes said otherwise.

"How old?" Jeff asked.

"Five years. And, yeah, we've been checking the retirement files. So far, Amy has gotten a great look at every operative we have all over the world, but recognizes no one. Let me mention that she's not leaving our control any time soon, if ever. All by herself she's a major security breach, even if she's innocent, let alone if she's deeply involved."

"Can't argue there." I cuddled the baby and tried to think of something that wasn't mommy related. "Amy said she thought he was a businessman."

"Covert ops field agents aren't supposed to be wearing signs that say 'Hi, my name is Bill, and I'm with the C.I.A.,' you know." Chuckie's sarcasm knob was up to full.

"No, really? Wow, I learn something new every day." I had a sarcasm knob, too.

Jeff sighed. "As enjoyable, and rare, as it is to watch the two of you bicker, could we maybe focus on the matter at hand?"

"I suppose. We have the other matter at hand, too." They both looked at me. "Ronaldo Al Dejahl? We are agreed this is a son of Yates' that we didn't know about?"

Chuckie nodded. "Your mother agrees. Yates was under surveillance for years, but he could have impregnated any number of women."

"Aren't we all so lucky? So, there could be more of them?"

"No idea. I'd have said that was Centaurion's business, but I can't really blame you all for not following the human side of things."

I looked at Jamie. She gurgled and grabbed at my hair. "But any child of his wouldn't be a human. It would be a hybrid or a full A-C."

CHAPTER 26

I LOOKED AT JEFF. He looked ill. Chuckie, same thing. "On record, that thought only just occurred to me."

"Hybrid males have no unusual talents." Jeff sounded like he was grasping for a good spin.

"But they can still have talents. Paul does."

"And you and White aren't exactly short in the talent department," Chuckie added.

"Yeah." Jeff heaved a sigh and pulled out his phone. "I want tracking for unknown hybrids. No idea of how. Take a sampling. What do you mean from whom? From the Gowers and Serene for starters. Then branch out—what? Really? Huh. Okay. What?" He looked over at me and Jamie and I recognized his expression—protective and possessive. "No." Whoever he was talking to was arguing, I could tell by the way Jeff looked. "Fine, we'll discuss it after you tell me what you have with the five adults we know about. Call me right away." He hung up and looked worried and thoughtful.

"Jeff? What's wrong? Aside from them wanting to test Jamie? Which, if it's a safe test, I can't understand why you said no."

"She's less than a week old," he muttered.

"What else is wrong?" I started to get worried, and it was clear it showed in my voice because Jamie began fussing.

Jeff closed his eyes. "None of the other hybrids are still alive."

That hung on the air for a bit. "Um, why not?"

He opened his eyes. "No idea. Praying to God it's not a shorter lifespan."

"You never checked this before you married Kitty and allowed every A-C under thirty to marry a human?" Chuckie sounded just this side of enraged.

"Before you both start, stop it." I took a deep breath. "Jeff, just call whoever does the statistical analysis and get them going on it."

He did as requested. Chuckie still looked ready to lose it. "Chuckie, stop. Whatever it is, we'll deal with it, okay? If it's scary bad, then we'll both need your help, not your rage, okay? Please? As my oldest friend?"

Chuckie nodded, and I saw him pull himself back under control. "Yeah. Sorry. It didn't occur to me, either, and since I would have loved a reason to tell you not to marry him, I can't really complain that none of us thought of it."

"None of the older A-Cs mentioned it as a danger sign, and I think they would have. Jeff's mother would have, for sure, at least when I first met her."

Jeff got off the phone. "Well . . . it's interesting. Reynolds, we need to somehow have Michael Gower under protection when he's back at NASA."

"Why?" Chuckie sounded confused. "Thought you cleared out the security issues there over a year ago."

"We did, but the statistics on hybrids are really interesting." Jeff let out his breath slowly. "None of them died from disease. None of them have made it into old age, either."

"Oh, I love this game, let me see if I can guess what comes next! They all had mysterious accidents, right?"

"I married the smartest girl in the galaxy."

"Nope, I've just been trained by the Conspiracy King."

Chuckie managed a weak grin. "Thanks. So, every one of them?"

"All but the Gowers and Serene," Jeff confirmed. "Every other hybrid is dead and buried."

"You said they were all men, right?"

Jeff nodded. "Yeah, which is a scary statistic in its own right."

"Why didn't anyone pay more attention to this?"

Jeff shrugged, but Chuckie looked thoughtful. "Maybe they did."

"Come again?"

Chuckie sighed. "You've been infiltrated before. Several times that we know of. It's likely there are more infiltrators than we know about. So, perhaps a study was done, and the results were destroyed or hidden."

"Who would do that?" Jeff asked. "Who would want to keep this information from us?"

"Beverly leaps to mind, and that's just for starters." I considered. "The current Diplomatic Corps might, particularly if the statistics indicated that interbreeding was good for both races."

"There weren't enough numbers for a sufficient test," Jeff protested.

Chuckie cocked his head. "Why did they stop then?"

"What do you mean?" Jeff actually didn't sound aggressive—he sounded confused.

I snorted. "Your race is extremely efficient. You test everything, at least as far as I've seen. You research. You do your homework."

Chuckie nodded. "So, why would they only interbreed a few couples?"

"It was every race and country," I offered. I remembered this well from Operation Fugly. "So, figure there was a sample of at least a hundred, maybe closer to two hundred." Jeff nodded.

"That's hardly enough to perform any useful analysis," Chuckie said. "What did the tests prove?"

"We were taught the tests showed no significant positives that made interspecies marriage worthwhile, which meant we shouldn't interbreed . . ." Jeff's voice trailed off, and he looked as though he was starting to get angry. "This is going to be one of those things they told us to control us, isn't it?"

"I think it's more that they told you to control you the way Ronald Yates wanted. We have to figure whoever was in on this willingly and knowingly was a Yates loyalist, like good old Beverly."

Chuckie shook his head. "If it's, as it always seems, a group of the older generation of A-Cs, we're going to have trouble finding them." He shot me a look I knew meant he felt that we potentially had some really excellent liars in the A-C community. "However, let's table the rest of our genetics worries. We need to move the murder worries front and center. How did the hybrids die?"

"Report's coming down to us, but it would be acceptable things. Car crash, superbeing, alcohol ingestion."

"Wait a minute. Jeff, no one knew alcohol killed A-Cs until I joined up and we all figured it out."

"Last male hybrid died from alcohol ingestion twelve months ago," Reader said as he came into the room carrying a file.

"You're the statistics guy?" Why was I always the last to know anything?

Got the cover-boy grin. "Why do you think I live for the light reading?" He tossed the file to Jeff and came over to me. Kissed my forehead, kissed the baby. Then leaned against the wall. "Our last hybrid was supposedly depressed, and the consensus was that he committed suicide."

"We don't commit suicide." Jeff sounded confused. "It's just not something A-Cs do, religiously or racially. I can't think of a suicide, ever, that I've ever heard of." I chose not to mention that Jeff asking ACE to kill him if I died was a form of suicidal thinking. I mean, he was stressed enough, Chuckie was right there, and they were both doing so well, I didn't want to wreck the cooperative mood.

"You don't do drugs, either. I point to White, who's locked up in your version of rehab, and mention that, yes, sometimes you do." Chuckie shifted in his chair. "But back to Kitty's point. Why would alcohol ingestion be an acceptable cause of death?"

Reader shrugged. "Guy was depressed. But let me have your attention before you go off worrying about that." He waited until we were all looking at him. "Every single hybrid, other than the Gowers and Serene, was living in Europe. And our last dead hybrid was living in . . . wait for it . . . Paris."

Silence. Jeff was an A-C, genetically quiet when thinking. Chuckie had learned to think to himself since thinking aloud got him beaten up when we were in school. Reader had been around the A-Cs a long time. As always, this left acting human to me.

"So how many hybrids were there, in total? To begin with, I mean?"

"Less than two hundred. And, yeah, girlfriend, in all of

those, the only female births were Naomi, Abigail and Serene. Only Americans had girls, I might add."

"Go U.S.A. But Paul told me that they tried every race and every country."

"They did. But the other A-Cs who married Americans didn't have children. There were several couples worldwide who never reproduced." Reader had obviously memorized the file.

"No one thought that was strange?"

Jeff shrugged. "It was a scientific experiment. Had the long chat with my dad about this when we told them we were pregnant. Any couple that didn't get pregnant, it was just assumed they couldn't—that our genetics and theirs didn't mix right. Enough couples did have children that it wasn't definitive proof of anything, good, bad, or indifferent."

"So none of the A-C scientists spent any time on this? At all? I get that it's likely that the original data was hidden or destroyed, but in all this time, it's never come up? No one's ever asked themselves or each other why it is that these experiments weren't continued? No one checked to see how the hybrids were doing? No one but me is interested in this stuff? How did I become the Genetics Queen?"

"You were interested in reproducing with one of them. What?" Chuckie said to the glare I shot him. "I'm not wrong and you know it. You were interested because it was all exciting and new, and you were hot for Martini and being told you couldn't marry him. I know you, that made you even more interested in him and finding out about this genetics experiment. But for them, it's just history."

"I didn't just want to marry Jeff because they said we couldn't." Oh, sure, that news had made me a lot more open to the idea, but it wasn't *why*. I didn't want to look at Jeff, though, because I was afraid he might think that was the only reason why.

"And here I thought it was only because I looked good in my suit." Jeff laughed. "I'll take whatever your motivation was and be happy with it, okay, baby?"

"Wasn't my only motivation." The great sex had had a lot more to do with it. I looked over at Jeff and realized he'd caught the great sex thought because he had a really satisfied smirk on his face. Wondered if it might possibly be safe enough to have sex the moment I could shove the other guys out of our room. Saw his smirk get a little wider.

"*Anyway*," Reader said, presumably because he'd seen the look on Jeff's face, too. "The A-Cs didn't leap into human relationships when they arrived here—their position with the U.S. government was too tenuous. The interspecies tests weren't approved until they'd been here a while."

"Remember, too, that we didn't come en masse. We were sent in waves. Diplomatic Corps for our race went first, to ensure we'd be allowed to stay. Give the home world that much credit, anyway." Jeff sounded only mildly disgusted.

"I'd give the credit to Richard and Terry and probably your dad and Stanley Gower. The ones with actual influence with the Royal Court, such as it was."

Jeff shrugged. "Probably. The first wave arrived in the nineteen-fifties. Established us as political and religious refugees, and then brought the next waves. We were all here by the mid-sixties."

"Which is when the interbreeding experiment was allowed."

Jamie started to fuss a little. Reader, still talking, came over and took her away from me. Put her onto his shoulder, and she was out like a light. Wondered how often he'd be willing to babysit his namesake. Hoped a lot.

"Stanley was pretty much the youngest person in the test group. That's why all the other hybrids are older than Paul—their parents started their families earlier. Oh, another fact you'll find interesting—the Gowers are the only couple who had more than one child."

"Did all the mothers die in childbirth?" I figured it was better if I asked that question.

Reader shook his head and kissed the baby. "Not a one. The pregnancies were harder on those couples with human females, but not life-threatening."

"So I was just special."

"I think of you that way, baby."

"Awww, so sweet. So, how many of them had special A-C talents?"

"Average number. The only thing normal out of the whole analysis." Reader shifted Jamie back into my arms. I cuddled her, and she snuggled into my chest. "About a third had normal A-C talents, and normal for males. So there were imageers, empaths, and troubadours. A couple of dream-memory readers, again, about average since that's the most uncommon talent, even though it's not male-specific. All of them were in active service. The imageers and empaths all died dealing with superbeings."

"Which isn't necessarily suspicious," Chuckie offered.

"True, it's not. The troubadours were a variety—accidents of some kind, usually automotive, superbeings, a couple from household accidents. Same with the dream-readers, other than our last one, who was our suicide."

"So, did they all know who was on the grassy knoll?"

"I'd assume it's more that they were being wiped out to prevent additional expansion of the species." Chuckie looked at Jamie. "I don't want her out of sight of at least two members of Alpha Team at any time."

"I agree." Jeff didn't even complain about agreeing with Chuckie. I didn't know whether to be happy or afraid. Settled for both.

"Here's the thing, though. None of the males showed anything different. Why wipe them out? I mean, I know for a fact that Yates and Mephistopheles both wanted to keep Jeff and Christopher from reproducing. But the Gowers were never mentioned. I don't think Yates even knew Serene existed."

Chuckie sat up straight. "No one knows who her father is?"

"No, only that he was human. Her mother died when she was a little girl; she was raised by cousins. Brian's met them—they didn't seem very invested in her, not the way Alfred and Lucinda are with Christopher, or Richard is with Jeff."

"Because Serene was born out of wedlock." Reader didn't make this sound like a supposition.

"You know this how?"

He snorted. "Girlfriend, they're all about playing the field and finding your ultimate love connection, I'll give you that. But be really thankful you got pregnant on your honeymoon. Their views about unwed parents make the Puritans look loose. Both parents, by the way, not just the mother."

I looked at Jeff. He shrugged. "Wasn't an issue." I managed not to say that it almost had been—I'd gotten pregnant a few days before our honeymoon, and if we'd been on schedule, we'd have been married after I was already six to seven weeks pregnant. He shook his head. "Get pregnant, get married, all is forgiven, never discussed, really. Just the kids making really sure. Get pregnant, say you don't want to get married? Then it would be a problem."

"Jesus, so you were banging Kitty when interspecies marriage wasn't allowed while at the same time unwed pregnancy would equal complete banishment, and you somehow think it's okay because your timing worked out?" Chuckie sounded just this side of enraged again. I hated to admit that I sort of shared his opinion.

Jeff's eyes narrowed. "From the moment I met her I wanted to marry her. It's not any of your damn business, but I was perfectly willing to be excommunicated, to use a human term, if we weren't allowed to get married."

Reader cleared his throat. "Guys, please. I don't want Kitty to have to flash the maternity rack—unless I have time to call the rest of Alpha and Airborne down to witness it. Let's get back to the matter at hand. What about Serene made you sit up and take notice, Reynolds? Haven't seen you that perky since we found Kitty's wedding dress."

Chuckie grinned. "Great dress."

"Yeah, *my wife* looked wonderful in it."

"Jeff!"

"He started it."

Chuckie shook his head. "I'll be the bigger boy and finish it. Simple question—how the hell do we know that Serene's father was really a human?"

CHAPTER 27

"SHE WAS TOLD HE WAS A HUMAN, and she has the expanded A-C talents." We'd never gotten any more out of Serene, and Brian hadn't been able to get more out of her relatives, either.

"Technically, Martini and White have them, too."

"No, they don't. They're just stronger than the others." This sounded somewhat lame when said aloud, but I decided that I didn't have to be brilliant this early into the Mommy Hood.

Chuckie sighed. "Let me say this in simple terms. Even before Martini got unwittingly loaded up on those A-C steroids and White shot himself up with them, they were both so much more powerful than any other empath or imageer that if you'd told me they were genetic mutations I wouldn't have argued. Now that the drug's been introduced? Martini's got expanded powers, and God alone knows what's happened to White. I don't even want to think about what Serene's got going, not that I'll be able to avoid finding out."

"So . . . what? Dude, if you have a theory, really, spit it out. The baby's gonna wake up for a torpedo soon." I knew this because my breasts were trying to burst out of the nursing bra.

"I want a full background check run on Serene, her mother, the cousins, everything. Try to pin down anything we can about her father." Chuckie sounded both worried and very in charge. "I also want a DNA test run as soon as possible."

Jeff looked like he was going to argue. I did my best to send an emotional signal not to start. "Chuckie . . . who do you think is Serene's father? I know it's just a guess, but I want to hear your guess."

He looked right at me. "Let's hear yours, first. Bet they're the same."

I swallowed. "Most of the A-Cs were told Richard White's father, the original exile, died when they first arrived. Only a handful knew that he was alive and calling himself Ronald Yates. Serene's part of the family is clearly not well connected—no one working at the top levels knew of her existence. So they probably didn't know Yates when he was on Alpha Four, or if they did, in the same way I'd have known the President, you know, before I found out my mom hangs with him on a regular basis—pictures from afar. Richard and Christopher both confirmed that Yates' looks had altered greatly by the time the rest of the A-Cs got here. Her mother was young when she had Serene, I know that much from talking to her. Very young. About twenty, no more than twenty-one."

Jeff looked sick. "Ronald Yates loved to spend his time with young girls."

"Yeah." All four of us looked at each other. "Well, on the plus side—at least Serene will have some family now. And she already has a daddy-crush on Richard."

"Who would be, in actuality, her older brother." Reader sounded about this as I did—sort of glad, sort of grossed out.

"Thank God she married Brian and not, say, Christopher." Jeff ran his hand through his hair. "Not that Christopher's ever shown interest in crazy chicks."

"He liked Kitty." Chuckie grinned at me. "But she's special."

"Awww, you're both so sweet, how do I keep the blushing away? Seriously, guys, what are the odds?"

"Gladys is really powerful," Reader said. "Everyone tends to forget she's Richard and Lucinda's half sister when discussing how the Martini family had no significant A-C talents in it before Jeff showed up, and how Christopher's mother brought in the A-C talents to the White side. I know why they try not to mention Yates. But it's the Yates half mixed with her mother that made Gladys strong. Maybe Richard's mother was the, pardon the phrase, weak link."

"And Serene's mother wasn't."

"Odds are long but also likely at the same time." Chuckie shook his head. "We have to find out as much as we can about Serene's parentage. Under the circumstances, we need a DNA test from the Pontifex."

Jeff opened his mouth. "Fine, I'm sure Richard won't object," I said quickly. Jeff's mouth snapped shut.

"I agree. The Pontifex does seem willing to actually help us solve mysteries instead of tossing himself in front of us like a roadblock." Chuckie said this staring right at Jeff, who had the grace to merely grimace. "And, frankly, we need to find out as much as we can about Ronaldo Al Dejahl. Discovering anything about his and Serene's parentage is going to be difficult. Which, in a way, brings us back to Amy. I still don't trust her part in this. At all."

"If Ronaldo's after me, or us, or whatever, then her involvement makes a lot of sense."

Chuckie shook his head. "It's too damned convenient. Especially using her father's name to lure the Pontifex."

"Maybe that's what we're supposed to think." I rocked Jamie. Not that we had a rocking chair, or anything else. The men looked at me blankly. "Guys, think. Whoever planned to take out the ETD and P.T.C.U., and let's assume it's our pal Ronaldo, has had some time to set it up. He's crafty. His father knew Amy's parents, meaning Amy might know him, or recognize him, but even if she doesn't, using Amy's dad's name to lure Richard isn't that much of a leap—I mean, if Richard had run it by me, I'd trust Amy's dad, right? If our Head Fugly makes it look like someone we think we should be able to trust is untrustworthy, we spend all our efforts on figuring out her deal, when we should be paying attention to other things."

Tito came in during the middle of my little speech. "Yeah, there's something else I really want us paying attention to."

CHAPTER 28

TITO LOOKED WORRIED.

"What?" Jeff looked worried, too, now.

Jamie started to cry. I got up, put her on my shoulder and did the Mommy Dance. All of the men were staring at me. "What?" I looked down. Nope, my clothes were on and my breasts weren't leaking. Saw no issues.

"Yeah," Tito said. "See what I mean?"

Jeff and Chuckie both nodded. Reader stopped leaning against the wall. All three men looked freaked. "I don't see what you mean."

"Look in a mirror." Tito didn't make it sound like a suggestion.

"Rather not, thanks. Last I checked I was down to moo-cow levels, and while that's an improvement over hippo, I just don't enjoy staring at myself looking like this."

"I didn't really notice," Jeff said, sounding confused.

"You've been with her constantly." Tito cocked his head. "I haven't, but I'm seeing her enough to note the dramatic change."

"I still have my hair—right?"

Reader grinned. "Thought bald was sexy."

"On Paul. And on you, when you were bald for, what, a week before your hair grew back? On girls it says militant or cancer patient."

"Yes, baby, your hair looks fine. Uh, let's go into the bathroom." Jeff got up, put his arm around me and walked me into the bedroom. "I want you to be really calm about this. In fact, let me hold Jamie." He took the baby from me, leaned her on his shoulder and kept his other arm around me.

"Is this supposed to be the Scare Kitty Hour?"

"No." He moved me in front of the mirror.

I looked. Saw me. Whoo hoo. "So?" Jeff took the back of my shirt and pulled, so that it conformed to my body. "Again, so?"

He sighed. "Baby, what's wrong with this picture?"

"Nothing. I look fine. I—" I stopped myself and stared. I looked more than fine. I looked pre-pregnancy, other than my breasts, which were still inflated to torpedo proportions. "Ummm . . . is it time to freak out or call Oprah and announce the best diet, ever, in the history of the world?"

"No idea." Jeff took my hand and led me back out to the living room. "Okay, Kitty's on board with the news. What's it mean?"

Tito shook his head. "No idea."

Chuckie's eyes were narrowed. "I think I have one." He stood up. "Do some kung fu move on me."

"You're kidding, right?"

"No. I think I can block you."

I shrugged and did my personal fave, Crane Opens a Can of Whuppass. I did it nicely, since I didn't want to kill or even hurt Chuckie. He was fast, but I was faster, and he was on the ground.

I put my hand down. "Why?"

He took it, and I could feel he was shaking as I pulled him up. "Martini, we need to run blood tests, right away. On all three of you."

Jeff was white. "No argument."

I looked to Reader. Wow, he was white, too. Tito wasn't pale, but he had his Serious Doctor Face on, which was never a good sign. I didn't like it when the most important men in my life were freaking out. All we needed was my dad to make it a full house.

"What's going on?"

Tito shook his head. "No idea. At all. Your charts show the same thing. You're back to pre-pregnancy status, other than your breasts, which are, thank God, making milk and acting normally. They're the only part of your body that is."

"I'm defective?" It figured.

"No." Chuckie's voice was shaking. "I think you've mutated."

"Oh, come on. I'm a human. I didn't get hit with any radioactive juice or get zapped by gamma rays."

"No. You just were carrying the baby of a mutated alien for the last nine months." Chuckie didn't sound accusatory or angry. He sounded scared.

"I can't believe I'm saying this, but Reynolds is right." Jeff sounded more scared than Chuckie. He was clutching Jamie and she started to cry again.

I took her from him and cuddled her, did the Mommy Dance, petted her back, and she calmed down. "Baby girl does not like it when her daddy freaks out, Jeff." I looked at the others. "Or when Uncle James and Uncle Charles and Good Doctor Tito freak out. She doesn't like that, either. Please calm down, guys, I mean it."

I found it hard to believe that Jamie was in life-threatening danger right now. So either everyone's emotions were so high that the blocks Jeff put in weren't working, or ACE was incorrect, which I doubted, or . . . something else. Under the circumstances, I felt it was probably a good idea to confirm if and what that something else might be.

Um, ACE? Are you there?

Yes, Kitty, ACE is here. Jamie is not picking up emotions. Jamie is hearing and interpreting sounds.

Wow, either I was broadcasting my concerns, which was, per Jeff, very likely, or ACE wasn't in the mood to make me work for it. I counted it as one for the win column either way.

So she's crying because all the guys sound freaked out?

Yes, and because of the tension around Jamie. Jamie cannot feel emotions as Jeff can right now, and Jamie cannot control the blocks as Jeff can, right now, but Jamie can feel things as all animals do. Not that ACE feels Jamie or Kitty are really penguins.

But we are animals, just more highly evolved ones.

Yes.

So she's acting like any baby would in a room full of freaked out men?

Yes.

Good to know. Thanks, ACE, you're the best.

"Blood tests. Now." Tito said, interrupting my chat with our higher power. He didn't make it sound optional.

"Oh, fine."

We went up to medical, and Tito did his vampire thing. I didn't like needles overmuch, but I could handle them by talking about something other than what was going on. "So, Chuckie, can I just run out to some baby store, buy a bassinet, and come right on home? I'll take a contingent of hunks with me, if necessary."

"No." He still looked freaked out.

"Jeff?" I tried whining.

"Hell, no." He looked more freaked than Chuckie.

"James?"

"I'd do it, but I think bassinets are the least of our worries, girlfriend."

Tito took the blood from Jamie, and she started to cry. "Oh, it's okay, Jamie-Kat. It won't hurt much and it'll be over fast. Tito just wants to take care of us." I kissed her head, and she calmed down a bit.

Melanie and Emily trotted in, looking strained. "Ready?" Emily asked.

Tito nodded and handed them three vials. "Do it fast and do it accurately."

They nodded and raced out of the room.

"So, to reassure everyone, I wasn't shooting up with Christopher."

"I know that." Jeff wasn't glaring but he was close. At least he didn't look freaked out for a few seconds.

"Already checked your arms out." Chuckie rubbed his forehead. "Look, Martini was altered from the drug the Club Fifty-One people gave him. So was Serene. The drug's not in their systems, but their systems were changed because of it. Their blood was, too, I'd assume."

"Safe bet," Tito said. "From what I've learned, A-Cs are more adaptable than humans in some ways, probably due to the faster regeneration based on the double hearts."

"Will that mean it's a problem if Jeff or Serene ever need blood?" Now I was worried and Jamie started to fuss.

Jeff managed a grin as he took her from me. "Jamie-Kat doesn't like it when Mommy's worried, either."

"No idea yet," Tito replied to my question. "That's a better question for one of the A-C gals. I've been kind of focused on human medical for some reason."

"Sarcasm is an ugly trait in a doctor."

"Only if you can spot it." Tito grinned. "Anyway, on the positive side, you're literally ready for action."

"Not that I'm allowing you to get into any," Jeff said quickly.

"Whatever. So, what's the thinking here? Jeff was altered, so Jamie was affected? And somehow she did, what, the mother and child version of feedback?"

"I'd assume so." Chuckie was staring at me, but I got the feeling I was being studied, versus checked out.

"What?" Jeff must have felt the same thing from him, because he wasn't snarling at Chuckie.

"Was she always fast enough to knock me on my butt?"

"I'm not without the skills, as I have to constantly remind all of you."

"My guess would be no," Reader said. I gave him a betrayed look. "Your skills are great, girlfriend. They're also not conventional."

Jeff handed Jamie to Reader. "Spar with me."

"Uh, no, you kick my butt every time."

"I'll be nice, like always."

"Humph." Decided to humor them and started fake-fighting with Jeff. Actually landed a couple of hits, but not too many. Could dodge or block most of his, which was nice. Not that he ever hit me with any kind of force, but I liked showing some kind of improvement.

He left himself open, and I landed a hit to his stomach at full force. Jeff went down. "Oh, my God, are you okay? Did I hurt you?" I was on the floor next to him, holding his upper body. "Jeff, are you okay?"

"Uhhh . . . yeah." He patted me. "I'm fine, baby. You just knocked the wind out of me."

"Sorry, I didn't mean to. You just left yourself open."

"Yeah." Jeff got to his feet and pulled me up. He hugged me to him. His hearts were pounding. "So, Reynolds, in answer to your question—no, she wasn't that fast, or strong, before."

"What do you mean?"

Jeff was still holding me tightly. "I wasn't at full hyperspeed, baby, but I was going fast enough that normally you wouldn't have been able to block me, let alone hit me."

"I never thought I'd be able to say this, but I'm shocked out of my mind." Chuckie sounded ready to lose it.

"Oh, come on. I don't have two hearts or two heads." I pulled out of Jeff's arms. "You're both overreacting."

"No, they're not," Melanie said as she and Emily came back. "Your blood's changed." She shook her head. "I don't know how to say this, but, Kitty? You're not fully human any more."

CHAPTER 29

LET THAT ONE SIT on the air for a moment. "So, you're saying . . . what?"

"You have A-C regenerative powers, and you're gaining speed and strength. No idea of what else yet." Tito was reading the results from Melanie's clipboard. "Standard recovery for an A-C female after pregnancy, by the way. Interesting."

He pulled his stethoscope out of his scrub pocket and took a listen. "But still only a single human heart. So she's not an A-C, just gained some of the abilities."

Melanie nodded. "Her blood is different, so is Jamie's. So is Jeff's, but we already knew that. Comparing to the Gowers' now, and Serene's."

Everyone, to a person, looked freaked out. "So, let me get this straight. I get hurt, I'm going to recover right away?" Heads nodded. "And I'm catching up to the A-Cs in the speed department?" More nods. "And I'm getting superstrong?" Nods again.

Considered all my reaction options. Wow, they were all the same.

"Oh, my God, are you kidding me? Are you serious?" I started jumping up and down. "This is the GREATEST! I'm Wolverine with boobs! I'm Wolverine with boobs! This is like the most exciting thing that's ever happened to me." Looked at Jeff's expression. "Um, well, other than marrying Jeff and having Jamie. But right after that."

"Stop jumping, it's giving me whiplash." Jeff shook his

head. "Only my girl. You're thrilled? The rest of us are ready to have hysterics, and you're excited by this?"

"Uh, comics geek-girl, remember? Hell, yes, I'm excited about it! I have my body back, and I didn't have to diet or exercise or *anything*. Name a woman who wouldn't be thrilled with that alone." This totally made up for the almost dying thing. Figured I shouldn't say that aloud, though. Wanted to continue to jump for joy. Since I'd been ordered not to jump, however, did the happy dance instead.

"You're doing the Purina Cat Chow dance." Reader started to crack up.

"Chow, chow, chow! I'm a super! I'm a super! God . . . who can I tell? Where're Lorraine and Claudia? And I gotta get a message to Jareen and Queen Renata and Felicia and Wahoa! *They'll* be excited for me!" My girlfriends from the Alpha Centauri system were all kick-butt types. Sure, Jareen was a Giant Lizard, Felicia was a Cat Person, Wahoa was a Major Doggie, and Queen Renata was the head of the Amazons, but they were still among my best friends ever.

"You know, I feel somewhat responsible for her reaction." Chuckie sounded like he was still wavering between amused and freaked out.

"Dude, you cannot stand there and tell me this isn't the coolest thing in the *world*! I mean, wow. I have superpowers. And I'm not evil or some horrible parasite host. I can kick serious butt now." Looked at Jeff. "I wonder if I can still drive and fly."

"Can't wait to find out." Jeff sounded like he could wait.

"You're not walking or talking faster. Maybe you'll be able to do both." Reader was starting to sound like this was no longer freaking him. "I wonder if it'll work that way for the human men, like Brian."

"Doubt it." Tito was still looking at my chart. "They aren't carrying the babies. I'm pretty sure the father's sperm were altered like the rest of him, which created the embryo and therefore mutated it. In the eight-plus months to go from embryo to fetus to baby, blood, and possibly cells, from the fetus clearly mingled with the mother's, which then created the mutation in the mother once the umbilical cord was severed. Of course, we'll want to run more tests." Emily and Melanie both nodded emphatically.

"How charming. Tito, could you have possibly made that any more clinical, gross, or weird if you'd tried?"

He shook his head, still engrossed in my chart. "Sorry, just fascinating stuff." He looked up and grinned at me. "You were right—I'd never have learned these kinds of things at a regular hospital."

"So happy it's all working out for you. We are rather attached to you by now. So, no worries about my torpedoes suddenly not working?" About the only downside I could see was if I wasn't going to be able to breastfeed Jamie. I liked it, a lot, and I knew it was good for her. And Jeff still loved watching it, too.

"No, at least, if you're now following standard A-C reactions," Emily said. "You should be able to breastfeed as long as you want. I recommend stopping between six months and a year, but it'll depend on how fast Jamie's developing."

"Do A-C babies grow faster than human ones?" And, if so, why hadn't anyone mentioned that in the last eight months?

"Not so much, no. But the double hearts do speed some things up. Teeth and such, as an example. Trust me," Melanie said with a grin, "you do not want to be breastfeeding when the teeth arrive."

I could easily imagine. "Good point. Noted." I was so excited I couldn't keep still. I was sort of bouncing.

"Baby, the whiplash, it's bad for me. Stand still."

Heaved a sigh. "Fine." Stood still. Excitement didn't go away. "Wonder how my parents are going to take the news."

"Take what news?" My dad's voice came from the doorway. "What's going on?" He went over to Reader and took Jamie. She woke up, cooed at him, and went back to sleep. "Oh, my little Jamie-Kat knows her Papa Sol, doesn't she?"

I watched my dad cuddle Jamie. He looked so happy and so did she, at least, as much as a newborn could. I was enjoying watching them so much I forgot what we'd been talking about.

Dad hadn't. He looked over. "Kitten? You had news for me and your mother?"

Jeff cleared his throat. "Yeah, Reynolds is still refusing to let us out of the compound to get a damned bassinet."

Chuckie blinked, but he went right into his part of this

act. "Yeah, it's dangerous. I don't want to risk anyone, Sol, especially Kitty, who wants to go baby shopping."

Dad shook his head. "Charles is right. We need to stay hunkered down. They can't hurt anyone that way. Poor Sheila! Those goons had knives to her children's throats. Naomi and Abigail had to alter their memories, it was that traumatic for them."

I took a deep breath. Jeff and Chuckie both gave me looks that shouted "shut up." Let the breath out. Geez. I was excited, not stupid. "Dad, what does Sheila think's going on? I haven't seen her yet."

He shook his head. "Not what I would have liked. We can't afford to have them forget the incident, because they may have information we need that they're not remembering, may be able to identify one of this network, and so on. So the girls took the fear of the event away from them. They remember it, but more like it was a movie they watched as opposed to an experience they lived."

"Sounds like a decent compromise."

"So live without a bassinet for a bit longer, kitten. Where is my little angel here sleeping anyway?"

Jeff and I looked at each other. Felt every eye in the room on us. "Ummm . . ."

"She's not in a Poof bed, is she?" Dad sounded horrified.

"Oh, no. Not at all." Jeff was able to answer that one with a cheery smile, because it was true.

"So, where *is* she sleeping?" Tito sounded like he was readying to go into Clinical Doctor From Hell mode again.

"Sleeps like an angel." Shot them the bright smile.

Tito looked at Jeff. "Where?"

Jeff looked at me. "Uh . . ."

"As the baby's doctor, I want to know where she's sleeping. And I want to know now."

Reader snorted. "How hard is this to guess? They have no bassinet, they have no cradle, they have no crib. Oh, girlfriend? I have you registered now. As soon as someone can get out of lockdown, some of this'll be handled."

"You're a god, James."

"True. Anyway, while Kitty might consider a Poof bed, Jeff wouldn't. They're not putting her on the floor, on the couch, or in the tub. Where the hell do you people *think* that baby's sleeping?"

Everyone gave him a blank look. Gee, nice to know they thought we were total morons.

Reader sighed. "She's sleeping in bed with them. And, no, I'm not sleeping in there with them. It's just really obvious. Why the hell do you think every other word out of Kitty's mouth is 'bassinet'?" That was Reader—gorgeous *and* brilliant.

Tito, Emily, Melanie, and my father all started in on the lecture about how it wasn't good for the parents to have the baby in bed with them. Reader looked at me and rolled his eyes. Jeff was muttering under his breath.

"Jesus, fine, fine." Chuckie sounded disgusted. "Far be it for me to actually consider the safety and well-being of people marked for death. Go ahead, shop away. Take the whole family with you, particularly the elderly and little children, since they can't run away from danger as fast. Make it a fun-filled holiday extravaganza. Possibly you won't be killed, maimed, hurt, kidnapped, traumatized, or terrorized. You know, it could happen."

Dad shook his head. "No, Charles, you're right. We shouldn't go out." He cocked his head and turned to Reader. "James, the registry—did you do it online?"

"Of course. I'm in the lockdown too."

"All from one store?"

"Mostly."

Dad looked at me. "You and Jeff want to check the registry first?"

We both snorted. "Uh, Dad? We've been arguing about what stroller to choose for three months."

"And that's the only thing they'd looked at." Reader sounded brisk, back to Drill Sergeant mode, just as he'd been for our wedding. "No, the registry goes as is. If I've somehow missed something, which I doubt, we can get it later."

"Fine, fine. So, Jeff, most of us didn't get to bring laptops along, and the few that were brought were confiscated, along with everyone's smart phones and handhelds."

"Why?" No one had ever confiscated anything of mine, other than to test it for bugs and bombs.

Chuckie heaved a sigh. "We're under the highest threat levels. This is a standard protocol, so no one can, say, send a text to their friends to let them know where they are, alert them to impending danger, give away our position, and so on."

"You know, like we did with you when you joined up, girlfriend," Reader added. Memory dragged itself up from its latest nap and reminded me that the only reason they hadn't taken my phone when I'd first run into Alpha Team was because Jeff couldn't find it in my purse.

Dad nodded. "Your mother gave the order, kitten. However, that means no one has any means of doing anything externally. So, are there any computers we can use?"

Jeff shrugged. "Library's got the most. Why?"

Dad handed Jamie to me. Leaned her up against my shoulder, she snuggled into my neck. Thankfully, this was just cuddly. Nice to know that Jamie and the Poofs could do what they wanted on my neck and it wasn't any kind of issue.

My father was on his phone. "Important things finally in motion. Yes, that's exactly what I mean. Don't faint. Yeah. Yes, head everyone to the library. I'm sure someone knows where it is. Yes, James has them registered. Who else? Yes, he's a godsend, I agree. Not sure, I'll bring him with me. I imagine it'll take you a while to get everyone rounded up and down there. Yes, we'll call them after James gives us all the information. Right, I'll call him next. No, I think he'll think it's funny, sort of fitting for them at this time of year anyway. See you shortly. Love you, too."

"Dad, what did you just tell Mom to do?"

Dad chuckled. "If the baby cannot go to the shower, the shower will come to the baby. The Internet's a wonderful thing. You kids should start using it."

"Thanks for the tip. Dad, we can't have a bunch of UPS trucks showing up here. It's a huge security risk, for us as well as the drivers."

"Oh, I know that. I wasn't going to have the merchandise delivered directly. It'll be picked up and delivered by people we can trust."

"Who might that be?"

Dad smiled at me. "Put it this way, kitten. Your Uncle Mort doesn't go into lockdown. Your Uncle Mort stays out and makes sure other people are safe."

"Oh, no. You're not serious. You're going to call in the Marines to deliver my baby stuff?"

He shrugged. "Your Uncle Mort is aware of the current security issue. He's also aware that his favorite niece just gave birth and has nothing for her baby. A baby he has not yet seen." Dad turned to Reader. "James, could you take me to the library? A large number of people want to tell you how relieved we are that you're around to take care of business."

Reader flashed the cover-boy grin. "Happy to be of service."

Dad looked at Jeff. "We'll call Alfred and Lucinda and let them know. Half of both families are with them, after all."

"Thanks." Jeff sounded dazed.

"Baby? They helped James plan our entire wedding in about two days. My family lives for this kind of stuff, and apparently yours does, too. Just go with it."

"You didn't even want a shower."

"True. But I can't begin to describe how much I want a bassinet, cradle, or crib."

He grinned at me. "Okay, point taken."

CHAPTER 30

DAD AND READER LEFT THE ROOM. I waited until Reader closed the door behind them. "Okay, why didn't you two want me telling my dad?"

"Because your parents are unlikely to think this is the coolest thing in the world, and it's smarter to keep you as a secret weapon than tell the world that you're now one of the X-Men." Chuckie looked around. "This information goes no further than the people in this room. I know Reader's already clear on that. Has Camilla seen Kitty or Jamie's charts?"

"Not sure," Tito replied.

"She's trustworthy," Emily said.

"Yeah, so was Beverly." Jeff's sarcasm was back up to eleven. "We'll check it out, Reynolds. Swear her to secrecy or keep it from her, depending."

Chuckie nodded. "Paul Gower can know, but not the Pontifex and, for the foreseeable future, not White, either."

"Christopher wouldn't do anything to hurt Kitty." Jeff didn't sound like he was arguing. I got the impression he just felt he had to support Christopher. I couldn't blame him.

"I agree. However, he's not in his right mind and hasn't been since he made the decision to shoot up. That makes him a security risk and a danger, to himself and everyone else. He needs to be focused on cleaning up, not on anything else."

"What about Tim and the rest of Airborne?" I asked.

"No," Chuckie said flatly. "What part of secret weapon doesn't click for you?"

"I trust these guys with my life, and they do the same with me. I've got powers now. I can agree with not telling Richard or Christopher. I disagree with keeping the rest of the team in the dark."

"I don't." Jeff didn't sound at all like he was saying this just to show willing. "Serene couldn't keep a secret from Brian if the entire safety of the world depended on it. She, Lorraine, and Claudia are all pregnant and don't need any extra worries—we have enough right now. Same for their husbands. Sure, Tim, Jerry, Chip, and Matt might be able to keep it to themselves—Tim's been with us a good while, and the flyboys are all military. But why ask them to? Tim has enough secrets from Alicia—why give him one more?"

I blinked. "Okay, lecture points taken, no more argument."

"What?" Jeff sounded as shocked as Chuckie looked. "That was too easy. What's wrong?"

"Where is Alicia? We pulled in families. Did we pull her in, too?"

Jeff was on his phone. He looked at me. "Tim's not answering."

Chuckie was on his phone now, too. He moved away a bit and started barking quiet orders.

"Com on." I didn't shout, I was proud of myself.

"Yes, Commander Martini?"

"Is Tim Crawford on premises?"

"Running search."

Took a deep breath and hoped.

"No, Commander. Captain Crawford is not." Oh, yeah, Tim had the Captain title, too. Not that I ever used it for him, either.

"Start scanning every Base we have. See if you can find Tim or his fiancée, Alicia Young. If you've got some way to track Tim, do it. Check the Martini estate, too."

We waited. "No, Commander, no sign."

I looked at Jeff. "We forgot her, didn't we? But I'll bet our enemies didn't. And I know Tim didn't. He probably thought she was taken to Caliente Base. We were busy—he called her or something, realized she wasn't where he thought she was, something like that." I felt awful. And scared.

Jamie woke up and started crying. "I have to feed her." I

wanted to, and I didn't. The mother part wanted to more than anything. The other part wanted to find Tim and Alicia and make sure they were safe and unharmed.

Emily gave me a sheet, and I covered up a bit, sat down, and unhooked. Jeff helped hold the sheet over me.

Chuckie hung up. "Just had her apartment checked. It's been ransacked, no sign of her, her car's still there." He looked confused. "There was something odd. My operative said they found a CD in the refrigerator."

"What was the band, what was the title?"

"Adam Ant, *Friend or Foe*."

"Tim's got her, thank God."

"You want to explain that?"

"Sure." Took the baby off one breast, gave her to Jeff, closed side A, opened side B, put the baby on the other breast. "Tim's leaving me a message. He runs my iPod half the time now, remember? Guy who apparently pulled me back from death by playing 'Nine Lives' by Aerosmith? He knows how I think, musically."

"Why leave a clue at all?" Chuckie still sounded confused.

"Because he knew I'd realize either that he was missing or Alicia was missing. Look, however we missed her was an oversight . . ." Thought about it. "No, it wasn't. It was on purpose." Wanted to curse, looked down at my newborn, controlled the impulse. "*Friend or Foe*, he's telling me that we have a mole."

"Can I arrest Amy now?" Chuckie was serious.

"We can't assume it's her. Even though, yeah, it sure seems likely. But let me think."

"All you're doing is talking."

"Dude, we've known each other half our lives?"

"Right. That *is* how you think . . . by running your mouth."

"You know it. Okay, so he could have left anything, at least, anything Alicia had or he had."

"Why didn't he tell anyone before he left?" Jeff didn't sound any more convinced than Chuckie. "Tim knows better."

"Jeff? When you broke out of Caliente Base to save me, did you stop to share that you were leaving, against direct orders, with anyone?"

"No. Fine, point taken, he's in love with her, it's his girl in danger, he's not going to waste time. Carry on."

"Chuckie, any guess as to when the apartment was ransacked?"

"Not too long ago. She had a small fish tank, it was overturned, but the carpet wasn't totally soaked."

I was impressed with C.I.A. thoroughness. "Okay, Gladys, you still there?"

"Yes, Commander."

"Can you verify the last time anyone can confirm Tim's being in the Science Center?"

"Last person was likely Captain Reader."

"Thanks. Jeff, need your cell." A thought occurred. "Can you please go get my purse?"

"Think Tim called you?"

"It's a possibility. Bring the Poofs along, too, please."

He sighed. "If I must." Jeff hypersped out of the room.

I called Reader. "James, when did you last see Tim?"

"This morning, why?" Brought him up to speed. He cursed. I moved the phone to the side away from Jamie. "I gave a direct order to have Alicia picked up."

"Figured you wouldn't have forgotten. So why wasn't she?"

"No idea. Did you ask Gladys?"

"No. Hang on. Gladys? Did someone override Captain Reader's order to have Alicia Young picked up?"

"Not that my records show, Commander."

Shared with Reader. "Okay, so someone talked directly to the agents who were supposed to get her. Need to know who they were, girlfriend."

I had another thought. "Gladys, do records show where Alicia Young was when we went into lockdown?"

"Yes, Commander. She was in the air, returning from . . . wait for it . . . Paris."

Chuckie groaned. "She's our mole?"

"Hardly. She thinks we're all P.T.C.U."

"Could still be our mole."

Brought Reader back up to speed. "Okay, so she's in the air when we go into lockdown. Tim would have known that, so he didn't panic until he realized she'd never been picked up, or gotten the message to go to a pick-up spot." Reader sounded calmer than me. Good, 'cause I wasn't calm. At all.

"They would have told her to go somewhere?"

He sighed. "Babe? Really. Think about it. She was in an airplane."

"Oh, duh. Left her a message on her phone. 'Go to this women's bathroom and call us when you're in.'"

"Right, standard procedure. So why the hell wasn't it followed?"

Had a horrible thought. "Maybe it was. Gladys! Do we have any agent teams who haven't checked in?"

Jeff was back and exchanged my purse for Jamie. "The Poofs didn't want to come. They were freaking out about something."

"What and where?"

"No idea what they were upset about. They were in their little condo you love so much."

"Tim left a clue there, go look for it, *now*."

Jeff sighed, handed Jamie back to me, and took off again.

"Commander? Several agent teams haven't checked in." Gladys sounded worried. "All teams were dispatched by Commander White. The team Captain Reader assigned to Alicia Young was sent home by the team assigned by Commander White," she added.

"Oh, great. White's our mole?" Chuckie sounded like he was going to kill himself.

"No, but it explains why we missed them—Christopher's not functioning, and he's not around to ask why the teams haven't checked in. Why did he switch teams?"

"Per the orders, Commander White felt the team he dispatched was better prepared to handle any issues," Gladys shared.

"Okay, so he wanted a more experienced team going out. Under the circumstances, can't blame him. So, Gladys, who were they going for or where were they headed?"

"The one replacement team was at Pueblo Caliente International, waiting for Alicia Young. The other three were in D.C."

I got a funny feeling. "Gladys . . . where are the A-C Diplomatic Corps?"

CHAPTER 31

"**THE DIPLOMATIC CORPS ARE SECURED** in the Embassy, Commander."

"All of them? You're sure?"

"Yes, Commander, I've scanned the building."

"I'd put my money on them, not Amy or Alicia, and sure as hell not Christopher." Reader's voice was clipped. "What's Reynolds think?"

"Chuckie, your thoughts?"

"Nice. Now we have so many mole options." He sounded tired. "Camilla could be the mole, too, you know. Jesus."

Jeff returned. "I vote for the Diplomatic Corps."

"James thinks so, too."

"I vote for locking everyone we know up in a Centaurion Base and just hibernating." Chuckie sounded ready to lose his mind.

"Dude, relax. Just let the conspiracy wheels spin for a bit. I'll handle the light thinking." Back to Reader. "James, thoughts?"

"Yeah. Tell Reynolds he could be the mole, too."

"Um, no, he couldn't. And why?"

"Yeah, fine, I agree. But why? Love to hear him sound like he's about to crack. Happens so never."

"You really have an evil streak, don't you?"

"One of the many reasons you love me."

"True. But I'm not saying that to him."

"Tell Reader he's hilarious. And that your mother checks

me on a monthly damn basis." Chuckie's tone was extremely snide.

"Geez, dude, did it sound like I thought he was right? Or that he was serious?"

"Didn't hear his side, just could tell what you two were talking about."

"Yeah, you're good, Secret Agent Man. Keep working on the theories. James?"

"I have no missed call or message from Tim. I don't know what that means." He sounded worried.

"Well, Tim has Alicia, or at least he got to her first."

"Commander? We have no contact with the four missing agent teams. Unable to raise on cell." Gladys sounded worried and pissed.

"The fun never stops around here, does it? Okay, lemme get my cell." Dug it out of my purse one-handed; Jamie didn't seem to mind. I had several missed calls from Tim's phone, but only one message, not from Tim's number. "Okay, James, handing you to Jeff. Gladys, hang on."

Tossed the phone to Jeff. "Yeah, you know, I think that's a brilliant idea." He hung up. "James decided since he's in the same damn building, he'd just come on back and talk to us in person."

"Whatever." Hit my voicemail and turned on the speakerphone.

"Kitty, I'm sorry. They're after us and I can't get to a gate. I think they've messed up Home Base's ability to track us somehow, too. My cell took a bullet. We're not hurt, yet. I'm on Alicia's phone, but the battery's going. Shit!" I heard what sounded like tires screeching, and then the phone went dead.

"Well, that was illuminating not so much." I looked at Jeff. "What did you find on the Poof tree?" He held up a CD. *Help!* by the Beatles. "Geez, couldn't get clearer than that." Another thought occurred. "Open it, what's the CD inside?"

Jeff did. "Not the Beatles." He handed the case to me and took Jamie.

"Chuckie, get your guys to open the CD they found." I stared at the disk.

"On it already." He was back on the phone. "Really?

That's weird. Okay, thanks, hold onto it. Yeah, run it for everything." Chuckie hung up. "What was inside the Adam Ant case was a CD of your wedding video."

"Huh? We had a wedding video?"

"Yeah." Reader ran into the room. "Remember? Our favorite 'investigative reporter' did all the photos and video at your wedding."

This was true. "But Mister Joel Oliver told me the video didn't come out. The *World Weekly News* only got the stills." I tried not to think about our wedding pictures having been in the tabloids nine months ago. Fortunately, as far as the photography had gone, we'd been boring and hadn't even made the front page.

Reader shrugged. "I paid him to lie. It was supposed to be a surprise for you and Jeff at the baby's induction ceremony. I gave Tim and the flyboys backup copies, just in case."

"Why?"

"Because they were the most unlikely to want to watch it early."

"Can't argue with the logic." I looked back at the CD Tim had put into the Beatles' case. "He was freaked and scared, but he took the time to set this up and drop it off. Why?"

"What? We're all waiting for you to tell us why and what it is you're looking at." Jeff sounded annoyed, but I knew it was because he was worried.

"It's the Beastie Boys' *License to Ill*."

Thudding silence. Waited for the sound of crickets. Amazing, none. "What's that mean?" Jeff asked finally.

"Hang on . . . I have to think the timing through." Which meant, out loud. "Okay, Alicia was in the air on her way back from Paris when we went into lockdown three days ago. Gladys, would she have just gotten in the air?"

"Most likely."

"Double-check that she was on the flight she was supposed to be."

Heard a sigh. "Hmmm. No, Commander. She was bumped from the flight."

"Mole." Chuckie sounded like he was getting a migraine.

"No," Gladys said. "She was flying on her airline pass. It's here in the records. She was on standby, therefore. She was bumped twice. Only got into the air, in reality . . . hmmm . . . last night. Flight landed at JFK this morning, then at Saguaro International in Pueblo Caliente this evening."

"Why the hell was she in Paris? Without Crawford?" Chuckie asked. "And don't say coincidence."

"She was nowhere around when we were dealing with the superbeing cluster," Jeff said. "And as far as I know, Tim didn't wander off to meet up with her, either."

"He didn't," Reader confirmed. "Oh, hell. I have an idea." He closed his eyes. "They're getting married soon. She has free airline flights. Fashion capital."

"She was shopping for her wedding dress." I wanted to run around and do something, but I knew Tim was counting on me to think.

"Right. I remember Tim saying they weren't doing anything for Christmas but really had some great New Year's Eve plans." Reader sounded as bad as I felt.

"Okay, here's what we have so far. Alicia was in Paris. I'm sure Tim checked with her, but he didn't ask to go get her or have the Euro team pick her up. Gladys, shout if that's wrong. So she wasn't in any danger while she was on that side of the pond. Which makes sense, if you consider that whoever's running this is gunning for me. It would take time to realize, okay, the immediate useful hostages are safe, let's start branching out."

"Possible." Chuckie sounded nowhere close to convinced but like the migraine was a given. "Or she's in it with Amy."

"Dude, really, let it go. Try to take Amy's reaction to how you are now as a compliment, okay?"

"Right. Still not seeing how Alicia's not the mole. Or Amy, for that matter."

Something was nagging at me. "Gladys, were there any other Youngs on any of the three flights that Alicia was supposed to be on?"

"Yes, Ralph and Margaret. Checking addresses . . . married couple, live in Long Island. Cross-checking . . . Alicia Young is their daughter."

"And now it makes sense. She went to Paris with her parents to shop for the dress and do Christmas there. Once in a lifetime, last time it's just the three of us thing. Barring

Alicia's parents being involved, Chuckie, deal with the coincidence. We're probably allowed one in the grand scheme of evil overlord plans."

"Whatever. Still not clear on the musical clues."

"Okay, Tim's in contact with his girl. Probably telling her and the 'rents to be careful, terrorist activity about, so they're on top of things."

"I know he called her when we were on the way to deal with the cluster in Paris," Reader offered.

"Good. Now . . . I'm going to play pretend for a minute here. I don't know that Jeff's an alien, I don't know what he does for real, but I think he's part of an elite counterterrorism squad. I've been sworn to secrecy, I'm in love with him and like his friends, so I'm a good girl and don't say a word. Now, Jeff calls me while I'm on a trip to Paris with my parents, says things are scary, stay aware and alert, and all that jazz. I mention this to my parents, who we are also pretending are normal folks. What do the three of us decide?"

Thudding silence. Was certain I heard crickets. No one in this room had a normal life? Looked around. Nope.

Tito sighed. "My parents wouldn't let me out of their sight."

"Bingo." One normal guy left. Wondered how long before we totally corrupted him. Gave it another six months, tops. "So Alicia's in New York, which was where the plane landed. She got off with her parents and stayed off."

"She shows as arriving at Saguaro International, Commander."

"Double-check it, Gladys. Make sure it's not an airline snafu or that it's her luggage that arrived or something." My money was on both. "Remember, she was booked all the way through. She could show because by the time they realized she wasn't getting back on, the plane was ready to leave."

"You used to work with the airlines, Commander?" Gladys sounded rather impressed. "Because you're right. She was booked; seat was empty from JFK to Pueblo Caliente. Her luggage, however, did arrive. It's still there, waiting to be claimed."

"Okay. So, why did Tim go to her apartment? And why did he leave me a warning before he left? He'd been tipped off about something. What was it?"

"His room's near Amy's." Chuckie was really hoping Amy was the mole.

"Yeah, his room's near a lot of people's right now, he's on the transient floor. Gladys?"

"Anticipating you, Commander. Due to protective custody and lockdown, Captain Crawford's nearest neighbors are Amy Gaultier, Captain Matt Hughes, Abraham and Sadie Katt, Doreen and Irving Weismann, Lieutenant Chip Walker, Michael Gower, Stanley and Ericka Gower, Captain Jerry Tucker, and Sylvia and Clarence Valentino."

"Who are those last people?" Names weren't familiar to me.

"My oldest sister and her husband." Jeff sounded as though he was catching Chuckie's migraine. "What the hell are they doing here? I thought they went back to my parents' house days ago."

"That's a very interesting question." My mind whirred. "And they're near Doreen and Irving . . . how close are those rooms, Gladys?"

"The Weismanns are across the hall from Captain Crawford, the Valentinos are next to them."

Before I could say anything else, there was a knock at the door and Denise Lewis stuck her head in. She was a gorgeous blonde with great teeth and bags of charisma. I liked her a lot.

"Kitty, I know everyone's doing some baby shower thing, but I figured you could use this right now. I brought it with us when they said we were going into lockdown." She grinned. Geez, beyond awesome teeth.

"Thanks, Denise. What is it?"

She came into the room and handed me a gift bag. "Open it now."

I could feel the rest of the room not wanting me to, but I wasn't coming up with what was going on with Tim yet, and figured the one minute might not hurt. Pulled out a yellow backpack-like thing. "Uh . . . pretty."

Denise laughed. "It's a baby carrier. Here, let me show you." She stood me up and hooked it around me, went to Jeff, took Jamie, gave her a kiss, and then slid her into the frontal backpack. Jamie nestled right in between the torpedoes and seemed quite happy there. "It's great for the mom, or dad, on the go."

"Denise, you're the best." I had to give her a side hug so as not to crush the baby. "This is great. Thanks for not waiting to give it to us."

She laughed again. "I've had it for three months, just waiting for a baby shower. But since the baby came first, the heck with waiting, right? What's a little rule break in the greater scheme of things?"

I stared at her. "I love you."

CHAPTER 32

DENISE LOOKED SHOCKED. "Um, love you, too."

"Can you ask Kevin to race over here? I think we need him."

"Sure." Denise looked around. "I guess the high-level meetings take place in the hospital wing when you've just delivered. You want Angela, too?"

"No, just Kevin. My mom can continue to do whatever they're doing in the library."

"Gotcha. Okay, see you later." She flashed everyone a killer smile and trotted off.

"Are you playing for the other side and didn't want to tell me?" Jeff sounded only mildly worried. "I mean, it's great, and lord knows having hands free will be nice, but I was worried you were going to kiss her with tongue there for a minute, baby."

I shook my head. "So sweet, really. No, she just explained what the hell's going on."

"And that would be?" Chuckie asked, with only a lot of impatience.

I moved around a bit. Just felt good to be walking normally, and I could tell it was nice for Jamie. "Here's the deal. Where's Alicia's luggage?"

"What?" Jeff and Chuckie asked that in unison. Oh, not the unison thing again. I'd had enough of that around our wedding.

"Her luggage is at Saguaro International. Waiting to be claimed." I looked around. No reactions, listened for the freaking crickets again. I heaved a sigh. "Okay, Tim was being a naughty boy."

"Crawford is the mole?" Chuckie sounded like he was ready to retire.

"No. Geez, you guys, think about it. His girl's in Long Island with her parents. All her stuff is in Arizona. Nothing is happening here. What would you do?" They all looked at me blankly. "Oh, for God's sake, Jeff. You did something similar with me within the first three hours we'd known each other."

The light dawned for Jeff, finally. "He snuck out to get her stuff. Do we hire idiots?"

I rolled my eyes. "No. We hire mavericks. At least, every human agent is someone who's incredibly capable, right, or we wouldn't *be* agents."

"So what was he warning you about, then, with the message on your Poof tree thing?" Chuckie didn't sound convinced of anything but the impending migraine.

"He wasn't warning me at all. He was asking me to cover for him." Blank looks all around. "He was asking for my 'help' and telling me he was going to New York." More blank looks. "As in, 'Kitty, I'm being bad, please help me, no sleep 'til Brooklyn, I'll be in New York, with my girl and her family, look for me at East Base. You gotta fight for your right to party, and I want to ring in the New Year with my woman.' Geez, why is this a shocker?"

"We're under lockdown." Jeff said it as if it were the definitive answer.

"Yeah, we are. And *nothing's happening*. We've been locked down for days. Tim's girl is not in lockdown, everyone else's girl or guy is, and he's kind of not happy about that. Plus, he was there when I did the extra special labor move. I'm sure he wanted to be with her after that. All the excitement happened on Christmas day, when he couldn't get to his girl anyway. The next days have been deathly dull. So he snuck out."

"Why the elaborate musical clue?" Reader didn't sound as if he were buying this theory, either.

"Because it's easier to leave a CD than a baseball program." Crickets abounded. "Tim and I freaking bonded over the witty banter about baseball and music. It's our 'thing.' He wasn't scared when he left the Science Center, he was being a bad boy breaking curfew, and he let his boss know it in a fun way."

"Okay," Chuckie said slowly. "So then what? How'd he get out?"

"How the hell did Kevin get out when he went to save Sheila and her family? He freaking went to the launch area, said, 'I need a gate to this bathroom stall,' and walked through. Tim's on Alpha, for God's sake. And, let's see . . . Commander White is in isolation and we are all afraid for him, Commander Katt-Martini just had a scary delivery and we're all trying not to stress her out, Commander Martini almost lost his wife, has a new baby, and now has his cousin in solitary. I could be a good little A-C and call Captain Reader to verify if I can let Captain Crawford out and get my ass reamed, or I can just calibrate the freaking gate to where my superior officer says he wants to go. Why do I have to explain this?"

"They don't break the rules like you do, girlfriend."

"Ha! Jeff breaks them all the time. All of Alpha and Airborne do. That's why no one questioned Tim's leaving or alerted any of us that he'd done so. For us, this is routine." Another thought occurred. "Gladys, is there a way to check on the status of the house where Mister and Missus Young live? Like, are there people in it?"

"What are you thinking?" Jeff asked quietly.

"Depends on who's home at the Youngs'."

Gladys came back. "Have dispatched a team from East Base."

I didn't like the time we were wasting, but I still didn't have a clear idea of where Tim was, or whom he was with. Needed to know where your guy was in order to perform even the lousiest rescue.

"Commander, no one home at the Young home. Place was ransacked. Agents were briefed to check the fridge. There was a CD in it—*Madman Across the Water* by Elton John. CD inside was *Traffic and Weather* by Fountains of Wayne. Is that a real band?"

"Yeah, they're great. Okay, geez, he's good. Gladys, please contact Martini Manor for me and see if the Young family has been checked in recently, like between the time you checked and now. Oh, and tell me what the weather is in New York, D.C., and Florida right now."

"Normally Security doesn't do the weather, Commander."

"I know. Isn't it cool to branch out?"

"I'm thrilled with the opportunity. Snowing in New York, raining in D.C., weather is fine in Florida." There was a pause. "Confirmation from the Martini compound—a family of three humans was delivered by two of our missing agent teams five minutes ago." Gladys sounded somewhat relieved. "Team assigned to Saguaro International and one of the teams assigned to D.C."

"Great."

"Do you want to talk to any of them?"

"Not right now."

Kevin Lewis came in. He was tall, dark, and totally handsome, dark skin like Gower's, great smile and teeth like his wife, bags and bags of charisma. "What's up?"

"We're not sure. Kitty seems to know something but hates to get to the point." Chuckie was rubbing his forehead.

"I know where Tim and the other agents are."

CHAPTER 33

"YOU GOING TO SHARE?" Jeff snapped. "Or will we just find his dead body later?"

Reader pulled Kevin aside and started talking in a low voice. I assumed he was doing the fast catch-up work. I would have been envious for the close proximity to Kevin, but I was willing to share. Besides, Jeff got so jealous when I drooled in Kevin's direction. No idea of why—wasn't like Kevin had eyes for anyone but Denise, and having seen her, who the hell could blame him?

"Okay, so the first musical clue was to get me to cover for him in a way you, Jeff, wouldn't figure out. I note also that Gladys had to tell the A-C agents to search the fridge, but Chuckie didn't have to tell his human guys to do it. I have a variety of guesses as to why, but it boils down to the fact that for the A-Cs, a fridge is where you go to get what you want, not store or hide things the way it is for humans. So Tim is being followed by A-Cs, not humans."

"Huh? How do you get that?" Jeff asked.

"No, makes sense. Go on." I could see Chuckie's conspiracy wheels starting to turn again. Hopefully they'd knock out the migraine.

"My guess is that he went to the closest gate to Alicia's apartment. From where I remember she lives, that's my parents' house. No worries, my family and pets are here. But between leaving his room and getting there, something occurred to him. I'm guessing it's something he heard or saw while he was still here. My CD collection is at my parents' house, and every CD we've seen so far is one I own—other than the two left with the Poofs, which I know are Tim's."

"You don't have them?" Jeff sounded shocked.

"No, I do. But I recognize this case; it's his, not mine, and the Beastie Boys CD is newer than mine—he bought it after Operation Fugly."

"Amazing attention to detail. We are where in the Science Center?"

"Oh, hush, Jeff. Tim tried to call me, but we were already here doing blood tests, and my phone was nowhere near me. He's broken the rules; he wants to talk to me, because as the head of Airborne, I can cover for him. So, spitballing on this one, but he grabs a bag and flings all the CDs in it he can, figuring, rightly, that he'll be able to give me a message somewhere along the way that only I will be able to understand."

"I can't believe you two use this kind of code." Chuckie seemed to be wavering between disgusted and impressed.

"You didn't figure it out. And no A-C would have a chance."

"We still don't know if you've got it. Please, go on."

"In order to claim Alicia's luggage, Tim would need some proof that he was authorized to get it. Presumably, an ID or something of hers that was at her place. So he goes there. He tries to call me again, I don't answer. I'm guessing that her place was not ransacked before he got there, but by the time he's there, he's feeling sure that they're going to be after her, and he's pretty sure he knows who 'they' are. So he takes the *Friend or Foe* case and sticks in our wedding CD. It's someone we know, and they were at or around our wedding. Meaning that Amy's out as the mole, Chuckie."

"Prove it definitively."

Kevin nodded. "Your mother and I aren't convinced either, Kitty."

"Working on it, guys. Tim heads for the airport. Two reasons, now. Get backup; get to Alicia, the hell with her luggage. We had two agents there. Because they were assigned by Christopher, they weren't called off. So they're dutiful A-Cs, they're waiting. Tim knows the bathrooms of choice, he finds them, or calls them, or something, but they connect."

"How do you know?"

"They're in Florida. Geez, pay attention, Chuckie. They take a gate and head to New York. I'd assume they go to MacArthur, since it's the airport on Long Island. They hyperspeed over to Alicia's family's house. Thank God, everyone's alive and well. Tim bundles them into a car—remember, Alicia doesn't know there are aliens on the planet. He knows that the enemy will be aware he's out of lockdown and after Alicia, so he's got to leave me a clue at her parents' house. So he makes sure I know this is about the Al Dejahl situation and then tells me where he's going."

"I get the Al Dejahl connection—*Madman Across the Water*. But the directions?" Jeff wasn't arguing, just asking.

"Fountains of Wayne are a New York-based band, and their songs are really East Coast focused. The advantage of that particular CD is that the titles of the songs are clues for what's going on. I'm not going to list every damn song, just trust me that Tim was telling me that the weather sucked, so they would be on the road, and that he was heading to Florida, because it was safer."

"No way they had time to drive from Long Island to Florida," Reader said.

"I'm sure they didn't. I'm also sure the agents called for a floater gate calibrated to Martini Manor. Gladys?"

"Yes, Commander, I've confirmed with Alfred."

"So Tim went for the gate because it was expose the truth or risk Alicia and her parents being killed. His cell phone took a bullet; my guess is it was while he was driving, meaning they were being pursued. He has Alicia's phone because she doesn't need it. But she was in Paris and delayed several days, didn't charge it or didn't have the right adapter to be able to charge it, and it's dead now, too."

"What about the other agents, who we can't raise on the phones?" Chuckie's eyes were narrowed.

"When Reid was pursuing me, he was tracking me based on my cell. I know Tim remembers that event. Figure they got rid of their phones or turned them off, for whatever reason."

"Commander, Alfred confirms that the Young family was pursued. They don't know by whom, they're still dealing with the gate transference."

"Don't let the agent teams with them do anything to alter what they're seeing. We need them to remember whatever they can."

"Alfred agrees, Commander."

"Please have him ask Alicia if she knows whether Tim was heading to East Base or to D.C."

There was a pause. "How did Tim get the D.C. team to him?" Chuckie's eyes were closed.

"Phone. Probably had one of the agents at Saguaro International contact the other teams. I mean, we do it all the time. Nothing Tim's doing is out of the ordinary for us. He's just doing it alone."

"At the worst possible time," Jeff muttered.

"Really? Alicia and her parents are alive, I'd guess just barely. I'm with Tim on this one."

"And he knew you would be, which is why you got the original clue in the first place." Reader looked thoughtful. "I wonder what he heard or saw that clicked for him. And when it clicked."

"It clicked by the time he got to the Katts' house." Chuckie looked at me. "You're sure he went there?"

"Pretty darned." Considered Reader's point. It was the key one.

Gladys came back on the com. "Commander, Alfred says that Alicia feels Tim and the other agents are trying to get to D.C. Confirmed with the four agents now in Florida as well. They are unsure of operation's status or Captain Crawford's plan past getting the Young family to safety."

"Yep, D.C., that's what I thought." I'd also figured Tim hadn't shared the overall plan with the agents going to Florida for a variety of reasons, the mole one being the biggest. "Thanks, Gladys, figured he wouldn't have told them much, especially with Alicia and her family right there. Make sure Alfred keeps his eyes peeled and phones are charged and such." I looked at Jeff. "How trustworthy are your brothers-in-law? And do any of them work with the Diplomatic Corps in any way?"

Jeff looked taken aback. "What?"

Chuckie rolled his eyes. "They hate you, and White, with a passion. They've been jealous of you two since, as near as I can tell, you were born."

"Why?" Jeff always sounded shocked by this. I found it kind of endearing.

Chuckie sighed. "I got to hear about it, for two hours straight, at your engagement party. They resent how much attention you got as a baby. Same with White. They resent that the two of you got to live at the Embassy when you were young. They resent that you and White are the ones in charge and were put in charge so young. They resent that they can't drive a wedge between the two of you, so they can't play one against the other. They resent that you've never hired any of them as agents, ignoring the fact that none of them have A-C talents. They seem to feel they should be in positions of importance merely because they married your sisters. Do I need to go on?"

"No, the rest of us know it. Jeff, how strong are your blocks against your family?"

He sighed. "Extremely strong. Okay, fine. But that doesn't make one of them a traitor."

"People have betrayed their country or race for a lot less than jealousy and hatred." Chuckie sighed. "Kitty, you think it's the Diplomatic Corps, right?"

"Well, Tim does, because he's heading for D.C." I dialed, she answered on the second ring. "Doreen, how're you doing?"

"Hi, Kitty, okay." I heard a sniffle. "What's going on?"

"I'm going to ask you something, need the truth."

"Okay."

"Did you and the Valentinos get into an argument earlier today about your being married to Irving and having a baby on the way?"

"Yes, God, does everyone know?"

"I don't think so. Look, was Tim Crawford around when you had that fight?"

"Yeah, he came out to tell Clarence to shut up, and got told he was a human and had no right to give any A-C orders for his trouble. Sylvia was so embarrassed, it wasn't her, just Clarence."

"Clarence like your parents?"

"Yeah, I guess. They told me they thought he was a social climber, but I don't know how they can think that, since he's married to a Martini. Then again, maybe that's why."

Huh. Interesting. "So that's considered a social status point?"

"Oh, yeah, why do you think my mother was trying to marry me off to Jeff?"

"Because he's the head of Field."

"That helped, but no, more because he's Alfred's only son."

"Any idea what the Valentinos are doing here instead of being back in Florida?"

"Sylvia wanted to come out to see your baby, and she feels she didn't get to spend any real time with you, Jeff, or Jamie, and she wants to. She insisted. Clarence didn't want to come. They've been fighting the whole time they've been here. It's hard to sleep they're that loud."

"Doreen, you're the best. Hang tough, okay?"

"I will. And thanks for calling, Kitty. I feel a little better."

"You weren't letting Clarence's opinion bother you, were you?"

She sighed. "No, but he reminded me so much of my parents. We've barely spoken since your wedding. It's been nice, honestly. They just refuse to accept Irving, even though he's the father of their grandchild."

"Yeah. Prejudice and bigotry's hard to fight." We hung up, and I turned back to Jeff. "Seriously, which of your brothers-in-law work with or near the Diplomatic Corps?"

He shrugged. "All of them, in a way."

"Want to explain that?"

"They're like Paul is to Richard, the adjuncts for each of our main Diplomats."

"Who are all lobbyists," Chuckie added. "What's their loyalty to your family over their own interests, man by man?"

Jeff shook his head. "Baby, I know where you two are going with this, and Christopher and I can't stand them, but I've never picked up traitor from any of them."

"Yeah? Let's go visit Clarence and see what you pick up, okay?"

CHAPTER 34

I GRABBED MY PURSE and left the hospital room. Had a vague idea of where the elevators were from here. Sadly, Jeff was right—I had no idea where I was in most of the Science Center.

He caught up to me and grabbed my hand. "How is this getting Tim, or the other agents, back safely?"

"Not sure, just know it is. I don't think we want to descend on the Embassy unless we know for sure that Tim's there."

He headed us to the elevator banks. Everyone was coming along, including Emily and Melanie. "Why didn't Tim go to the Martinis' with Alicia and the other agents?" Kevin asked as the elevator doors closed.

"No idea." Well, that was a lie. I had an idea. Just wasn't sure if it was right yet.

Jeff gave me the hairy eyeball, so I knew he'd picked up that I was hiding something. But he didn't push it. "What are we doing, besides descending on my oldest sister and her husband like a lynch mob?"

"I'd love to lynch someone," Chuckie muttered.

"Amy's not the damn mole, okay?"

"We'll see." He stretched. "Of course, at the moment, we're spoiled for choice."

Kevin looked at me. "How many are working on the same plan?"

I managed a laugh. "God alone knows."

"Yeah." Kevin shook his head. "Reminds me of Florida.

Too much." It did me, too, but I chose to keep that to myself for this moment.

Reached the transient floor, got out, headed toward Tim's room. Heard the fighting before we got halfway there. Wow, Doreen hadn't been kidding. Sylvia and Clarence were in full-on domestic dispute.

"You know, my first superbeing was making a scene like this one. Guess we should be relieved we took the ozone shield down on Alpha Four."

Jeff's eyes were narrowed. "I hope he doesn't talk to her like this in front of their kids." He was growling, already at "rabid dog."

I hoped my grandparents were in the library. I'd never heard my Papa Abe raise his voice to Nana Sadie. My father never raised his to my mother or me. Jeff bellowed, but never at me. He bellowed orders, warnings, and my name, but out of protection, not anger. Even when we were fighting, he didn't scream at me.

I let go of Jeff's hand and grabbed Chuckie. "Did you find out if anyone's been pushing that drug?" I kept my voice low. Kevin moved up next to us.

"Not that we can tell." He kept his voice low, too.

"We're still searching, all covert ops, all Centaurion Bases," Kevin added. "But it's hard to do fast without alerting the people you want to catch that you're after them."

Chuckie cocked his head at me. "You thinking Clarence is trying to enhance himself?"

"No idea. But I should think Alfred would have done something about this if it was ongoing."

"Never assume that. Families are different."

"And what a man says in front of his wife's father and when he's alone with his wife can be very different." Kevin wasn't smiling. I got the impression hearing the Valentinos fight was upsetting him as much as Jeff. "What's behind closed doors is very different from what the public sees, many, many times."

"True." Left my Feds and went back to Jeff. He was in front of the door, and I could tell he was furious.

"Why are you always taking their side?" I could just recognize this voice as Clarence's. I'd only talked to him a couple of times, but it was a safe bet since it was coming from the room they were in.

"Because they're my family! You know, Jeff has never said a bad word about you to me, and neither has Christopher. Why do you think you can just sit here and insult them to me?" Sylvia's voice, for sure.

"Oh, God! Yes, yes, Mister Wonderful and his sidekick, Mister the Other Wonderful. You know, Jeff's been carrying Christopher for years. Takes his eyes off him for one minute, and Christopher shows how weak he is."

I started to get pissed off. More than I already was.

"He made a mistake! You couldn't handle the pressure either one of them have for a week, let alone for the past dozen years!" Sylvia sounded furious and ready to cry. What she didn't sound was surprised. This was an old, old argument.

"So it's the pressure thing again. Jeff's under pressure. Christopher's under pressure. You never care that I'm under pressure!"

"What pressure? You work for a diplomat! You take notes at meetings and run a calendar. How is that comparable to protecting our entire race and this planet on an hourly basis?"

I noted that Jeff seemed shocked by Sylvia's comments. I sidled closer to him. "I'll explain later, but trust me when I tell you that your sisters think you walk on water, Christopher, too, even though they've really hidden that from the two of you."

He nodded. "Can I kill Clarence, do you think?"

"I think it would upset Sylvia. Let me handle this, okay?"

Jeff looked at me as if I were crazy. "No."

"You have no idea what kind of pressures I have! You just sit around all day, making demands and worshiping your father, brother, and cousin!"

"I take care of our children. And I work, and you know it!"

"What does Sylvia do?" I kept my voice low, not that there was any need.

"Handles minor science stuff out of D.C. She's got five kids, it's not as though she has a lot of time to do much else, even though most of them are older. None of them are out of the house yet."

"Are any of the kids here?"

"No, they'd be in a different section if there were more

of them, toward where your parents stay, the larger rooms." I could tell Jeff was controlling himself from breaking down the door. I was very impressed.

I looked down. Jamie was fast asleep. I had to figure ACE was blocking this from her, because there was no way she could miss hearing this, and her baby animal senses couldn't miss picking up the levels of stress that were raging through this area.

"Wonderful. And we're here, away from where we both work, why? Oh, wait, I forgot. So you could fawn over that human bitch your idiot brother married and their spawn. And, God forbid, we miss visiting your pathetic cousin. How many times are you going to go down there to see what you can do? All he wants is another shot of Surcent-humain."

"Which should concern you! Someone addicted my cousin, and all you can do is belittle him for it."

"He addicted himself, and willingly."

I put my hand on Jeff's arm. "Stay. I mean it. Chuckie, I just found our dealer."

"Yep. What do you recommend?"

I considered. Jamie was still asleep. What a good baby. I considered my options and decided it was too early for Jamie to get in on the action with me. Maybe when she was more than a week old.

I unhooked the carrier and handed Jamie to Emily, who gave me a look that said she was fully aware of what I was about to do and that she approved. Melanie stepped in front of them and gave me the "go girl" look.

"What I always recommend. Don't piss off the comics geek-girl." I went to the door and kicked it in. Hey, I was impressed with Jeff's restraint. Didn't mean I had any to spare. Wood splintered and flew everywhere. Very cool. Happily, it missed the room's occupants. Well, happily that it missed Sylvia. I was okay with it impaling Clarence, but no such luck. I walked in. They were both staring at me openmouthed.

"Clarence, never a pleasure. Hey, Sylvia. I'd like you to, you know, leave the room for a minute."

"Kitty, we were just . . . arguing." It was clear Sylvia knew how lame that sounded.

"Yeah. See, I know why the cops avoid domestic disputes.

Married couples shrieking and yelling at each other bothers everyone else a lot. Cops show up, married couple now have a mutual target." I looked at her. "But I'm not a cop."

I moved, and I knew it was fast, and kicked Clarence right in the gut with one of my best side-blade kicks ever. He flew back and doubled over. "My spawn and I would like to introduce you to Kevin Lewis of the Presidential Terrorism Control Unit and Charles Reynolds, head of the C.I.A.'s Extraterrestrial Division. Chuckie and Kevin have interesting views on how to extract information. But you can be happy with this knowledge—they're both a lot nicer than I am."

Clarence might have been a lot older than me, but he was still an A-C. He got up and lunged. Never got near me. Because Jeff grabbed him and threw him into the hall. Chuckie caught him and used his alien-nerve pinch, or whatever it was that pretty much ensured he, as a human, could take out an A-C if he needed to. Kevin cuffed Clarence in less than a second. My men were impressive, I had to admit it.

"Keep him awake, Chuckie, I have some questions. Sylvia, has Clarence been this much of a jerk all your married life?" She looked shaken, and she didn't answer. "Babe, we have that whole fate of the world and all the people we like in it thing going on again. Really, stop acting like you're an idiot and get with the program. Answers, now. How long has your husband been like this?"

"For years. But if you mean to this level, only since we met you." Her voice was low and her eyes were cast down.

"Yeah, I figured. I do bring out the best in people. Talk to your little brother for a minute, I think he's going to pop a vessel and could use some big sister soothing. And vice versa, Jeff."

I went out and grabbed Clarence by the throat. I lifted him off the ground. "Wow, James, this is just like when I had that weird dream during Operation Fugly."

"It's freaky from this vantage point, girlfriend, I can tell you that. What's the plan with our favorite drug dealer here?" Reader sounded almost as angry as I felt.

"What are you talking about?" Clarence gasped out.

"AMY!" I bellowed. Not up to Jeff's standards, but no one in two solar systems was.

I heard a door open. "Kitty? Is everything okay?" She sounded as though she'd been hiding in her room. The door on the other side opened, and Doreen and Irving peeped out. Yeah, domestic disputes did that.

"No. French class is a long way away for me, but not for you. Check my translation. Surhumain means superhuman, right?"

"Right."

I started to squeeze Clarence's neck. "Alpha and Airborne don't have a special name for that crap you gave Christopher. We just call it the Club Fifty-One drug. But you called it Surcenthumain. Super Centaurion human, if I want to be literal. A French name for the most dangerous drug available to an A-C. Lord knows what it does to a human." Though I had a good guess. I was holding a guy double my size off the floor, after all. "So, who's making it, and how much is out there already?"

He glared at me. "You have no idea of what you're dealing with."

"No? I think I do. You're dealing with Ronaldo Al Dejahl. In fact, all the Diplomatic Corps is. They don't mind that he's the son of Ronald Yates—they're all for it. Because they're on some purity of the race kick . . . still. Not that this plan works well for you all. But, boy, are some of you really hooked into it."

"You're single-handedly destroying our race."

"Blah, blah, blah. I'm the single-handedly-ruin-it-all girl, go me. You're using Christopher as a guinea pig. It's been tested on Jeff and Serene, but not by A-Cs. In order to counter something, you have to know what it can do, and you have to have enough of it around to test. Then there's the whole pure versus synthetic issue. We need to find out if Christopher's been injecting pure or not."

"I have no idea." Clarence, like most A-Cs, couldn't lie. He was looking anywhere but at me.

"Right. So, Al Dejahl's offered, what? Money, power? So you can sell him this drug or, lord knows, just give it to him, and he can create a race of super-Centaurions? So they can take over the world?"

Clarence glared at me. Not up to Christopher's standards. No one was. Jeff had bellowing, Christopher had glaring—they were both the unquestioned champions of their events.

"You people are aware that Ronaldo's the product of a human mother?" Clarence's mouth twitched, but he got it under control. I stared at him. "Jeff? I need to talk to Richard, immediately."

A cell was offered. I dropped Clarence and took it. Chuckie had the nerve-pinch thing going. Kevin punched Clarence in the gut, I figured just because he wanted to. I loved my guys.

"Missus Martini. Jeffrey sounded very tense."

"Yes, well, we've discovered the usual ugliness. Mister White, how old was the man you met with, the one who said his name was Gaultier?"

"He was an older man. However, Mister Reynolds felt I wasn't meeting with the, as you put it, Head Fugly, but one of his associates."

I watched Clarence carefully. "So he was a young man, around, oh, twenty-five?" Clarence twitched and looked away.

"Beg pardon? I said he was older. About my age."

"And he gave you a feeling of familiarity?" Clarence's whole body was tensed, I could see it and Chuckie nodded to me.

"Missus Martini, perhaps I'm not coming through?"

"Perfectly, Mister White. Perfectly. I'll fill you in later. I have some traitors to deal with first, however."

"I see our luck holds firm."

"You know it." I handed the phone back to Jeff. "Ronaldo's not a hybrid, is he?"

"He's not?" Jeff sounded confused.

Chuckie gave me a long look. "He's Serene's older brother, isn't he?"

CHAPTER 35

"GOT IT IN ONE! Not that I doubted you for a second, Chuckie." Clarence's reaction had been pretty much textbook A-C trying to lie, and it said very clearly that we had a bigger problem than we'd thought. Par for our course.

"Yeah." Chuckie looked toward Amy. "Still say you're too trusting."

"Possibly. But I doubt it. Take my relative by marriage down to a nasty cell and do the C.I.A. thing, will you? Be sure to stay available by phone."

"Happily. I'd like some company."

"I want to keep you or Kevin with us, and you interrogate better, so . . ."

"Tito, go with him." Jeff looked to Reader. "James—"

"Staying here." He pulled out his phone. "I need two teams, transient floor, ASAP." Waited a couple of seconds, four guys in the Armani fatigues appeared. "Help Reynolds and Tito. Do what they say."

They nodded, and the pack of them went off, down to the fifteenth floor, I was fairly sure.

Sylvia was sobbing quietly. "He's not a bad man." Jeff had his arm around her. It was the closest I'd ever seen them.

"Most traitors aren't. They just convince themselves that doing the wrong thing makes sense."

Doreen came out of their room. "What have my parents done?"

"You know what I love most about you, Doreen? Your ability to know exactly who's behind this crap every time."

She sighed. "I grew up with them." She shuddered. "I hope our baby's nothing like either one of them."

"Your baby will be like you and Irving." I sincerely hoped. I had another thought. "Did Tim call you?"

"Yeah, hours ago, though. He wanted to know what the security was on the Embassy. Said he wanted to verify it was working. I told him. Was that wrong?" She looked worried.

"No, it's great." I hugged her. "Look, do me a favor. I have to talk to Jeff. Can you two get Sylvia calmed down and, I don't know, take her somewhere else?"

"We were going to go down to the library. That's where your grandparents said they were going. And it sounded like they were kind of having a party."

"Great! They'll love having the three of you. Sylvia, be sure to spend some time with my Nona Maria. She'll be happy to tell you about my Aunt Carla's ex-husbands, all of whom will make Clarence sound good." I actually felt for any man stupid enough to marry my Aunt Carla, but my Nona had a different take on it.

Jeff hugged Sylvia tightly, then Doreen and Irving took her and went off. I looked around. "Amy, have to ask you something."

She was staring at me. "I think I should be asking you. How did you hold that man off the ground? Like it was nothing?"

"Long story. Look, I wasn't kidding, we're at our usual crisis. I need you helping us, because I think we're going to hear a lot of French, and no one's fluent other than you."

"You're kidding. You want to bring her along?" Jeff sounded incredulous.

"Yeah, I do."

"Keeping in mind that you, and our baby, are not going anywhere."

"Sure we are. We're going to go visit Uncle Christopher while you guys act like the cavalry and go help Tim."

"Help Tim do what?" Jeff sounded confused and frustrated. I had to remind myself that I'd been the one who'd spent the years with the Conspiracy King. "And I hate it when you think about him like that."

"Chuckie's the best at what he does, Jeff. Just like you."

"I can't believe Chuck asked you to marry him and you might have considered it for, like, a second." Amy sounded repulsed.

Jeff gave her a very friendly look. "I like how she thinks."

"Uh-huh. Ames? He's freaking brilliant, okay?" And he hadn't been awkward for over a decade and had been pretty darned handsome for that long, too. He'd also been damned good in bed, but I wasn't going to mention that aloud.

"I *hate* it when you think about him like that." Jeff was on "rabid dog" again.

I looked at him. "Who did I marry? Why did I marry him? Discuss."

"Fine, fine." It wasn't, but at least we weren't going to have our domestic dispute in front of the whole transient floor. Sylvia and Clarence fought about Jeff and Christopher, Jeff and I fought about Chuckie. Some things seemed universal between spouses.

"Anyway, here's what I hope Tim's in good enough shape to tell us. He heard Sylvia and Clarence fighting. Heard that drug name mentioned. It didn't register. Did his thing in our room, went to my house. The gate in my parents' house lets you out in their guest bathroom, 'cause, you know, why mess with the theme?"

"There are pictures of Paris in that bathroom," Kevin said. "I've seen them. Eiffel Tower shot is the first thing you see when you exit the gate."

"Yep. I'm guessing that the word clicked for him then. He's been to the house; he knows where my room and my music are. Trotted in there. I'll lay money he looked at my bookshelf, which happens to have a French/English dictionary sitting on it. Took a look, said, 'crap,' and put Operation Solo in action."

"I'm still not clear on why he's not in Florida." Jeff ran his hand through his hair. "It would have made more sense to get there and advise us."

"Variety of possibilities. I'm going with the fact that he's hoping to stop whatever else is going on—because, trust me, there's always more than one thing going on, don't forget—before it gets more out of hand. I stress again, he's not alone. He's with four other agents. He said they weren't hurt, at least, not when he'd called." I chose to ignore the fact that the last thing we'd heard from Tim's call was the sound of screeching tires.

Jeff took a deep breath. "Okay. James, call Paul, and let's get moving." He grabbed my hand and pulled me aside. "I'm serious, baby. I want you staying here, where it's safe. I don't want you leaving Jamie; I don't want you, either of you, in danger. We'll talk about your door destruction and prisoner interrogations later. At least you weren't holding our baby while you did them."

"I'm not a total idiot, Jeff. Besides, she's in the sack, safe in Emily's arms, fast asleep."

"I can't believe she didn't wake up."

I leaned up and kissed his cheek. "Her daddy was here to take care of her and her mommy. No reasons to worry."

He kissed me back, full on the mouth, and I relaxed and enjoyed it. "Promise me."

"Jeff, I'm not going to do anything to endanger myself or Jamie. I promise."

He didn't look as though he believed me at all. "Okay. What are you doing with Christopher?"

"I'm going to see if he can tell me anything else. I can't believe he'd take anything from Clarence. He can't stand your brothers-in-law, possibly more than you can't. So there's some intermediary somewhere, maybe more than one. We have to find out how widespread this is—were they just testing on Christopher, or do we have more A-Cs out there slowly turning into mutants?"

Paul and Michael Gower arrived. Michael was a younger version of his older brother—big, black, built, bald, and totally gorgeous. He was also The Player of the A-C community. If there was a single woman around, human or A-C, Michael was batting with intent to score. "We're leaving lockdown?" Michael sounded relieved.

"Yeah, rub it in. It's a big place, but the term 'stir crazy' is starting to apply."

"New mothers are supposed to stay in bed." Gower looked more closely at me. "Uh . . . Kitty?"

Michael was staring at me. "Wow. You look fabulous as always, Kitty." He didn't let the married gals feel unappreciated, either. Sometimes it was too much, but I'd gotten used to him now, and he didn't really faze me.

"Thanks."

"We'll explain on the way," Reader said, voice crisp and no-nonsense. He looked at Melanie and Emily. "Ride herd on her. Trust me when I say she's crafty." Melanie laughed while Emily gave Jamie back to me and helped me hook the Snugli back on.

"Love you, too, James."

Got the cover-boy grin. "Yeah, don't tell Jeff why you named the baby after me."

Jeff rolled his eyes. "Hilarious. Amy, you up for this?"

She nodded. "Am I dressed okay?" She was in jeans, sneakers, and a sweater.

"Yeah, take a jacket, but otherwise, why not?"

"Think you look great," Michael said. He hypersped next to her. "I'll just make sure nothing happens to you."

"We're going to an Embassy, right?" Amy seemed flustered by Michael, but I couldn't tell if she was interested or annoyed or both. "That's where your diplomats are locked down."

"Yeah," Kevin said, eyes narrowed. "How did you know that?"

Amy rolled her eyes. "Those people were fighting for hours. I think I know everything about Jeff's family now. Poor Christopher—his mother's dead, no wonder he turned to drugs." Amy's mother had died during sophomore year of college. Her father had remarried, and supposedly she liked her stepmother. But she never came back to the States for holidays.

Jeff and I exchanged a look. "You explain it to her."

He sighed. "I'm hoping to be too busy."

"I'll handle it." Reader kissed my cheek. "Be good."

Michael took Amy's hand, and I felt myself relax. It was stupid, but I didn't want Jeff holding another woman's hand if he could help it.

Jeff grinned at me. "I like it when you actually worry about something that's so out of the realm of possibility." He stroked Jamie's head and gave her a kiss, managing to nuzzle the torpedoes at the same time. Then he kissed me again. "Stay safe, baby. I almost lost you this week. I can't face that again." He grabbed Kevin, Gower grabbed Reader, and the six of them disappeared.

I reached into my purse and pulled out the Poofs. Interestingly, I had four, not two. I recognized my additional Poofs as Toby and Gatita, Christopher's and Reader's, respectively. Figured Toby had been sent to me when Christopher went into isolation, and Reader had told Gatita to take care of me. Extra Poofs were not a problem.

"Harlie?" The head Poof purred at me. "I want you to follow Jeff and protect him, and James, Paul, Kevin, and Michael. Amy, too, if she's being good. Help them get Tim back safely, okay?" Harlie mewled. "Is Fuzzball with Michael?" Got another mewl. "Great. You make sure you two work together, okay?" Mewl, purr, rub, Harlie was gone.

Took a deep breath. Turned around and looked at Melanie and Emily. "Now that the menfolk are gone, while we go down to check in with Christopher, tell me what's really going on with me and Jamie."

CHAPTER 36

MELANIE NODDED. "NOT HERE." We all headed off for the elevators. Got inside, Melanie hit the button for the medical level that held the isolation chambers. "I'm worried about the strain on your heart."

"Yeah, I figured there would be a downside."

Emily shook her head. "But, so far, there's not. I watched you the entire time. If you had a problem with the physical exertion you just did, it doesn't show." She took my wrist and checked my pulse. "Normal."

I ran a private body check. "Yep. I feel fine. Better than fine, honestly." Thought about it. "Does Jamie have two hearts?" I thought I felt a tiny version of Jeff's heartbeat next to me, but I'd never held an A-C baby before I got one of my own.

"Yes, she's perfectly normal internally for an A-C and externally for a human." Melanie sounded like she wasn't telling me everything.

"But?" They looked at each other, but not at me. I hit the Stop Elevator button. "Really, there's so obviously a 'but' that's hanging on the air here."

"Her brain activity is extremely advanced." Emily sighed. "Several years advanced, not just months."

Considered this. "Well, first off, she's a hybrid, and from what we can tell, that means expanded A-C talents. And whatever the Surcenthumain did to Jeff affected both her and me. Plus, Chuckie feels both Jeff and Christopher were already pretty much mutations. So it's not a surprise. My concern, though—is it dangerous for her?"

"I don't think so." Melanie didn't look or sound like she was lying. "We're monitoring her development closely, though. But, you may have to deal with her in solitary."

"I'm sort of surprised Jeff hasn't had to take her in there already," Emily added. "Alfred and Lucinda had to put him into solitary almost immediately after he was born."

Any time I thought about what Jeff's childhood had been like, my heart wanted to break. But he was a great adult and didn't seem to carry too many scars from his youth. Oh, sure, the strained relationship with his family and trauma over losing Christopher's mother, Terry, when the boys were ten were the biggies. But he didn't seem damaged otherwise.

"Tito is doing tests and research, quite a bit of both," Melanie went on. "Much of it related to genetic mutations. We're assisting him. We just don't have any conclusive evidence yet."

"Or much to compare to," Emily added. "Human mutations are much slower than anything you and Jamie have gone through. Even A-Cs mutate at a slower rate than what's happened with you."

"Have her talents manifested?" Melanie asked. "We want to compare her talent manifestations to the other hybrids' as well as to Jeff and our standard talented people."

"Sort of, but Jeff implanted blocks, so that's keeping her talents in check right now. When Christopher's better, he'll implant some, too."

Melanie raised her eyebrow. "That's news."

Whoops. Forgot, they hadn't told anyone they'd done this with all of their nieces and nephews. All of Alpha and Airborne knew, but I guessed the girls hadn't shared with their mothers, which meant they were doing a lot better with that whole "top secret" thing than I was. Shocker. "Erm . . ."

Emily laughed. "How'd they figure out how to do that?"

I knew Jeff didn't want me telling anyone about the glowing cube Terry had given him, and Melanie and Emily were unlikely to have been the ones who took it way back when, so bringing it up wouldn't help solve that mystery, either.

"Not sure. I know they had to implant blocks in all of Jeff's sisters' kids. I don't think they've done it for anyone else. I think they were afraid to." I also wasn't sure if they could only implant into those with a close DNA strain or not. All the A-Cs were related to each other somewhere back there, so that might be a moot point. But it was a point I'd have to discuss with Jeff.

Melanie nodded. "The older generation is very resistant to doing anything we haven't done for centuries. As Clarence exemplified." Wow, Melanie had a sarcasm knob, too. Knew I loved her.

Emily sighed. "I can't believe Clarence willingly helped turn Christopher into an addict. I mean, that's carrying pathetic jealousy a bit too far. Not that he hasn't always been a world-class jerk."

"All of Jeff's brothers-in-law seem to hate him and Christopher."

"Jonathan isn't so bad." Melanie sighed. "No one's as bad as Clarence."

Emily snorted. "That's like saying a regular superbeing is better than an in-control one. Jonathan's okay, but that's about all I'll say." Loved Emily, too. My favorite mothers after my own and Chuckie's.

"Did Ericka Gower have any kind of reaction to carrying her kids?"

Melanie shook her head. "None. She's still fully human. It's got to be the drug, Kitty. We've been monitoring the rest of the babies coming; only Serene's seems . . . different."

"Different?"

"More like you and Jamie," Emily answered. "Not like Claudia's, Lorraine's, or Doreen's babies. Nor any of the others' who are pregnant." She sighed. "And now Christopher's altered himself."

"Which means any girl he marries is going to be affected, just like me, right?"

"We don't know. Maybe, maybe not. One test case isn't enough to base concrete assumptions." Melanie was a scientist first, I had to remind myself. All the Dazzlers were, really.

"What about the addiction factor with him?"

They both shook their heads. "Again, we don't have enough experience with this," Emily said. "We're looking into it, of course, but unwitting addiction is different from willing. Serene wanted to get the drug out of her system."

"Are you saying Christopher doesn't?"

"No," Melanie said quickly. "But from what I've read up on human addictions, he's acting more the way a human addict would than Serene did, in terms of cleaning up, I mean. If we had more help, we'd probably be making faster headway."

"Why don't we get more help on this, then?"

"Tito doesn't want too many people working on this project," Emily explained. "I can't blame him. Right now, it's just the three of us, and I think it needs to stay that way. This information in the wrong hands could be incredibly dangerous. Fortunately, we have a large team working on understanding and countering the drug itself, so we have that knowledge. But as for having them work on this with us?" She shrugged. "We're talking about the Heads of Field and Imageering and their families. Discoveries about Jamie's development, your mutation, the outcome of Christopher's addiction—all that information needs to remain highly classified, for your protection if nothing else."

"Can't argue with the logic."

"No, but that means that while the three of us are good, we're not going to get the answers as quickly as if we could assign a whole team." Melanie shook her head. "I just hope we figure it all out before anything terrible happens."

CHAPTER 37

"UM, EXCUSE ME? I THOUGHT you said no bad was happening? When did the situation status change?"

Melanie managed a chuckle. "It hasn't. We're trained to look for all possibilities."

"And the possibility of things going badly always exists," Emily added. "Right now, though, everything seems fine, and we have a lot of other issues going on."

"Can't argue with the logic or the accurate summation of our business as usual." I hit the Stop Elevator button again and we continued on. A thought occurred. "What's your estimate of my being able to drive or fly now?"

Melanie shrugged. "No idea. We'll find out whenever you next try to drive or fly."

"Can't wait." I made the decision that I'd try driving first, and it wouldn't be in my car. I loved my IS300, and I didn't want to discover I was now too freaky-fast to handle human machinery by dropping the transmission. Lexus repairs weren't cheap.

We got out of the elevator and headed for the isolation area. It was big—it housed well over a hundred isolation chambers—because we had a lot of empaths, and they all needed to use these chambers to regenerate. None as often as Jeff, though. I couldn't help it; every time I was in this area I worried about him. Possibly because it was the creepiest place in any A-C facility—like being in a cross between Frankenstein's lab and a haunted Egyptian tomb, with a lot of extra tubes and needles added in just for fun.

It occurred to me that Jeff had run off on a mission and no one had adrenaline with them. What if he needed it and no one was there to stab the adrenaline harpoon? All our medical people were here, I was here, and Jeff was out there, surrounded by hostiles.

Jamie woke up crying. I took her out of the sack with Emily's help and cuddled her. Diaper seemed fine, no interest in a torpedo, which made sense because they weren't fully inflated yet. Figured I'd stressed her out worrying about Jeff. Did my best to calm down while doing the Mommy Dance and wondering if either ACE or the blocks were doing a damn thing.

We reached the chamber where Christopher was. I was surprised to see Naomi and Abigail Gower there. They had the same ebony skin as their mother and older brothers, but now that I knew their father, I could see Stanley in them. Naomi saw us and grinned. I could see a trace of Jeff in her smile—genetics always impressed me. They were typical Dazzler gorgeous and also typical Dazzler nice.

"Glad you're here, Kitty. I think Christopher needs someone to talk to." Naomi reached for the baby. "And I'll take your little Jamie-Kat." I handed her over, and Naomi cuddled her. "Precious girl," Naomi cooed.

"Awww, she loves her Auntie Naomi," Abigail said with a giggle. "And her Mommy, too. And her Aunties Melanie and Emily and Abigail." She winked at me. "I can feel it. She's a happy baby."

There were gases naturally in Earth's air that could be manipulated to cause humans to "see" or "remember" events differently. The male A-C agents, including Jeff and Christopher, had implants in their brains that allowed them to manipulate the gases to prevent panic when superbeings formed, or for other crowd control and safety measures. Abigail was able to manipulate these gases without outside assistance. She was also a sort of reverse-empath; unlike Jeff, who picked up what someone was feeling and why, Abigail's emotions were affected by the people around her. If you were angry, it made her angry, and so forth.

Naomi's talents were like her big brother's—dream and memory reading. But she could also manipulate and change those memories. The girls worked as a team more often than not, though they'd never done any real fieldwork, unless you counted my wedding, which was an A-C talent boot camp all by itself.

Naomi kissed Jamie's head, and her eyes went wide. She looked at me. "You know she didn't understand." She sounded just like ACE had when I'd asked him if Jamie had almost killed me, and I knew she'd seen something in Jamie's mind.

"I know. ACE is watching over her, just like he did for you two and Serene."

Naomi relaxed. "Yeah. It was nice to find out who our 'voice in the sky' was."

Abigail nodded. "Should have guessed, especially after ACE went into Paul. But I think he didn't want us to know."

"ACE was afraid we'd hate him for taking care of you."

Both girls shook their heads. "I can't imagine what we would have been like if ACE hadn't helped," Naomi said softly.

"I know. We're extremely lucky ACE is our loving observer."

Abigail stroked Jamie's head. "Interesting." She looked at me. "She's really processing things well."

"I've just been told that her brain functions are advanced." Melanie and Emily both nodded their confirmation.

"Yes, but that's not what I mean. There's a lot of emotions going on and she seems very . . . calm." Abigail cocked her head, and Naomi leaned hers against Jamie's. "She's definitely empathic," Abigail said slowly.

"There's imageering ability in there, too," Naomi added. "More talents, too, at least possibly. I think she's going to be more advanced talent-wise than any of us so far."

I wasn't sure if I should be incredibly proud or worried. Settled for both. "Is she having trouble handling everyone's emotions or whatever it is imageers have trouble handling?"

"Imageers have to stop themselves from touching pictures before they can handle the feedback," Melanie said. "So just keep her away from pictures and she'll be fine."

"If she's as advanced as Christopher, she might make pictures in the air," Emily added. "But those are usually nothing to worry about. And they can be helpful."

Naomi nodded. "She's very well controlled." She looked

as if she were going to say something else, but Abigail nudged her, and Naomi quickly nuzzled Jamie instead. I got the impression the Gower girls had spotted the blocks Jeff had installed somehow and were also fully aware of how much watching over ACE was actually doing. I also got the impression they didn't want to talk about it here, for whatever reason.

"Speaking of which, we weren't joking," Abigail said briskly. "Christopher needs someone in there with him. He asked Richard and Paul both to leave him alone."

"And they did?"

Abigail snorted. "Look, as a race we don't have a lot of experience with addiction. But spending time with Chuck has taught the two of us a lot."

CHAPTER 38

MY WHOLE BODY WENT TENSE, and Jamie started to cry again. "Is Chuckie addicted to something?"

Abigail shook her head. "No. Relax, really. He's like the cleanest guy out there. I've seen him take one drink in the entire time we've known him. He could be an A-C, he's that clean. Well," she looked into Christopher's chamber, "that's a bad example, but you know what I mean."

"He taught us about addictions because we had a lot of issues when we hit minds addled by alcohol or drugs." Naomi was rocking Jamie and got her quieted down. They both seemed very happy. "It helped a lot. I know Jeff and Christopher resent him, but he's the best friend Abby and I have ever had."

"Abby?" Not that I minded, but only Jeff used a nickname, since the A-Cs lived for certain formalities.

Abigail grinned. "Chuck calls me Abby and Sis here Mimi."

Naomi shrugged. "We both like it. He treats us like normal adults."

"Everyone thought you were normal before."

"Yeah, but we're the babies. You know, I'm twenty-four and Mimi's twenty-five, but we're infants to the others. Besides, I think Jeff's right. We need to adapt to humans because we're never going back to Alpha Four."

"I don't know, the current monarchy is very pro Earth

and Earth A-Cs." The king had been in our wedding party, after all.

Abigail shrugged now. "Don't know, don't care. We belong here. I wish more of the old folks would catch on and stop pretending it's the same here as the home world."

"Your parents aren't like that."

"No, thank God." Naomi said with a laugh.

Abigail jerked. "You need to get in there, Kitty."

"I didn't think emotions could get in or out of these things."

"They can't, really. But I'm very close, and the drug's not out of Christopher's system. I think that's why Jamie's been crying."

"Really, not my reactions to things?"

"No," Naomi said quietly. "I'm sure she's picking up some of what Christopher's going through, like Abby is."

"Everything is heightened by the drug, as far as we can tell, including what's sent out, not just what comes in, if you know what I mean," Abigail said.

"Yeah, I think I do." Which meant my emotions were likely broadcasting on a stronger frequency now than they had been before. Lucky Jeff.

"I can just pick him up," Abigail went on. "Trust me, he needs someone who's not afraid of him or willing to put up with his crap."

I managed a laugh, kissed Jamie's head, and then Melanie opened the chamber door. Christopher was strapped down on a large medical table that rested on a pedestal, so that the table could move in pretty much any way and rest at any angle. It was slanted so his feet were just slightly lower than his head. He was tied down, had tubes and needles in his arms, and what I knew was a feeding tube in his mouth. If he'd looked hideous, I'd have been staring at Frankenstein's monster before the electric shock treatment.

As it was, seeing him like this just reminded me of how often I saw Jeff like this. Not as much as I was willing to, because my reactions when I saw him in isolation were very similar to my reactions right now. I wanted to rip all this stuff out of him, get him out of the restraints, and drag him off to safety.

Only this *was* safety. I'd have lost Jeff in the first two days I'd known him if it weren't for isolation. I knew my baby would have to spend time in here, too. Maybe I would also, now. The idea terrified me.

I went to Christopher. His eyes looked tortured and angry. I took the feeding tube out of his mouth, and gave him some water from the pitcher on one of the tables. I held his head while I helped him drink from the specially designed cup. I'd gotten good at this with Jeff, the few times I could calm down enough to be in here with him.

Done with the water, I kissed Christopher's forehead. "How're you doing?"

"It's hell. Get me out of here."

I looked at his eyes. They looked better, a lot less bloodshot. But they also looked wild. "I can't."

"Please. Kitty, I can't stand it." I could hear the pain in his voice.

I stroked his hair. "I know. It's horrible. But we have to get the drug out of you."

Christopher shook his head. "It'll never be out of me. I know what's happened to you because of what this did to Jeff."

"How?" Who would have been stupid enough to tell him against Chuckie's direct order, which Jeff had agreed with?

"I can see it. I can see what's happening inside you. I can see your cells rearranging."

"Umm . . . Christopher? Managing not to have hysterics here, but only just."

He took a deep breath. "Remember I told you I could see the people I cared about if I concentrated?" I nodded. "Well, I can. It's so awful in here—I've never understood how Jeff could stand it. He's braver than me, I guess."

I kissed his head again. "He wouldn't agree. Now, please, before the hysterics start, finish up the scary explanation that probably won't make me feel any better."

"I was . . . scared," he said in a low voice. "So I tried to see you and the baby, just to pretend things were normal. I concentrated so hard, I could see you, and then I could really see you. It's never happened before, but I've practiced while I've been in here, and if I want to, I can see what's happening in your body."

"Desperately focusing on the positive here. So you're about to become the king of the brain surgeons or something, but what's going on with me?"

"You're a superhuman. I know you've already figured it out, but your cells have altered to the point where I don't think you're going to go back to the old you."

"Is it going to kill me?" Wow, asked that without my voice shaking too much. So proud of myself.

"I don't think so. Your body's adapted to it really well. I think it's because the drug was originally based on what our people were working on for both human and A-C suspended animation. I think it's a combination of both, and that's why it's not hurting you. I mean, if you consider becoming superhuman not being hurt."

"Dude, I consider it the most awesome thing ever, as long as I'm not gonna die from it in like a month or something and as long as it's not hurting my baby."

"I looked at her, too. Jamie's fine. She looks like Jeff inside, same cellular changes."

"Christopher, this is both the most interesting and most gross conversation I've had since Tito described how this happened to me. Where is my snarkmeister? I'd love a snarky comeback instead of Doctor McSteamy."

He managed a grin. "Too tired to snark. I just want out of here, so badly."

"I know, honey." I stroked his head some more, and he closed his eyes.

"That feels so nice."

A thought occurred. "Christopher, can you see the makeup of things that aren't human? Like, can you tell if what you injected was pure or synthetic?"

"Haven't tried." His eyes were still closed. "Where's Jeff?"

"Um . . . out."

Christopher's eyes stayed shut. "Is he going to help Tim?"

"Yeah. How did you know about that?"

"Tim came to see me yesterday. Kind of following up on whatever I might have let slide because of being locked in here like an animal. He was upset that Alicia still wasn't home, happy we still had a team at Saguaro International, that sort of thing. So I've been watching him. He's okay, at least he was the last time I checked."

Made sure my voice was really casual. "Honey? How far is your range?"

He opened his eyes. "Alexander and Councillor Leonidas are having some trouble, but not with each other. Otherwise, they and Victoria are doing okay. Jareen and Neeraj are expecting, but they don't know it yet."

CHAPTER 39

"OH, MY GOD. YOU'RE SEEING people in the Alpha Centauri system?" I managed not to shriek. Good, good. I was calm, cool, and collected.

"Yeah." He swallowed. "Is this the part where I make that horrible laugh and turn evil and then try to kill everyone I love, right before you and Jeff kill me to save the world?" He was serious, and trying not to cry.

"Oh, honey, no." I hugged him as best I could, stroked his hair, and kissed his forehead. "Having power is one thing. Using it unwisely is another. Honey, you've always been powerful. And all you and Jeff have done with that power is protect people and worlds, and you both could have taken over without even trying hard. Chuckie thinks you and Jeff were already genetic evolutionary steps."

"You mean mutations."

"I was trying for the positive, comforting spin. Besides, I'm a mutant, now, too." I kissed his head. "I'm totally jazzed about it, by the way, especially since you said I'm not going to die from it and that Jamie's safe."

He managed a weak chuckle. "Glad one of us is."

"Honey, this is why you were shooting up, remember?"

Christopher heaved a sigh. "Yeah. Oh, and I don't need you to mention what an idiot I was. I'm clear on that." He was quiet for a few moments. "Kitty . . . I'm terrified."

"I know." Stroked his hair while I tried to figure out how to say what I needed to without making him feel belittled. "Jeff was scared, too, when this happened to him. I know

Serene was also. But they both got past it and learned to deal with new powers. You will, too." I kissed his head. "How did you get the Surcenthumain?"

"The what?"

"That's the drug's official name."

"Never heard it before."

"How did you get it?"

"I . . . don't remember." He sounded confused. "I remember watching Reynolds do some work with Abigail and Naomi. James was there, and he made a joke about how those two could probably shift galaxies if they had that Club Fifty-One drug. Reynolds got pissed and went into his antidrug rant. I thought it could be a good thing if we did it right . . . and then, I can remember the second time I injected myself."

"The second time?"

"Yeah. Not the first. I remember being really pissed at Reynolds for something—I think he'd made some comment about Jeff getting to you in time because of the drug and that being the only reason he didn't just order it wiped off the face of the Earth." He sighed. "Can't wait to have to deal with him after this."

"He'll be fine." I kissed his head. "Chuckie's really freaked that you did this, Christopher, but that's because he respects you. If he didn't respect you and Jeff, he never would have let Centaurion leave ETD control." Or let me marry Jeff, but I didn't figure that was relevant to this conversation.

"If you say so."

"Known him half my life. I say so."

"I don't think he's ever going to get over you."

Great, how had this moved from important things to my love life? "We'll always love each other, Christopher. It's not really important now."

"Why does he hate Amy so much?"

I found myself wondering if Christopher had lost his mind. "Because he never liked her, and she never liked him. She thought he was a drag on me socially, and he thought she exemplified everything wrong with wealth."

"Who was right?"

"Neither. I met more interesting people because of Chuckie than anyone else in my life, at least until that superbeing formed. I tried things I never would have because of him and learned things that have helped me survive in my second career. Amy's not nearly as stuck up as Chuckie's always thought, and she's worked for everything she's gotten, though most people assume her parents paved the way. But she went to college on a full merit scholarship, worked like a dog to pay for law school, and then got her job based on skill, not connections."

"So they fought over you?"

"Geez, dude, you make it sound like Amy's my special girlfriend. She's straight. For what it's worth, she thought Brian was a great boyfriend and was upset with me for breaking up with him. Everyone but me thought Chuckie was nuts . . . you know, because he believed you and your family were living on Earth."

Christopher actually laughed. "Yeah. Wonder if he's going to rub that in to her."

"Dude, they are not hanging out reminiscing and bonding over newly found shared interests. He wants to arrest her as a mole and lock her away. He can't stand her, and nothing she's said or done since you and Jeff brought her in from Paris has changed that mind-set. She still can't stand him, either. It's been a long time since I've seen them act like we were all still in high school, but I'm not looking forward to putting the three of us along with Brian and Sheila in a room together."

Thought about how I hadn't seen Sheila yet. Got the "worst friend in the world" feeling. Decided saving the world might make up for it. Never had yet, but maybe I'd be lucky.

"Is that because it'll be all of them against Reynolds?"

"Insightful. Yes."

"How many years did you spend defending him?"

"Dude, I've never stopped. I have to defend him every damn day to Jeff."

"Jeff's never going to have the jealousy chat with Reynolds."

I snorted. "They have it all the time. Not like his jealousy chat with you and James, more like a constant stag fight."

"Do you like it?"

I thought about it. "It doesn't bother me the way it did when you and Jeff were fighting over me. That freaked me out."

"Why?"

I kissed his head. "Because you mean so much to Jeff, and vice versa. I was afraid I was going to ruin your relationship, and then you'd both hate me."

"Lissa said the same thing." He sounded despondent. "She was almost right. If Jeff hadn't put up with me treating him like my worst enemy, she would have been right."

"She was murdered before she could tell you she was going to marry you and while she was with Jeff. I can understand why you took it out on him."

"I can't. Not any more."

"You're a bigger boy now." I leaned my head against his. "I guess asking for my old Christopher back's kind of impossible, huh?"

"Can't have my old Kitty back, either."

I moved and looked into his eyes. "I want you to promise me something."

He sighed. "I'm not going to shoot up again, no matter how tempting it is." He sounded like he'd been saying this to people for days.

"Great, not the promise I'm looking for." He raised an eyebrow. "Recovering from addiction's one step at a time. Sometimes it's not even one day at a time, sometimes it's like one minute at a time. You can't promise that you'll never do it again. You can only promise that each minute you'll do your best to not give in to the demon."

"That . . . makes sense. So, what promise *do* you want?"

"Help me get used to being a super. Jeff's frightened, Chuckie's frightened, I think James is frightened, too. I'm not, and that frightens them more. I don't know how to be an A-C, so to speak. I have no idea how much more I'm going to mutate, what powers may come. I need to have someone I can go to when I'm scared, someone who's going through the same thing but is willing to talk to me about it. I need you to be my A-C version of James—the guy I can go to who understands what I'm going through and will also tell me the truth."

"Jeff won't, and can't, lie to you."

"Jeff can't, and won't, tell me the truth all the time, either. He's my husband. There are things he won't tell me because he thinks the ignorance will protect me. He might be right. But we're going down a scary road together, and there are times when I need to talk to someone who won't get jealous or upset and who understands what I'm going through at the same time. I couldn't have survived in this new world I'm in without James. I'm not sure I'll survive the newer one without you."

Christopher gave me a crooked smile. "You're right. I'm not in love with you any more. But I still love you. You can run to me if I can run to you."

I kissed his forehead. "That's what friends, and family, are for."

"I'm glad we're both."

"Me too."

CHAPTER 40

CHRISTOPHER SIGHED, AND I felt him relax. "How much longer do you think they're going to keep me in here?"

I looked at the various instrument panels that lined the one wall the patient couldn't see. "I have no freaking idea. The pretty lights are all doing their flashy thing, like whenever Jeff's in here. Still have no idea of what they mean."

"Guess I'm not surprised. And also guess you're not going to turn the table so I can see the lights."

"I don't think I'm supposed to."

"And this has stopped you before when?"

"Good point." I turned the table. I mean, he was restrained and calm.

Christopher stared at the light board. "Why am I still in here?"

"Because you need to be."

He shook his head. "No, I don't. The lights indicate I'm cleared . . . and have been for, God, hours."

"Hang on." I ran to the door and pounded.

Melanie opened it. "Are you okay?"

I dragged her inside. "Look at that board. What does it tell you?"

She stared at it. "Emily!" Emily ran inside, the Gower girls and my baby following. "Am I reading this right?"

Emily looked at it. "Why the hell is Christopher still trussed up in here?" She sounded furious. "He should have been taken off hours ago, maybe even yesterday."

Melanie grabbed me. "You didn't tamper with anything?"

"I took the feeding tube out and gave him some water. That was it."

Emily was on her phone. "I need an analysis team down to Isolation, Commander White's chamber, immediately." She hung up and took every single needle and tube out of Christopher.

Melanie put her hand on Christopher's shoulder. "Just need to verify some things, then we'll get you out of here."

I turned to the Gower girls. "Who was here, other than Paul and Richard?"

"Michael, but he didn't go inside. Paul wasn't here very long, from what he said." Naomi sounded confused. "Paul would know what the lights mean, wouldn't he?"

"Maybe." Emily sounded brisk. "But his focus when he's been here has been helping Christopher deal with withdrawal symptoms and soothing him. He might not have paid the status board any attention."

"Richard would, wouldn't he?"

"I don't think he looked at it," Christopher said. "He's spent all his time in here talking to me, like you did, Kitty. Paul, too. I didn't even ask them about the board, they were both so upset."

Naomi handed Jamie to me. "Need to concentrate, don't want her affected." She leaned against Abigail.

Jamie gurgled and cooed at me. "There's my baby cat." Kissed her, did the Mommy Dance. It kept me from totally panicking.

I heard a mewling, and a Poof head stuck up out of my purse. "Man, I'm glad you have Toby," Christopher said, sounding relieved.

"You didn't send Toby to me?"

"No. I wasn't supposed to bring it with me, but it was nice not to be completely alone. The Poofs aren't exactly stress creators."

Toby jumped out of my purse and onto Christopher's shoulder. It started purring and nuzzling his neck.

"So, someone let Toby out. Or Toby let itself out." We weren't sure what the Poofs could or couldn't do. They were androgynous and only mated when an Alpha Four Royal Wedding was imminent. Other than that, their ability to go huge and toothy, and their ability to travel at some kind of Poof hyperspeed, we knew almost nothing about them—except that they were adorable.

The analysis team arrived. All younger Dazzlers. Emily had them check everything, including the water, for contaminants. Everyone breathed a sigh of relief when all were pronounced normal.

Melanie let Christopher out of the restraints. A part of me was waiting for him to actually do the evil laugh, attack us, and run off to start world domination.

What he did was stretch, bend over, and get the kinks out of his neck. Then he kissed the baby. And hugged me. "Thanks."

"Any time I can stare at something with no comprehension but save the day, I'm glad to do it."

Christopher laughed. "Good to know. Now, what I want to know is who the hell kept me in here, and why?" His Commander voice was on full. I felt tons better.

Naomi opened her eyes. "Chuck's heading for us, dead run."

"He's furious, and worried about Christopher," Abigail added.

I gave Jamie to Christopher. "Hold your goddaughter." I trotted outside of the chamber to see Chuckie running toward us at full steam. He could have been on the track team with this kind of speed. "Ahead of you, only just."

He skidded to a stop. "I hope to hell your husband's kicking the asses of every one of your so-called Diplomatic Corps. How's White?"

"I'm good. Sort of." Christopher walked out, Jamie leaning against his shoulder. "Freedom. It's so nice. Who did this to me?"

"The same damn people who hooked you in the first place." Chuckie was so angry he could barely talk. "You don't remember how you started shooting up, do you?"

Christopher and I exchanged a glance. "No, I don't. Kitty asked me about that, and it's all . . . not there."

"Yeah, it's not there because you didn't actually do it willingly." He took a deep breath. "Let me rephrase that. You did agree to take the drug, because they couldn't have forced you unless you'd been willing in some way. But you were manipulated into it, and your memory was wiped.

Once you'd shot up the first time, the drug kicked in and the subliminal suggestions they gave you helped make you want more. By the third time, you were hooked. Anyone would be, it's that powerful."

"Who, exactly, did this to Christopher?"

Chuckie looked at me. "Put it this way. I should have killed them at your wedding, not just arrested them."

CHAPTER 41

"WE HAVE A DIPLOMATIC CORPS WHY?"

"They help us in Washington." Christopher didn't sound enthused.

"Uh-huh, yeah, I'll bet."

"Tradition," Melanie added, also sounding unenthused.

"They provide that so-called needed check and balance," Emily offered, sounding the least enthused of the three of them. I agreed with the lack of joy.

I looked around. "Let's get out of this area."

We headed back to the elevators. Christopher kept hold of Jamie, and Toby stayed on his other shoulder. They looked kind of cute and funny. I figured he wouldn't want me to mention that aloud.

"So, what's the full story on the drug?"

"Most of what we got we already know. The drug was originally created to put both humans and A-Cs into suspended animation for long-range space flight. It was altered to focus on an individual's strengths. In the case of regular humans, it makes them more like A-Cs if they have the capacity for it. In the case of regular A-Cs, it makes them stronger. In the case of those with talents, however, the results are less consistent but also much more advanced."

"What about how the drug focuses on the negative emotions? Was that planned?" I wondered if it would affect me in the way it had everyone else. So far, I hadn't noticed any unusual emotions, even taking my pre- and post-pregnancy mood swings in stride. I hadn't had all that many, really. So maybe the drug was helping. I didn't count on it, of course. Our luck almost never ran that way.

"No. The fact that the drug focuses on the id and enhances negative emotions is a by-product, not the main intent. They're happy with that result, of course, but I'm fairly sure they want to find a way to control it."

"Are they involved in the supersoldier project or projects?"

Chuckie shook his head. "No idea. I don't think Clarence knows everything, and he certainly doesn't know how the drug was perfected. However, I do think he knows who else may have been used as a test subject, in addition to Serene, Martini, White, and, essentially, you, Kitty."

"More of our people are being drugged like this?" Christopher sounded pissed. Couldn't blame him; the feeling was clearly mutual among our group.

"Can't tell yet. There's more there, but I think we need Martini or Mimi and Abby to try to read him. Later," Chuckie added, as we reached the elevator bay. "I think we need to get the Diplomatic Corps under lock and key first."

I pushed the button for the fifteenth floor. I wanted to go to the Lair as fast as I could get there. "Chuckie, is Fluffy with you?"

"Yes." He mumbled it.

"Good."

Upon hearing its name, Fluffy stuck its head out of one of Chuckie's suit pockets. Purred at me, then spotted the Gowers, mewled with what I took to be joy, and leaped out of the pocket onto Naomi's shoulder. Purred, rubbed, jumped to Abigail, did the same, jumped back to Naomi's shoulder and sat there purring.

Naomi laughed. "Hi, Fluffy, missed you, too."

"What's the plan?" Emily asked me. "I mean, are we assuming Jeff and the others are okay?"

"I never assume that." I didn't. Our plans went awry at the drop of a shoe.

Left the elevators to see several Security A-Cs guarding one of the interrogation cells. Tito was with them. He came over as soon as he saw us. "How're you feeling?"

Christopher shrugged. "Okay."

"Kitty?" Tito had his Doctor Face on.

"Great. Worried but great."

"Yeah." Tito looked more worried than I was.

"What is it?"

He sighed as we went into the Lair. "I can't reach any of them."

I stopped walking and turned around. "By any of them, I assume you mean Jeff, Paul, James, and the others?"

"Right."

"Com on!" Chuckie, Christopher, and I shouted that in unison. Too worried to let it freak me out.

"Yes, Commander Martini, Commander White, and Sometime Supreme Commander Reynolds? You bellowed?"

"Gladys, what's the status at the Embassy?"

"We've been monitoring since Commander Martini left. No change. We still have the Diplomatic Corps inside and no one else."

"Hang on. How many people is that?"

"Twelve. We have six diplomatic couples."

"So there are no servants, no children, no adjuncts, no random A-Cs or humans who were there when it locked? Just the twelve of them?"

"Yes."

I looked at Chuckie. "How easy would it be to fake?"

"They've had plenty of time to plan for it. I'd figure easy."

"Christopher, can you see Jeff?" I did my best to sound calm and cool, not panicked and freaked. Failed.

He closed his eyes. I considered taking Jamie from him, but they both seemed okay. "Yeah," he said slowly. "He's outdoors."

"How can you tell?"

"He's wet. I can see rain hitting him."

"Landmarks?"

"Not . . . really. I can see a circular turn with cars in it. Paul's with him, James is too. Who else could be with them?"

"Michael, Amy, Kevin, Tim, and four of your A-C agents."

"I see Kevin. But not Michael, Amy, or Tim. At least, not with Jeff." I could tell he was concentrating. "Jeff looks angry, but he's not hurt. Same with the others with him." He winced. "Amy looks terrified. Michael seems scared. They're with Tim. He's hurt, but not badly." Christopher was quiet and then opened his eyes. "They've tortured and killed the other agents."

CHAPTER 42

"HOW DO YOU KNOW?" Chuckie's voice was low.

"I just watched them kill the last one. They're using them as lab rats." Christopher handed Jamie to me very carefully. "We need to get to Jeff and then get to where they have the others."

"Where is that?" Chuckie had his patient voice on.

I answered. "Jeff's outside the Embassy. They think the others are inside. But no one's inside, it's a trap, rigged to get whoever goes inside it. They weren't chasing Tim, they were herding him."

"That's a pretty big leap, Kitty." Chuckie didn't sound unconvinced.

"Dude, you trained me up in the conspiracy theories, and there isn't a psycho or megalomaniac around I can't feel the love with. The others are in France, probably Paris. But why can't we reach Jeff by phone?"

"Weather?" Tito asked.

"Proximity," Chuckie replied without missing a beat. "Whatever's causing Security to 'see' twelve people in there is probably interfering with the phones."

"James just crossed the street," Christopher said.

I dug my phone out and dialed. He answered on the second ring. "James, don't go in the Embassy!" Jamie fussed at my voice level. Christopher shook his head and took her back from me.

"Stop screaming, girlfriend. What's going on?"

"Get the others over to where you are, away from the Embassy!"

"Stop shrieking, I need my hearing." I heard him shout something.

"They're moving to where James is." Christopher sounded relieved.

"James, I need to talk to Jeff."

He sighed. "Sure, break my heart."

"Still love you best, want to keep you all alive, that sort of thing."

"So you claim. Here he is. Your woman." I heard the phone pass.

"Why are you calling us? We're in the middle of an operation."

"Don't go in the Embassy!"

"Baby, why the hell are you screaming at me?"

"Do not go in the Embassy! It's a trap."

"Yeah, well, we figured something when Michael and Amy tried the subtle approach."

"What did they do?"

"Went to the door and pretended to be stranded and seeking shelter from the storm."

"Whose idea was *that*?"

"Amy's. She's not as good at this as you, but she can sure get into the same amount of trouble."

"So what happened?"

"Door opened, they went in, door slammed shut. Called Michael, cell phone dead or inactive."

"Yeah, they've got something on or around the Embassy scrambling signals. We couldn't reach any of you until James crossed the street. There's probably no one in the Embassy, but it's a trap. By the way, get the hell out of the rain before you get sick."

"How do you know it's raining? I mean still. I know we got the weather report hours ago."

"Christopher has new, fun talents, similar to Serene's. Look, it's scary bad, only, thankfully, not where you are. Get back here, fast. We have to get to Paris."

"No 'we' involved in that." I heard him bark some orders, and I was pretty sure I heard the word "floater." "You are staying put with Jamie. Do you understand me?"

He had his "growly man in charge" voice on. It was the voice he somehow always thought I'd obey, even though I never did.

"Yes, I do. Jeff, they're experimenting on them. If you barge in, they'll experiment on you, too." My voice was heading to the dog-only register.

"We'll be fine."

"Like hell! You'll be in trouble. Tim's hurt but still alive, Michael and Amy are alive; they've already tortured and killed the four agents with them, though."

Jeff was quiet for a few moments. "How do you know this?"

"Christopher. Scary expanded talents. So expanded he knows we should send a baby gift to Jareen and Neeraj so it arrives when they discover they're pregnant."

"How is he?"

"Happy to be out of isolation hours later than he should have been, undoubtedly due to that bastard your sister's married to. Of course, from what I can tell, all your sisters married jerks."

Chuckie shook his head. "Jerks, yes. Traitors, no. At least, not all of them."

"Chuckie says not all your sisters married badly. Hurrah. Get out of the rain, and please, please come back here and go to Paris from a gate out of the Science Center. *Please.*" Normally I begged like this when we were having great sex. This was not my preferred trade off.

Chuckie took the phone from me. "Or you can let her stay here with me. I'll protect her. Better than you. And, you know what? I'm betting there are plenty of things I can do for her better than you can. Things I know she likes." The way he said it, it was obvious he was insinuating bedroom things.

He held the phone away from his ear and looked bored. I could hear Jeff bellowing but couldn't make out what he was saying. "Yeah? Go ahead, race off like a moron. The baby may be amazing and talented, but she's less than a week old. She won't remember you, and she looks just like her mother, so after a while we won't be reminded of you at all, and I'll treat her exactly as if she's mine—she'll call me Daddy, and I'll be sure to spoil her and her mother. I think Kitty and Jamie will love it in Australia." He hung up the phone and handed it back to me. "Expect your husband any moment."

Christopher handed Jamie to me again. "I can't believe I'm going to have to do what I know I'm going to have to do."

I took Jamie, Christopher moved between Chuckie and the door. He caught Jeff as he came barreling through at hyperspeed and got him into a chokehold. "Stop it."

Jeff was snarling. "Let me at him."

"Why? What he did was the only thing that was going to make you listen." Christopher tightened his hold on Jeff. "It's adapted to my system, just like it did to yours. I'm stronger now, too. Do you want to spend the time to find out if I'm stronger than you while we have our people in mortal peril? And while your wife's just holding it together? Or do you think you can wake up and realize there's a reason we wanted you back here, first?"

Jamie started to cry. I tried to comfort her, but it didn't do any good. I was close to crying, too, so that might have been why. I saw Jeff pay attention to what we were feeling instead of being enraged. His body relaxed, and Christopher let him go.

Jeff came over to me and took Jamie. He cuddled her and hugged me. "I'm sorry."

"Let's get you into dry clothes. Where are the others?" I felt panicked that they'd gone to Paris already.

"Here, girlfriend." Reader walked in, Kevin and Paul right behind him. "Hard to catch up to Jeff when he's doing the enhanced hyperspeed." He grinned at Chuckie. "Gotta hand it to you, you sure know how to push his buttons."

Chuckie shrugged. "Some people make it easier than others."

"Look, everyone get into dry clothes, make sure your cell phones are charged, and then, for God's sake, regroup here before you go racing off." I figured it couldn't hurt to remind them not to be foolhardy. I mean, better late than never.

"Get weapons," Chuckie added. "I'm sure we're going to need them."

Christopher nodded. "Yeah. I can't see much, other than the room they've got them in. It's big, but I can't tell how big. I can only see it because . . . of the bodies."

"Change, back here in ten minutes or less." Jeff had his Commander voice on full.

Everyone scattered, women included. I got the impression that Melanie and Emily were planning to come back. Well, like daughters, like mothers. Lorraine and Claudia were off fieldwork, but maybe their mothers could cover it. They were doctors, after all, and we clearly needed medical along.

We went into the bedroom. I put Jamie down in the middle of the bed and helped Jeff get out of his jacket and shirt. I got a towel and started to dry him off. He took it from me, wrapped it around my back, and pulled me to him.

"You'll go to Australia with him over my dead body."

"That was Chuckie's point."

"Yeah, yeah, fine." Jeff bent and kissed me. I melted against him. When he finally ended our kiss I nuzzled into his chest and buried my face between his pecs, one of my favorite places to bury. Didn't have time to bury in my other favorite place. He kissed the top of my head. "You're staying here. With Jamie. Where it's safe."

"It wasn't safe for Christopher here." I brought him up to speed fast on what we'd learned. "Chuckie will explain it all in fuller detail, I'm sure."

"I hate him. I really *hate* him."

"As I said to him the other day, I'm glad you're both straight, or you two would probably be married."

"Hardly."

I kissed Jeff's chest. "I wish everyone was safe. Because I know I can have sex now."

He laughed. "No one focuses on the priorities better than my girl."

CHAPTER 43

JEFF PUT ON A DRY SUIT—the Elves never failed to produce. His long Armani trench coat was hanging in our closet. It looked great on him. Then again, everything looked great on him.

I changed Jamie's diaper. She was going to need to eat soon. I hoped it could wait until everyone left. I picked her up and considered that I also needed to give her a bath and do all those other good mommy things I was most likely failing at. I'd been on the ball a couple of days ago, when nothing much was going on. Add life-threatening dangers, though, and I was already in need of assistance.

"Oh, by the way," Jeff said as he took Jamie from me and cuddled her. "Why did you send Harlie after me?" The Poof popped out of the trench coat pocket and mewled at me. Poofs really had amazing abilities.

"To protect you."

"It's a Poof, not a machine gun. There's only so much protection they can provide. Keep Harlie with you and Jamie. That's an order. And, before you can argue, we're in a Field situation, and that means you are required to obey me because you report to me."

"That's so cute. When you get back, you can try to order me around again. The only time it works is when we're having sex."

He grinned. "I like ordering you around best then anyway." Jeff wrapped his free arm around me and kissed me deeply. "She's too young for you to leave her, and it's too dangerous for you to bring her. Remember that, baby."

"I know, Jeff. I'm not an utter moron."

"No, but you're brave and impetuous. You have to sit this one out, baby."

"I guess." I heard people coming into the Lair. "Showtime, Jeff."

He sighed. "Yeah." We walked out of the bedroom. He kept his arm around me and held onto Jamie. I knew he didn't want to leave us, and it occurred to me that he probably hadn't wanted to come back here because it would be harder to go to Paris for him now. Felt worse and just totally in love with him at the same time.

Did a nose count. We had Chuckie, Christopher, Kevin, Tito, Reader, Gower, Naomi, Abigail, Melanie, and Emily, all looking ready to go. I anticipated Jeff's words.

He pointed to the four women. "No. You're all staying here."

"Jeff, women can vote these days and hold jobs." Did my best not to sound sarcastic. Failed, if Chuckie's fast grin was any indication.

"Yeah, I know. They can also get killed. However, not tonight. We have Amy already in danger and covering the female side of the house."

Melanie and Emily exchanged looks with me. "Jeff? Who's going to do medical?" Emily asked it calmly, but I could tell she was angry.

"No one. We're getting in, grabbing our hostages, and getting out." Jeff sounded like he believed that.

"Right. Uh, just how do you think you're going to do that? Christopher has only a vague idea of where they are." And I knew how our team's luck ran.

Jeff shrugged. "We've worked with a lot less."

I looked right at him. "Name a time."

There was a lot of silence in the room. I looked around. All the men were doing a good job of not looking at any of the women. Melanie and Emily crossed their arms and glared at Jeff. Not up to Christopher's standards, but still, pretty good.

"You're not field trained," Jeff said, trying to maintain authority. But, these were mothers he was having the stare down with—they'd had a lot more years with authority than he had. "It's dangerous."

"You take our daughters all the time," Melanie said calmly.

"Kitty does. I don't. I never approved having female operatives." I could tell Jeff knew how that sounded as soon as it left his mouth because I saw him wince.

"The C.I.A. has female operatives," Naomi said. "In fact, if I recall, the head of the P.T.C.U. is a woman. Why, I think she's your mother-in-law, if memory serves." Wow, everyone had a sarcasm knob. I was impressed.

"Angela's trained." Jeff was grasping, I could tell.

"Are you saying we aren't?" Emily's voice was at that dangerous, silky level, where any man who opened his mouth was going to be in trouble.

"Uhhh . . . " It was clear Jeff had come to the same conclusion I had.

"Jeff, you need to have medical. I know I'm not going. I hate it, but I'm clear. But right now I think you need all the backup you can get."

Christopher closed his eyes. "Tim's hurt, not life-threatening, yet." He jerked. "Oh, God, they're dissecting our agents' bodies in front of Tim, Amy, and Michael. Not sure why, but the three of them look horrified."

Jeff looked at me. "You want to let your best friends' mothers go along with us why?"

"Because you need us," Melanie said. "We know it, and we're going. It's that simple."

"Us, too," Naomi said.

"Absolutely not." Chuckie's voice was calm, but I'd heard that tone from him before. He meant it. "You two aren't going anywhere any more than Kitty is. You have no training for anything like this, no experience, and this isn't the operation to learn on."

"They might be able to find everyone."

Chuckie gave me a long look. I knew he was angry. "They might be killed, too. Or captured. Why don't we take the baby along, Kitty? She's worth a lot to whoever's in charge, I'm sure."

"We could also argue about this for the next several hours and lose more of our people. Or, we can go." Jeff wasn't arguing with Chuckie. I didn't want to fight both of them. Besides, Jamie needed to be fed.

"Fine. You're the ones in charge. I'm on maternity leave. I get it." Everyone, to a person, geez, to a Poof, turned and stared at me, in obvious shock.

Jeff gaped at me. "Who are you, and what have you done to my wife?"

"I don't like it, okay? I'm just accepting it." Ungracefully, but at least accepting it.

Jeff stroked my neck. "You're sidelined for your safety and Jamie's safety, not because you're not a good leader." He looked back at the Gower girls. "I agree with Reynolds. You two aren't going anywhere."

"What about us?" Emily looked ready to keep on arguing.

Jeff sighed. "I'll concede, only because it may take us longer than we want to find them and medical could be an issue. I'd like to remind the two of you, though, that we have a chain of command, and you're at the bottom of it. You're not married to me, so don't think you're going to order me around and have it work the moment we leave this room."

Melanie nodded. "Agreed."

"Yes." Emily gave me a sympathetic smile. "We'll do our best to cover your side of the operation."

"You mean you're going to get into trouble, fall from a great height, and ignore everything Jeff, Reynolds, or I say?" Christopher's snark was back, just in time for the offensive. How nice.

"Whatever. Let's get going. Everyone get to the launch area." Jeff kissed me, not nearly long enough. "You behave," he whispered in my ear. "We'll be back as fast as we can be. I love you, baby."

"I love you, too." I held him as tightly as I could. We broke apart; he kissed Jamie and handed her gently back to me. Then the A-Cs each grabbed a human, and they all took off, leaving me and the Gower girls to hold down the boring fort.

CHAPTER 44

I HEAVED A SIGH. "I need to feed the baby."

"We'll help." Naomi seemed as let down as I felt. "I guess they're right. We don't have any field experience, and you have the baby."

"Yeah, it just sucks." I went into the bedroom, and they came with me.

Abigail cocked her head. "You know, maybe you should change, just in case."

"I look that bad?"

"Well, the outfit's a little baggy now." She grinned at me and went into the closet.

Did the torpedo thing. Naomi was a great help. Abigail rummaged for clothes for me. "You want your usual jeans and a T-shirt?" she asked from inside the closet. "Or a sweater? Or, wow, you have an Aerosmith thermal. That's what you want, isn't it?"

"Have you been shadowing me for like all my life?"

"No. Chuck talks about you *all* the time. I mean, all the time. All. The. Time."

"Doesn't that get old fast?"

Naomi shook her head. "I think it's helping him get over you."

"Talking about me constantly? Sounds like just the opposite to me." I was getting worried about Chuckie. What if Christopher was right and he never did get over me? I loved him, and I wanted him to have a good, happy life.

How could he do that if he remained romantically in love with me forever?

Naomi took Jamie and burped her in between torpedo switching. "He's been in love with you for over half his life now. And he's been in love with *you*, not what he thinks you are or would become, but as you were, for every stage of your life."

"Great. I feel like the worst woman in the world now, thanks ever." Took Jamie back, put her on torpedo two. She ate like a horse. Of course, her daddy was hung like one, so maybe that was why. Started thinking about sex with Jeff, managed to drag my mind back to the present situation. Sort of wished I hadn't—my old buddy Guilt was making a surprise reappearance. Guilt loved the idea of Chuckie never finding anyone else, because Guilt really enjoyed its career.

"Don't. Chuck understands." Naomi sat down on the bed next to me while Abigail brought my change of clothes over. "He won't let you go, ever. But that's not a bad thing."

"Uh, how? I mean, how does him being obsessed with me equal not a bad thing?"

"He's not like Brian was." Abigail sat down on my other side. "Kevin told us about that. Now, Brian was obsessed and not over the real you. Glad you worked that out with him, because he and Serene are so into each other."

"Mutual obsessives obsessed with each other. Yeah, match made in Heaven or Hell, depending. Heaven, in this case, thankfully."

"Right. But Chuck's not obsessed with you." Abigail took Jamie and burped her this time, while I started to change clothes.

"What you two are saying sounds obsessed to me."

"No, he's just thorough." Naomi sounded thoughtful. "He accepted that you were marrying Jeff, and why, over a year ago. The moment you two were married, his focus was to make sure you were going to stay married, happily."

"Okay, I can buy that. I mean, he told me he could be married with a ton of kids and would still do what he could to keep Jeff on his toes. But I don't see how this focus on me is moving him on to someone, anyone, else."

"I do," Abigail said calmly. "Before, he didn't talk about you at all, to anyone."

This was true. Chuckie was a very private person to most. Until a year and a half ago, really, to anyone other than me and his parents. "So?"

"So he didn't talk about you because he was keeping you to himself, locked away, where all the things you did that he loved, or made him laugh or feel special, all your shared experiences wouldn't be shared with anyone else. They were his, and yours, alone. And if you'd picked him over Jeff, they'd still be his and yours alone."

Naomi nodded. "But because you didn't pick him, he's actually letting you go by talking about you. It's not like he talks about your past together to just anyone, but we're close to him. He tells us about you, and because he's opened that locked part of himself, it's also relaxing the hold you have on him, so to speak. The more he tells us about you, the more the romantic love part fades."

"The friend part's still there," Abigail said quickly. "He'll never stop loving you as his best friend. But I think he's already well on the way to not loving you romantically any more." She grinned. "Based on the fact that I know by heart how many times you made him listen to Aerosmith's *Toys in the Attic* and *Rocks* albums until you made him agree they were the best rock albums of all time."

"And then you made him choose which one was best between the two," Naomi added with a laugh. "And then argued about how he was wrong."

"I just think *Toys in the Attic* is a little better," I mumbled.

"We know," Abigail said. "Trust us, we *know*."

"Which is why we know it's helping him," Naomi said.

"I hope you're right." I wasn't convinced, of course, in part because Guilt liked the idea that Chuckie was talking about me because I'd broken his heart.

"Give it time," Naomi said. "He'll work his own way out of it into where he should be. Don't worry, don't push him. The harder you push for him to find someone else, the harder he'll resist it."

"Yeah, sounds like Chuckie." I contemplated whether to tell them, but I figured they might know anyway. "He was alone on Christmas."

"We know. We invited him to be with our family. Our mother still likes to celebrate it. He didn't want to. We understood. I think his parents did, too." Naomi laughed. "They know he's working through the situation in his own way."

"You've met his parents?"

"Oh, yeah. Chuck doesn't treat us like lab rats. And I think he wants to keep an eye on us, so no one else can treat us like lab rats." Naomi checked Jamie's diaper.

"Or worse," Abigail said darkly. "I've heard some fights he's had with others in the C.I.A." She shook her head. "I wish Jeff and Christopher and the rest of the guys would stop treating him like the enemy. Sometimes he's the only friend we have."

"Yeah. Your diplomats pulling this stunt is one of the worst things for A-C safety, too. Earth governments don't like it when the crafty aliens try to take over the world." I sighed. "So, what're we going to do to try to keep our minds off worrying?"

Naomi shrugged. "Your family's still in the library, I think. Why don't we go there? Might at least distract us."

"Works for me."

Abigail gathered the few baby things we had for Jamie, including the Snugli, at hyperspeed, I realized. "Wow, I can see you. I mean, going fast. You're clear, not blurry and not invisible. And I can tell you're moving at hyperspeed, too."

"I wonder when your mutation is going to stop." Naomi sounded thoughtful.

"What if it doesn't?" Abigail sounded worried.

"What if it regresses?" Naomi asked.

"Cross that bridge when I go to the dark side or when I turn all 'Flowers for Algernon.' For now, let's go see what my family and yours have been up to." I was dressed, stuff was gathered. I took Jamie, slung my purse over my shoulder, did a Poof check, and we took off for the library.

CHAPTER 45

REACHED THE LIBRARY and realized Doreen hadn't been kidding—it was a full-fledged party. It looked like everyone other than the few A-Cs on agent or Security duty were in here. Jamie cuddled into my neck—I got the impression she didn't like the noise and crowd, but I could have been putting my own feelings onto her.

Spotted Sheila and decided now was as good a time as any to stop being the worst friend in the world. The Gower girls said they'd catch up to me after I got some time with her and wandered off toward their mother, who was with Denise Lewis.

Trotted over to Sheila, did the squeal and hug thing. She had her youngest on her hip, and I had Jamie in my arms, so the hug wasn't what it could have been, but it wasn't a hug from someone who resented or hated me. She looked great. She'd always been between Amy and me in height and had dark hair and eyes to our fair.

We then did the fast catch-up thing, and while we did it, all our old jokes interspersed throughout, I felt myself relax. It was almost as if we were back in high school, but better, because we were both adults, settled into our lives, and, happily, those lives, while different, weren't mutually exclusive.

"I can't believe what you do now," Sheila said with a laugh as I finished my really fast explanation of what the last couple of years had held for me. "Just glad your mom sent all those great-looking guys to rescue us."

"Yeah, the visual benefits are wonderful."

"I saw a picture of your husband. Boy, talk about gorgeous."

"Yeah, Jeff's a total hunk."

"I'm sure you've heard this too much, but I was surprised you went for him and not his cousin. Saw him, too. Totally your type."

"So the world seems to feel. If I was going to stick to that type, I'd have married Chuckie." Whoops, that was a slip. Guilt high-fived itself.

Sheila shook her head. "I don't know what's more shocking—what you do and who you married, or how Chuck turned out."

"Wow, you're not hating on him?"

She laughed. "Uh, no. I married a nerd, remember? They make great mates." Reader had said the same about A-Cs. Found myself wondering if Jeff counted as a nerd. He was really smart and funny. Couldn't imagine awkward. Then again, if I'd met Chuckie now, I'd have trouble believing he'd ever been awkward, too. Resolved to ask to see Alfred's pictures of Jeff and Christopher through the years. Thought about Alfred—something tickled in my mind. Couldn't figure out what or why, though.

"I guess I don't think of Roger as a nerd."

"Me either, anymore. Honestly, if you'd told me you and Chuck were getting married, it wouldn't have surprised me. He's always been in love with you." Guilt did a back flip while shouting "go team."

"Thanks, I need that guilt from someone else."

Sheila laughed again. "My mother said you have to marry who you're really in love with, at least the first time." She shook her head. "Amy thinks her dad loves his second wife more than her mother. I wouldn't know, but she seems so adrift."

"Ames? Adrift?" Maybe. I hadn't seen her much in recent years, after all. "She never said anything like that to me." Worry raced over to hang out with Guilt and chat.

"I'm probably just seeing things that aren't there."

"And maybe you aren't. You were always Miss Insightful in school. What's Ames shared with you that she hasn't shared with me?"

Sheila looked thoughtful. "She said that your mom and

Chuck had suspected her dad of being involved in whatever's going on, and while she felt she had to defend him, especially against Chuck, in reality, sometimes she wonders how much he's changed since we were young. It sounded like she never sees him, even though he goes to Europe all the time. I didn't get the feeling they talk much, either."

I talked to my parents all the time, at least several times a week; sometimes several times a day. The idea of not being in contact with them, or them being nearby and not stopping to see me if we were living far apart, seemed almost unthinkable.

"Amy talks to my mom regularly."

Sheila grinned. "So do I. Your parents stay in touch with us and, from what your mom's said when we've chatted, your best friends from college, too. In addition to Chuck, I mean."

This I knew to be true. Frankly, Mom kept in better touch with my friends than I did, which I chose to see as her being a great mom and helping me out, as opposed to me being a total loser as a friend and Mom desperately covering for me. "Well, my parents love you guys."

"I know. Amy knows, too, so don't worry about it. I want an important question answered, young lady."

"Shoot."

"How are you liking married life? You got the instant baby, that can be kind of hard." Sheila looked ready to console me if I wanted to whine and to shake the pom-poms if I was cheering about it. That was one of her best qualities, her ability to support her friends no matter what.

"I like it. A lot. Jeff's a great husband, and he's a natural daddy." Had a thought while I shoved Guilt and Worry away, hard. "You know, Jamie eats like a horse. My doctor was concerned she wasn't getting enough milk, but she seems to be doing fine, at least so far. Did you go through anything like that?"

"Oh, yeah. Number Two was a chowhound. He still is." She grimaced. "Look, I know you know they're all buying baby stuff for you. I ordered something, too, but lord knows when it'll get here. We used to share stuff all the time—you still up for it?"

"Sure, what?"

Sheila grinned. "Gonna help you stock up for the long winter." She grabbed my arm and headed us off.

Sheila was carrying a huge diaper bag. I was envious. She led the way to a bathroom I didn't even know existed in the library area. She looked pretty good for having four kids—I guess running after them kept her in shape. She reminded me of her mother. Amy reminded me of her own mom, too. And I was my mother's little clone, apparently. Wondered if Jamie would be just like me. Sort of hoped so. But that made me want a little Jeff, too. He'd really gotten me focused on lots of kids over the less than two years I'd known him. Then again, maybe it was just because I loved him so much.

"What's it like having four?"

"Never buy the lie that it's easier the more you have. But, you know, they're great. Each one's different, but it's neat to see yourself, your husband, and your families in them."

There were some people in Jeff's family I knew neither one of us wanted to see in our kids. My mind tickled again. Again, no idea of why.

"Where are Numbers One through Three?" They had names—Roger, Jr., David, Martin, and baby on the hip was Gerald—but they called them Numbers One through Four. It was their thing, and I'd always found it funny. Still did.

"Roger has them. Your dad's having a field day with them. I think he's hoping you have a boy next." Sheila dumped her baby bag on the counter. This was a nice bathroom—tried to mark its location for the future. Gave up.

She dug something out—a lot of something. "What is that?"

"Nursing mother's best friend. An electric breast pump."

"Oh. Um. Ick."

She laughed. "Your boobs look ready to explode."

"I just fed Jamie, too."

"So, pump. You can store up—it freezes, for at least two weeks without a lot of issue." She winked. "It's great if you want to have someone watch the baby while you and the husband practice making another baby."

"You speak my language. Gimme the pump."

The less said about the joys of pumping breast milk the better. Having Jamie right there was a help, according to Sheila of La Leche League, which is what I started calling her the moment the pump began. I felt for milk cows.

I was making boatloads of milk. It was almost horrifying. Sheila was really impressed. "God, you could be a professional wet nurse."

"I think I'd almost rather die. I love breastfeeding Jamie. But I think Jeff would draw the line at sharing the rack with anyone other than his own child."

"Oh, so he's your usual then."

"What is *that* supposed to mean?"

She gave me a sly grin. "Possessive, protective, jealous—you know, what every serious boyfriend you ever had was like. What Chuck was like, only in a low-key way, at least, whenever you were around. If I'd known that, I wouldn't have questioned the physical choices."

"Jeff's not . . . totally . . . um . . . okay, he's just like that, yeah. But it's sweet."

"Yeah? You didn't think so when you'd had it with Brian. So, who was better in bed, Chuck or Jeff?"

"Beg pardon?" I hadn't told her I'd slept with Chuckie.

"Oh, come on. It's me. He was hot for you from day one. And he's tall, handsome, your normal physical type now, maybe a tad taller than your average, but I doubt that was a deterrent. You two went to Vegas together for a week. I remember talking to you about that trip. 'Best vacation of my life' were your exact words. The way you think, I know that meant you screwed like rabbits."

"Yeah, okay, fine. Until I met Jeff, honestly, Chuckie was the best. By far."

"Jeff's better?"

"Jeff's a freaking sex god."

"You're such a simple creature."

"Almost male in my needs. Yeah, yeah, heard it from you before. Bitch."

We both laughed. "I miss this," Sheila said.

"Me too. Is it hard, being a wife and mother first?"

She shrugged. "Sometimes. But it's usually worth it. But that's me. Everyone's different. I have a hard time imagining Amy as a wife, let alone a mother. But I think she really wants to find that special guy."

"Yeah, well, they show up when you least expect them. I sure wasn't expecting Jeff when he appeared." Literally and figuratively.

"Yep, like the song says, you can't hurry love."

Finally done. I had pumped something like twenty bags of milk. "This looks like I'm starting my own dairy. Do you have any bags left?"

"Sure. In fact, you keep the rest of this box. You can always express by hand if you have to."

"Ugh." I took the box from her. The way she handed it to me, I saw the bottom. There was a mark there that looked vaguely familiar. I brought the box closer to my face. There was a circle divided into three parts, with the letters A, B, and C in each piece of the pie. Underneath were the words Aquitani, Belgae & Celts. I read them aloud.

"Three tribes of Gaul in Julius Caesar's day. Why?" Sheila was changing Number Four's diaper. She'd always been a history buff.

"They're on the bottom of this box. You get Gallic breast milk bags?"

She laughed. "No, silly. I'm just a loyal shopper."

"You're Polish, married to an Englishman. If you can even count that, since you're both like fourth generation Americans at least."

Sheila looked over her shoulder and gave me a "duh" look. "That's the baby products division of Gaultier International, idiot. Amy's dad's company?"

"He imports milk bags from France?"

"I doubt it." She turned back to the diaper situation. "That's his logo. Duh, Gaultier—three parts of the Gauls. Get it? He's just proud of his heritage."

"I thought he was an importer and exporter."

"Sure, he is. But he's almost as big as Proctor & Gamble. He's got a lot of different businesses. One of them covers a lot of baby products. We buy his company's generics, too."

"Generics?"

She looked over her shoulder again. "You sure you should be out of bed so soon after delivering? Generic drugs, idiot."

I stared at her. "Oh, my God."

CHAPTER 46

I LOOKED AROUND. Worth a shot. "Com on!"

"Yes, Commander Martini?" Gladys sounded tired of hearing from me. I almost couldn't blame her.

"Two things. I need someone to come and collect the incredible number of bags of breast milk I just squeezed out, get them into a freezer, and make sure that whoever has Jamie can get them as needed."

"Not really Security's job, but, as always, we'll humor you. What else?"

"I need to know where Herbert Gaultier, of Gaultier International and a whole lot of other companies is, and I need to know immediately. Oh, and I'm leaving this bathroom. Have whoever's coming to get the milk step on it."

Two big Security A-Cs came in, looking embarrassed, carrying a cooler. I gave them the milk. "Take care of that, freeze it in a safe container pronto—safer than this cooler, by the way."

"Yeah, that stuff's worth its weight in gold." Sheila shook her head. "I can't believe what you do for a living now."

The Security guys left, carrying my tonnage of milk. "It's going to get more unbelievable fast." I dug my phone out of my purse. Called Jeff. Nothing. Managed not to curse, only because Jamie was in my other arm.

I needed the team assembled fast. Considered my options. Dialed. "Lorraine, Code Red. Need you to get all of Airborne that's in the facility into a conference room in the library, pronto. Make sure we have med kits."

"On it."

I looked around, then remembered I had their numbers programmed. Dialed again. "Abby, need you and Mimi to find me like now. We're at Code Red."

"Already picked up your panic, we're heading to you now. Have your mother with us, by the way."

"Love how you think."

"Mimi already tried to call Chuck, no answer."

Managed not to curse again. "Yeah, welcome to DEF-CON Worse."

"This is that field situation Chuck and Jeff were trying to keep us out of, right?"

"Got it in one." I could see them now and hung up. We were near one of the larger conference rooms, and I headed inside, Sheila and Number Four trailing me. Mom and the Gower girls came in, the rest of the team right on their heels. Pregnant women can't move all that fast, but even going at the slow version of hyperspeed, an A-C is faster than most humans.

Hughes was last in, and he shut the door. Happily, the room was soundproofed, and the noise level went down considerably. Did the latest nose check after everyone was seated. All five of my pilots, all three of my girls at various pregnancy levels, Brian, Abigail, Naomi, Sheila and Number Four, and my mother. Not enough A-Cs by far, but what we were going to have to go with.

Mom got up and took Jamie from me. She looked me up and down. "Clearly you've had the best pregnancy recovery in the world."

I noted that the team were all staring at me. "Yeah, okay. I'm not supposed to tell you, per Chuckie and Jeff. But—"

"You've been affected by whatever the drug was they gave Jeff, because it's in his DNA and so in Jamie, and Jamie was in you." Lorraine said this as though it was obvious. It was, but everyone else had been shocked.

"Um, yeah. Did your mom tell you?"

She snorted. "Remember what Claudia and I were doing when we met you?" She'd always been buxom, but pregnancy really agreed with her. Unlike me, her blue eyes really sparkled, her blonde hair looked luxurious, and she glowed, even while snorting at me.

"Erm . . ." Sort of not so much.

"We were on the Exoskeleton team," Claudia answered for me, managing to look as good as Lorraine and managing to also remain almost as willowy as normal. She was a brunette, her brown eyes were freaking dewy, and her hair practically glistened. "We were trying to figure out why and how the parasites turned a human into a superbeing without killing the human. One figures that out by doing work at a genetic level."

I comforted myself with the reminder that they were my best A-C girlfriends and maybe I'd look that good the next time around, now that I had all the Surcenthumain doing its thing inside me.

That I could keep on considering having more when Jamie wasn't a week old probably wasn't so much desire as having heard Jeff discuss "lots of kids" from the first hours I'd known him and constantly thereafter. He'd programmed me to plan on having an entire litter of children and, apparently, I was quite receptive to it, too.

Thought about a little Jeff again. Then thought about big Jeff and how he was in mortal peril and dragged my mind back to present terrors. I'd thought it was pregnancy that had made my mind wander. Wondered now if it was the drug. Forced myself to not think about it right now.

"Oh, right. Fine. Um. Great. Everyone says I'm not going to die early from it." Well, I wasn't thinking about it too much.

"I think it might extend your life, actually." Lorraine had her Dazzler scientific mind tuned to high.

Mom coughed. "You mind explaining that for the laypeople in the room?"

"I'm Wolverine with boobs, Mom." I didn't add that I didn't have the claws. For all I knew, they were coming.

Every human did the same thing—went bolt upright, leaned back, considered, nodded, and then relaxed. "Great. So, what's the situation? You didn't call us all in here to share that your comic book fascination has once again paid off." My mother's sarcasm knob went well past eleven. Then again, she wasn't crying. I was good with the sarcasm.

"Alpha Team, with the addition of Kevin, Melanie, Emily, Amy, and Michael, are pretty much in life-threatening danger they aren't prepared for."

"So," Jerry said. "Routine. By the way, looking great,

Kitty. Love the way you're filling out that top." I really felt Jerry and Jeff had somehow been separated at birth.

"The usual elaborate plans intersecting on top of us?" Lorraine asked.

Claudia gave a mirthless chuckle. "I'm putting money on it."

Did a very fast recap of everything that had happened. "So Alpha Team's working under the assumption we have our standard megalomaniac trying to take over the world while at the same time we have everyone's favorite Purity of the Race proponents doing their thing in support of said megalomaniac. But, sadly, the actual elaborate ruse is different."

"How so?" Lorraine asked. "Seems pretty clear they wanted guinea pigs."

"Yeah. So why Alpha Team as said piggies? I mean, no one will notice that Jeff and Christopher are dead, right? No human would notice Chuckie's disappearance? No biggie, grab the top dudes and go to town."

"You think it's like Florida?" Hughes asked. "You think a human's in charge?"

"In charge of what?" Randy asked. He was absently stroking the back of Claudia's neck. I missed Jeff. "The elaborate ruse or something else?"

"Amy is the ruse."

"You think she's the mole after all?" Mom sounded sad.

"No, I think she's been an unwitting pawn. See, it's too freaking convenient. Amy's sent off to do some weird work thing and finds a connection to a known but supposedly defunct terrorist organization as well as information that says the heads of the P.T.C.U. and ETD are targets. Then she's allowed to escape with this information, is given a number to call by a guy you and Chuckie cannot find, alive or dead, is pursued by double digits, manages to get rescued just in time."

"Sounds like she's the mole." Mom, like Chuckie, really was into the mole idea.

"No, it sounds like she's a patsy. And she's been set up by someone who knew exactly what she'd do, every step of the way."

CHAPTER 47

SHEILA SAT UP STRAIGHT. Her eyes were wide. Interesting—then again, she'd been in the bathroom with me and, clearly, she was still Miss Insightful. "Kitty . . . is this going where I think it's going?"

"Probably."

Everyone looked at Sheila. She shrugged. "I have four kids, but that doesn't make me a moron."

"I think they're waiting for you to share, Sheila."

"Oh." She blushed, then swallowed and looked at me. "You think it's someone in Amy's dad's company, don't you?"

"Not someone."

Mom dug her phone out. "Where is your target? What? Why wasn't I informed? Fine." She covered the phone. "Herbert Gaultier is in D.C."

"No, he's not. He's in Paris. He went into the Centaurion Embassy, didn't he? Which means he's gone to wherever they took Amy and Michael." Mom went back to the phone.

"Amy's own father? Kitty, how could that be?" Sheila sounded horrified.

"He doesn't plan to hurt Amy, at least I'm sure that's what he's told himself. He doesn't care about the rest of us. Maybe he would if his first wife, the one who knew me and you, was still alive. But she's not. We haven't seen him since her funeral. We're not important to him at all. Plus, whoever's behind this knew my closest friends from high school but has left my closest girlfriend from college completely alone, and said girlfriend is a senator's Girl Friday. So whoever's behind it only knows me from the high school years, which is why your family was targeted, Sheila. You're a weakness for me *and* for Amy. And, let's face it, there's nothing wrong with capitalism. Until you find the most amazing drug in the world."

"But what's he going to do with it?" Randy asked. "Having it's useless unless you have some use for it."

Mom hung up. "Good lord. Yes, Gaultier went to the Embassy. No idea of why my team thought that wasn't something to warn me about."

"You told them to guard him, he wasn't in danger."

"Kitty, we need more info." Hughes had his eyes closed. "I know you usually do this with James, but I'll do my best, because I think I see where you're going with it. But if you're going to bring down an influential businessman, and figure out where the hell he is, you have to have more than a logo." My flyboys—great-looking and brilliant. Loved them all.

I took a deep breath and let it out. "Okay. What is standard procedure for a known threat? Exactly what we did. Total lockdown, pull everyone, and I do mean everyone, in. Teams will inch out and about, but carefully. Only team likely to be out without a lot of permission is Alpha."

Just as I'd confirmed for the C.I.A. folks the other day. I wasn't sure if they were involved, but I was willing to accept only one coincidence per Operation, and Alicia being in Paris when this all started was it. Not that I had a clue yet if they were actually involved, had shared this info, or had an alternate plan running we'd find out about along the way. The fun truly never stopped for us.

"So it's the usual destroy Alpha team ploy. Not seeing a connection. Or a motive." Walker's eyes weren't closed, but I could tell he was willing to see if he could figure it out before Hughes. Healthy competition was never a problem. It was the unhealthy competition I was worried about.

"No," Joe said. He was standing behind Lorraine, rubbing her shoulders. "Because there are easier ways to get rid of them than having them in lockdown. Besides, look at Kitty. It's the drug that's the root of this plan, right?"

"I'm pretty damn sure, yeah."

"But if they don't want to destroy Alpha, what do they want to use the drug for?" Jerry sounded thoughtful.

"Florida was a lot of plans, but they all led back to the same guy." Brian was getting in on the act. Serene was on his lap. I stared at her.

"What, Kitty?" She looked down. "Is there something on me?"

"No, in you. In me, you, Jamie, Jeff, and Christopher." I looked at my mother. "A superhuman, superalien drug. Mom, what would that be worth on the black market?"

She snorted. "You wouldn't have to black market it. Every government would pay billions to get their hands on it. The bidding war would be insane." Mom looked at me, and her face drained of color.

Hughes' eyes opened. "Oh, shit. Well, there's the motive." He looked at me. "But why all the elaborate steps?"

"Originally? To get us out of the way and set up the Diplomatic Corps to oust the Sovereign Pontifex or insist he demand the patent rights be turned over to Gaultier International or whoever the Corps thinks is in charge. Now? Well, now they have the hostages they need to force the patent-holders to give up those rights."

I looked around, everyone looked blank. "Okay, here's what's going on and why. The stuff with Amy was to get us all herded into place. The stuff with Sheila was to enforce our fears and pull in anyone else who might still be loose. This would have worked great if Tim's girlfriend hadn't been in Paris waiting for a standby flight."

"But Tim's captured, and that's why Alpha's in trouble." Lorraine sounded confused.

"Tim being out is the only reason we know what's going on."

Hughes nodded. "They were never after any of us originally, they just wanted us out of the way, right?"

"Originally, I think so, yeah. See, the one thing no one ever asked during Operation Drug Addict was who, exactly, made the Club Fifty-One drug cocktail they gave to Serene and Jeff."

"It was based on drugs we were working on for NASA," Serene said.

"Based on. Movies based on books have an original book they look at. So, who put the drug together the first time, in the combination and strength to affect Serene and Jeff biologically?"

"Wasn't NASA," Brian said.

"I'm betting it was Gaultier International, or some subsidiary branch."

"Not sure, but Alfred said—" Brian stopped speaking and looked at me in horror. "Oh, my God."

CHAPTER 48

"YOU THINK ALFRED IS INVOLVED in this?" Mom sounded shocked.

"No. Alfred holds the freaking patents on everything the A-Cs do out of NASA. Because the Martinis are royalty, right? But when they got here, they landed in Capitalism Unlimited. I'm sure it was an easy decision, since Alfred already had scientific aptitude, to send the patents through him—meant he would maintain wealth and, for this country, that would equal our version of royalty. Jeff said they use his family's home as one of their showcases for humans. The Embassy is another, I'm sure."

"They have everyone Alfred would care about." Walker sounded sick.

"Not quite, but damned close. Okay, listen. The person behind this knew not only Amy well, but *me* well. Well enough to know what my mother and oldest male friend did for a living. Well enough to know where and whom I was working with. And well enough to predict most of what was going on. But *not* well enough to know who my college or work friends might be."

"Tim's the mole?" Mom was starting to sound like Chuckie. Tried not to worry about him, and Jeff, and the others. Failed utterly.

"Mom, for the last and final time, there *is* no mole! The mole idea *is* the elaborate ruse, just like I said to Chuckie, Jeff, and James, geez, only earlier today." Felt like it had been days ago. "The mole idea focused everyone away from what's really going on."

"Which is?" Lorraine asked.

"Chuckie's always said that there are only two reasons why anyone pulls the elaborate ruse—to gain money or power. This is a money grab, the first one we've ever gone through together, which is why it didn't dawn on anyone. There is no mole—there are people set up to look like moles. And this elaborate plan has been in effect since, at the latest, we went through Operation Drug Addict. The person who created the original Club Fifty-One drug, which has become Surcenthumain, realized way back then that this was a freaking gold mine, as long as it didn't kill the users. Trust me, when we have time to research it, we'll discover that Herbert Gaultier is the one who created the right drug cocktail or that the flunky who worked for him who created it is dead."

"But the operation in Florida was almost a year and a half ago. Why is this happening now?" Claudia asked.

"Perfecting drugs takes time," Mom said. "Think about how long it takes the FDA to approve anything."

"But imagine if you can speed it up by testing it on A-Cs who are close enough to humans to breed just fine with them, but different enough that they have regenerative properties. Jeff was the target for Operation Drug Addict—both Leventhal Reid's target and our current Head Fugly's target. If they'd succeeded in killing Jeff and/or the rest of Alpha Team, no worries, there were all those thousands of Club Fifty-One loons to test the drug on—who cares if some of them die? Just don't want the soldiers from the country that wins the bidding war to die."

"So Jeff and Serene were the test subjects?" Lorraine pursed her lips. "That's not enough."

"They used Christopher and observed him somehow. His talents are so strong it's frightening. But healthwise he seems fine. Meaning that you can give this stuff to people a lot, and it'll just make them more super. Meaning that you can sell it to every country out there, and have repeat buyers, and so forth."

Hughes looked at me. "You're a test subject, too. So's Jamie."

I nodded. "Gaultier would have known I was married to

an A-C—Amy would have told him Jeff's name, somewhere in there, I'm sure."

"He sent a gift, remember?" Mom's voice was like ice. "A silver frame."

"Oh, wow. So that's how they were spying on Christopher."

"If there was a camera in the frame, wouldn't it have been spying on you?" Mom sounded like she was worried the drugs had affected my brain.

"Yes, except that we gave it to Christopher because we liked the ones we got from Sheila and Roger better, and we only have so much space in the Lair. It's the frame on Christopher's nightstand." I chose to save the anger and hatred—I was sure I'd need it later, in a big way.

"So, who or what is the target?" Jerry asked. "I can buy all the rest of it, but not why the Diplomatic Corps is involved or why Tim and the others were kidnapped."

"And how does Ronaldo Al Dejahl fit into this?" Mom asked.

"He's the other elaborate ruse."

CHAPTER 49

EVERYONE STARED AT ME. "Come again?" Jerry said.

"There is no Ronaldo Al Dejahl. There is some guy playing him. Perhaps the same actor who played the older businessman who gave Amy the old covert ops number and was 'murdered' in front of her."

Naomi shook her head. "Clarence firmly believes this man exists."

"How do you know?"

She shrugged. "I'm looking into his mind right now. He believes."

"Bet the Diplomatic Corps believes, too. You know, Centaurion's not the only group with lobbyists. I'm sure Gaultier has a lobbyist or two, and I'm sure they've become good pals with the A-C Diplomatic Corps."

"Probably," Mom said. "I've mentioned I can't stand Robert Coleman, right?"

"At my wedding, yeah. I hate his wife a lot more. Look, they may be A-Cs, and maybe they've learned how to fake it better than the rest of them, but the entire race literally cannot lie, at least believably to humans." I knew Chuckie disagreed, and I also knew he was probably right, but now wasn't the time to focus us all on finding the A-C liars, since it was clear to me that we knew who the main ones were anyway.

"It makes them vulnerable to lies, though," Walker said slowly. "I mean, look at the Pontifex."

"Richard. We need him. Gladys, any sign of Herbert Gaultier?"

"No, Commander. Which is why I haven't alerted you. We're still searching. Should I assume you want me to send the Pontifex to you?"

"Yes, thanks. Tell him it's extremely urgent."

"He already knows. He's been on the com with me since your call from the bathroom."

"Nice. Mister White, please hyperspeed down here."

"At your beck and call, Missus Martini." No sooner had his voice died on the speaker than he was at the door.

"Why is it you hyperspeed faster than the Security guys?"

"I'm in better shape. I told you when we first met, I can perform at active agent levels."

"Good, we may need you to come along with us."

"Kitty, are you crazy?" It looked like Hughes was speaking for everyone. "Every scheme is designed to put the Pontifex in danger. He was already at risk, remember?"

"Well, see, the thing is—"

"As Commander Martini has been saying, this is an elaborate plan to make billions of dollars selling a dangerous and severely undertested drug." White sounded calm, which was good. I wondered if he was clear on how much danger his son and nephew were in and figured he was. "As such, I was never in danger. You all were supposed to think I was in danger, so you would continue to work to find the nonexistent mole."

"Mister White, thank God you've come."

He nodded. "I've also already alerted Alfred. As of yet, he has not received a request for patent rights."

"Where are his daughters and, more importantly, their husbands?"

"Sylvia is here, and Clarence, as you know, is in solitary confinement. Jonathan is with Marianne at the Martini estate. The other three told their wives they were at the Embassy."

"So they're either hostages or in on it."

Naomi closed her eyes. "Can't get it out of Clarence. He's really into the purity of the race thing, though. He seems to believe Al Dejahl is going to rescue him." She opened her eyes. "Right after Al Dejahl kills Richard and takes over as the new Sovereign Pontifex."

"Wow, usually they want to kill Richard to just not have a Pontifex any more. Mister White, you're moving up in the elaborate ruse world."

"Truly, I'm thrilled. However, this entire plot seems to me to be centered around you, Missus Martini."

"As flattering as it won't be, why so?"

"The threats were all to people in your orbit. I am in that orbit, let me remind you."

I thought about it. "Gladys? What do you think?"

"Beg pardon? You want my opinion?"

"Yeah. Because you're sort of our A-C God in the Machine."

"I'd suggest calling the real one."

I looked at Naomi and Abigail. "Duh." Said in unison. Too busy to care.

I closed my eyes and concentrated. ACE, can you hear me?

Yes, Kitty, ACE is here. Please hurry.

Hurry to where, ACE? I think we know what's going on, but we don't know where you all are.

ACE is not with the others.

What do you mean? Where's Paul?

Paul and ACE are together. They attacked Paul and ACE first, because of ACE, he wailed. Paul is unconscious, and ACE must stay with Paul or Paul will die.

ACE, they're the evil ones, not you. Don't blame yourself. Where do they have you and Paul stashed?

In an airless chamber.

Managed not to scream, either out loud or in my head. Why?

So ACE would be unable to help the others.

ACE, where are you all? Are you in Paris?

Not any longer. ACE and Paul are in something that is moving. It stops, then starts again.

And the others?

The only thing ACE and Paul saw before the attack was a circle with letters in it.

A-B-C?

Yes.

I'm on my way, ACE. Hang on.

I opened my eyes. "They attacked Paul first because of ACE. He's doing a Houdini, so ACE can only concentrate on him."

"Pardon?" White asked, but the others looked just as confused.

"Sheila, look at the milk bag box. I need the address for that division of Gaultier International." I looked around. "I have to save Paul. The rest of you have to get to Jeff and the others."

"Kitty, you can't be serious." Mom sounded as though I'd just suggested I was going to shack up with a drug addicted car thief instead of go to college.

"Mom, I promised ACE when we first found him that I'd never desert him. If I don't get to them, then Paul dies, and ACE will die, too. We need ACE."

"I have the address, Kitty. It's in France, I think it's outside Paris."

"Makes sense." Since I was pretty sure Paul and ACE were on a train or the Metro.

"I'm going with you," Naomi said.

"Me, too." Abigail stood up.

"No. You two have to find the others. They're most likely at the Gaultier location, but I have no idea if they've been moved or not. You two have the strongest talents, since Jeff and Christopher aren't here."

"You can't go alone, Kitty." Mom sounded like she was going to stop me physically.

"She won't. I'll accompany her." White sounded very calm. "I would like to request that the three pregnant women stay here as well."

"I agree. Look, before the arguments start, if they catch you, your babies are going to be experimental fodder. Let's avoid that, okay? Mom, you're staying put. If something happens to me and Jeff, I want Jamie with you and Dad, okay? Living will, witnessed by everyone here."

Mom looked as though she was trying not to cry. "We thought we'd lost you earlier this week."

"And during Operations Fugly, Drug Addict, and Invasion. Face it, Mom, I'm the best there is at thinking like the loons, and that means I'm in danger. So what? Everyone's in danger right now. ACE and Paul don't have a lot of time. I don't know what time the others have, but we don't know what that PPB net will do if Paul dies with ACE inside him."

White coughed. "Actually, we do." Everyone stared at him. "The net will collapse and destroy the Earth." There was dead silence for a few moments.

"Okeydokey! Richard and I are going to go off and save the world, while the rest of you, you know, save everyone else we happen to love. Chop, chop, time's a wastin'. Oh, and Sheila, welcome to my world."

She shook her head. "In a weird way, it's kind of nice to know Chuck was right all along as opposed to totally deranged."

"Yeah, let's hope he's still alive." I went to my mother and took Jamie. I held her as tightly as I could, which wasn't as tightly as I wanted to. "You be good for your Nana Angela, okay, Jamie-Kat? Mommy has to go find and save Uncle Paul and your fairy godfather ACE and then, hopefully, everyone else can find Daddy and save him and everybody else we love who's in danger."

I kissed her and looked at her face. I wondered if I'd ever see it again. She blinked her big, blue eyes, and something flashed in them. I saw a train car with a human-sized box in it. I also saw the words on the side. She blinked again, and I saw a Gothic structure I, and any other person who'd ever taken a day of French, knew well.

I kissed her again. "You are such a good baby. Mommy loves you *so* much." I handed her back to Mom. "Serene, please look into Jamie's eyes if one of us calls and needs help."

"Okay, Kitty. Why?"

"Because Jamie knows where everyone is."

CHAPTER 50

WE HYPERSPED TO THE launch area. I was able to keep up with everyone without holding onto an A-C. I felt a tiny bit of nausea, but nothing like I was used to. I had a little trouble stopping, but White grabbed me before I barreled into or through a gate.

"Okay, Gladys, where did Jeff have you send them?"

"We marked on Captain Crawford."

"How?"

"All personnel have transmitters installed. His went live again just before Commander Martini requested location."

"I have a transmitter?" Jeff hadn't told me about this.

White sighed. "Yes, Missus Martini. Jeffrey had it put into you after, as you call it, Operation Drug Addict."

"When? How?"

"Kitty, is now the time?" Hughes' voice was strained. "We all have them, they aren't dangerous."

"Who knew to unscramble just before Jeff wanted a location?"

"Missus Martini," White said patiently, "I believe we agree we've been infiltrated? I thought the goal was to save our people in peril before we hunted said infiltrators down."

"Fine, fine. So, they got Amy and Michael and realized they wouldn't be working alone—frankly, realized that neither was an active agent and so they were the decoys for Alpha Team. So they let Tim's sensor go live, however they scramble and unscramble, so that Alpha could find them easily, either because they were advised or just because their timing worked out."

"Makes sense," Jerry said. "I'm betting on advised, by the way. So, where are we going? Same mark?"

"No. That's another trap point. That's how they hit Paul—they knew they'd be coming and had some kind of weapon or gas or whatever that got him. For all we know, they got all of them. ACE has to focus on keeping Paul alive in an airless chamber."

"Oh, that's what you meant by Houdini." Walker sounded relieved. "Makes more sense now."

"Whatever." I looked to the A-Cs manning the gate calibrations. "We need a gate to send everyone but me and Mister White to Notre Dame Cathedral in Paris. Make sure they land either outside or on the top where the gargoyles are." Hands started spinning at hyperspeed—I could watch them, and it didn't make me sick.

"Why?" Naomi asked. "Why not land where the others are?"

"Because I just know they're in Notre Dame, not where. Outside means they can't catch you instantly, and they're inside somewhere. Christopher was seeing Tim and the others inside a big room."

"Is there a dungeon in Notre Dame?" Joe asked. "I've never been there."

"I thought it was join the Navy, see the world?"

"We joined the Navy and have gotten to see other worlds," Randy said. "We're okay with that, of course."

"Good to know."

"I don't think there are dungeons, Kitty," Brian said. "And, remember, we're arriving in the day there, early morning, I think."

"Why are they in a tourist spot?" Jerry asked. "That seems stupid."

"I have no idea. As I say all the time, I don't make up these plans, I just have to foil them. Stay in touch; stay together if at all possible. Girls, remember that none of the guys can move at hyperspeed, so you have three guys each to keep somewhat safe." They nodded. Naomi took Joe, Randy, and Brian, and Abigail took Jerry, Hughes, and Walker.

"Gate to Notre Dame exterior is ready, Commander Martini," the A-C in charge of the bigger gate said.

"Be careful, you guys."

"Have guns, med kits, and two cute A-C girls, will travel," Jerry said with a grin. Then the eight of them stepped through.

"Okay, need a gate for me and Mister White, going through together. We need to land on a moving object."

"Difficult, Commander," the gate A-C handling our transfer said. He was young, but then again, a lot of the active agents were. He also looked vaguely familiar.

"Wow, really? Don't care. Make it work, make it so, do it now. We need to land on the Transilien Paris-Lyon. It makes stops, but I'm not betting our luck will be any good, so figure it's between stations right now. Move it or we all die within, I'd guess, fifteen minutes."

"Transmitting train stats to you now," Gladys' voice came over the com. The A-C looked at something on the floating info board near his head and started calibrating.

I hooked my purse over my neck. "I think, under the circumstances, we want to be very sure we stay together, Mister White."

"Just out of curiosity, why do you call me Mister White whenever you're in an active situation?"

I shrugged. "Makes me feel more official, I guess."

"Whatever works. They're after you, you know."

"Yeah, I figure you're right. Why do you think, though?"

He sighed. "You're the real test case. They knew it wasn't killing Serene, so they knew the slow method worked. They couldn't kill Jeffrey with a massive dosage, and we found the antidote, or at least the counter. So they already knew how it would affect A-Cs. My guess is that they still believed Christopher was in love with you. Get him insane enough, have him kidnap you and bring you to them. Something along those lines."

"Maybe. Do you think they knew Jamie would be affected and that it would affect me?"

"No idea. If I were a risk taker who was also scientific enough to create this drug in the first place, I'd bet on the side of yes."

"You know, you really should do more fieldwork, Mister White."

"I have a suspicion I'm about to do quite a lot right now, Missus Martini."

"Gate is ready, Commander. Do you want a team to accompany you and the Pontifex?" The way the A-C asked, I knew he wanted me to say yes.

"No. We don't need cannon fodder. They're killing the guys who aren't big shots. Let's keep our grunts safe, and let the folks in charge do the fighting, okay?"

The A-C gave me a long look. I looked back. He looked upset, in a quiet way, but still, upset, worried. He was working a gate, which meant he didn't have any A-C talents. I usually didn't see a lot of emotion out of the gate A-Cs; they were part of the Security team, trained to stay cool under pressure. But there was one gate agent who was really aware of when the Commanders went through and was awed by our presence and standard politeness. I knew because his brothers had told me.

"You have immediate family involved in this, don't you?" I asked. He nodded. I took a shot. "William and Wayne?"

He swallowed hard. "Yes. Good luck, Commander. Please come home safely." He didn't add that he wanted me to bring his brothers home safely, too. He didn't have to.

"We'll do our best."

"They have to go, now," Gladys said urgently.

White and I didn't hesitate. He took my hand, and we ran through the gate.

CHAPTER 51

SADLY, GOING THROUGH A GATE still made me sick to my stomach. Figured.

Then again, it might have made me sick because we landed on the top of a speeding train. "Down!" White pulled me and we fell onto the roof, just before we went whooshing under a bridge.

"Love their freaking timing!" I had to shout, the train was going so fast.

"Can we get inside?"

I looked around. No bridge, lovely countryside. Stood up, helped White up, and then realized we were in the middle of the train. Had no idea where Gower was from here. "Hang on." I got back on my stomach and crawled to the side of the car.

Thankfully White grabbed my ankles as the train curved, and I started to slide off. Got an interesting view of the side of the car. Wasn't the car Jamie had shown me. Indicated White should pull me back.

"Well, that was fun, and I have no idea where to go." Remembered I'd been a hurdler. Still no sign of a bridge. Got up, ran to the end of the car, hurdled the scary open space, landed, managed not to twist an ankle. White showed up next to me, we did the look over the side thing again.

"I think we're going the wrong way." Turned, ran, hurdled, kept on running, hurdled again, got to the next car. White arrived, over the side. Stood up, flung ourselves down. Reminded myself to look for freaking bridges before standing again.

"I think they're toward the front."

"Presumably the cargo is stored there. Lead on, Missus Martini."

"You okay on the roof? I think we'll go faster."

"I live for danger and excitement."

"Mister White, you're learning how to lie."

"No, Missus Martini, I just enjoy sarcasm as much as the rest of you. Will our passage alert the other passengers?"

"Don't care. Besides, I haven't seen many when I've looked in. For all we know this train was commissioned specifically. Or else everyone's up front or something."

He nodded. "We'll cross that metaphorical bridge when we come to it. Presuming a real one doesn't take our heads off first."

Looked ahead, no bridge. At least we were running toward the front, so we could see if a bridge was coming.

This was a long train, naturally, because our luck wouldn't let us be on a two-car vehicle unless it was hurtling down the side of a mountain. Did the run, hurdle, run thing over and over again. Stopped to check a couple of times and felt pretty sure we were heading for the car closest to the engine. Saw a few people scattered in the cars. They seemed unperturbed by the sound of pounding feet on the roof or my face staring at them upside down. Either things like this happened all the time, they were in the employ of Gaultier Enterprises but not paid enough to take an interest, or Parisians were really as blasé and "been there, done that" as they were reputed to be.

Only had to fling ourselves down for bridges a couple more times, got to grab each other once each to keep from falling off when the train curved, and I only missed one jump. White was, fortunately, right behind me, so he hit me in the air and we both hit the top of the next car. Rolled to the side, but I managed to grab the air filtration unit on the top, and he grabbed my purse before he went over the side. I was definitely stronger than normal, because I pulled him back to me without any issue.

"Are we there yet, Missus Martini?"

"I think so." There were only two cars left, the one we were on and one in front of it. Stayed on our stomachs and scooted to the back of this car. Thankfully, there were railings to hold onto between the car connections. Unhappily, there were no ladders. It so totally figured I didn't even bother to complain about it.

Grabbed a railing, did a sort of flip and landed on the platform. The door was locked. I looked through the little window—yep, luggage. Did a Jeff and wrenched the door open. Was so impressed with myself.

"Missus Martini, could you go inside so I could get off the roof?"

"Oh, sure, sorry." Trotted in. White joined me. "Look for a Paul-sized box."

"You take the front, I'll take the back."

"Works for me." I ran to the front. "There's no door leading to the next car."

"I anticipate another roof frolic with great joy, Missus Martini."

"Yeah, I'm not seeing anything big enough either." White was picking things up and putting them back. I was ransacking. Whatever worked. There was nothing in here that was big enough.

We met in the middle. "Next car, Missus Martini?"

Had a thought and slammed my foot on the floor. It made a funny sound. "Hidden compartments."

We bent down and ripped the carpet up. Superstrength was awesome. Found the hatch, White ripped it up. I got in. "Wow, absolutely nothing in here."

"Good practice for your new career in destruction, I'm sure."

"Ha ha, funny. Let's get to the other car."

Raced out, stood there trying to figure out how to get onto the roof. White picked me up and lifted me over his head. Okay, that way worked. Had to duck because of another stupid bridge.

"Can you scream a bit less loudly?"

"No, not that I've ever noticed."

"Yes, true. You know, babies can be awakened by loud noises."

Crawled onto the roof, stayed on my stomach, put the hand down, pulled White up. "You know, we live in the Lair. Unless you're all listening in on the intercom, I can't believe our sex life is disturbing anyone anymore."

"Just mentioning it, parent to parent. Shall we?"

Checked for bridges, cursed, ducked, got up, ran, hurdled, didn't miss or fall this time. Turned around to see White lower himself from the other end of the last car. Show off. He'd already ripped the door open and was inside by the time I got down.

I was really surprised, but there were no goons in here waiting to attack us. Just a lot of big boxes. "Great."

White slammed his foot on the floor. It sounded like the other car had. "Let's err on the side of overly suspicious."

We ripped the floor up. There was one big box in this secret compartment. "You a betting man, Mister White?"

"No. I assume it's rigged?"

"I'd think so." I had no experience with how to defuse a bomb or a booby trap. "You see anything?"

"Not that I can spot."

I pulled out my phone. "Mom, need help with what could be a bomb."

"Nice to hear you're still alive for the moment. What's the target?" Brought her up to speed with what it looked like. "Have Richard check the other boxes, just in case. This could be the decoy."

"Good point." Told White, and he started opening things at hyperspeed. Come to think of it, we'd been doing everything at what I'd call slow hyperspeed. I hadn't noticed. At all. "So, what do I do?"

"Look around the box. You're looking for anything unusual or that seems wrong."

Climbed down into the hatch. It was pretty cramped with the big box in it. "It's metal, that's all I've got." Mom cursed. "Hey, not in front of Jamie!"

"Serene has her."

"Tell her to ask Jamie if there's something that's set to hurt her Uncle Paul and fairy godfather ACE. Use those words."

Mom sighed, but relayed my request to Serene. I heard voices. "Huh. Well, if we're to trust that your child is now the all-seeing one, there's a gas that will release when you unlock the box. It's deadly, of course."

"Of course. Okay, thanks, Mom, I'll call back. If, you know, I'm still alive." Hung up. "Mister White! Need the muscles. We need to get this box up out of the hatch."

It was heavy, but A-Cs were strong and now so was I. I could tell I wasn't as strong as White yet, because I had a harder time with my end of the box. But there was no way I'd have been able to do anything if I hadn't been enhanced.

Managed to get the box out, but we had to flip it. "Not a problem. We need to place the top in the open door anyway." Explained the deadly gas thing.

White looked from box to doorway and back. "I don't believe we can do it, and still not take a full shot of the gas." He took a deep breath. "Please tell Christopher that I love him and, of course, forgive him for the addiction. Please tell Paul, should he survive, that I expect he'll make an excellent Pontifex."

I didn't like where this was heading. I looked at the box, on its side, the bottom facing me. For whatever reason, it reminded me of the Escalade that Reid had tried to kill me with. The one Jeff had flipped on its side. The one he'd ripped the undercarriage out of. "They said the gas would come out when we unlocked the box . . . not when we opened the box."

"Pardon?"

"Take a deep-ass breath and hold it, Mister White." I did, and then I slammed my fist into the bottom of the box.

CHAPTER 52

JEFF HAD NEVER MENTIONED that hitting things still hurt when you were an enhanced individual. Wished he had. However, my hand wasn't broken, and the box bottom was bending. I hit it again, and the seam along one side started to separate. Grabbed it and pulled.

The back of the metal box came off. No gas, at least, nothing I could see. Had to take another breath. White did, too. There was what looked like the bottom of a coffin in here. Hilarious sense of humor Gaultier and his goons had.

Slammed my hand into it, hit through the wood and landed on metal. Figured. A few more slams and I could rip the wood part off. A bit more and the metal gave. I pulled the bottom panel off and flung it away as Gower's big, heavy body rolled onto me.

I was slammed onto the floor of the hidden compartment. Gower wasn't moving. The fun just never stopped. I listened for heartbeats—faint, very faint, but there.

"He's alive, I think. Get him off me!"

"Working at it, Missus Martini." Gower was lifted off me. I helped White get him out of the compartment.

I got out, too, and looked around. "Where's the coffin?"

"I tossed it, just in case."

"Wow, seriously, consider going active. You rock, Mister White."

"I take that as a great compliment. Let's bring Paul back from the edge of death first, shall we?"

We didn't have a med kit with us, which was my oversight. What a surprise. White did the slam the hearts thing while I did the mouth-breathing thing. Managed not to wonder if Gower and Reader had ever seriously considered the whole going bi and adding me in thing, though, even scared, it took effort.

A few minutes of this and Gower started coughing. Coughing was good. No air for so long could mean brain damage, though, and that would be unbelievably bad.

Gower's eyes fluttered open. "Kitty? Richard?" He sounded shocked and confused. "Where are we?"

"God, am I glad you're not brain-dead."

"Nice to see you, too." Gower looked at White. "What's going on?" He blinked. "Everyone's in danger."

"We know, Paul," White said reassuringly. "You were in worse danger, however."

"How's ACE?"

Gower closed his eyes. "Relieved." He chuckled. "ACE says he knew Kitty would save us." His eyes opened. "You saved us over Jeff and James."

I shrugged. "Jeff trained me really well on that good of the many idea."

"Yeah. We were in a warehouse."

"That was Trap Point Two. Everyone's in Notre Dame, or they were last time I checked." We helped Gower to his feet.

"Why are they at one of the biggest tourism spots in France?"

"No idea." I blinked. "Oh, my God. I have a great idea. Well, it's a horrible idea, but still, great if you're a freaking megalomaniac looking to make a bazillion dollars."

"Mind sharing?" White put Gower's arm around his shoulders. "I feel okay, Richard."

"You don't look okay. Missus Martini? The horrible plan is, what?"

"I think they're going to test the drug in its gaseous form."

"Why?" Gower didn't sound convinced. "On a bunch of random tourists? Why would they want to do that? There's no control, no way to follow the test subjects."

"No idea. I'll find out when I get there."

"When we get there." Gower twitched and sighed. "ACE agrees with you."

"Good. Mister White, can you please call for another floater gate? I want Paul back in Dulce pronto." White pulled his phone out and dialed. "Interesting that we're still alone in this compartment."

White shrugged. "We were moving more quickly than I think you realized. It's doubtful that anyone in any individual car heard us long enough to worry about it. And clearly our enemies felt that even if we found Paul, we'd be killed while trying to rescue him."

"Good point. Let's keep Paul nice and safe and disappoint them completely."

"Kitty, I don't know why you want me, and ACE, to go back. I have to think we'd be able to help you."

"Paul, if you die while ACE is inside you, the PPB net will collapse and destroy the Earth. Call me crazy, but that makes you more indispensable than Richard."

"Oh." Gower looked shaken. "Maybe . . . maybe ACE shouldn't be in me?"

I hugged him. "ACE belongs in you, Paul. It'll be fine. I'll get everyone, foil the plan, and we'll be back before you know it." I was human, I could lie well.

"Or you could be killed." Couldn't lie that well, apparently. Gower shook his head. "I don't like it. You shouldn't be here at all."

"Could have let you die, voted against it. Take care of everyone, my baby in particular."

"I'll do my best."

There was something in the way he said it. "Um . . . are you really okay, Paul?"

"Yes."

Still something. Gower sounded doubtful and worried, and he wasn't looking at me. "Paul, what's wrong?"

He sighed. "ACE wants us to go back and go into isolation."

"Um, why?"

Gower took a deep breath. "ACE had to use . . . resources he's not . . . used to in order to keep me alive."

I thought about this. "Is ACE hurt?"

"Not like we'd consider hurt, but, yes. Drained, might be the better way of putting it. ACE needs to recharge, and he's saying in order to do that, I need to sleep, heavily."

Gower swallowed hard. "That means we can't help you, at least not until ACE is recovered at least somewhat."

I'd accepted from day one that ACE wasn't going to save us unless he could be settled in his collective consciousness about it. And when White had shared that if Gower died, the PPB net that was the "physical" part of ACE would collapse and destroy the Earth, that had made sense to me, but only because I thought ACE would be essentially trapped in the vessel that was Gower's body.

The idea that ACE, a superconsciousness, could be drained or damaged just like anyone else wasn't one that had ever occurred to me. Now that it had, I had to consciously force myself not to freak out.

I cleared my throat. "Ah, what about Jamie?"

Gower managed a weak smile. "ACE says that the blocks Jeff put in are protecting her well enough. He also says that Christopher should wait to put in the imageering blocks until everyone's safely home again."

So that was why and how Jamie could actually tell me where everyone was—ACE wasn't muting her imageering powers, which, clearly, she had. I decided I could marvel about this, freak out about this, or get back to the business of saving the day and marvel and freak about everything at a later time. I went with the latter.

"Okay, we'll handle it. You get yourself and ACE back to the Science Center and into a nice isolation chamber pronto."

"Gate coming in a moment," White said.

I looked over to where he was standing. "Wow, I can see the gate. I mean, not some shimmering or trick of light, the real gate itself. Awesome. This drug's fab."

"Please, one addict on Alpha Team was enough," Gower muttered.

"Dude, I didn't shoot up, and I'm not ingesting more. I just like the results. Not all the lab rats get the cancer, you know."

Gower looked at me. "That may be the test, at Notre Dame."

"Yeah, good point. I'll keep my supereyes peeled. Love to all, have medical check you over while in isolation or something, and let us know when you and ACE are feeling better." I didn't add that I hoped this would be soon. Healing took however long it took, and wishing it would go faster never sped anything up—I had lots of experience with Jeff in isolation to know that by now.

"Paul, go through now," White said. Gower hugged me, nodded to White, who was still on his phone, then walked through the gate. "Good, thank you. We would like to go to Notre Dame now. Oh, really? Interesting. Then, land us elsewhere. Perfect." He looked at me. "The team has been, as near as Gladys can tell, captured. No idea of how. They landed in the square in front of the cathedral and went off the grid then."

"So, where are we going?"

White was back to his call. "Wonderful. Yes, going through together. Thank you." He hung up and took my hand, then we walked through the gate.

And out into a bathroom.

CHAPTER 53

AT LEAST, I THOUGHT it was a bathroom. It was a small, disgusting room with a hole in the tiled floor, and that was about it. The smell was horrifying, almost as bad as the smell of dead fugly. "Where, in God's name, are we? Besides the grossest exit point of my Centaurion career, and since I've been in a variety of Third World airports now, this is really saying a lot."

"Bathroom in a little café down the street from the cathedral." White edged us around the hole. "There are many times I'm thankful the Ancients landed in the United States."

"Dude, I am so with you. Let's get out of here."

Opened the door, walked out. No one even blinked at us. Paris was a lot like Vegas in that way—anything went.

I dragged us to the counter and ordered two chocolate croissants and two café au laits. In decent French. I mean, it had been years, but it's not hard to get that particular order out in native tongue. While we waited for our order, I forced White to take off his jacket and tie, which I used as an impromptu belt. Made him unbutton his shirt a bit and roll up the sleeves. Order arrived, White paid. Somehow, he had Euros, not dollars. I decided not to ask. Maybe he had his own personal A-C Elf.

We munched and sipped as we walked outside. "Not that I mind the snack, since I was a bit peckish, but why?"

"Everyone else barged in. Everyone else looked like a Centaurion operative, including Chuckie, since he seems to have adapted and wears an Armani suit all the time now. Which is freaky, in that sense."

"You look like a tourist who likes rock and roll. What do I look like now?"

I snuggled next to him. "My sugar daddy."

"I await Jeffrey's reaction with mild terror. Though I'm relieved the weather isn't too cold. However, this feels quite awkward."

"Pretend. Because I think the only way we're getting in there is if we look like tourists."

"Won't they recognize us?"

"Maybe. Maybe not. Not sure how they're identifying our agents, other than dress and showing up via a gate right where they expect us."

We took our time eating. Well, sort of. We were both hungry, so the croissants disappeared fast. Sipped the coffee while we looked around. "Missus Martini, do you spy what I spy?"

"Yeah. A tonnage of children in uniforms. It's school field trip day at Notre Dame, isn't it?"

"Looks that way. Meaning the best test subjects in the world are about to be infected."

"I agree. By the way, since we're going undercover and all, at least until we're blown, which, for us, could be in two seconds, call me Kathy and I'll call you Rick."

"Why?" He didn't sound thrilled about the nickname.

"Because everyone calls me Kitty, and no one calls you Rick. It's part of our supercool disguise, Rick honey."

White managed not to wince. "Are you sure people won't just assume, far more correctly, that I'm your father?"

"Rick, this is Paris, land of mistresses. It's different for A-Cs, I guess, but trust me—as long as I put my arm around your waist, you put your arm around my shoulders, and we act lovey, everyone will assume you're a typical cradle robber and I'm your sort of trophy wife."

"A quick brush of your hair might make that more believable."

"Wow, I see where Christopher's snark comes from." Pulled out my brush and did the hair thing. Noted I had all six Poofs with me. "Huh. Fluffy, Fuzzball, and Toby all did a runner. They're with us, Mister . . . ah, Rick."

"I see you're as comfortable with the subterfuge as I am . . . Kathy."

"You can call me honey, too. Just avoid 'baby' and maybe Jeff won't care."

"Truly, death by suffocation might be preferable. What is your thought about the Poofs?"

I considered them. "They like me best?"

"That I have always taken as a given."

"No guess beyond that. But, you know, have Poofs, will travel." I finished my coffee. "Ready to go visit the King of Gothic Architecture, Rick?"

"No." He stood up, took our cups and napkins and threw them away. Came back, helped me out of my chair. Carried his jacket in one hand over his back, put his other arm around my shoulders. I put mine around his waist. "How's this?"

"Honestly? You look like Timothy Dalton, only younger and hotter. Believe me, no woman's going to question why I'm with a guy old enough to be my father."

"No wonder Jeffrey was willing to do anything to marry you. My ego hasn't been this inflated since we first met you and you insinuated I was a male model."

I laughed and leaned up and kissed his cheek. "Hey, it's true." We strolled to the cathedral. It was hard to not just run like a crazy person, since I had no idea of what they were doing to whom but could pretty much bet that Jeff, Christopher, and Chuckie were going to be taking the brunt of it. However, we weren't captured yet, so maybe our plan was working, or at least not failing miserably.

Sauntered up to the ticket counter. No issues, White paid for the tickets, we got in line to go in. Because it was the end of December, there weren't too many tourists here, not like there would have been in summer. There were just tons and tons of kids. I didn't know how French schools worked, but in America, they would have all been on vacation.

I spotted what looked like a teacher and did my best. "Pardon, um . . . je suis Americaine, et . . . um . . ." It had been a lot easier to order the food.

She was younger, dark, and pretty, and she laughed. "I speak English, Madame."

"Oh, great. My husband and I were wondering, don't you have a holiday break for schools like we do?"

She nodded. "We do, but this was a special treat from one of our philanthropists. The children are getting a special tour, sweets, and other gifts. Because of his schedule, we had to agree to have everyone come today. The cathedral wouldn't close to the general public, but there aren't many tourists here at this time of year."

White and I exchanged a glance. "What a wonderful benefactor. Who is it?"

"Monsieur Ronaldo Al Dejahl. He runs several local and international companies."

"Ah, well, thanks for the info."

She nodded, then her class was called in. White and I were asked to wait in the nonexistent queue for the next free slots.

"I see you continue to be able to think like the megalomaniacs, Kathy."

"It's my gift, Rick. I wonder if they've spotted us yet."

The door girl came back. "Entré vous. You may go in."

We stepped through. Right behind the kids. A few other tourists raced up and were let in as well. I checked—they didn't look like anything but tourists.

I'd never been to Notre Dame, but I'd seen a lot of pictures, and Amy had sent a ton of shots of every single Paris landmark when she'd first gotten the job overseas. So I had a familiarity with where we were. I knew something was wrong, because we weren't going up the steps, which was what the brochure we'd gotten when we bought our tickets said we'd be doing. The idea was to get up to the top, look at the city and the gargoyles, then go back down. We weren't doing that.

We were instead going right into the main chamber of the cathedral. I scanned the room. Tons of children, adults scattered here and there, no one I recognized. "We paid to go up, right?"

"Right. Per the brochure, cathedral entrance is free."

"Then why are we in here?" I looked at the brochure. "There's an underground crypt," I murmured to White.

"That will be where everyone is." He looked around. "But do we go down there or evacuate here?"

"No idea. I don't think you and I can evacuate. We'd

have to be able to do the thing with the gases, and even if I were somehow capable of it, I have no idea of how to do it."

"And I have no implant." He moved us casually to the side. "How do we get to the crypt?"

I studied the brochure. "Great. I think we have to go outside again. It seems that the entrance is across the plaza."

"That may be, but there should be a way in there from here, too."

"Maybe, but I can't find it. Let's go. We have to get to the others before we save the kids, I think. Besides, it doesn't look like anything's happening yet." We went out the way we'd come in. The girl working the door looked shocked. "We wanted to go see the towers."

"The towers are closed right now." She didn't seem concerned that we were leaving.

"Okay. How do we get into the crypt?"

"It is closed today, too."

"Gee, honey, let's get our money back." I dragged White off. "Okay, so our people are in the crypt and they're going to gas the kids in the cathedral. I feel so stressed."

White held me back. "Look around."

I did. "Um, what am I looking for?"

"A way in."

I looked, didn't see anything. "Seriously, you should be Field." I scanned the brochure. "I think we're supposed to go into the underground garage, over there." I nodded my head toward it. We started the saunter. "Wow, and we could have bought a combo ticket, too. Bet they didn't mention it when you got our tickets."

"My mind was elsewhere, dear, please forgive me for missing out on the deal."

"Rick, really, I may have to hurt you."

We got into the parking garage and followed the signs. Crypt was closed, as promised. But the door was unlocked. We opened it carefully. White held my arm. "Stay here and on guard, just in case." He went inside. I did as requested. It was creepy in the parking garage, which was pretty empty. I wasn't sure how long to give him before I charged in like cavalry.

Didn't matter, he was back in less than a minute. "It's closed and there's no one in there. I looked in the tombs and such, carefully. Nothing and no one."

I looked around. "It doesn't make sense."

"Back into the cathedral?"

"Maybe. I don't want us running around in circles. We have all the clues, I'm sure of it. We just need to figure out what's actually going on."

"Do we have the clues? All I see is confusion, started by Tim leaving without telling anyone what he was doing, where he was going, or why he was doing it. And I fail to understand why he didn't take the opportunity to get himself and four of our agents to safety, either—since Miss Young and her family are confirmed as safe, he certainly had the opportunity. While all our human operatives are, as you put it, mavericks, they aren't stupid. And, don't take this the wrong way, but you're the most impetuous and foolhardy of all our human operatives. All our operatives, really."

"Yeah, true." I pondered. "So, maybe our real question is this—has Tim ever been working on the same plan as we have been, or did he see something else the rest of us have missed?"

CHAPTER 54

"I FEEL CONFIDENT I've missed most of the clues," White said with a sigh.

"But have you, really? I didn't ask before, but where were you when you came to Paris? I mean when Chuckie's C.I.A. guys found and saved you?"

"At the airport. It was suggested by my contact as a safe place it would be easy for both of us to get to."

I stared at him. "You were at the Paris airport when Alicia was." He nodded. "Did you see her?"

"No. I saw the man I described to you; he said the Gower girls were very talented and that he was concerned about their safety. He insinuated someone of great authority wanted to get them hidden away—away from C.I.A. and Centaurion control, essentially—in order to protect them. Then he spun on his heel and walked rapidly away, right before a swarm of C.I.A. operatives arrived, who said Mister Reynolds was concerned about his lost little lamb." He shook his head. "They actually said I was their lost little lamb."

"Chuckie has a interesting sense of humor. So, okay . . . Alicia isn't me, but she's not a total wimp, either. What are the odds she spotted and recognized you, saw what went on, and followed your contact? I say they're decent. So, she saw him, and she saw . . . what? Where he went or who he talked to after you were taken back. And she told Tim about it."

"If it was dire, why didn't Tim break protocol when Miss Young and her parents were in Paris and just bring them to safety?"

I thought about it. "Maybe he wasn't sure where safety was."

"Explanation, please?"

"Why was Tim only trying to contact me?"

"Not an explanation."

"Tim spoke to Alicia, probably several times between Christmas and when he left the Science Center, so he knew something was up before he ever took off. Which means he was always working on a different plan. He was never sneaking out to break the rules; he was sneaking out to save the day. But why didn't he tell anyone straight out? Or leave me clearer clues?"

I closed my eyes and tried to think like Chuckie. What was at stake? No, who was the person with the most to win or lose? Gaultier had a lot to gain financially, if he could sell this superdrug. But my mother had said he was clean. Why wouldn't she know he was in illicit pharmaceuticals? Why didn't Chuckie mention it? And why did Tim think he had a better chance of saving the day alone? I opened my eyes and looked at White. "Name your enemies."

"Beg pardon?"

"Enemies. You have them. Who are Centaurion Division's enemies? All of you have told me more than once that not every agency out there likes you. Who doesn't like you? Or, let me ask it this way—why, during Operation Fugly, did Beverly call in the C.I.A.? They weren't there to help—if my mother hadn't been there, they'd have carted all of Alpha Team off."

White stared at me. "You, your mother, and both Abigail and Naomi have said this, many times—the only friend we have at the C.I.A. is Mister Reynolds. Of American organizations who know of us, our relationship with them is the most strained."

"When you described the person you thought was Gaultier, Chuckie described the real Gaultier. Who is Chuckie's height, and has blue eyes, like Chuckie, and who could put on a blond wig and pass as Chuckie, at least from a distance."

"I don't follow you."

"Alicia saw you and was alerted that something was off. She followed the person you were talking to, and I'll bet she saw him meet up with someone who looked just like

Chuckie, especially from a distance. Maybe she took a picture; most phones have cameras in them these days. So, Tim sees Chuckie in Paris, where he shouldn't be, talking to a guy we all think was trying to kidnap you."

"But Mister Reynolds was in the room with you when I was in Paris."

"Yes, he was. Because Amy was able to warn us in time." Which begged its own set of questions I wasn't ready to deal with. "I'm betting you were supposed to 'witness' his murder in Paris—remember, we're dealing with people who are good enough actors to convince Amy she saw a man killed in front of her. Chuckie was supposed to be dead—he was alone for Christmas and I'll bet more than his parents and the Gowers knew that. But what I know is that he hasn't told anyone he works with that he has gates in his office, home in Australia, and apartment in D.C. Without those gates, he'd be dead."

"Why?"

"No freaking idea yet, just know it's so." I pondered. "That's why they called the meeting."

"Beg pardon?"

"Chuckie and I had a meeting while the superbeing cluster was going on in Paris. One or all of the people involved wanted said meeting to ensure Chuckie would be exactly where they wanted him—with me, having a pointless video conference, instead of potentially in Paris where action was going on." I thought about the questions. "And they confirmed exactly what we'd do if we were threatened *and* that Christopher, who they've been drugging, would take over if Jeff and I were out of it."

I dug in my purse and pulled Harlie out. "Harlie, can you take us to where Jeff and Chuckie are?" Harlie mewled and didn't move. "Oh, right. Jeff told Harlie to guard me and Jamie. I guess Jamie's safe, so Harlie's with me." No worries, I could stay calm during this scary crisis. I dug through again and tried with each Poof. They all mewled and didn't move.

"Perhaps they were told to guard you as well."

"Maybe." Pulled out Poofikins. "But no one's told my Poofikins anything, have they? Poofikins, we need to find Jeff and Chuckie. Can you help us?"

Poofikins mewled and stayed in my hand. There was much Poof mewling now. I looked back into my purse. The

Poofs looked fine, but I noticed something else in there. Sure, my purse had been jostled a lot, particularly on the train, but my iPod was out of place, even for that.

I pulled it out and turned it on. "That's weird."

"What?"

"I know the last thing I listened to was the Counting Crows. But my iPod's tuned to the Nine Lives Mix."

"So?"

"I don't have a Nine Lives mix." I took a look. "Oh, man, I am such an idiot. Tim expected me to go for my iPod a lot sooner, I'm sure. He must have made this mix. Jeff said the Poofs were freaking—bet he told Poofikins to make sure I saw my iPod." The first song was 'Nine Lives.' The other songs from the CDs he'd identified as clues were there. But there were other songs, too. "Damn. He expected me to listen to this and catch on. And we don't have the time."

"Titles might spark something."

I put one earpiece in my ear and one into White's. "Let's have a listen." I scrolled through "Help!," "Time to Get Ill," "She's Crafty," "Friend or Foe," "Material Girl," "Levon," "Tiny Dancer," "Traffic and Weather," "I-95," "Cinderella Undercover," "You Can't Always Get What You Want," "Runaway," "Dr. Wu," several others. We listened to snippets of the songs. Some of this made sense, some still didn't.

I looked at White. "I don't get it. He took the time to put other bands in here—Oingo Boingo, the Stones, Steely Dan, geez, even Dion. But he didn't give me their cases or CDs as clues. Why not?"

White considered this while I scrolled through the songs again. "Perhaps he feared someone would break the code if they had all the music."

"But he was pursued by A-Cs."

"Was he?" White looked around. "We stand in the middle of a parking garage. My people don't normally do their business in underground parking garages. However, I've seen many movies, and humans love to do covert business in underground parking lots. Why, I don't know."

"Because you can't see well. So you could fool someone into thinking you were someone else, like the head of the ETD, if you were in the right place." I stared at the music mix. At one title in particular. Hit play. "Oh, wow. You know . . . we have a mole."

CHAPTER 55

"YOU'VE BEEN SAYING we didn't have a mole. I agree that we do, just pointing out that you are contradicting yourself."

"Yes, because I thought this was only a money play. But it's both—one partner gets money, one partner gets power."

White looked at the songs. "I don't know most of these, other than by association with you. However, that title sounds promising." He pointed to "Cinderella Undercover."

"Yeah. We're listening to it. Check the chorus."

He was quiet. "Cinderella undercover, workin' for the C.I.A. Truly, rock music at its finest. Who's Cinderella? In this situation, I mean."

"Cinderella is our mole. Gaultier's partnered with the C.I.A., which makes sense in an odd way. They protect him—the P.T.C.U. has no idea of what he really does, ETD is kept in the dark about him, too—and he gives them what they want—the A-C War Division—and everybody makes money."

"Mister Reynolds is the mole?"

"No. He's a target. So the question is, is she an enemy or a double agent?"

"Who?"

"The person Tim realized *was* the mole. I'll bet he saw her around Christopher's isolation chamber. She could go in, but she shouldn't have been there. Maybe she used the official name for the drug, maybe she talked to Clarence in too familiar a manner, maybe he saw her fiddle with Christopher's grid down there. And because no one but me likes Chuckie, he wanted only me to know—if Chuckie's not involved, I can protect him. If he is involved, then I can set Jeff on him. Also, if we had one mole, how many others might we have? Clarence is a traitor, who else, right? Tim bet on the side of major infiltration and got out to be able to do something to save the day."

"Not following you. At all."

"Why was Camilla my doctor? I don't know her, and Tito, who's essentially an intern, ran everything. Why did Chuckie even mention her as a possible mole? He didn't want her to know I'd turned superpowered, but he also said she could be the mole—why? If he knew for sure, he'd have arrested her. So she triggered some memory in him. I'll bet he's seen her at C.I.A. headquarters and didn't remember consciously. And Tim wasn't in the room then, so he had no way of knowing if Chuckie was the one who put her in place or not."

"Camilla is our mole?" White asked hopefully.

"Yes."

He sighed. "Not happy, just relieved to know. She was originally stationed out of East Base and was moved to Dulce right after Operation Drug Addict, as you so charmingly call it, because she was part of the team working to determine how the drug could be removed from DNA. It can't be, so far as we can tell," he added softly.

I turned off the iPod and pulled out my phone. "No service. Bet you don't have any, either." No phone service meant no way to call Mom or Serene and see what Jamie might know, let alone to verify how Paul and ACE were doing. This was typical for our luck, of course, so I chose not to be surprised.

White looked as he handed me back the earpiece he'd been using. "True enough. So, are they in here somewhere or is it just that there's so much steel and concrete here?"

"No idea." Think, think. "Why did Chuckie send Fluffy to me? Same question with Michael and Christopher. They're in grave danger, why not see if the Poofs can do some damage?"

"Because your danger is greater."

I stared at the music mix. "Our danger. If we're back to

our usual, you're the target. You're always the target. The Diplomatic Corps is helping Gaultier, or, rather, the C.I.A. operative who they think is Ronaldo Al Dejahl. He's supposed to take over as Pontifex after they get rid of you. And me, Mom, and Chuckie. Because we're the three humans who can stop that."

"We seem remarkably unmolested."

"Yeah." I laughed. "Because of you."

"Pardon?"

"Dude, I'm not kidding. You're better than Jeff. Who stopped us from running into a trap?"

"Gladys."

"Well, yeah, but you, too. You were smart enough to ask for a gate somewhere far enough away to keep us safe, you were willing to do the disguise, you kept me from running across the square and alerting whoever's watching that another Centaurion agent was blundering around. And no one knows how you'll act in a danger situation because this is the first one in what I'd guess was a long time that you haven't had Jeff, Christopher, and Paul running interference for you."

"Possibly." He didn't sound convinced.

"Who, besides me, knows you plan for Paul to be your successor, not Christopher?" Dropped my iPod back into my purse while trying not to stress.

"No one. Christopher does not have the right make up to be Pontifex. I know he dreads it, as well. Paul has the right mind-set, and I thought so even before you put ACE into him."

"Right. But everyone else thinks it's going to be Christopher—you succeeded your father, after all. So, when the A-Cs split again over who should be Pontifex, those who were loyal to you would support Christopher. Whom the Diplomatic Corps and C.I.A. had drugged out of his mind and therefore believed they could control."

"How will Gaultier make money this way?"

"Seriously, we are going to team up from now on. How? By being the exclusive provider to the U.S. government, via the C.I.A., of the superdrug. Take over this world, and all of the Alpha Centaurion worlds, become wealthy beyond imagining."

"You really think that's the ultimate goal?"

"Christopher can see Jareen, on one of the farthest inhabited planets from us in that system. The gate is open between Earth and Alpha Four. Yeah, I'm freaking certain. I'm Megalomaniac Girl, remember?"

"So, where are they and how do we foil this plan and save everyone, including those innocents in the cathedral?"

"Damn, I knew you were going to ask the hard question next."

"Do you have the hard answer?"

"No, I have another question, one I asked before but which we haven't answered. Is Camilla merely a mole, or is she a double agent?"

"Why do you even assume double agent?"

"Because Amy was triggered to warn us. Chuckie would be dead for sure if she hadn't told me what she'd discovered. Mom might be, too."

"I thought our original assumption was they wanted us herded into one place. Meaning Amy was triggered by those who mean us harm."

"Yeah . . . but why give her information that would pull the two humans you want dead into safety?"

"It wouldn't have mattered if you'd died during delivery. Did Camilla have something to do with that?"

"No. But, I wonder . . . ."

"Wonder what?"

"Tito said babies come when they want to. I wonder if Jamie came early on purpose?"

"To what end?" White wasn't arguing with me.

"Saving her parents, saving the world, that sort of thing." I looked back at the Poofs. "Where is everybody? Protecting me and Richard's useless if everyone else dies."

Harlie mewled but didn't seem upset.

"I don't care what Jeff or Chuckie told all of you. They lied. They're in danger. So are Christopher and James and Michael. Where are they?"

More mewling.

I looked at White. "Your turn."

He shook his head. "I'd like to save everyone more than merely find them." Six Poofs jumped onto the ground and scampered across the garage. White grabbed my hand, and we ran after them.

"Dude, seriously, you might be able to single-handedly

do all the field work yourself. I know it's been a long run as Pontifex—retire to the active lifestyle."

He laughed. "If we survive and save everyone, feel free to forward the suggestion again, Missus Martini. If I can stop the subterfuge now."

"Well, stay looking Timothy Dalton-ish. And call me Kathy if anyone's around. Otherwise, I'm with you, Mister White. Besides, this is sort of like being in our own version of *The Avengers*."

"All you need is the catsuit. Which would, I must say, look excellent on you."

"Wow, hope Jeff's still alive. Otherwise, I may have to shock my parents with who I marry next."

CHAPTER 56

THE POOFS LED US ACROSS the garage to a different set of stairs. Went down, and the Poofs jumped back, Poofikins on my shoulder, Fluffy on White's. The others went back into my purse.

"Chuckie told Fluffy to protect you."

"I hope we'll be in time to save his life by way of thanks."

"Yeah. Let's just plan on it, okay?"

We were moving at the slower hyperspeed again. I wondered when I was going to peter out. I'd been up to five miles without too much problem before I'd gotten pregnant. Jeff hadn't allowed me to run since our honeymoon, however. Tried not to think about what they could have done to or be doing to him, just concentrated on moving as fast as I could. Wasn't up to full hyperspeed, but it was faster than the best human sprinters could go.

"We aren't in the parking garage any more," White said as we went lower. No sooner were the words out of his mouth than the stairs stopped and we hit a corridor. It turned left almost immediately, and we ran down it, though at a slightly slower pace.

"How can you see?" The corridor wasn't lit, which was why I assumed White had slowed us down a tad.

"How can you? We have improved night vision over humans."

"Superpowers rock! I'm amazed you guys didn't just take over and rule the pathetic humans the moment you arrived."

"My father wanted to."

I squeezed his hand. "I know. I know why they want to kill you, Richard."

"Why is that?"

"You're too good a man. You always have been. You're what keeps all the A-Cs working with humanity instead of taking over. You're what keeps your people safe, too."

The corridor turned, left again. "We're heading back to the cathedral, I believe."

"Why does something like this exist? I mean, a dark, scary tunnel going not much of anywhere?"

"It's a tunnel leading, I'd guess, from the cathedral out."

Thought about history. "Oh, right. In times of trouble, you ran to the church. But maybe you needed to get out again and didn't want to go through the front doors and be killed."

"Correct."

"Geez, you a history professor on the side?"

"No, but I've spent a lot of time with one recently. Your father."

"That's his cover. He's a NASA cryptologist. You were there when I got to discover my parents weren't who they said they were."

"He's still a professor, and he's also a history buff. Fascinating, your world history. I've enjoyed reading about it, much based on your father's suggestions."

This corridor was longer than the other one. "When does this thing end?"

"You studied French. How big is the cathedral?"

"Big." I thought about it. "We're going into the center area, the big part of the cathedral, aren't we?"

"I'd assume so." There was something darker up ahead of us. "Jump!"

I did as he said, hurdled, really, but it wasn't my best. Fortunately, White landed without issue on the other side of the huge hole and hauled me back next to him. We kept on running. "What was that?"

"Cave in, trap, something. Nothing to worry about."

"You're a natural. Thankfully, or I'd be dead already."

He laughed. "Perhaps. I hate to admit it—in an odd way, I'm enjoying this."

"Because you're so damned good at it."

"I'm sure the company helps as well." We kept on running. "One thing still confuses me, Missus Martini. Well, more than one, but this in particular. Who was after Tim, and why were Miss Young's apartment and her parents' home ransacked?"

"My guess? They want our DNA. It's a standard evil medical supergenius plot in the comics. Get the DNA of the major good guys, create the clone army programmed to destroy the good guys with their own powers."

"Not following you. At all."

"Tim spotted Camilla, heard Clarence use an official drug name, maybe saw some other things, put two and two together. The wedding video's the tip-off. He wanted me to focus on people who were at or around our wedding—the Diplomatic Corps, I'm sure, even though they were thankfully, removed before the 'big event'. But also Chuckie and you, people Alicia would only have seen there. They were after her for one main reason—she had something with our DNA on it, at least, so they believed."

White was quiet. "Oh. She caught your bouquet, and Jeffrey took the garter off your leg with his teeth. Michael, who caught the garter, put it back onto Miss Young's leg. I remember the guests found that all quite hilarious."

"Truly, you're going to join active field duty after this. Yeah, because whoever catches the garter's supposed to be the next to get married. Alicia kept the garter—it actually has none of our DNA on it any more because I know she washed it. She's going to wear it at her wedding for good luck. However, Tim was looking for it, because he could offer it to the baddies—doing his own version of double-agenting. Maybe he made a deal before he left, just to be on the safe side. He's the one who ransacked her place, to find the garter and also to leave a big message for us. Nothing says 'danger' like someone's place being trashed."

"And her parents' house?"

"I imagine he and the other agents did that, too. Again, sticking with the theme. The A-Cs could trash it in about five seconds, we knew to look for clues there, since he freaking told me with the musical clues that I was so slow to catch on to."

"So, who was after him? How did his phone get shot?

Why did he finally leave a message when a voicemail earlier would have been more helpful?"

"Figure the bad guys caught on. Guns are human weapons . . . the C.I.A. was alerted by Chuckie sending his guys out. The ones trying to kill Chuckie and my mom sent goons after Tim. He left a message because he was pretty sure he was going to be captured. And, since he likely had the garter on him, the bad guys know it's useless by now. But it bought us some time."

"Makes sense, Missus Martini."

Had to jump a few more holes, climb over some rocks, and in one case, move a rockslide while we were discussing Tim's ability to outthink the rest of us. "Guess it's a safe bet that whoever has our people isn't using this route."

"It does appear that way." White tossed another big hunk of rock, climbed up, hauled me up, jumped down, lifted me down, and we kept on moving. I was totally impressed. Tim needed a promotion, and White needed to get out and kick butt a whole lot more.

We reached an intersection. We could go straight or turn left. "Poofies?" Harlie jumped down and went to the left. We followed, Harlie jumped back into my purse. "Interesting. Where are we going?"

"No idea. You're the one who studied French, supposedly."

Thought about it as we ran on for what seemed like another forever. "We're still on Ile de la Cité. So, what else is here? Oh, duh. The Palais de Justice." Thought about it. "And the Conciergerie. Where they held prisoners during the French Revolution. You know, right before they beheaded them. Tourists are kept out of most of it. I'll bet the philanthropist Ronaldo Al Dejahl gets to visit when and where he wants, though." We sped up.

We finally reached another set of stairs. These led up. They also looked ancient. "The stairs can be slippery," I shared.

"Oh? How do you know?"

"The brochure said so about the ones in the cathedral going up to the gargoyles, would make sense these are the same, and they look like the ones in the pictures."

"Then we'll exercise caution."

We started up. Stair charges had been a part of my life for years, because I'd had the most sadistic track coaches in history. There were no railings to hold on to, and the stairs were indeed slippery. They were also covered with dust. No one had been here in years, if not decades or more. We were moving fast enough that slipping wasn't too much of an issue. Of course, I slipped, but White kept a firm hold on me and kept us moving upward. I remained overwhelmingly impressed.

We hit a ceiling. White felt around, located the trapdoor, and opened it, carefully. He pulled himself up, then pulled me up. We were in a medium-sized room and were, thankfully, alone. White closed the trapdoor quietly, took my hand again, and then we moved through the room.

As we got to the door, Harlie jumped out of my purse again and started leading. We followed. I looked around and pulled White's head down. "We're in the cellars," I whispered in his ear. "Where the prison was." He nodded.

It had been warm in the tunnels, and we'd been running. We were moving slowly now, and it was freezing in here. I started to shiver. White stopped and put his jacket on me. Felt warmer and grateful both. He took my hand again, and we started off after Harlie.

It was a big building. Perhaps if we hadn't been trying to save everyone, I would have enjoyed the architecture. As it was, I was trying to come up with a plan. Neither White nor I had an actual weapon on us, we had something like two dozen people to save, and we had no idea how many bad guys we were dealing with.

White squeezed my hand and leaned down. "Light ahead." Harlie jumped into my purse. It was clear where we were supposed to go now.

We slowed down and started creeping. As we got nearer, I heard the sound of someone shouting in pain. My grip on White's hand tightened—it was Jeff.

CHAPTER 57

"STOP IT!" AMY'S VOICE. She was screaming and crying. "Why are you doing this to them?"

"There are reasons." Recognized this voice, too. Amy's father. Hadn't heard him in years but could still recognize it.

We got to where we could see but remain in shadows. Big corridor, rooms off to the sides, bars. Every male was stripped to the waist and chained to the bars, pretty much spread-eagled. Would have spent a lot of time drooling if they weren't in mortal peril. The women were all in one cell together. Apparently they weren't strong enough to bend these bars, because I could see Emily and Melanie trying to pull them apart, and the bars weren't budging.

Herbert Gaultier was between the cell with the women and where the men were pretty much on display. He wasn't alone. I could see Robert and Barbara Coleman and several other A-Cs with them.

White leaned down and spoke in my ear. "All the Diplomatic Corps are here. The smaller, darker-skinned man is the one I met at the Paris airport."

I moved my mouth to his ear. "Figure he's who's pretending to be Al Dejahl."

White nodded, and we both continued to look at the scene. I couldn't spot any of Jeff's other brothers-in-law. What that meant, I didn't know.

"Really, Jeffrey," Barbara Coleman said with false sweetness. "Just bring your wife and baby here. That's all we ask. Then we'll stop hurting you." I found myself wishing I'd killed her during Operation Drug Addict.

Jeff just glared at her. She smiled, and then I could tell she sent an emotional blast at him, because he shouted in pain again, and his whole body jerked. Not just her, I realized. All of them, all twelve of the Diplomatic Corps—they were all attacking my husband with the intent to torture him to death. Forced myself not to see red, not to just run in there, but it felt like the hardest thing I'd ever done.

Chuckie was next to Jeff—still alive, but he'd had the crap beaten out of him. Christopher was on Jeff's other side. He looked as though they'd used him for sparring practice, too.

The rest of our guys were spread out, all looking like they'd been on the wrong end of a gang war. "Why do you want a baby?" Tito, interestingly, was still able to talk. Cage fighting had its benefits. He was next to Christopher.

"Oh, not just any baby. Theirs. And the other enhanced hybrid when it arrives. For study." The man whom White identified as our fake Al Dejahl moved closer to Tito. "Why do you care?" Tito didn't answer, which earned him a punch in the gut. He shouted, but it was a shout I was familiar with—martial arts taught you to let out air and shout when you were hit, to deflect the pain. Probably why Tito looked better than most of our guys, which was the textbook example of damning with faint praise.

"Stay away from my wife," Brian managed to growl. He was on Tito's other side. Al Dejahl backhanded him.

"Stop it!" Amy was close to hysterical.

I could see Kevin, Michael, Reader, and Tim clearly—like the others, they looked like crap. Those four were on Chuckie's other side, so closer to me and White. The flyboys, who were on Brian's other side, looked no better, but it was hard to be sure from this distance. But they all seemed alive. Tim was closest to us, Jerry farthest. I had no idea how to get any of them out of here safely, let alone all of them.

Another thought occurred, and I pulled White's head down. "How in the world did they catch all of them? Tito can take an A-C without help, let alone the rest of them working together."

"Perhaps whatever was used on Paul was used on the others."

"Where are the rest of the people who would have kept the women in line? Or carried the unconscious bodies?"

We looked. I couldn't spot anyone else. Meanwhile, Jeff was being tortured, and I knew he was going to be close to dying soon. Everyone loved to hurt my men, Jeff in particular.

Ran through my inventory of what I had to use. Me, White, six Poofs, an iPod, hairspray, cell phone, and the adrenaline harpoon. None of these screamed "cavalry coming" other than if I lucked out and got to Jeff before he died. I'd seen the Poofs devour a man in front of me, but that man had been trying to kill me. Had a crazy thought I decided to table for later.

They sent another emotional hit at Jeff, and his whole body writhed in agony. He was panting from the pain.

"Leave him alone," Christopher snarled.

"Oh, we can't do that," Robert Coleman said. "We have a new leader, and we need to make sure no one is stupid enough to suggest Jeffrey as the next Pontifex."

"My father's not going to let you get away with this."

Coleman snorted. "Please. He's only survived this long because he's had you and Jeffrey to protect him. Gower's dead, so the one weapon you had has gone back to the cosmos, or dissipated."

I yanked White's head down. "You said the PPB net would collapse not dissipate."

"Yes, because I know and they don't. One thing I did learn from my father—tell your diplomats only what they need to know in order to do their jobs. High-level secrets are for those who can keep them."

"Your new leader's a fake." I wasn't sure how Chuckie was managing to talk, but he sounded insolent, too.

"Yes, of course he is." Coleman laughed. "I do share one viewpoint with Jeffrey and Christopher—I'm sick of having to take any kind of order from you." He walked over and hit Chuckie in the ribs. I heard a crack. Chuckie hissed in pain. I shook from rage, and White squeezed my hand. I forced myself to relax.

The sound of footsteps reached us. White and I moved

back farther into the shadows. What looked like a platoon of men entered the room on the opposite side from us. I knew some of them, and the rest looked vaguely familiar. They were C.I.A. people I'd met over the course of the last year or so. None of them were part of the ETD, nor were they the top dogs elsewhere, but then again, the top dogs weren't usually the ones who had to do a power play to get on top, just to stay there. All of them looked nasty, and there were more of them than there were of our guys.

"Why are they all still alive?" the last man into the room asked. I knew the voice, and I knew him, at least, now—Cooper. He looked smug and bored. I managed not to hiss and attack, but it took the most effort so far. So now I knew who was in charge of all of this, at least from the C.I.A.'s side.

"We don't have what we need yet," the fake Al Dejahl said.

"Have one of the diplomats go to the Science Center, grab the spawn, grab the pregnant idiot, and nuke the place." Cooper said this as if he were giving an order for a latte. I already hated this guy, but now I hated him even more for that and also for calling Jamie names. I was getting tired of everyone calling my baby "spawn." They didn't mean it in the cool, superhero way.

"Katt's there. She won't let her daughter or granddaughter out of her sight." I recognized this voice, a woman's. Camilla stepped into the light. "You'll need to draw them here, just like I told you."

"How the hell did they get warned, that's what I want to know," Cooper snarled. "I'd still like to know who fucked that up." White and I looked at each other. He raised his eyebrow, and I shrugged.

"I wouldn't know," Camilla snapped. "She went into labor early, not like I could pay attention to anything else and not have my cover blown."

I looked at the cell where the women were. It was hard to see from where we'd moved to, but I got the impression someone had her hand over Amy's mouth.

"My part worked as planned," Gaultier said.

"Really?" Cooper had a sarcasm knob, it seemed. "So it was part of your plan for your daughter to discover who we were actually targeting? And for her to alert every damned alien that it was time to go into lockdown?"

Gaultier shrugged. "You wanted them herded. We herded."

"We didn't want Reynolds or Katt alive when the herding started, you idiot."

"Your people left the clues for Amy to find. I just made the arrangements for her to go where it would be simple for her to make her discovery." I could hear Amy crying. Apparently her father could, too. "Oh, stop blubbering. What did any of these people mean to you? You haven't seen your supposed best friend for years. The rest of these are alien scum that don't belong here anyway. Don't worry . . . you'll enjoy being princess of a new world."

"They're good people, the humans and the aliens you're torturing both. They saved me, and they didn't have to. How can you do this?"

Gaultier walked over to Chuckie. "As I recall, Amy, you always hated this one."

"Leave him alone!" Amy flung herself at the bars. "He was right, he was always right! He told me you were a greedy son of a bitch when we were in tenth grade. He knew what you were when we were children!"

Interesting. I'd had no idea. Explained a lot of their mutual animosity.

Gaultier laughed and leaned into Chuckie's face. "Every businessman is a greedy son of a bitch. You're one of us now, you know that." He leaned closer. "You're greedier than me, Reynolds. Coveting another man's wife. It was so easy to center things around her—she's the belle of the alien ball, isn't she? She was a slut when she was in school, and she's a slut now."

Chuckie lunged toward Gaultier and slammed his forehead into Gaultier's nose. Blood spurted as Gaultier staggered back. "Kill that bastard!"

I got ready to run, but Cooper shook his head. "Need him until we get the slut and the spawn."

White leaned down. "Good control. Proud of you."

"I was *not* that much of a slut! I mean, it's not like I was the only girl who did the deed before I was married."

"They're baiting men who love you. No man wants to

hear the name of the woman he loves or cares about dragged through the mud."

"Why?" Coleman asked. "We could kill all the humans right now."

"You're all morons." Al Dejahl sounded disgusted. "Kill them and we have no leverage."

"You let us kill the others." Barbara sounded like she'd enjoyed that.

"For scientific purposes, yes." Cooper sounded as if he were explaining something to a five year old. "We've studied all the hybrids other than the five, excuse me, six now in existence. It'll help to compare standard empathic and imageer brains and bodies to the others. But until we have what we want, Mister Al Dejahl is right, the rest of these are too useful."

"She'll come for just one of them," Barbara said. "Kill the others, let Jeffrey hang on until she arrives." Nice to know they were expecting me.

"She won't come. She's not that stupid." Jeff could barely talk.

Barbara laughed. "Your little feminist throwback? Of course she'll come. She's on her way. Baby in tow, I'm sure. After all, there's no baby formula in the Science Center, is there? We made sure of that. So it's mother's milk, or the baby starves. Though she might be a poor enough mother to allow that, I'm sure her own mother won't. So, I'd expect the whole little family to arrive."

I could see how this would have made sense, and I might have even suggested it if Sheila hadn't been there with the breast pump. Got a huge love for La Leche League all of a sudden. But these people didn't seem to know us at all. So whoever was feeding them their information was doing a great job—of helping us.

Camilla nodded. "I'm sure Missus Coleman is right—Missus Martini's been complaining about not being allowed to do anything since the baby showed up. Look, I can't stay here too long. They'll notice I'm gone soon enough."

"We're almost ready to put Operation Expansion into effect, Mister Cooper," a different C.I.A. operative said.

"You're sure they're not inside?" Cooper sounded frustrated.

"No, sir. We've checked all adults inside the cathedral. No sign of Missus Martini or Mister White."

"Maybe they're still trying to find Gower's body." Cooper shrugged. "Okay, keep on torturing Martini here until the baby can't take it and shows up, with or without her mother. Mister Al Dejahl has to start the ceremony."

They were ready to leave, and that meant we were out of time. I had no sane idea of what to do. Pulled my iPod out, took my purse off. Tuned to Tina Turner's "Steel Claw" and put it on repeat.

"Any ideas, Missus Martini?" White asked in my ear.

"Only the crazy one."

CHAPTER 58

I LET GO OF WHITE'S HAND and walked into the room. "Hey, I heard there was a cool BDSM party going on that I just couldn't miss."

Well, that got the full room's attention. All the C.I.A. guys had guns it seemed, and they all pulled them and pointed them at me.

"How nice of you to arrive," Cooper said to me. "Excellent timing."

"Well, we sluts hate to miss it when all the hot guys are tied up waiting for us. So, let's see. Humans have the guns, A-Cs have the speed. Should be fun." The music was, in my opinion, Tina's most rocking song ever, and it started to work on me. I could barely keep still. "You know, at a time like this, I just have to ask one question of you vicious bastards—WWWD?" I heard Chuckie start to laugh.

"What's that stand for?" Barbara Coleman sneered. "How stupid am I?"

"Nah. What would Wolverine do? Oh, by the way, Professor X? Probably need your mad skills, too. And the answer to WWWD, Babs? He'd kick ass."

I saw the humans start to fire their guns. I ran, at a hyperspeed I knew was faster than I'd gone yet because I ran around the bullets. Kung fu moves were flowing like never before, possibly because I was doing them at what seemed like a hundred miles an hour. Guns went flying and so did humans. White was in here, too, I could just see him. He was also kicking butt as though he did it every day. Maybe we *were* the new Avengers. Needed to get him a bowler hat and an umbrella.

The A-Cs leaped into action. Coleman was after me. I ran up the side of a wall, did a midair flip, caught his neck between my legs and squeezed. As we landed, I twisted. His neck looked funny.

"Hey, Babs!" I picked up her husband and tossed him onto Barbara. She screamed as she hit the floor.

"Poofs assemble!" I couldn't help it, my first superhero fight was beyond what I'd ever imagined. I saw the six Poofs go huge and toothy as they poured in. I heard screams from the humans.

Decided it was time to get the rest of Girl Power going. Grabbed one of the Diplomatic Corps and slammed his head into the bars holding the women. Had to slam him a couple of times, but he finally opened the door. Sure, he was dead, but who had time to look for keys? Noted the Gower girls had some weird metal things on their heads. "Bombs?"

"Control devices." Naomi was trying to get it off. "We can't do anything with these on." Guessed Chuckie and I weren't the only ones who read the comics.

Three of the A-C female diplomats tried to gang up on me. This was fine. Did Dragon Guards the Well, which was a great form for multiple attackers. I found myself wishing my kung fu instructors were here to witness this. This was a black belt performance for sure. I did a leaping splits kick and hit two of them in the head. Maybe double black belt.

Melanie and Emily were pissed, and they waded in and started beating the two women I'd just kicked. I punched the third so hard she flew across the room, slammed into the bars above Jeff's head, and then hit the ground.

Turned around and pulled the metal controllers off the Gower girls. Considered that I could use a weapon. Reached out, grabbed one of the iron bars, pulled. It flew into my hand.

There were several people ganged up on one, which one I realized was White. Spun my iron staff and waded in. It was a lot like when we'd fought the Alpha Four invasion—but I was better now. I cartwheeled through the air, landed with the staff point on the ground in the middle of the melee, and used the momentum to kick the head of the nearest bad guy. He went down, I stood on top of him and slammed the staff up and around. I aimed for heads—I didn't want any of these people alive to do any more dirty work on the people I cared about.

I heard screaming and saw the rest of the bad guys who were still standing holding their heads and crumbling to the ground. Glanced toward the Gower girls. They glared in concentration, and their expressions said they were as pissed as me. I counted bad guy noses. We were missing Cooper, Gaultier, the fake Al Dejahl, and Camilla. It figured.

"Kitty, we can't get the chains off!" Melanie was trying to get Jeff unbound, Emily was working on Chuckie, and Amy was with Christopher, but no one was effective.

I looked at the three men. My men. All of them were my men. And they'd been tied up, beaten, tortured. Any one of them could have won a fair fight. But our enemies never fought fair.

The anger came, and it was massive. I saw Jeff's expression—his eyes were wide, and he looked afraid. Of me. I didn't want him to feel anything like this; I didn't want to hurt *him*. I wrapped my mind around his and held it in a safe place, where nothing could hurt him. Then I looked at the chains holding him.

They flew off and slammed against the wall of the cell behind him.

Cool.

CHAPTER 59

I CONCENTRATED. ALL THE CHAINS holding the guys flew off and away, to slam against the back wall. Double cool.

Ran and caught Jeff as he was falling. Laid him gently on the ground. Raced around and caught all the other guys before they hit the ground, too. Everyone was in slow motion, I was moving so fast.

They were all hurt, some worse than others, but all badly. I grabbed Christopher's hand. "Show me everyone here we care about." Christopher closed his eyes, and I could see everyone's internal damages. I grabbed Tito's hand in my free one. "Fix them. Closest to death first. Abby, Mimi, link to me." Naomi put her hand on my head, she and Abigail held hands, then Abigail touched Chuckie.

His lungs were punctured, and his other internal injuries were horrifying. I concentrated as information flowed from Christopher and Tito through me to the Gower girls. Chuckie's head went back, and he shouted from pain—the repairs were hurting him. No anesthetic. I did the same for him as I had for Jeff, wrapped his mind in mine and kept it in a safe, loving place.

It took a bit—or maybe not, I couldn't tell how fast things were moving any more—but Chuckie's injuries were repaired. I released his mind gently.

We moved to Jeff next. For once I didn't have to stab him in the heart, but only because we were restarting his hearts this way. His blocks were shot, so his mind was hurt as well as his body. Stayed calm while the repairs went on, just kept his mind wrapped in mine, soothed him, fixed his blocks and put them back up, while I caressed his mind and kept the pain and fear away from him.

And so it went. Fix one, move to the next, protect him from pain, do the repairs, move on. Christopher and Tito had to be repaired before some of the others, but it was a tossup as to who could claim to be the least injured.

After what seemed like hours, we were done. We got out of our weird Wonder Quintuplets link, and I looked for White. "Where's Richard?"

"He said he wasn't hurt. He went after the ones who escaped." Emily's voice shook.

"We need these bodies for anything, proof, burning in effigy, that sort of thing?"

"No," Chuckie said. Naomi was helping him stand up. "Disappeared without a trace would be easier."

"Poofies, enjoy your well-earned snackage." The Poofs devoured. "Careful with Barbara, Poofies, she might give you indigestion." Poofikins looked at me, purred, and crunched Barbara up. Loved my Poofs. Dead bodies were gone fast. Much Poof belching occurred, but I decided to ignore it and focus on the easy cleanup.

Melanie was staring at me as though she'd never seen me before. "Kitty . . ."

"Superpowers and Poofs rock. Going after Richard, he's going to need me. Oh, by the way, Chuckie? You were, as always, right. We had a mole, but she was a double agent, which is why you were all still alive. Jeff and Christopher? For the last time, he's the best and only friend we have in the C.I.A. Start treating him as such. James? Paul's alive and well. Tim? You're smarter than me, dude, good job. Love all of you, all my boys, very much. Stay here, I'll be right back."

I took off after my partner.

CHAPTER 60

I DIDN'T KNOW WHERE I was or where White had gone, but it didn't matter. The Poofs were with me, and they clearly knew. We didn't go the way the others had, we went the way we'd come in. Down through the trapdoor, which I didn't bother to close, down the stairs, along the dark corridor.

I still had my iron staff, the Poofs were still large and in charge. I didn't worry about altering memories when we arrived—I was too worried about children being altered for life.

Used the staff to semi-pole vault over the problems in the floor. I was so fast I probably didn't need to, but better safe than sorry. Hit the intersection, went to the left. Came to stairs, old stairs like I'd seen in that brochure. We ran up them like they were nothing.

Reached a trapdoor and the Poofs stopped and went small. They jumped into the pockets of White's jacket. I'd forgotten I was still wearing it. Opened the trapdoor carefully.

Unlike the Conciergerie, this room wasn't empty. On the plus side, the trapdoor was in a corner where no one was. Managed to get the door opened quietly, pulled myself up. Pulled the staff out but laid it on the ground right away. I couldn't imagine the reaction if I sauntered out with an iron staff in hand, but pandemonium leaped to mind.

Needed to slow down again. Changed my music to the first slow song I hit, Trik Turner's "Friends and Family." Fitting, really.

The place was packed to the gills. I noted the doors were closed. I would have bet money they were locked tight, too.

Moved slowly through the throngs—it was packed with an unreal number of people. Headed toward the nave, where it looked like at least one of my targets was. I was pretty sure the fake Al Dejahl was there.

I stayed near the side so I'd hopefully not be spotted. I was close enough to see Al Dejahl clearly but not close enough to do anything when someone grabbed me, put his hand over my mouth and pulled a headphone out of my ear.

"Kathy, how good to see you."

I relaxed and he let go. "Rick, you continue to impress and amaze." Turned off my iPod and put it in one of the pockets. Patted the Poofs in there, too.

White moved us back against the wall. He put his arm around my shoulders, leaned down, and spoke softly in my ear. "I believe we're back to your original theory. When I was fighting with Ronaldo there, I noted he had two heartbeats."

"Huh. He's not great looking."

"Assume his mother wasn't attractive. Presumably she had other positives."

"Suppose so." Interesting to be right, then wrong, then right again. My head hurt thinking about it. "Where're Gaultier and Cooper?"

"No idea."

"I hope Camilla's gone back to Dulce."

"As long as she's a double agent, not a triple agent."

"Good point. You know, you totally rocked in that fight."

"Not as much as you. I'm terrified to ask how."

"I'll give you my guess later. Is Al Dejahl going to allow himself to be enhanced, too, do you think?"

"Doubtful. If they're still doing experiments, then they don't know long-term ramifications. By the way, I assume the plan is to kill everyone other than Jamie, so Alfred only has one living family member left. He would be willing to do anything to protect her, I'd assume, including give up patents."

"Well, that may be their plan. We're not letting that plan go any further."

"I agree. Just wanted to share my thinking."

"I'm so not kidding. You're the freaking best agent we have."

"Flattery will get you everywhere. What baby gift would you like?"

"I want us to kick these people back to the Stone Age."

"Happy to do my best."

We both scanned the room. No sign of obvious bad guys, no sign of Cooper or Gaultier. "Who put Camilla in place?"

"No idea. I would have suggested Mister Reynolds, but clearly not."

Wanted to ponder that a bit more, but now probably wasn't the time, at least not out loud, so, for me, definitely not the time. Spent some time looking around; people were milling about, shifting, clearly waiting with a good degree of anticipation, meaning no one was likely to wander off and out of range of the bad guys. Pity.

Just when I was about to suggest hyperspeeding it and grabbing Al Dejahl, things got started. "How are we going to protect the kids? I can't figure out where stuff's coming from, let alone come up with an idea of how to get everyone out of here safely."

"Maybe all we'll be able to do is help them deal with their mutation. Not my preferred plan, but I'm not coming up with anything either."

I felt someone come next to us and I nudged White. "Rick, honey, when do you think this ceremony's going to start?"

"Soon, I think, Kathy. Let's get closer."

"Or you could, you know, let those of us trained to do this handle it from here." I looked to my right. Jeff was standing there, looking particularly annoyed. He was also in a T-shirt that said "Faire l'amour avec moi." I looked down. He was in jeans and Vans sneakers. My jaw dropped.

He closed it gently. "We bought out the gift shop down the street." He looked at White. "Richard, get your hands off my wife." He handed me my purse.

"Sorry, Jeffrey, we're undercover. Meet my trophy wife, Kathy." White lifted his arm so I could put my purse over my neck, then put it back around my shoulders.

I nodded. "Rick's my sugar daddy."

Jeff shook his head. "I'm out of it for a little while and my uncle steals my girl."

I looked around. The rest of the team were in here, spread out. They were all in T-shirts. I'd never seen a group of A-C agents so casual in the entire time I'd known them. Christopher was across from us, Amy was with him. Abigail and Naomi were flanking Chuckie. The girls were in T-shirts and jeans, too. Jeff hadn't been kidding, there was a happy gift store owner out of merchandise.

"How'd you get in?"

"Got out of the prison the way we'd been brought in, realized we looked like refugees, bought clothes, went to the ticket window, bought tickets. We got a group rate."

"I can only imagine. So they're letting people keep coming in?"

"Can't keep anything from you, can we?"

I noted Reader sauntering up the middle aisle. Unsurprisingly, he looked awesome and like he was on the runway. People looked at him, to the point where conversations stopped and heads literally turned. "Is it safe for James to be basically standing there saying, 'Look at me, go for it, shoot the hottest guy in the room first'?"

"My ego is what's shot. My wife's been stolen by my uncle and is casually telling me my gay friend is the hottest thing on two legs."

"I'm not the one wearing the pick-up shirt."

"What's that supposed to mean?"

"I'll translate it for you later, Jeff. Are you guys going to do something, or should Rick and I go back to handling it?"

Christopher looked over at us. He shook his head. "Good. No one's altered yet." Jeff sighed. "I think we can handle it."

"Christopher's powers are scary."

"We'll discuss scary once we're out of this. I may never sleep again."

"Not to worry, Jeffrey. I'll keep Kathy with me." I could tell White was trying not to crack up.

"Thanks so much."

"Oh, Jeff, Rick says Ronaldo up there is really Yates' son, but likely not from Serene's mother."

"Yeah, he hit like an A-C, so not a surprise. So you were right, then wrong, then right? Geez, that gives me a headache just thinking about it."

Reader took a seat in the front row. Literally. I wasn't sure if there'd been a free one or he just moved someone over with the force of his cover-boy smile, but he was right up front. "Seriously, why is James the sitting duck?"

An older man got up and started speaking in French. I could make out one word in about ten. However, it wasn't hard to guess what they were saying. Only, words weren't computing. My French wasn't that awful. The person speaking wasn't making sense, though. As far as I could tell, he was talking about Reader, not Al Dejahl.

I looked over to where Christopher was. Chuckie and the Gower girls were next to Amy. I could see her talking to them. I watched her mouth move, then heard the words I was pretty sure she'd just said come out of the man who was giving the introductory speech.

Wild cheering started, and then Reader stood up, turned around and waved. He was wearing a "Paris, je t'aime" shirt. It looked like designer-wear on him. The kids went nuts. The adults went nuts, too. "What's going on?"

"Top international male model, remember? *The* top. Before he retired?" Jeff was grinning. "He's not quite as popular here as Jerry Lewis, but apparently that Calvin Klein ad you loved so much and was so controversial back home is considered high modern art over here."

"That's awesome, but how does it get the kids out safely?"

"You know, it's amazing how many humans one A-C can drag and still go fast."

"Not every single person in this room, I can guarantee that."

"Don't need to get them out if things are handled properly."

"You don't want to tell us anything, do you?"

"I'm reveling in having something I'm in charge of actually work out right, yeah."

White chuckled. "James seems in his element." He also seemed fluent in French—he was speaking now, fast and clear, like a native.

"Is there anything James can't do?"

"Turn straight, thank God." Jeff sighed. "Look, seriously, can I have my wife back?"

White sighed. "Well, it was enjoyable while it lasted."

I started to move to Jeff when I saw something up in the higher level, where I thought the brochure had said the choir was. A figure, holding a rifle with a silencer on it. Aimed at us.

Aimed at only one of us.

CHAPTER 61

I SHOVED JEFF AND WHITE, hard. We were near pillars, and I managed to get each of them behind one before the bullet left the gun. I did the splits. I'd never been able to do them before, but clearly they were part of my repertoire now. The bullet hit the wall above my head.

Jeff grabbed me and pulled us to the same pillar as White. His hearts were pounding. "Are you okay, baby?"

"Yeah. Is this part of the plan?"

"Hilarious. Not quite. Richard, you okay?"

"Yes. I really think we need to get her a catsuit." White looked around the pillar. "The man with the rifle's moved."

"Chuckie's going to be his next target."

"How? He's on the same side." Jeff looked around. "Thank God for the silencer, no one noticed."

I looked around Jeff. "Chuckie noticed." He was in the middle of the room, heading for us at a run. For whatever reason, there was a gap, and no others were close to him. I knew what this meant. I pulled away from Jeff and ran as well. Tackled Chuckie and brought him down. The next bullet hit the ground. I could tell it would have hit his head if he'd still been upright. "James, we have a sniper!"

Reader shouted in French as he grabbed Al Dejahl. I was pretty sure he'd told everyone to hit the ground, because they did, with a lot of screaming.

I was still on top of Chuckie. "Not that I don't love this, but I think we need to move." His eyes widened. "Or not."

I looked over my shoulder. Cooper was standing there,

rifle pointed at us. "It won't matter," he snarled. "You'll all be dead soon."

Chuckie shoved me one way and rolled the other. Next bullet hit the ground, pretty much where our hearts had been. I thought the next bullet would go into one of us, but Cooper jerked, flung the rifle up, and fired straight ahead.

I looked, expecting to see Reader go down. What I saw instead was Al Dejahl throw himself in front of Reader and take the bullet. In his head.

I heard the rifle clatter to the ground. Chuckie had spent his time tackling Cooper. They were fighting, but Chuckie was winning. Cooper managed to pull a smaller gun. I screamed, Chuckie grabbed Cooper's wrist, and I heard bone snap.

The gun fell to the ground. Then Chuckie twisted Cooper's head in a way I knew meant we had another bad guy down. He let Cooper's body fall to the floor as Michael and Brian ran up.

The crowd stayed reasonably calm. I looked around—it was clear Jeff and Christopher were doing crowd control. Jerry and Hughes ran in with Paris police. Reporters were right behind them. I recognized one of them.

"Chuckie, what are we going to do? In addition to everyone else, our buddy Mister Joel Oliver is somehow here, too."

He reached down and pulled me up and into his arms. "Leave Oliver to me and the rest of it to your husband," he said quietly. "Don't talk to anyone. Thanks for the save. All the saves." I hugged him back. I managed not to shake, but only just. He rocked me, and I felt a little better.

White ran over and pulled me out of Chuckie's arms. "Kathy, you were so brave."

Freaked but not dumb. "You know, Rick, one of those once in a lifetime things." I pulled his head down. "What's going on?"

"Pretty much what Jeffrey and Christopher had planned."

"You mean me, Chuckie and James almost being shot in the head was supposed to be happening?"

"Tell you later. Just be my good little trophy wife, we're going to get interviewed shortly."

"Are you kidding me? Chuckie told me not to say anything!"

No sooner had I hissed this into White's ear when a microphone was shoved in our faces and a reporter was talking to us, rapidly, in French.

"Tourists. American tourists," White said, sounding like a confused regular guy. I decided burying my face girlishly in "my husband's" chest was a better option than opening my mouth, so I did.

I heard more voices, one of them familiar. Looked out, to see Reader being interviewed. Good, our spokesmodel was handling things. In perfect French.

Chuckie had Mister Joel Oliver by the arm and was leading him away. Oliver didn't look to be fighting it. I had no idea if Chuckie was handing him a line of bull, promising an exclusive later, threatening his life, or having Jeff or Christopher do a mind alteration attempt. Decided the *World Weekly News* getting this story was the least of our immediate issues.

I looked around, and Tim caught my eye. He gave me a small nod and looked up. I looked up, too. To see a lot of clear balloons resting against the ceiling. Knew where the gas was. Figured they'd added helium to it to keep the gas conveniently out of the way until they were ready to start the test.

Paris police performed crowd control. I noted that Tim, Tito, all the flyboys, Jeff, and Christopher weren't anywhere around any more. Neither were Melanie and Emily, though the Gower girls were with us. No Amy, either.

Our group, or at least the portion of our group here, was herded elsewhere while medical arrived to take Al Dejahl's and Cooper's bodies away. Reader was still talking to the police and reporters. Michael and Brian were with him. I got the impression our story was the brave American astronauts on holiday saved the day, but I couldn't be positive. I couldn't see where Chuckie and Oliver had gotten to.

Naomi grabbed me and pulled me to the side, away from the others. "Sorry. We lost concentration at a bad time. But we have to get out of here."

"What the hell was and is going on?"

"Abby and I tapped into Cooper's mind. He was going to shoot the balloons to release the gas. Our plan was for me and Abby to control Cooper, have him shoot Al Dejahl and then we kill him, thereby stopping the terrorist from killing anyone else. Gets them both out of the way and us out of it reasonably well."

"So Cooper shooting at me and Chuckie was there for added excitement?"

Naomi gave me a dirty look. "No. Abby and I lost concentration when . . ."

"When what?" I got the usual bad feeling in my stomach.

"When Mister Gaultier grabbed Amy. Christopher doesn't know, he was already in place to do crowd control. Chuck does, but he was more concerned about you, Richard, and Jeff. It was hard to tell which one of you was the target."

"Me." I knew Chuckie had known that, too. "Why did Al Dejahl take the bullet intended for James?"

"James is good at fake throwing. First grab looked like he was protecting Al Dejahl. Then he tossed him so it looked like Al Dejahl was being a hero and saving the handsome celebrity." Naomi managed a small smile. "James is really amazing."

"True, very true. Anyway, how did Gaultier take Amy? No way she went with him willingly."

"Uh, gun to her temple? He didn't shoot us only because we didn't try to stop him."

"Great. Yeah, we have to get out of here." I looked up at the ceiling. The guys looked precariously perched around the upper levels. I concentrated, and a shimmering bubble went around the balloons. I squinted, and the bubble started to shrink. The balloons popped, but noiselessly, and the gas didn't escape. Made the bubble smaller and smaller, until it disappeared.

"How did you do that?" Naomi sounded freaked and impressed.

"Tell you later."

Jeff and the others joined us shortly. Figured they'd used hyperspeed. He came up next to me. "How in God's name—?"

"Really, tell you later. We have a bigger problem."

"Two of them," Melanie said as she and Emily joined us. "We went with the medical team to check and make sure Cooper and Al Dejahl were really dead. They are, but the one who looked like Al Dejahl only had a single heart."

"How can you tell when he's dead?"

Emily shrugged. "Have scalpel, will travel."

The rest of our group, other than Reader, Michael, and Brian were with us now. I spotted Oliver in the crowd of reporters, mostly because Michael was standing next to him. "Chuckie, what's up with Mister Joel Oliver? Why is he here?"

"He's here because of the clustered incident from last week. He's getting this story and will print what everyone else prints."

"Why is that?"

Chuckie managed a small smile. "Because I promised him a bigger scoop later." I raised my eyebrow, and he sighed. "I'm giving him intel on Cooper. Nothing classified, but I'm going to be sure Cooper's reputation's trashed. Michael Gower's agreed to see that our favorite reporter gets an exclusive shot of the astronauts to seal this deal. We're good on the paparazzi front."

"I'm all over speaking ill of this particular dead. Okay, great. So back to the bigger issues. The real Ronaldo Al Dejahl is out there somewhere, and, realistically, we have no idea what he looks like."

"What do you mean? We've all seen him." Christopher looked around. "Where's Amy?" We brought the others up to speed, fast. Christopher's jaw clenched. "Let's get out of here."

"No," White said calmly. "I want to hear Kathy's explanation for why she doesn't think we know what Al Dejahl looks like."

I was worried, but I had to laugh at everyone's expression. "Have you all met my husband, Rick? Look, the real Al Dejahl is an A-C, because Richard felt two hearts when he was fighting him, and Jeff said he hit like an A-C. A-Cs have talents, and I'll wager he's a troubadour with imageering ability. He's making himself look like who or what he wants. For this particular operation, he made himself look like the actor or agent the C.I.A. hired to impersonate him. We have no idea what he looks like, but I'm putting money on him resembling Richard in some way. Serene resembles Richard, if you know what to look for."

"Where would he go? Or Gaultier?" Jeff had his Commander voice on.

"They want Jamie." I said that calmly. I was proud of myself.

"Yeah, who's going to let them in?" Jeff didn't sound nearly as calm.

I looked at White. "What are the odds?"

He nodded. "Good, very good."

I put my hands in the pockets of his jacket. "The Poofs are gone."

"Good. I think we know where they went." White looked at Jeff. "Gaultier isn't going to the same place. I imagine Christopher can track where he's gone, or at least where Amy is. You take them." White took my hand. "Your wife and I will handle my half brother."

Jeff shook his head. "It's my daughter they're going after."

"Yes, it is. It's my grandniece. And my half sister—they want Serene as well." White gave Jeff a long look. "You have to trust us right now, Jeffrey. You need to find Gaultier and Amy and keep Christopher under control. You're the only one who can, and he's the only one who can find her now, isn't he?"

"Jeff, I won't let anyone get our baby." I put my hand on his arm. "Richard's right. And we have to go, now, or all of us will be too late."

"She's just a tiny baby." Jeff sounded like he was going to lose it.

"Yes, she is. She's also so powerful Cooper was expecting her to warp over from Dulce to Paris to save her daddy. My mother's with her, and so are the girls. Trust me—nothing's scarier than a mother protecting her young." I could feel the power building. I leaned up and kissed him. "I love you, Jeff. Go save Amy and keep Christopher and the others safe while you do it."

I pulled at White, and we raced out of the building.

CHAPTER 62

I RAN US TO THE PARKING GARAGE.

"Why here?" White asked when we stopped running.

"So no one but you sees. Hold onto me." I wrapped my arms around him, he wrapped his around me, and I concentrated. I knew where I wanted us to go. I felt the power build and expand.

We moved, fast as a gate, but with no nausea. The movement stopped, and the power faded. We stepped apart and looked around. We were in the Lair.

"Why here?" White asked. "Why not right by Jamie?"

"I assume we need to sneak up on the situation. Seeing two of you in one place will freak everyone out."

He took my hand, and we moved out of the room. "Elevator?"

"Stairs. I don't know what level they're on. So we search each floor." We hypersped through the lower level. No one was there—including Clarence. Not a good sign, but not a surprise, either.

Moved up, no one on any of the lower levels. "This is just like Operation Fugly. Everyone was up top. Why do the bad guys like to herd everyone into one damned spot?"

"Easier to perform genocide. Or make the pronouncement that there's someone impersonating your Pontifex and he should be killed on sight."

"Yeah, I was sort of expecting that, too."

"I assume he's told everyone that the others are being mind-controlled or impersonated, which is why you sent them after Amy."

"That and, frankly, you and I seem to be doing pretty darned okay on our own."

White laughed. "You do make becoming a field agent sound more appealing than it ever has before."

Reached the library level. Lots and lots of people in here. But they were quiet. They were listening. "And, unfortunately, Gower is unable to function now. We'll need to pull the entity out of him in order to keep his mind from destroying itself." It sounded like White, unless you actually knew how he talked.

I pulled his head down. "At least some of them have to be wondering what's wrong with 'you.' You don't talk like this."

"Enough will be too frightened to notice." We were in the back, behind a pillar, and we both scanned the room. "I don't see your parents. Or the baby."

I closed my eyes and concentrated. "Oh, God. He has them locked into isolation chambers. Paul was already there, but Serene, Lorraine, Claudia, my mother and father are in chambers, too. I don't know how he did it."

"He's a hybrid. We have no idea what his talents are. He may have mind control abilities. Do you see the baby?"

I moved us a bit. Now we could see Al Dejahl. He looked just like White normally did—full Armani suit, handsome, kindly. And he was wearing a Snugli carrier. With my baby inside it. I was ready to lunge.

White squeezed my hand. "Not without a plan. He'll kill her or escape with her."

I nodded. "Okay. I'm open to ideas."

White was quiet for a few moments, while Al Dejahl spent some time discussing how badly demolished Alpha and Airborne teams were. "Are you able to go so fast that you can run on the ceiling?"

I thought about it. "Yeah, I'm pretty sure." Pulled out my iPod, tuned it, set for repeat. "Under the circumstances, anyway."

White took a look. “Elton John, ‘The Bitch is Back.’ I was expecting Aerosmith.”

“I like to mess it up, keep the bad guys guessing.” I looked at him. “Ready, partner?”

“Lead on, Missus Martini. Remember to tell me what size catsuit you wear.”

CHAPTER 63

TOOK A DEEP BREATH and let the music play. Didn't take long to rev me, I was already running on waves of fury.

Turned us and ran, fast. Hit the wall and went up it. Kept moving as we hit the ceiling and perspective turned. It was a little like when I'd fought Uma in the bubble created by ACE and the other PPB entity, Lilith. Didn't matter, wasn't going to be up here long.

The library was huge, and Al Dejahl was at the far end. He wasn't using a microphone to project his voice—more proof he was a troubadour. More reasons for the people in here to not believe him. But then again, they were all quiet, all acting too sheeplike. My family, in particular, were acting far too docile.

Reached the target and dropped. We spun in the air and landed right behind him. I grabbed his arms. "Get away from my baby, you bastard."

"Gladys!" Al Dejahl shouted. "Need Security!"

"Gladys, belay that! He's an imposter . . . and your half brother."

"Richard *is* my half brother." Gladys sounded angry, but also confused.

"Yeah, Richard is. The guy with me, not the guy holding my baby." Al Dejahl was fighting me and he was really strong. The people in the library weren't moving. "Gladys, why are they all acting like sheep? Why are you? Think dammit!"

White unhooked the baby carrier and got Jamie. This was the trigger—the rest of the A-Cs and humans started to move forward, like zombies. "Mister White, run, get out of here."

He nodded. "Hurry." If I looked at it like a human, he disappeared. But I could see that he was just running very, very fast. Superpowers were fab.

Distractions, however, weren't good. Al Dejahl got loose, spun and swung at me. He was fast, too, and we were fighting furiously in a moment. "How did your mother keep you hidden and under control all this time, Ronnie?"

He grinned. "Call me Ricky. I'm in charge now." He swung at my face.

I blocked, ducked, and kicked at his legs. "Your plan won't work."

He snorted a laugh as he jumped to avoid my leg sweep. "You're all so naïve. My father raised me in secrecy, so I'd be protected . . . and ready to carry on his master plan." His eyes narrowed as he brought a hammer fist down toward my collarbone. "I'm going to enjoy avenging his death, believe me. And what I do to my little sister will make it even better. My father didn't want her, but I have plenty of uses for her planned."

All the theories gelled into one certainty as I spun out of the way and managed to kick his butt at the same time. "You're a full A-C, not a hybrid. In fact, you're Serene's brother, aren't you? Same mother, same creepy father."

"Same powerful father, same latently powerful mother. Yeah. One of the many reasons I can control all these sheep." He faked a punch and, when I blocked it, grabbed my upper arms.

"Zombie mind control won't last long."

"It'll last long enough. Kill her!" He shoved me into the crowd and took off running.

I landed in a group of people I knew well—my family. I realized the Martinis were here, too. He'd called everyone to Dulce, presumably to do whatever horrible thing his master plan called for. They were lunging for me—I couldn't hit my grandparents, and now that we were past all of Jeff's childhood issues, I couldn't hit his parents, either.

Someone landed next to me, and a hand reached down,

grabbed, and pulled me up. We slammed through bodies. "Camilla, great to see you."

"Yeah, wonderful. You guys couldn't kill him when he was right damned there?"

I pulled off my iPod and dropped it into a pocket. "Who put you in place?" We were heading for the isolation area at full speed.

"Who do you think?"

"I only have two guesses, since I know it wasn't Chuckie. My mother or Alfred. And, I have to go with Alfred."

She grinned. "Yeah. Royalty's used to people trying to off them."

"How do you get away with the lying?"

"Training. Trust me, we can do it, but it's almost like our other talents, it's a specialized gift, and it's very rare—most of us can't lie, at least not to humans. Those of us who can? Well, we learn how to do it effectively."

"The Diplomatic Corps is good at it, aren't they?"

"Some of them. Not all."

Reached isolation and decided to table this discussion. No one was there. "Where are they?"

"He's hiding." Camilla looked around. "But where?"

"Which he?"

"Both, probably. But Richard's the one with the baby. So he has more reason to hide."

"Let's get the others out of isolation. They may be able to help us."

"They may be mind-controlled. Al Dejahl was back and had them locked up before I got here."

"Yeah, 'cause they were using a body double at Notre Dame."

"Figures." We reached the isolation chamber with my mother in it. Camilla did something with the door. It didn't open. She cursed. "They changed the sequence. We don't have time to break it."

"Gladys! Open the damned isolation chambers."

"Commander Martini, the Pontifex has advised us you're under mind-control. Cannot take your orders, therefore."

Camilla and I started off, looking for where Al Dejahl or White could be. "Gladys, for God's sake. Aren't you watching? You don't sound mind-controlled, maybe he can't do it to you. He couldn't control Serene, don't think he can control Richard. Maybe it's a blood thing, though Lucinda seemed all over beating the crap out of me."

"Who is 'he,' Commander?"

"Ronaldo Al Dejahl. Illegitimate son of Ronald Yates, also known as your father. Same mother as Serene. He's a troubadour and an imageer and God alone knows what else, and, like your father, he's pure freaking evil."

"You are working with an identified mole, Commander. Your views cannot be trusted."

We spun around a corner and saw two men. "Oh, hell, not this again." They both looked exactly alike—both had the Timothy Dalton look going, both were holding Jamie. I knew Al Dejahl was faking it, but it was a damned good fake.

"Who's who?" Camilla asked.

I could hear pounding feet in the distance. "The anti-cavalry's coming. And I have no idea."

Both men were fighting, sort of. They were both holding the baby, in that sense, so she wouldn't get hurt. They were both decent at fighting one-handed, but I had no guess as to who was who. The footsteps were louder; we were almost out of time.

"Rick!"

The one who was likely the real White turned toward me. Unfortunately, this gave the other one the chance to both hit him and move them around so fast that I couldn't follow who was who when they separated. I figured we could do the name and speaking stuff, but the real White was going to be killed before I could figure it out.

The zombie army was almost to us, and I had nothing but the crazy left. I ran toward both of them. "Poofs assemble! Save Jamie and the real Richard White."

Out of nowhere six large, toothy Poofs showed up. They surrounded one of them, and I tackled the other one.

We hit the floor, hard, and he shifted. It wasn't White, or the little dark guy playing Al Dejahl. This man was handsome—typical A-C handsome. He was older than Serene but not by too much. I saw resemblance to her and to White and realized I was finally looking at the real Ronaldo Al Dejahl. He flipped us, pinned my legs with his knees, and grinned as his hands went around my throat.

"Maybe I'll keep you around, have you pop out more kids. More of my kids. She'll know me as her father and do what I say. They all will. You'll like being the mother of the galaxy, won't you? You don't have to have a functioning brain to pop out the babies, did you know that? At least, not with the advances in medicine Gaultier's made."

He was incredibly strong, stronger than Jeff, which was saying a lot. So much for the idea he wouldn't take the drug until it'd been tested—I could tell he was enhanced, probably using Christopher's method. Camilla was shouting, but I got the impression the zombies had captured her. I could hear the Poofs growling.

"Poofs—"

Al Dejahl tightened his hands on my throat, choking me so I couldn't talk and could barely breathe. "No, no, no. I think we'll leave your pets confused."

"Poofs, help Kitty," White said. The growling continued, but the Poofs didn't move.

Al Dejahl leaned closer. "Your baby's trying to help." He looked over his shoulder. "Good girl, Jamie. You keep those fluffy monsters from hurting your mommy just like I told you to." He looked back at me. "You got empathic blocks into her mind somehow, but that's all right. It actually helps me, because she can't feel anything. She can hear, though. She's a good girl and does what she's told."

I really wanted to kill this guy, but, enhanced or not, I was definitely losing this fight.

"Let her go, Ronaldo. You can have me, take my place. Just let Missus Martini and the baby go free."

Al Dejahl laughed. "You really think I'll take that offer, big brother? I already took your place. They all believe, even Gladys. She was hard, but even the strongest minds can be controlled." He grinned at me. "Young minds are so impressionable. And, in the case of my soon-to-be-daughter, quite powerful."

Rage helped me jerk my neck out of his grasp, albeit only a little. "Loser," I managed to gasp out. "Mind controlling a newborn is the best you can do? You couldn't control my parents or my girls."

He tightened his grip again, and I went back to wondering if he was going to break my neck or just asphyxiate me. I already knew I had about five seconds left before I blacked out. "They need a little more time, I'll give you that." His smile went wider. "Can't wait to see Martini's reaction when he watches me fuck you in front of him. Right before I kill him, of course."

A fist slammed into Al Dejahl's head. He let go of my throat and went flying. "Yeah? Let's discuss that possibility."

CHAPTER 64

JEFF LOOKED AT ME. "You okay, baby?"

"Scary man attacking!" Al Dejahl lunged for Jeff.

Jeff grinned and slammed his fist into Al Dejahl's face. "Really? Hadn't noticed." He turned and gave Al Dejahl his full attention. "You think you can show up and just walk all over my people?" His roar was already past "rabid dog" and "enraged bear." Jeff was at "lion takes over the veldt," which meant Al Dejahl was toast. "You think you can threaten my uncle, terrorize my child, and attack my wife?"

Al Dejahl was landing some hits, but Jeff wasn't tied up. I got to my feet and pulled Camilla away from the people holding her. They looked like they were waking up—I had to figure Al Dejahl needed to focus on Jeff's fists. Went to White. "You okay?"

He nodded. "Good thing you arrived when you did. I'm not quite as good with the fighting as you and Jeffrey are." He handed Jamie to me. "I'm a bit concerned about the Poof situation, of course."

I couldn't be sure, but Jamie also looked worried to me. "It's okay, Jamie-Kat. You were right to keep the Poofies around you and your Uncle Richard. Daddy was here to save the day, wasn't he?" I kissed and cuddled her. She gurgled happily, heaved a little sigh, closed her eyes, and went to sleep.

I put the Snugli back on with Camilla's help. "We'll deal with what damage your loser half brother did to the Poofs later. For all we know, they were just waiting for the right order, and neither one of us gave it to them. And, dude, you were fighting a guy at least young enough to be your own son, while holding a newborn, and you remained standing and said newborn remained completely unscathed. I say again, you totally rock."

"As much as Jeffrey?" he asked with a chuckle.

Turned to watch Jeff continue to beat Al Dejahl to a pulp. "Okay, not quite as good with the fisticuffs as Jeff, but, you know, he's enhanced." And totally, drool-worthily hot. It never failed—when he was protective, I got weak in the knees. And this was the example of protective to the tenth degree.

"Stop lusting after my uncle." Jeff tossed this one off as he picked Al Dejahl up bodily and slammed said body into the door of a nearby isolation chamber.

"Had to pick my next husband in case you and my other options were all dead."

"Nice. Gladys, you'd damn well better be off the mind control. I want everyone who was locked into isolation out, NOW." He bellowed it. He was so good with the bellowing. Jamie made a few fussy sounds. I realized it was probably close to time for her to eat.

"Jeff, can you finish him off? It's torpedo time."

"Oh, sure, no problem. I'll just hurry it up and stop being fancy. Richard, you want him dead or alive?"

"Did Mister Reynolds have an opinion?"

"Don't know. He's with Christopher and the others."

"Um, what? You were supposed to stay with them and save Amy."

Jeff slammed Al Dejahl against the door again. "Yeah? Well, I could have let him kill you, I suppose. I happened to remember, though, hey, I'm in charge and, therefore, I don't have to be a good little soldier and follow orders."

Al Dejahl was limp. Jeff was still pounding. "Son, I think he's out of it." Alfred looked shaken.

"He's still breathing." Jeff looked at his father. "You know, I can see every damn emotion she has, and most of the thoughts when they're strong. Nothing like seeing my parents do the mindless automaton attack on my wife to make me feel great about the next family get-together."

"Speaking of which, Clarence is out of solitary."

Alfred sighed. “Yes, Sylvia couldn’t take it. We let him out.”

“Beg freaking pardon? He was trying to kill Christopher and my baby!”

“No. He was being deceived.”

“He wasn’t mind-controlled. He was using his own free will.”

“Yes, he was,” Alfred said patiently. “However, people do make mistakes.” He gave me a rueful smile. “And my eldest daughter loves him, despite the fact he’s an utter moron and a traitor. He’ll be watched, believe me.”

“You’re nicer than I am.”

“Yes, I believe I am.” Alfred grinned. “Not that I’m suggesting for one moment that you soften up.” He sighed. “I think we want to keep him alive.”

“Clarence?”

Alfred gave me the “duh” look. “No, Ronaldo Al Dejahl. Richard, what do you think?”

White shook his head. “I can’t give you an answer to that, Alfred.” He was looking past me, and I saw Gower. He had one arm around Serene and one around Lorraine. My father had his arms around my mother and Claudia.

“Paul, Dad, are you guys okay?”

My father nodded. “Yes, kitten, we’re fine. A little shaken—nothing like being in solitary and hearing the same message over and over again.”

“What message?”

“You will obey me.” Dad shrugged. “It’s an old trick. Your mother and I know how to ignore it. And our girls here were all little tigers.” He hugged Claudia. “Never make the mothers mad, that’s my advice.”

I hugged all of them. “Mom, you sure you’re okay?”

“Yes, we’re fine. He didn’t want to hurt us—I know he wanted the babies, and I think he wanted me to take care of Jamie. Lord alone knows. Don’t care. Why isn’t Jeff just breaking his neck?” She sounded annoyed. Knew where I’d inherited my desire to kill the baddies and save trouble.

“He’s enjoying himself. You should have seen what they did to him and the other guys. Let him have a release.”

“Right. Where are the other guys?”

Oh, right. Most of our team were still out there, somewhere. “Jeff, we have to get the others.”

"I'm not done killing him yet."

White was speaking to Gower. I could see they were arguing. I went to them. "Richard, it's not time for this, and I'm not the right person." Gower sounded upset.

"Paul, you are the right person. By the way, how is ACE?"

He sighed. "Better. Not fully back to normal, though. He had to protect me again while we were in isolation so Al Dejahl's mind control couldn't work on me."

"So ACE wasn't, ah, spotting me during any of this?"

Gower shook his head. "ACE says that you were able to do what you did because of all the hormones running around in your body right now."

"Don't piss off the new mother?"

"Exactly."

"The drug does work on the id, doesn't it? And I'm seriously pissed."

"Yes. Your rage was definitely helping you." Gower cleared his throat. "ACE also says to expect to be extremely tired once your rage fully wears off."

"Can't wait. How long before ACE is better?" It was bad enough when someone was hurt, but it wasn't as though I could tuck ACE into bed and give him juice and aspirin to make him feel better.

He twitched. "ACE says that he should be fine shortly, so, and I quote, Kitty can stop worrying about ACE."

"Okay, as long as both of you are going to be alright soon, I'll focus the worry elsewhere. But I think Richard's right. Who we protect needs to change. And the best way for our people to understand that is if you do what he's asking."

Gower shook his head. "I'm not the right person to be Pontifex. It should stay within the family line."

I snorted. "Like Christopher has the Zen to be the religious leader? From the first day I was with you guys, I knew who Richard's successor would be. At least, who it should be."

"But you have to accept it, Paul." White's voice was gentle. "And I must insist you decide quickly. The Pontifex needs to advise Jeffrey whether we should let our enemy live or not. I can't make that decision objectively any longer—I know what that means."

Gower swallowed. "I promised to protect you with my life, Richard."

White nodded. "Protect me now as our religious leader. Protect the world by working with the superconsciousness that loves us." He stroked Jamie's head. "A new day is coming, Paul. Change is here, and we have to adapt to it properly or we will perish. Please—I ask this as my last act as Sovereign Pontifex, that you succeed me while I live, not after I die."

Gower looked at both of us. Then he nodded and turned around. "Jeff, let him live."

CHAPTER 65

JEFF HEAVED A SIGH but he stopped slamming Al Dejahl into the wall. "Oh, fine. I want him locked up and not on the same floor where I live."

"That won't be an issue, I'd assume, Jeffrey." White gave me a small smile. "Let's get the rest of our people, shall we? Then we can discuss personnel changes."

A contingent of big Security A-Cs showed up and carried Al Dejahl off. Camilla shook her head. "Killing your enemy is a lot safer."

Gower nodded. "In self-defense, yes. Just because you can? No."

Jeff came over to me. He picked me up and kissed me. "I suppose telling you to stay here while I go back to the others is useless."

"You know it. Mom, do you have any milk left?"

"Plenty."

Jeff put me down, helped me take the Snugli off, then he cuddled Jamie and kissed her head. "Mommy and Daddy will be right back, Jamie-Kat." Mom took her, and we strapped the Snugli on her. Jeff looked at White. "You're sure?"

White nodded. "Yes." He looked at the others. "We'll do this more officially, I'm sure, but as of now, I am no longer Sovereign Pontifex. That honor, and all the authority and respect that comes with it, now belongs to Paul Gower. Listen to him as you've listened to me all these years."

Jeff nodded. "Anyone who doesn't will be considered a

traitor. I don't like traitors, in case anyone wasn't sure." He looked at me. "Let's go."

I looked at White. "Embassy, Mister White?"

White smiled. "I'd assume so, Missus Martini."

I looked up at Jeff. "Meet my newest recruit."

Jeff shook his head. "You're like Typhoid Mary for adrenaline junkies."

"It's a gift." I took White's hand. Jeff raised his eyebrow. "Hey, he's my partner."

Jeff took my other hand. "So am I. And I have to guess you can handle a double dose of hyperspeed now." We headed off to the launch area. "Embassy, now, all together."

"Yes, sir, Commander." The A-C was the same one who'd worked the gate when White and I had left hours—or was it days?—ago. It seemed like days, but reality told me it was just hours.

I looked around. He was the only A-C on the job in this area. "You're back on duty fast."

He flashed a quick smile. "My brothers always said I ignored directions really well. I was able to resist the order to assemble and stay in the launch area." He looked down. "I did give in to the mind control, though, finally."

"So did everyone else, including the Head of Security. I think you did pretty damned well, all things considered."

Jeff grunted. "I agree."

He looked proud for a moment. "Thank you, Commanders. Please be careful . . . again," he said to me.

"Will do." My throat felt tight. "Do you know . . . were your brothers with Captain Crawford?" I held my breath. Maybe they'd been sent to Florida.

He swallowed. "One of them was, yes."

I had to know. "Which one?"

"Wayne."

The empath. The big, fun, nice empath who knew me well enough in a short time to know where I'd hidden a file. One of the only two who could back me and Chuckie on the superbeings as supersoldiers thing. "Why didn't he go to Florida with William? Why did Tim break them up? They were a team."

"William's married and has a baby due soon. He . . . he told me Captain Crawford said you'd want the expectant father to be safe."

"He was right." I'd wanted all of them to be safe, though.

The A-C looked at Jeff. "Gate's ready, Commander."

Jeff nodded. "Thank you."

We walked through together. It occurred to me that I still didn't know Wayne's younger brother's name. I didn't have time to dwell on that, though. The gate still made me sick, and this time we weren't landing on a moving train. I might be superenhanced, but gates were apparently going to stay the bane of my existence.

It was dark, but I could see decently, only there wasn't much to see, just a lot of boxes and the gate we'd exited through. "Where are we?" I whispered.

"Basement." Jeff was speaking softly. "Stay together. Richard, they won't know you're not Pontifex any more. Have no idea what that will or won't mean, just be aware of it. Kitty, seriously, let me run in first, okay?"

"Man thing?"

"Yeah, I don't want to see my wife killed, call me a caveman."

"Later, when we have a bassinet and the baby's asleep."

White chuckled. "It's nice to know she always focuses, Jeffrey."

We went up three sets of stairs to the second floor. I could hear raised voices. "How is one human managing to hold off our entire freaking team?"

"We're not as good with hostage situations as you are." Jeff's sarcasm knob was back to eleven.

"Guess not."

We rounded a corner and ended up in a doorway to what I realized was a ballroom. Why the A-C Embassy had a ballroom I didn't know, but I also didn't have time to worry about it, because I saw how Gaultier had our team pinned.

He didn't just have Amy—he had all of Jeff's family.

CHAPTER 66

EVERYONE BUT AMY WAS HELD in what looked like an electronic pen that locked them against a wall with no door or windows. The pen glowed and shimmered—I got the impression touching it was a bad idea.

On the plus side, in addition to all of Jeff's sisters, nieces, and nephews, the rest of his brothers-in-law were in the net as well, meaning they might not all be traitors like Clarence. I decided not to dwell on my new definition of "plus side."

Gaultier was in front of the pen. He had Amy in a chokehold and a gun at her head. We were in a doorway that was in the middle of the long room—Gaultier and his mass of hostages were to our left, our team was spread out to our right, Christopher in front of them.

Jeff was ready to leap into the room, but White and I held him back. "Wait," I whispered.

Gaultier hadn't spotted us. "You can't win."

Christopher snorted. "And you can? By doing what, exactly? You kill her, kill any of them, and I kill you. How do you win that way?"

Gaultier laughed. "If I die, the pen will kill them all. You want to be the one who kills all those little children?"

"How did you turn into this?" Amy snarled. "You weren't always like this."

"Sure he was," Chuckie said. "I told you, you just didn't want to believe it. Your mother died, and his only restraint died with her. Speaking of which, where's the trophy wife?

She in on this or sitting home thinking you're on a business trip?"

Gaultier smiled. "She's perfectly safe." He shook Amy. "She's not against being queen of a new world. What's wrong with you?"

I studied the pen. "Where's the switch, do you think?" I whispered in White's ear.

"I'd imagine on his person somewhere. Do you notice anything odd about him?"

I looked carefully. "His nose isn't broken any more."

White nodded. "He enhanced himself. The drug is popular."

"Your wife might enjoy life on a new world, but you won't," Christopher snarled. "It's eating you up."

"What?" Gaultier laughed. "The Surcenthumain? Hardly. I feel great."

I knew what Christopher wanted to do, but I didn't see a clear way for him to do it without Amy or all of Jeff's family dying. Which meant we needed to disengage the net and create a distraction.

Moved back a step and spoke softly. "Poofies." Six Poofs showed up, silently, at my feet. I went down on my knees. "Can you get to Alfred's family, Harlie? Behind the net?" No Poof mewling or purring. I took that as a "no." Limitations to Poof talents was not the news I was hoping for.

White stepped back and squatted down. "Can you rescue all of Alfred's family who are held here in the net in this ballroom?" The Poofs bounced up and down, then disappeared.

"Dude, again, you rock beyond all others."

Jeff pulled me and White to our feet. "What do I have to do to get that kind of hero worship from you?"

"Tell you after I help Christopher."

"Me, not you."

"No, me. I'll explain why later, okay?"

Jeff opened his mouth to argue, but White put his hand on Jeff's chest. "Please, Jeffrey. Trust us." He looked at me. "Missus Martini, your plan?"

"Going with the crazy again. It's working so well for me right now." Dug into my purse and pulled out my portable speakers. Plugged in my iPod, programmed the song, handed it to White. "He has a gun, so put this in the doorway, but be sure you and Jeff are against either wall when you turn it on."

White nodded. "I approve of the song choice."

I took my purse off and put it down and to the side. There was a door opposite us, I ran around to it. Got there in about two seconds. Hyperspeed was awesome. Christopher and Gaultier were still talking. He'd learned something from hanging out with me for the past couple of years. Keep the bad guy monologing, keep everyone alive.

"Is it the drugs making you act like this?" Amy asked. "Or are you actually enjoying it as much as you seem to be?"

Gaultier chuckled. "There's nothing more enthralling than power. You used to understand that."

"That's not how I was raised. You were never like this when Mother was alive."

"You need to stop mewling for a woman who's been dead for years. She lacked vision, something I see you've inherited from her."

"Right now, I'm praying I've inherited everything from her." I recognized the expression on Amy's face—I'd seen it at her mother's funeral and a few other times in our lives—she wanted to cry and was determined not to.

"Including an early grave," Gaultier said with a sneer.

Hoped the Poofs were in place, because I could see Gaultier getting antsy. Had to figure he'd learned how to calibrate a gate, and I was confident there was more than one gate in the Embassy. Meaning that if he got away, we were going to have a hard time finding him, or stopping him from getting to Alpha Four.

"What are you waiting for?" Amy said. She sounded scared, but more, she sounded angry. "Why don't you just kill me and all the others?"

"He's waiting for me." I walked into the room, but not too far in, close enough to leap back out through the doorway if I had to.

Gaultier laughed. "I knew you'd come. Yes, I am waiting for you. Come here, or I kill Amy and the others."

I shrugged. "Go ahead. Al Dejahl might recover from the beating Jeff gave him, but I wouldn't count on it. Cooper's dead, Chuckie took care of him. Mister White and I took out all the Diplomatic Corps and all your C.I.A. buddies. That pretty much only leaves you."

"And you're here to take care of me?" Gaultier sneered. "You might be enhanced, but I have the upper hand."

"Dude, seriously, upper hand? Who says that crap any more? You're reading too many old megalomaniac how-to books. The modern megalomaniacs prefer something more effective than holding a bunch of little kids behind an electronet."

"The old ways are still effective."

"Yeah?" I studied my fingernails. "Take a gander." The net was empty. My Poofs had done their job.

Gaultier didn't look pleased. "No idea of how you did that, but you apparently can't whisk Amy away as easily, can you?"

"Nope. Besides, I'm figuring you and the rest of the Psycho Squad rigged the Embassy for bombs and such. Otherwise you wouldn't be so confident standing there alone with a whole lot of younger, stronger, and seriously more pissed people in front of you. So, uh, guys? Do the bomb squad thing, will you?"

"Move and I set them off," Gaultier said quickly.

"Blah, blah, blah. You can't set them off because you're in the freaking building, and we're all really clear that you want to live forever. That's what you think the drug will do, ultimately, right? Extend life—unlimited strength, regeneration, power."

Gaultier shook his head. "You wasted your mind. You actually can think, can't you? But you've wasted yourself with these people and their quixotic need to save the world."

"Only world we've got." I looked at Reader. "Seriously. Bomb check, unscramble the signals, and so on. Chop, chop, time's wasting."

He grinned at me. "Sorry, just love watching you work." Reader barked some orders and the team left, other than Christopher, Chuckie, and the four women.

"Chuckie, get the girls to safety, would you? Science Center's clean, finally. I'd suggest going through the gate in the basement, but if you want to see what they did to your apartment first, I have no objection; just keep the ladies with you."

"You're sure?"

"Positive. Get Abby and Mimi out of here, and get Melanie and Emily back to their daughters, who have made them proud but could use their kickass mothers right now, trust me."

Naomi grabbed his hand, and the five of them zoomed off at hyperspeed.

I figured White had to be holding Jeff back by this time, but I tried to send an emotional signal that Jeff would be more useful defusing bombs and such. Wasn't sure if he got it or would listen to it, but a girl could only try.

"So, just the four of us. Cozy." I yawned. "Damn, I'm tired." I really hoped I wasn't going to have to do anything, because that exhaustion Gower had told me was likely seemed to be coming on fast. "Really, you're going to off your own daughter?"

"She's weak. I'll have stronger children, children who won't question me."

"I liked you better when I thought this was all about money. Seriously, you suck at the megalomania. Believe me, I've seen some pros, and you're like amateurville. Ames, try not to be too embarrassed by him. I'll tell you about Jeff and Christopher's grandfather some other time—talk about a guy who turned megalomania into an art form."

"Do you ever shut up?" Gaultier asked.

"No," Christopher said with a laugh. "She never does."

"Part of my charm." I hoped the team had the brains to figure out to tell White, not me, when all the bombs were found. Also hoped they'd find them soon—my breasts had been near my baby, and they wanted to do their job in a big way. "So, while we stand here in what I like to think of as the Psycho Standoff, how'd you make Christopher forget he shot up the first time?"

Gaultier snorted. "He was willing. Every time it came up, he was fighting with Reynolds about it."

"C.I.A. have Chuckie bugged, huh? I'd have thought he'd sweep for that regularly."

"He does, but your boy here carried the bug in with him."

"Really? Wow, how did you get him to do that?" I could tell Christopher was furious and getting more so. Good. He was going to need the anger soon.

Gaultier laughed. "One of his nieces gave him a keychain he carries with him."

"Which niece?"

"Stephanie." Christopher's teeth were gritted. "Sylvia and Clarence's eldest."

"Oh, yeah, we've met. She's the one who told me your father would never let me marry Jeff. Got it on you?"

Christopher never took his eyes off Gaultier. He reached into his pocket and tossed the keychain to me.

"Interesting. Most of Alpha and Airborne have this same thing. She gave them to everyone for Arrival Day this year." A-Cs didn't celebrate most Earth holidays, but they were big on the official day they'd first landed on Earth. "I didn't get one."

"Jeff's niece didn't give you a gift?" Amy sounded shocked. I was impressed—even during this kind of hostage situation she could focus on propriety. Amy would never jog around during a solemn ceremony, and she knew all the forks to use, too.

"Oh, I got a gift." I saw someone's hand wave to me from the opposite doorway. Hoped it was the "get ready" signal, not the "run away" signal. "She gave me some tunes."

CHAPTER 67

ON CUE, A HOWLING like only Screamin' Steven Tyler could make blared out, loud and, in this room, echoing, as Aerosmith rolled into "Nine Lives." Gaultier jerked and Christopher moved.

I could only see him because I was enhanced. He ripped the gun out of Gaultier's hand and away from Amy, crushed it, shoved her out of the way, and then started pounding. As everyone said, Jeff was bigger and stronger, but Christopher was nastier.

I trotted over and grabbed Amy before she hit the ground. Christopher had moved her gently, but an A-C moving fast is hard on a human. I put my arm around her and got us to the wall to watch. I leaned against said wall. I'd only been this tired after being forced into a 10K run when I'd just been recovering from the flu. I wanted to lie down, but it didn't seem like the right time to nap.

The music stopped. I assumed White was clear we didn't need it any more.

"What if he hurts him?" Amy sounded panicked.

"I think that's the idea."

"But Christopher almost died. I know you healed him, but we don't know if he's really okay." She sounded close to tears again.

"Oh, sorry, got the 'he's' and 'him's" confused. Trust me, Ames, your dad's toast. Um, you want him alive? 'Cause if you do, Jeff's going to have to stop Christopher." I couldn't, it would take a lot more strength than I had if ACE wasn't assisting.

She shook her head. "That man's not my father. I don't know who that man is, or thinks he is, but he's not my father. My father loved me; he loved you, too. My father would never have done this to any of us, especially not me."

I didn't know if she meant this figuratively or literally, and I decided not to care right now. I was quite clear about how evil people could be, but one of my parents wasn't the Head Fugly. If Amy needed a little delusion to get through this, I wasn't going to take it away from her.

Christopher was beating the crap out of Gaultier. They were rolling around on the ground, but he was winning, not that I'd had any doubt.

"That man died a long time ago, then."

"Yes, I think he did." Amy took a deep breath. "Is it wrong that I want him to die right now?"

"No. It wouldn't be wrong if you wanted him to live, either." I cleared my throat. "Of course, I sort of fall on the 'kill 'em all and let God sort it out' side of the house these days. Seriously, if you want him alive, I have to get Jeff, right now. Because Christopher is definitely going to kill him."

Christopher slammed Gaultier's head against the ground. He was doing a lot of snarling—most of what I could hear in reference to Amy and what Gaultier had done to her.

"No. I'm . . . I'm glad he's going to kill . . . that man. If he didn't, I'd have to."

I hugged her. "Then no worries." At least, no worries right now. Figured we'd deal with emotional fallout later.

"Why didn't you marry Chuck?" Odd question, but I considered her mind-set and the situation, so maybe not so odd.

"He asked at the wrong time. I was already too in love with Jeff to marry someone else."

"Chuck's always been in love with you."

"Yeah, and I'll always love him. He's still one of my best friends. We just have to stay friends, but that's okay. I think he'll get over me."

Christopher had them off the ground and was slamming Gaultier against the wall. Apparently, this was a family move. I had to admit I always found it manly and impressive.

"When did you know you were in love with Jeff?"

"Oh, I realized it during the 'my guy's tied up and they're trying to kill him' portion of the festivities. Possibly because it says a lot when the bad guys have to tie your man up in order to do any kind of damage to him. But if you want the truth, I fell in love with him in the first minute I knew him."

"So that's normal?"

I managed not to grin or laugh. "Yes. You know, they make great mates. Really great. Sure, it's an adjustment, being with a guy who knows what you're feeling or how your body's functioning or everything about you just from touching your picture, but it's kind of nice, too. To have someone who loves you and understands you so well. And everyone has something to overcome. Plus, they really do recover quickly."

"No fights?"

I managed not to bark a laugh. "Ah, sadly, plenty of fights. Might just be me and Jeff, though. James and Paul don't fight much. I don't think Brian and Serene do, either. Just depends on the personalities." Lorraine and Claudia had had plenty of fights with Joe and Randy, but, as with me and Jeff, it didn't mean they didn't love each other or weren't right together.

"I suppose. Jeff seems like a wonderful father."

"He is. The kind that would die for his child, not hold a gun to her head." Thought about something else. "The superpowers are pretty cool. Supposedly Jamie and I won't die early from them. You get used to the talents, too."

"I saw you fight. I don't think I could ever do that."

"No worries, don't figure I'll do that too often. Sometimes you have to break the rules to save the world, that's all."

"I have no idea what you mean."

"Few ever do, Ames. Few ever do." Gaultier wasn't moving anymore. I got the impression he was quite dead. Christopher dropping him to the floor was an indication, too. "Oh, wow, there's Jeff. Be right back."

I zipped over to the other doorway, then turned and watched. I mean, why not? Jeff came up behind me and pulled my back against his chest. I leaned against him, heaved a sigh, and let my body relax. I was down to merely really tired, which was a nice improvement over exhausted. White stood next to us.

Christopher turned to Amy and stalked over to her. "Are you alright? Did he hurt you?" His voice was shaking. She started to cry, and he reached for her. Amy flung herself into Christopher's arms and buried her face in his neck. He held her and rocked her while he stroked her back. "It's okay, I'm here. I won't ever let anyone hurt you."

"When did you know?" Jeff asked me quietly.

"Oh, when we got Richard back from Paris. He was defending her, snarling at my mother over her, it was kind of obvious once I thought about it."

"I didn't pick up any of this. I thought she was going to end up with Reynolds."

I managed not to snort a laugh. Didn't want to ruin the romantic atmosphere, particularly since Christopher had moved Amy's head so he could kiss her. Nice kiss—at least she seemed to like it, if her body melting against his was any indication. He was good, as I recalled. Not up to Jeff's standards, but I had a feeling Amy might not agree. Not that I was going to let her test Jeff out.

"Baby, I call that wishful thinking on your part. Chuckie and Amy will be civil after Operation Confusion, but the best we'll ever get is mildly friendly, potentially the exchanging of small gifts at the holidays to show willingness. And you didn't pick it up because Christopher can now hide his emotions from you, and Amy was doing the same thing I did when I first met you—telling herself there was no way she'd fallen in love with some guy just by looking at him."

"You really fell in love with me the first time you looked at me?" He sounded like he didn't believe it but hoped it was true.

I turned and looked up at him. "The moment you smiled at me, I was hooked, and by the time you told me your name, I was yours."

Jeff picked me up, and I wrapped my legs around his waist. He kissed me, and finally we could take our time and let it be a real kiss.

CHAPTER 68

"BOY, WE LEAVE TO TAKE CARE of things, and everyone's making out." Tim sounded like he was laughing.

"Well, hard to call it everyone." Reader was definitely laughing. "I mean, you and I are not making out, because our mates are elsewhere."

"Jeff and Kitty always make out," Jerry said.

"I see Christopher bagged the latest hottie," Michael said with a sigh.

"How do you boys think I feel? I've had to watch them far longer." White cleared his throat. "Ah, Jeffrey? I need to speak with my partner for a moment."

Jeff ended our kiss slowly and with clear reluctance. "How did this happen?" He set me down gently. "How did my wife end up turning my uncle into a field operative and her partner?"

"I'm just good that way. What's up, Mister White?"

"Oh, I just wanted to discuss a number of possibilities with you, that's all." He looked around. Christopher and Amy were still kissing, quite passionately.

"If they start to go for it, we all leave the room."

"Ah, not exactly where I was heading, Missus Martini, but I appreciate your version of discretion."

"Any time. By the way, are we sure you guys found all the bombs?"

"Well, Gaultier's dead and we're not blown up, so we're

betting on us." Kevin grinned. "I have to admit, it's never dull working with Centaurion."

Tito gave me the hairy eyeball. "When was the last time you fed your daughter?"

"Geez. Sheila had a freaking electric milking machine. I pumped out a dairy's worth, Mom said they had plenty left." My breasts indicated they didn't care.

"Uh-huh. Mister White, can we either have the discussions back at Dulce or have Missus Katt bring the baby here?" Tito was back to full Doctor From Hell mode.

"Oh, this won't take too long." White took my hand and led us out of the ballroom. "I just want to show you the Embassy. I don't believe that in all this time you've ever been here."

"No, though Jeff and Christopher have told me about it. They liked it here."

"I know. There are actually seven floors, and as you may have noted, it covers a full city block."

"Yeah, it's impressive." I hadn't noted, of course. I had an eye for certain details, but not the ones that everyone else seemed to.

"The basement is, of course, for storage and the main gate. The ground floor is where business is normally conducted, main parlor, diplomatic offices, group kitchen and dining area."

"Uh-huh." I had no idea why he was telling me this. We were at an elevator. Got in, he hit the button for the seventh floor.

"I'll mention that the alarms do not go off if you stop the elevators midway. Also, the Embassy has more than one set, on opposite sides of the building."

"Classy, and thanks for the tip. Richard, why are we taking a tour?"

The doors opened, and he led me out. "We normally have up to six diplomatic families living here at any given time. Needless to say, those families need their own privacy. The top three floors are divided in half—one half each is given to a diplomatic couple or family."

"Check."

He walked us through this particular half. It was huge—easily bigger than my parents' house. Nothing compared to

Martini Manor, in that sense, unless you realized there were five other set-ups just like this one. Huge master bedroom with all the niceties, including a tub for six and a shower for twelve in a bathroom bigger than the Lair. Wondered if they'd used the same architect as the Mandalay Bay but decided now wasn't the time to ask.

"The soundproofing is excellent."

"Good to know. They have the A-C Elves here, too?"

"Of course." He cocked his head. "Jeffrey still hasn't told you how that's done?"

"Nope. You want to tell me?"

Apparently I sounded too eager. "Sadly, no. I'll leave it to him."

"But you're my partner now. Partners are supposed to share those key secrets."

"In a sense." Several other bedrooms, living room, library, what I thought was a den, family kitchen and dining room, playroom, some other rooms whose purpose was unclear. You could house a family of eight here with no issues at all. "I'd like to mention that as Mister Reynolds and your mother have pointed out, our diplomats function at least as much as lobbyists. It would be beneficial, I believe, to have some diplomats who could actually tell a believable fabrication, now and then, at any rate."

"Better hire some humans, then. You all still can't lie to save anyone." Well, other than Camilla and the Chosen Few, but they weren't figuring into the equation at the moment.

"Note the lovely view." I picked up the sarcasm.

"Yes, lovely. Look, snow. Snow is nice if I don't have to be in snow."

"Are you chilly? We can turn up the new invention we have here, called the heater. We also have air conditioning." White's sarcasm knob went to eleven, too.

"No, I'm fine. Why are you showing me this?"

"The fourth floor is a gym and entertainment area. The third floor houses staff, including medical and security. The second floor, as you saw, holds the ballroom, as well as music rooms and some salons given over to Washington parties and such."

"Fabulous set up. Impressive in all the right ways. Uh,

nice drapes. What reaction are you going for here? I'm just curious."

"And dense. Though I mean that in the best way possible." He sighed. "The entire A-C Diplomatic Corps has, ah, disappeared. We cannot function in this country or world without diplomats and lobbyists, nor can our own government function without them."

"Oh, got it." He smiled. "We need to find the right folks to move into the Diplomatic Corps. Got it. What about Paul and James?"

White closed his eyes. "How does Jeffrey not strangle you?"

"I beg your pardon?"

He opened his eyes. "Jeffrey was very happy living here. So was Christopher. You and Jeffrey are new parents. I would like to point out that your baby is less than a week old, and you have not seen her for more than a few minutes for the last many hours. Christopher has, I truly hope, found the right girl who is both not in love with his cousin and able to look past his indiscretions."

"Indiscretions?"

"Drug addiction."

"Oh. Well, yeah. I mean, Ames did her share of pot, don't let her fool you."

"Uh-huh. Good to know. I'll be sure the smoke alarms are up to spec."

"Dude, she doesn't smoke *now*." It was, however, another reason she and Chuckie didn't get along. He'd been there when she'd offered me a joint. I decided Jeff wouldn't like me thinking about that incident.

"Oh, what a relief. Am I getting through?" His expression reminded me of my mother's during Operation Fugly, when she was desperately trying to get across that Christopher was snarling at me because he was interested, not just a total jerk.

"Erm. No. Not so much. I'm not good with the regular people innuendo."

"Perhaps I'll call Mister Reynolds and ask him to translate it into comic-book-speak."

"I'm good with that. Of course, Chuckie's done some innuendo I didn't catch, too, so it probably won't work."

I heard a chuckle and turned around. Jeff was leaning against the wall, arms crossed. He looked amused and possessive. "She needs some things spelled out. Baby, he's trying to suggest we retire."

"But I just got him as my partner!"

White laughed. "I'll be happy to still partner with you, Missus Martini. I just believe it might be wiser to do so as, ah, more undercover agents, if you will."

I looked back to Jeff. "No clue. Sorry. Densest girl on the planet. What are you two talking about?"

Jeff laughed. "Uncle Richard wants us to head up the Diplomatic Corps, baby."

CHAPTER 69

"EXCUSE ME?"

Jeff grinned. "Well, us and Christopher. Who's now got a girl who comes from money. So as soon as we race them down the aisle, we'll have someone who actually knows the ins and outs of how to set the table and plan the menus and do the fancy invitations."

I let this one settle in. "Who else?"

"Who do you suggest?" White asked.

"You, for sure."

"I'm willing. It will be much easier for Paul if I'm not underfoot."

"Paul and James can't be diplomats?" I was whining, I could tell.

Jeff sighed. "Baby, the gates. James can get to you in three seconds. Besides, the Pontifex has a residence here, too."

"Things were always far too turbulent to use it when Theresa was our head diplomat." I heard regret, so much regret, in White's voice. It dawned on me why he wanted us here. To give Jeff and Christopher's children the chance at what their fathers had never had—a stable life without fear.

"Doreen grew up here, and she and Irving hate the desert."

"A wise choice. I'm sure she'll bravely carry on her parents' work while we desperately search for them to no avail."

"You're actually the best liar, too. Wow, Richard, you totally rock."

"Really, baby, stop lusting after my uncle. It bothers me on the same level you saying my dad's hot bothers me."

"You worry too much. So, we need two other couples?"

"Yes, two or three, depending on what official role I take, but not all the positions need to be filled at this moment. As long as we can announce that you and Jeffrey will head up the Diplomatic Corps in the Colemans' absence, all will remain reasonably calm."

"Who's going to head up Field, Imageering, and Airborne, though? Let alone Recruitment?" I looked at Jeff. "I can't imagine you willingly taking orders from someone."

He shrugged. "I can take them from James."

"Seriously? You'll put a human in as the head of Field?"

"And as the new head of Airborne, yeah. Tim deserves the promotion."

"Considering we're all pretty much alive because of him, yeah."

"More because of you and Richard, but I'll give you we'd be in a lot of trouble if not for Tim."

"We'd be like dead. But fine. So, who's going to head Imageering?"

Jeff coughed. "I can't believe I'm going to say this, but . . . Serene."

"You're high."

"No. She held out against Al Dejahl's mind control. Gladys couldn't, but Serene, Lorraine, and Claudia could."

"But she has a baby coming, too."

"You're arguing against us putting a woman in a position of power?" Jeff sounded shocked.

"No, not so much. I just thought this was a 'protect the babies' move."

"There are always going to be babies," White said quietly. "Some will have to grow up faster than others, some will not."

"Plus, with almost no parasites showing up, Imageering is going to have to work more closely with the other government agencies. It's already become a less active position—Christopher was complaining about it a few months ago. Then he started shooting up and his focus changed, but since he's clean now, I think we'll hear him whine about it soon."

"Geez, Jeff, he was tricked into it."

"Yeah, yeah. Anyway, Serene won't be in the danger Christopher was before you cleared out good ol' granddad and brought the ozone shield down on Alpha Four."

"Okay. I can see most of this. James is a great leader and focused on protecting the new Pontifex in all sorts of ways. Tim's shown super ability to cover the Airborne role of thinking like the psychos. And Serene has those nifty and expanded imageering powers. I'm clear on all that. But who's going to do Recruitment? Paul can't, ACE shouldn't, and besides, Recruitment also functions as protection for the Pontifex."

White coughed. "You."

"I thought I was supposed to be the diplomat's wife? I'm getting confused here."

"You're supposed to be the diplomat." Jeff didn't sound like he was joking.

"Jeff, really. What is my role? I'm tired, and the torpedoes are anxious."

"You and Jeffrey both will need to function in a diplomatic capacity. You, however, have hired better and faster than anyone else. You've identified talent and brought it on when we needed it. You've trained operatives to the point where they can assume leadership positions. In addition to Tim and James, I believe we will be moving Lorraine and Claudia into positions of Captains, to fill the slots James and Tim's promotions will leave open. As such, we need you to move to the head of Recruitment. This will force you to spend time with Paul, James, Tim, and Serene as well as the rest of your former team. I do hope you can handle it."

"Sarcasm is such an ugly trait in a former Pontifex. Fine, but you're helping me with it. I think we work well as a team."

"Yes, got it, you're attached to my uncle at the hip now and refuse to let go. He'll be living in the same building. I draw the line at our bedroom."

"He's so possessive. It's sweet, though." I heard a baby crying, screaming, really, and my breasts started to leak. "I hope that's Jamie." Ran to the entry door to see Tito escorting my mother and screaming baby in. I grabbed Jamie and cuddled her. She was still crying but a little less. "Mommy's here, Jamie-Kat."

"She refused the bottle," Mom said with a sigh. "I think she knew things were fine and wanted you."

White led me into a room off the master bedroom. "Nursery."

"Wow, there's everything here, isn't there?"

"Including an isolation chamber."

I felt my throat get tight. "Oh. Good."

White opened the nursery door opposite the one we'd come in through. Jeff stroked my back. "They're not that bad, baby."

"This one in particular." White ushered us inside.

"Wow." Instead of one of the horrific Coffins of the Damned that I was used to, this room looked remarkably like a nice, well appointed, very cozy hospital room. "There are three beds."

"We don't know what the mutation will do to you," White said softly. "However, this room is equipped for any and all talent-related issues and is also, I'm sure, far less frightening to be within."

"You can say that again. So, did the Colemans have an empathic family member or something?"

White coughed. "No. Theresa, however, was empathic and had a son and nephew who were quite strong in their talents. This used to be her quarters, before . . ."

"Ah." I looked up at Jeff. "You sure you're okay coming back here to live?"

He nodded. "I was happy here. And Uncle Richard's right—this room isn't a frightening place to be, at any age. I'd much rather have Jamie in isolation here, when it's necessary, than pretty much anywhere else."

I decided that making the comparison between this isolation chamber and the ones I was used to seeing Jeff in was probably a bad idea. I looked around the room some more. "That's good. And I'm pretty sure I could be in here with Jamie, if necessary, and not freak out." I looked at White. "You're sure this is the right decision?"

White kissed my forehead. "Yes. I'll leave your little family alone and speak with your mother about our new world order."

We went back into the nursery. Jeff escorted White out, shutting the door firmly behind him, then helped me out of my shirt and into the lounger. Jamie started eating as if she hadn't had food for days. He squatted down next to us and stroked her head. "I wasn't sure I'd ever see you or her again."

I ran my hand through his hair. "I know. When I heard them hurting you . . ." I stopped and swallowed. "You okay doing this, though?"

He nodded. "Yeah, I am. Richard's right—our original purpose on this world has been handled. We need to adapt or we'll be exterminated or turned into what you, your mother, and Reynolds are trying to protect us from."

"You going to manage to stop treating Chuckie like the enemy?"

Jeff grinned. "I'll do my best." He sighed. "It was interesting to hear what Cooper and his gang were saying to and about Reynolds. They hate him for all the reasons you love him. I think it's smarter for me to work with the man you respect and love, not against him, since without him, I don't know that you would have ever wanted me."

I pulled his head to me and kissed him. "Jeff, I love you for you, not because you're a supercool alien sex god, though, you know, that's a major contributing factor. But I'm happy you're going to have the jealousy chat with Chuckie and stop being a total jerk to him."

"I didn't say *that*." Jeff laughed. "He doesn't get the jealousy chat yet. Soon, I think, but not yet."

"Whatever. Just stop being mean to him."

"He likes it, to a certain extent. I don't know that he and I will ever feel comfortable being buddies. But I'll give him what he's deserved from me all this time—my respect and cooperation."

"That's good enough for me, and probably for him, too."

Time to change torpedoes. Did the switch. Jeff perched on the armrest and watched us. "I don't think I'll ever get tired of seeing this. My wife and baby." He stroked my hair. "You're the most amazing woman in the galaxy, you know."

I leaned my head back against him. "I'm just me, Jeff."

He bent down and kissed me. "That's what I said."

CHAPTER 70

WE FINISHED FEEDING JAMIE, did the diaper check. Fortunately she didn't need a change because we had nothing here. It was kind of strange—there was nothing in the rooms that would indicate anyone had been living in the Embassy.

Jeff kept Jamie on his shoulder and his other arm around me. It was such a relief to be together and feel normal for a few minutes.

We joined the others, well, most of the others, in the living room of this penthouse. Christopher and Amy were conspicuously absent as I looked around the room.

Caught Reader's eye and he grinned. "You did tell us to leave them alone if they started to go for it."

"I'll be sure to use the stairs," Tito said with a laugh.

"Are you going to be our in-house medical?"

"Yeah, Richard seems to think it would be a good idea." He shook his head. "Can't believe how fast my life's changed since running into you guys."

"I know exactly how you feel." Looked around the room again. "Where're Kevin, Brian, and Tim?"

"Back at Dulce. Alicia and her family are there and getting the indoctrination into our world. Brian was worried about Serene. And Denise was getting a little anxious about her husband, especially after the whole mind-control thing." Reader stretched. "Man, I'm tired. When the heck did we last sleep?"

"I have no idea. All the running back and forth to Paris

has my internal clock on the fritz." I heard my phone ringing. "Where's my purse?"

Reader handed it to me. "We know not to let it get lost, girlfriend."

Dug my phone out. "Hi, Dad, what's up?"

"Kitten, could you all hurry up and get back to the Science Center?"

"Is everything okay?" I started to give the "hurry up" signals and all the guys stood. Other than Reader, who just grinned.

"Yes, yes. You're just going to be late."

"Late for what?" I saw Reader's expression. "Oh, no, really? Right now?"

"Yes, right now. Hurry, I don't want you to miss your Uncle Mort."

"Okay, Dad, we'll be right there." We hung up. "I see it's time for the baby shower." I could tell I hadn't said this with the right kind of excitement by the way my mother rolled her eyes.

"Induction ceremony," Jeff corrected.

"Big ol' shower with everyone invited," I countercorrected.

"Some girls are excited to have a shower," Michael said with a laugh.

"Oh, I love showers. Think they're the best things in the world." Jeff coughed. "But we're going to a big party where everyone's going to stare at me, and I'm going to have to squeal like I just won the lottery over every single item. Including the ones where I have no idea of what it's supposed to do or be, or the ones I would rather die than use, or the ones that are ugly— "

Jeff put his hand over my mouth. "Baby . . . bassinet."

"Let's go to the shower!"

"Who's going to make sure Christopher and Amy are, uh, through?" Jerry asked. He clearly represented everyone else's concern.

I sighed, opened my phone, and dialed. It rang and went to voicemail. Hung up, dialed again. Same thing. One more time, answered on the last ring. "WHAT?"

"Christopher! Great to get your attention. We're all about to go back to Dulce. I hate to drag you two away from the study of etchings or betting on the submarine races or whatever it is you guys call it, but we're all about to walk past wherever you are."

"So? We'll catch up to you later."

"Uh, really, listen to me, I'll talk slowly. We—and by we I mean me, Jeff, Jamie, my *mother*, your *father*, Tito, Jerry, Matt, Joe, Randy, Chip, Michael, and James—are about to file past you, slowly, and with a strong likelihood of comments and, perhaps, even recommendations or requests. There would be more of us in the parade, but Kevin, Brian, and Tim already left. I'd bet they walked by you, however. Be glad I had Chuckie take the gals home. Am I getting through?"

"Yeah, thanks for the warning."

"How long do you two need to get dressed? Of course, by that, I don't mean how much longer would you like, but how much longer do I stall before I merely take streaming video and ensure Jamie's college fund?"

"I hate you."

I heard Amy asking what was going on. "Tell Amy the eagle is landing."

"You're kidding."

"No. Do it." He did. I heard her shriek.

"Okay, uh, fine, the mood's sort of spoiled now, thanks a lot. Who the hell is the eagle anyway?" I heard Amy shriek my mother's name. "Oh. Come on, she was okay with you and Jeff doing it anywhere and everywhere." I heard Amy scream that my mother was not okay with it.

Mom put her hand out and I gave her the phone. "Christopher. Yes, hello. We all—and by all, I mean including you and Amy who, let me mention, Sol and I think of as one of our 'other' daughters—are heading back for Jamie's induction ceremony. You have one minute to put your damn pants on, or I'll use your balls for target practice." She hung up and handed the phone back to me.

"I'm glad Brian missed that. I don't think that kind of nostalgia would be good for him."

"I hate hearing about things like this," Jeff muttered. "Be kind, don't talk about Reynolds. Or my uncle."

Mom smiled at him. "I never said those things to you, Jeff."

"That Kitty ever heard, yeah."

"Mom, you didn't threaten Jeff, did you?"

She laughed. "What's the good of being Mossad trained if you never use it? Let's go. Amy, at least, will be presentable. She might have cleaned the room by the time we get there, too."

"You are an evil woman."

"And you take right after me." Mom kissed my cheek, then strode off.

Reader ran and opened the door for her. "Going to escort Angela because I love watching her work, too."

The flyboys looked at each other. There was a small stampede to catch up to Reader and Mom.

Tito shook his head. "Like they've never seen it?"

"My mother's got . . . style."

Michael laughed. "Yeah, trust me. I know when to hang back and play with the baby." He was making goo-goo faces at Jamie. She seemed to like it. "See? She likes her Uncle Michael."

"All the girls do, Michael."

White went to the door. "Shall we? I'm hoping Angela has things under control so I don't have to show displeasure or relief. Or offer tips."

I snorted but managed to keep my mouth shut.

"I hate it when you lust after my uncle. Possibly more than when you lust after my father. Go back to lusting after Kevin, it was easier to take."

"Wow, I have your permission to lust after Kevin? What next? I get to go to Australia with Chuckie?" Jeff tickled me and I squealed. Jamie made baby sounds, but she didn't seem upset.

Got to the elevator. I gave it a closer look now that it looked like I'd be living here. It certainly had possibilities. Decided Jeff and I should test it right away. He moved his hand to stroke the back of my neck. "Love how you think."

We stopped at the second level to pick up the rest of the team. I could hear them as we walked down the hall. "No, really, Angela, we were just talking." Amy sounded panicked.

"Uh-huh. Brush your hair." Mom sounded pissed. I knew she was laughing inside. "Christopher, tuck in your shirt. Do you really want your days-old niece to see you like this?"

We walked into the ballroom. "Mom, really, they're

adults." Amy was dressed and brushing her hair. Christopher was tucking his shirt in, fast. James and the flyboys were doubled over.

Amy sprinted over and grabbed my arm. "Kitty! Shower time! Great!"

"Oh, come on, Ames. You're a big girl."

"Yeah, uh, right." She looked over her shoulder. "I was scared of making your mom mad when I didn't know she was the head of antiterrorism." She looked at the brush in her hand and gave it back to Mom. Mom snatched it in the "annoyed parent" way she'd perfected years ago.

"She's also a crack shot," Jeff offered. "Good thing Christopher got his pants on in time."

"We were just talking!"

"Ames, really. Even Jamie's not going to buy that one."

"Why not?"

I coughed. "Well, your new Paris T-shirt is inside out, and your bra is, if I'm any judge, shoved into Christopher's jeans pocket. Either that or he's scary happy to see the rest of us. Christopher's shirt is both inside out and on backwards. Proud of you both for getting your jeans back on, facing front and everything. You're in his shoes, though. Either that or you really like your shoes bigger and he lives to scrunch his toes up."

Amy blushed bright red. Jerry and Hughes were collapsed against each other they were laughing so hard.

Christopher shot patented Glare #5 at everyone. "You know, is a little privacy that hard to come by?"

"Most of us don't do it in the middle of a huge ballroom. Sorry, but even Jeff and I have more self-control than that."

"Yeah, and they'll go for it pretty much anywhere," Walker offered.

"We do not."

All five of the flyboys looked at me. Jerry cleared his throat. "The elevator in Dulce, like every other ride, the women's bathroom in the Paris Metro, the men's bathroom in the Guadalajara airport, the Pontifex's office, a maintenance closet in Saguaro International, conference table at C.I.A. headquarters, limo in Vegas, taxi in Montreal, cave in the Grand Canyon, top of the Empire State Building, and in every aircraft type we have at Area Fifty-One, though always safely on the ground."

"You forgot that side street in the French Quarter," Walker said.

"And in the back of that rib joint in Saint Louis," Randy said. "Food there was great, too."

"Oh, and inside Big Ben," Joe added. "Can't forget that.

"Meat locker in Texas," Hughes offered. "I get my steaks well done now."

"Made me want mine rare, for some reason," Jerry said with a wide grin.

"You forgot the head in the Russian whaling vessel." Michael shook his head. "That was a fun vacation. I'm still making money from the pictures."

"Locker room for the Arizona Diamondbacks," Tito added. "A little further along during pregnancy than I'd have recommended, too. For the location, I mean."

"It was a really good game. Geez, thanks for the listing, guys. I'd like to mention, again, that we were never in a huge ballroom."

"We'll give you time." White shook his head. "The guest bathrooms are through that door and to the right. Perhaps you two could take another minute or so and put your clothes on correctly? Oh, and, I'm sorry, Miss Gaultier, but I believe these are yours." He handed Amy a pair of lacy panties.

She grabbed them and ran for the bathroom.

"I think I'll go help her." I went to Christopher and pulled Amy's bra out of his pants. It matched the panties. He shot patented Glared #3 at me. "I'll find out if the Earth moved for her or if you need to get tips from Jeff or your dad."

With that I ran at hyperspeed for the bathroom.

CHAPTER 71

"KITTY!" CHRISTOPHER WAS right behind me.

"Can't come in the girls' room when there's two of us here!"

"I need my own shoes."

I stopped running. "Oh. Okay. Give me Amy's, I'll get yours."

"You did it in my dad's office?" He handed me the shoes.

I coughed. "More than once."

Christopher shook his head. "Unreal." He shot me a worried look. "You don't think she'll be too embarrassed to come out, do you?"

"Oh, she'll be fine. I'll handle it."

He nodded and stood there, looking really nervous. "I think she likes me."

I managed not to snort too loudly. "I think she's crazy about you. You don't seriously think Amy gets down and dirty with every guy she meets, do you?"

"Well, no, but . . . I've never dated a human girl." I raised my eyebrow. "You don't count."

"Humph. But, true. Hang on." I opened the bathroom door. "Ames, I need Christopher's shoes." They flew out. "Thanks." I tossed hers in and shut the door. "Look, go get properly dressed. Jeff and I will wait for you guys, and I'll have him send everyone else on, okay?"

Jeff strolled up and handed Jamie to me. "Already handled." He kissed me and gave me the Snugli. Then he grinned and put his arm around Christopher's shoulders. "Let me explain the human female to you."

"Oh, please." Jeff winked at me. I laughed and went into the bathroom. "Ames, no worries, it's just the four and a half of us here; everyone else is on their way to Dulce."

She was still blushing. "Everyone thinks I'm a slut, don't they?"

"I think I have that title sewn up, at least per your late and very unlamented father."

"Is your mom mad at me?"

I snorted, big time. "Uh, no. She was having fun. She really does think of you as one of her other daughters."

"That would make her more mad with me, then." Amy still looked worried.

"Hardly. Ames, she wanted me to marry Christopher when I first hooked up with this crew. She adores him. So, good choice."

Amy gave me a sidelong look. "Did you sleep with him?"

"Geez. I see my reputation precedes."

"He's your type."

"Was. Was my type. Brian was, too, and I haven't banged him since senior year."

"You slept with Chuck."

"Good lord, who sent the group memo?"

Her turn to snort. "Uh, you said it was the best vacation of your life. For you, that meant killer sex for at least fifteen out of every twenty-four hours."

"Yeah, yeah, fine. Until Jeff, yeah, Chuckie was the best. By far."

"And you didn't marry him."

"Had he asked before I'd met Jeff, I'd have said yes." And, of course, if I'd comprehended that he was so asking. Sometimes, I didn't even catch a straight-out statement, as Chuckie could absolutely attest. My superhero name could be Density Girl. "But once I'd met Jeff . . ." I shrugged. "I don't know how far you two actually got, but unless Jeff's an anomaly, trust me—once you go alien, you never, ever go back."

"We've only done it a couple of times," Amy said while she stripped and put her underwear back on.

I recognized the look on her face—it was a combination of pleased and guilty. "How many times? Exactly?"

She blushed. "Three."

"Kind of fast, for how long we left you two alone, I mean."

She turned bright red. "We only did it twice here."

The light dawned. "Aha. So, where did you two find time to fit in the dirty deed during all the excitement?" She mumbled something. "Sorry, can't hear you."

"The changing room at the gift shop by Notre Dame."

"Wow." Marked this as a great idea.

"He almost died! And he was so brave—you missed most of it, but he was just so amazing, and then they had him hanging there and he was hurt but still trying to protect us and . . ."

"And staring at him half-naked and spread-eagled was more than the ol' libido could take?"

"I'm a slut, aren't I?" She pulled her jeans on, but she wasn't looking at me.

I couldn't help it, I started laughing. "Ames, geez. You're twenty-nine, he's almost thirty-two. I couldn't resist Jeff, at all. Still can't, not that I want to. They're gorgeous, and you love the brooding, serious types."

"Why didn't you go all the way with Christopher?" Shoes on, still not looking at me.

"Because we weren't right together, and I was already in love with Jeff, even though I didn't want to admit it. Why didn't you sleep with Michael? I know he gave it his best shot."

She shrugged. "He's gorgeous, but he's a player. I . . . I don't want to just be someone's . . . experience." I heard the fear in her voice.

"Christopher's in love with you."

"I know he likes me, but I don't think he loves me." She pulled her shirt on. "I mean, he doesn't really know me."

I sighed. "He's an imageer. Among the many talents is the ability to touch a picture or video of someone and know everything about them. He touched the picture of me, you, Sheila, and Mom and Dad from my sweet sixteen."

"To find out about you."

"Yeah, true." Oh, well, she'd find out sooner or later anyway. "I look like his mother, Ames. So does my mom. Christopher was interested in me because I reminded him of his mother, and he attached to Mom for the same reason."

"A lot of guys want to marry a girl just like their mother."

"Maybe. I'm betting she was more like you than me. Jeff says I think the way Terry did, but I'll bet cash money I don't act like she did. Christopher and I are great as friends, as family, as someone to cover each other's backs. And, trust me, I need him, because the superpowers are weird and scary. Awesome, but scary, too, and I need him to help me when Jeff can't or won't. But we would never have worked. The things I do that Jeff thinks are adorable Christopher is amused by only because it's not his girl doing them. Christopher hasn't been interested in me for a long time now."

"But he was in love with you for a while." She looked sad.

"So what? Jeff and Christopher were both in love with an A-C girl named Lissa. She was going to pick Christopher, but she was out with Jeff when she was murdered in front of him. I could spend the rest of my life wondering what things would be like if that hadn't happened. But what good is that?"

"He's only known me for a couple of days."

Her hair was messed up again. I dug my brush out and handed it to her. "Ames, did you listen? He touched that picture and others. He touched every person in the pictures too. I know because, shocker alert, I never dust. That means he's always known you, since he met me. He just hadn't met you in person yet. But I think he wanted to. And I know once he did, he confirmed it."

"Confirmed what?" She gave me back the brush, and I dropped it in my purse. Noted all six Poofs were there, snoozing.

I put my free arm around her shoulders and looked at her in the mirror. "That you're the girl he's been waiting for."

She leaned her head against mine. "Are you sure? Because . . . I'm so in love with him." She started to cry a little. "And . . . I don't know what I'll do if . . ."

I heard the door open. "If he decides he'd rather be alone, lonely, and unhappy instead of with the girl he's in love with? He's an alien, not an idiot." I hugged her, then let go and walked out. Christopher held the door for me. "Really, this is romance, not sex, time. We're on a schedule."

"Got it. Kitty . . . thanks."

I kissed his cheek. "You did the same for me, if you recall."

Jeff was leaning against the wall. "Were we this stupid?"

"You were, if memory serves."

He laughed. "I told you I was going to marry you within, what, ten minutes?"

"I think it was thirty, but who's counting?" He took Jamie and put her on his shoulder again while I snuggled up against him and buried my face in his shirt. "So, how did you pick this particular T-shirt?" He wrapped his free arm around me.

"It was the only one that fit me."

"Being totally ripped and all big and brawny does limit your clothing choices, I guess. Have I mentioned that you look so hot in these clothes?"

"I feel stupid."

"You look great. How many women flung themselves at you on your way into Notre Dame?"

"I was running to get to you before you got into trouble. Didn't stop to flirt."

"You don't need to. Your shirt says it all."

"What does my shirt say?"

I looked up at him. "Make love with me."

His eyelids drooped, and he got the half-smile, half-snarl on his face that always reminded me of a jungle cat about to strike. "Maybe I'll keep the shirt." His voice was a purr. I started to grind against him, and he slid his thigh between my legs while his hand stroked the small of my back. "Maybe I'll have you wear the shirt . . . and nothing else." My breath was getting ragged. "What do you want, baby?" His voice was a low growl as he slid his hand over my bottom and squeezed.

I moaned softly. "You."

Jamie made a baby sound and started fussing. We both took a deep breath and then shifted back to good parenting positions. Jeff cuddled Jamie while I put the Snugli on and tried to get my nipples to stop poking through my shirt.

Just in time, as Christopher and Amy came out of the women's bathroom. He had his arm around her shoulders, and she had both arms around his waist. I finally paid attention to their shirts. His said "Fall in love in Paris" and hers said "Parisian Princess." Fitting, really.

"All set?" Jeff asked.

Christopher nodded. "Yeah." He looked around. "Kind of nice to be here again."

"Get used to it."

He gave me a confused look. "Why?"

"Oh, right. You two were, ah, busy when your dad explained all the new, fun things we're going to be doing." Jeff slipped Jamie into the Snugli, then put his arm around me. I wrapped my arm around his waist as I leaned against him. "We'll tell you on the way to the shower. Ceremony. Whatever." I couldn't help it, I yawned. Widely. I was still tired from the Surcenthumain Rage High.

We took the elevator down to the basement. "You really did it in all those places?" Amy asked.

"More than they listed." I shrugged. "What can I say? My needs are simple, my wants are few."

"Yeah," Jeff said happily. "It sucks to be me."

CHAPTER 72

WE ARRIVED BACK at the launch area. Same A-C on gate duty. "Nice to see you back, Commanders." He had a brave little smile on his face. "Is the situation under control?"

"Nice to be back, and it's under control now." I took a deep breath. "I'm sorry we weren't in time to save Wayne or the others."

He shook his head. "Wayne was Field, ma'am. He knew the risks. They all did."

I doubted very much that Wayne or the others had expected what they had gotten, but I chose to keep that one to myself. "What's your name?"

"Walter."

I studied him. I'd been too late to save Wayne, but I could do something for his brothers, so that maybe they'd have something positive to discuss at a future family dinner. William and Wayne had said they were one of the best Field teams, after all, and I didn't doubt it. And Walter, with no A-C talents, had managed to hold out against Al Dejahl's mind control at least as long as Gladys had, maybe longer.

Walter shifted. "Is something wrong, Commander?"

"You like it in Dulce, Walt?"

He looked confused. "I go where I'm assigned, Commander."

"Yes, yes, good man. I'm asking if you want to be in

Dulce, or Caliente Base, or if you would prefer to be elsewhere. If given the choice."

"Oh. Well." Walter looked hesitant.

"Go on, I'm sure she has a reason." Jeff looked down at me. "No idea what it is."

I gave Walter the expectant look. He cleared his throat. "I grew up at East Base."

"Miss it?"

He nodded. "Sort of. I . . . miss the snow and the seasons."

"What about William?"

"His wife works at the Space Center. It's kind of hard for them being in Caliente Base."

"Was Wayne married?"

"No, Commander. He didn't have anyone steady, either."

"William's an imageer, and Wayne is . . . was, an empath, right?" I felt Jeff stiffen as Walter nodded. "Do you have a talent?" I knew he didn't, but I felt it was polite to ask. He liked that we were polite, after all.

"No, ma'am." He managed a weak grin. "Other than being annoying. At least, that's what . . ." He looked down quickly. I chose to refrain from commenting on the tears I saw roll down his cheeks.

"Big brothers are like that," I said softly. "He loved you very much."

"How would you know that, Commander?" Walter didn't sound accusatory; he sounded sad.

"Wayne was ready to one-up you at the next family dinner." Everyone else looked at me with varying expressions of confusion.

Walter didn't. He smiled. "Yeah, I sent them both to Saguaro International. They told me they'd gotten to hang out with you." He seemed to realize what he'd said, because he blushed bright red.

"Hanging out was more what I was doing. They were working. Well and hard, I must add. I really . . ." I'd really liked them, both of them. Wayne had been a smart, fun, funny guy. And he was dead now. And I wasn't really sure why he'd been killed, why his death had been deemed necessary or expedient by our bad guy cadre. The only things I was sure of were that I'd let him down, somehow, and that it had to be rectified.

My throat was trying to close up again, and mommy hormones meant I'd have no control if I let the tears start. I cleared my throat and shoved on. "Walter, I'd like to ask you to consider going to work at the Embassy. I'll talk to you about it in more detail later."

He looked dazed. "Embassy duty is usually considered a top assignment, Commander. I haven't been active long enough." Walter looked about twenty-two to me, give or take.

"Yeah, well, we're kind of on new rules now. So think about it."

"Yes, ma'am."

We went to the elevators. No one spoke until we were inside. "What happened to the bodies?" Jeff asked as soon as the doors closed.

"No idea. Didn't you ever see them?"

"No," Christopher said, his voice tight. "I saw them when I was in isolation, but when we arrived in Paris, they weren't there. Or we were never where the bodies were."

Amy looked ill. "It was horrible, what they did to them. They . . . they waited and killed them in front of Tim, Michael, and me. They tortured them first. And then dissected them. I couldn't figure out why. I still can't."

"Who did it?" Jeff asked.

"My so-called father," Amy snarled. She shook her head. "After what I saw him do, what he said his plans were, and what he did to me, I'm glad he's dead. I wish I'd killed him myself."

"No, you don't," Jeff said quietly. "You think you do, but be glad you didn't have to make that choice."

"I made it for you," Christopher said, even more quietly than Jeff.

"I know. Thank you." Amy flung her arms around Christopher and buried her face in his neck.

Christopher looked incredibly relieved. I figured Amy was going to have some issues later, but that's what my mom and dad were for. Mom seemed to be good at covering the Replacement Mother role, and I was happy to share her with the people she, Dad, and I loved. Dad, of course, would not only follow Mom's lead, but he'd be there if Amy wanted someone who actually loved her to walk her down the aisle and so forth. Besides, as Ericka Gower had told me, once you were in with the A-Cs, you were family forever. Amy would, ultimately, be okay.

While Christopher consoled Amy, my mind went back to what Gaultier and the rest had done. It was bad enough hearing what had happened to any of our people. But hearing what they'd done to someone I knew and liked made me want to throw up and hit something. Neither option seemed wise at the moment.

Instead, I took a deep breath. "Let's get through the induction ceremony and get some sleep. Then we'll figure out where they are. I'll want you three to tell the rest of Alpha and Airborne, as well as Chuckie, what you saw. Might figure it out that way."

"What's your plan with Walter?" Jeff asked as the doors opened.

"I want people around us we can trust."

"Why can we trust him?"

"Just know we can." Like I'd known I could trust his older brothers.

"Great, I feel so secure."

The library area was packed and it sounded like people were having a wild time. I spotted a lot of guys in uniform, and not Armani fatigues. Marines in dress blues were everywhere. I noted a large number of the younger Dazzlers sidling up to quite a number of them. The Marines didn't seem to object.

I forced myself to focus on the party, mostly because I knew Jeff cared about this ceremony much more than he wanted to admit. Waded through the crowd. It was packed so much that Jamie got jostled quite a bit. Jeff growled, lifted me up and put me onto his shoulders. "This is different." I had to shout. Realized if he was turned around and the baby was asleep, I wouldn't have the slightest objection. He stroked my thighs. Boy, did we need a bed for the baby.

Jeff carrying me like this was a huge hit. We got lots of cheers and catcalls. Jamie didn't like the noise, but she didn't seem too upset. Finally got to the part of the room where my and Jeff's parents were. Most of our friends and family were close by. Everyone was staring at us, and I started to get really self-conscious.

Reader stood up on the same platform Al Dejahl had been using. He flashed the cover-boy grin and damned if the entire room didn't start to get quiet. There were chairs here, so Jeff lifted me off his shoulders but kept me on his lap. Christopher followed suit and pulled Amy onto his lap.

The room had a huge screen, and it lowered as Reader spoke. "Hey there, party animals." Everyone laughed. He had a microphone, but I did wonder if he had troubadour in him somewhere. Because it was almost impossible to look anywhere but right at him.

"Stop lusting after James."

"He's gay. Totally hot, but gay."

"Yeah. It's a toss-up, whether it's worse to have you drooling after my gay friend or my uncle."

"Look at it as giving me an appetite only you satiate."

"Huh. Nice spin. Which one of them suggested it?"

"I came up with it on my own, used to work in marketing, remember? Now, hush, James is talking."

"In keeping with human traditions, we made a video about nine months ago." Lots of cheers. "And I know the general story was that it didn't turn out." Some good-natured boos. "But . . . that wasn't exactly the truth. We've been saving it for this important ceremony. So, everyone, let's take a short trip back in time and see the new parents' wedding highlights." Reader grinned right at me. I tried to smile back. Failed.

"Oh, goody!" Amy was serious. "I can't wait. I'm still upset I missed it."

"Me too." Christopher stroked her face and then pulled her to him. They smooched, and I decided to watch the video.

Of course, shortly after it started, I wondered if I could pay Christopher and Amy to make out so I could watch them instead. At the start, it was fine. I got to see Jeff and his parents enter. He looked so great in his tux I forgot to worry about what was coming. I focused on not drooling on Jamie instead. I did notice that he looked nervous and uncomfortable. It wasn't too obvious, but I did know him well.

I also got to hear all the various blessings everyone in the wedding party other than Jeff had missed, though I noted that Reader must have had Mister Joel Oliver edit them down, because this part didn't last as long in the video as it had in real life.

Then we were on to everyone walking in, looking wonderful and stately. True, they were walking around for what seemed like forever, but everyone was graceful, smiling, and looking good.

I had to hand it to Oliver's paparazzi camera crew—they were really good. I'd never noticed them, but they'd gotten literally everything and had clearly been using several cameras. I tried not to anticipate what was coming that they'd also undoubtedly caught all of. Failed.

"What a beautiful ceremony," Amy said rather wistfully.

"Um, yeah." We cut to follow Chuckie, aka our wedding Majordomo, get to his seat. There was some ceremony with this no one had told me about, and I tried to focus on it to distract myself from what was coming.

But that only worked for about half a minute, and then it was time for my entrance and I cringed. Mom and Dad sailed in and did their thing, and there was me, closing the door. I looked like an idiot. Watched myself trip and recover while I heard the chuckles starting. Wow, this was fun. They were laughing on screen and in the room. We had the next comedy blockbuster on our hands.

Oh, great, we were now at the point where I'd given up and started running. I risked a look at Amy. Her mouth was opened. In horror. Well, she wasn't laughing.

I tried not to cringe again as I rounded the corner and did my "deer trapped in headlights" thing when I spotted Jeff. I started to wonder if I'd really pissed Reader off in some way. I also wondered how long it was going to be before I gave up and just let the tears of embarrassment fall.

But then the video cut to Jeff, and I got to look at him more clearly than I'd been able to during the actual ceremony. He was looking for me, I could see it now, and he looked nervous and frightened.

The camera caught the moment he saw me, and his expression shifted—he looked shocked. I still wasn't sure if I should crawl under the chair or not when I saw him shake his head and then, the next moment, he was next to me. His whole demeanor changed. He looked proud, confident, protective, happy. Then he flashed his killer grin, and the running of the bride and groom began.

Jeff nuzzled my ear while the audience roared. "It's even better on video. I could only see your head bobbing up and down. My God, I can't wait for you to get into that dress again and run around the room."

"I really didn't embarrass you?"

"Baby, this is the only wedding video that's going to be worth watching years from now. God, I want stills of that shot." I was over Jeff's shoulder and the camera had zoomed in on my butt. "Oh, God, and that one, too." Zoomed in on my upside-down chest. "I could kill James . . . why didn't I have a copy of this for the last eight and a half months?" He was serious. I felt great all of a sudden.

Watched the ceremony, still teared up but for good reasons. Then we got to the reception. Christopher's toast still got the crowd sobbing, Amy too, I noted. All the various fun activities. Got to see Jeff's expression as all the guys kissed me during Reader's "Kiss the Bride" number. He tried to hide it, but I could tell he was jealous. Felt flattered.

The camera caught me and Jeff saying good-bye to Reader and then sneaking out. Caught my grandparents leaving to go gamble. Then it panned to more guests, all over the room. Our personal paparazzo even managed to get a shot of himself, surrounded by a bunch of Dazzlers, grinning like he'd won the lottery.

The shots went around the room again. In the back one man and woman were sitting at a table. The woman was a thin bleached blonde, and the man was about Jeff's size, with dark hair. They were both attractive, for humans. He looked midtwenties; she looked late twenties to early thirties.

I heard Amy gasp. "What was *she* doing there?"

CHAPTER 73

"WHO?" I STARED AT THE COUPLE. As I looked more closely, there was something familiar about the man. Very familiar.

"That's my stepmother. What was she doing at your wedding?"

"Who's with her?" Christopher asked. "That's not your father."

"It's our buddy, Ronnie. He altered himself a little to, I guess, be incognito, but I saw him up close and really personal, and that's pretty much him."

Jeff leaned over. "I want a copy of this. Immediately." He wasn't asking for enjoyment any more; his Commander voice was on full.

Christopher nodded and pulled his phone out. I looked around for Tim. Interestingly, he was looking for me, too, it was clear. He was with Alicia, and they started heading toward us.

"Jeff, our families will kill us if we go into mission-mode right now."

"I know. We'll get through this, sleep, and then figure out what else is going on."

I felt a hand on my shoulder. "We have a problem, don't we, Missus Martini?"

"Yes, Mister White, I think we do."

"You'll be relieved to know that James is aware of what you don't care for in terms of baby showers. And despite your justified concerns based on, as you put it, all the wedding rigmarole, the induction ceremony is quite short. We'll all be able to regroup sooner than you think."

The video ended, and Gower was up there with the mic, looking mildly uncomfortable. He cleared his throat. "My first real act as your new Pontifex is a joyous one." There was a smattering of applause.

Gower looked at us, at Jamie really, and the discomfort was gone—in its place I saw the next religious leader of our large and now-extensive tribe. "Welcome to the family, little one. You're one of us, now and forever, and we will never forsake you."

The A-Cs all stood and clapped. The humans followed suit. Reader went back to the dais, and Gower got down.

"That's it?" I whispered to Jeff.

He grinned. "That's it."

"Why didn't you tell me?"

He shrugged. "Sometimes I like to watch you try to wriggle out of something you'll actually enjoy."

"You know, they all say I'm the crazy one, but sometimes I really wonder about you."

Jeff chuckled as Reader took the mic again. "Folks, you know a girl who can still sprint during her wedding likes things to move fast. To that end, and because, as most of you know, it's been an exciting week here, we're going to do things the A-C way—which, for us humans means we eat, drink, and be merry and let the parents open the gifts when the baby's napping. Should only take them to her first birthday to go through all the gifts, right?"

This earned laughs and my total relief. Okay, Reader still loved me, and I still loved him. The world was okay.

My Uncle Mort took the stage and the mic. "The United States Marine Corps would like to congratulate the Katt-Martini family on their newest addition."

The Marines all over the room stood up and did a loud cheer in unison, earning wild applause from the rest of the attendees. It was impressive. Jamie only fussed a little over it, too.

Uncle Mort winked at me. "We also heard the new parents were missing a very important item."

Four Marines walked in solemnly, carrying something on their shoulders. They reached us, did the whole military thing, and placed it in front of us.

I squealed at the top of my lungs. “I love you, Uncle Mort!”

This was better than winning the lottery. It was beautiful, tricked out with everything, at least, everything I could think would make sense to trick it out with.

“What is it?” someone shouted from the back of the room.

Jeff and I answered in unison. “It’s a bassinet!”

CHAPTER 74

WE WERE ABLE TO USE the hungry, fussy baby excuse to leave after a little while. Jamie seemed to have reached her limit, and I was ready to lie down, too.

The issue was, where were we supposed to go to sleep? Turned out Al Dejahl was indeed locked up in a very secure containment cell on the fifteenth floor. For whatever reason, Jeff therefore refused to sleep in the Lair. I felt weird going back to the Embassy, but according to Gladys, it had been swept for any form of bug, bomb, or tripwire, so it should be secure.

The rest of Alpha and Airborne and what I now considered our extended team gathered around us as we argued about where to go to sleep for the night. Jamie was fussing, and I was close to lying down on the floor—I was too big for the bassinet.

I grabbed White as he joined us. "Richard, why was there nothing in the Embassy? I mean, if you were showing us the Colemans' penthouse, it sure seemed devoid of any personal items."

He shook his head. "No idea, Missus Martini. The rest of the Embassy was also devoid of belongings."

"Maybe they figured they were going to skip town," Tim suggested.

"Or the planet. Still, seems kind of . . . odd."

"I'd suggest my place," Chuckie said, "but it's trashed, and I can't guarantee it's safe, either."

"Your parents' house, or mine?" Jeff sounded as tired as I felt.

"No, we went into lockdown for a reason."

"Thought that reason was handled."

"Not for sure yet. I'm just too tired to deal with what I think most of us noted during the showing of James' Documentary in Embarrassment."

Reader grinned. "You looked great. But, yeah, hadn't paid any attention to our mystery couple before."

"Caliente Base?" Jeff was at least focusing on sleep.

"Gave up our room there, remember?"

"Yeah. I remember being told that we had too many places to live and the Lair was more than sufficient. Which is why we don't have a room at Caliente Base, or an apartment in New York, or one in Pueblo Caliente, either." Jeff's sarcasm knob was on eleven again.

"I'm not the one refusing to sleep in the Lair." Jamie started screaming, and I had to do the Mommy Dance. "Okay, either this means she is demanding the Lair or that she wants to be nowhere near it."

"Or that she's wet, hungry, or just tired beyond belief." Jeff rubbed his forehead. "Isolation chamber."

Christopher answered before I could. "No. Absolutely not."

Jeff shrugged. "They're not that bad once you get used to them."

"They don't sleep a family," Christopher snapped. I decided not to mention that the one in our rooms at the Embassy did, since I was freaked out about going over there. "What's wrong with the Embassy? It's empty, literally." It was as if Christopher were reading my mind. I hoped he hadn't gotten that skill along with all his other new ones.

"You know how Jeff doesn't want to go to the Lair? Well, I'm afraid to go to the Embassy by ourselves, okay?" Everyone looked at me. "It's big and . . . creepy without other people in it."

"We used to be alone in it all the time." Christopher shook his head. "And we were little kids."

"I'm with Kitty. It's strange to be in an unfamiliar place with no one else around." Amy looked totally innocent saying this. I knew where she was heading with it, of course.

"Maybe some of us should go over with Kitty and Jeff, just to make them feel safer."

Bingo. She might look innocent and be far too worried about her reputation, but no one was better at the "but it's for everyone's safety, Mom" technique than Amy.

Not that I objected. Christopher seriously needed to get laid, repeatedly, if I was any judge. It had seemed to do Amy a world of good, too. Plus, I wasn't going over without at least two other people with us. "I'd be okay with some other people with us. Preferably people I felt really, really comfortable with."

"Why would you need anybody other than Jeff?" Christopher asked, looking blank.

Jeff nodded. "Everything's cleared out, baby. We'll be fine."

Reader and Tim were both trying to keep straight faces and failing utterly. Joe had his hand over Lorraine's mouth, and Claudia had her face buried in Randy's shoulder. The rest of the humans and A-C females were all also trying not to bust a gut, even Serene whom I normally thought of as innocence on the hoof.

Amy gave it another shot. "Kitty's afraid." She enunciated carefully, I assumed because she figured she hadn't spoken clearly before. "I think some of us should go over there with her."

Interestingly to me, while Gower, Michael, and White all had knowing, amused looks on their faces, Jeff and Christopher didn't seem to get it.

Christopher sighed. "They're grownups."

"Yeah, I really think we can handle it there, baby."

Amy shot me a look I knew was asking me if she'd landed a beautiful but dumb one. "Naïve to our ways, Ames, that's all."

Claudia had managed to recover enough to talk. "Kitty, I would love to offer to go and stay at the Embassy with you, but I think, since I'm pregnant, I should stay here. Plus, my mom hasn't finished telling me all about what you guys did in Paris. So I'm really sorry, but I don't think Randy and I can go with you." She said this slowly and carefully, as if she were explaining something to kindergarteners.

Lorraine nodded and spoke in the same "language for the slow of wit" way. "The same for me and Joe. We can't go with you because I'm pregnant and need to spend quality time with my mom." She nudged Serene.

"Right! I need to make sure Brian's really okay, and so, um, we can't go with you, either, Kitty." Serene sounded like she always did, but she gave me a bright, "didn't I do it well?" smile.

Jeff and Christopher were still the Clueless Twins. "Great, really, Kitty's just having new mother worries."

Christopher nodded. "Look, just go and get some sleep."

I looked at Reader. No help there, he and Tim were leaning against each other, they were laughing so hard, albeit silently.

Michael cleared his throat. "I'd love to go and make Kitty feel safer, but some of her single cousins are here, and I think I need to stick around in case any of them are afraid or bored or just want to talk about etchings or submarine races."

Even with that broad a hint, my husband and his cousin were still not catching on. "Don't take this the wrong way, but why would I want you to come guard my wife while I'm right there?"

"What, you're going to suggest Matt, Chip, and Jerry next?" Christopher snarked.

"I cannot go to guard my leader because there are hot girls here who demand my attention, sir." Jerry managed to get this out without barking a laugh. I was so proud.

"Same for me, sir!" Hughes said, staring ahead as if he were under military review.

"Ditto!" Walker apparently didn't trust himself to more than two syllables.

Tito sighed. "Actually, wherever Kitty and the baby go, so go I. But, I have my own room there. On the third floor. Where staff lives. Far away from the seventh floor."

They still didn't get it. Jeff sighed. "Okay, Tito, no argument. Wherever we end up, I'll make sure you have a room."

"I have a room at the Embassy already, Jeff. However, it's so far from yours and Kitty's. Maybe someone should go along so they're closer. To make the new mother feel safer." Tito was amazing. He got this out with a total poker face.

Naomi got into the act. "Abby and I could go." She nudged Chuckie, pointedly.

"No. I don't want the two of you out of the Science Center without a full guard." Chuckie was giving me the same look that Amy was—why did you marry an idiot and fix your friend up with his idiot cousin?

Christopher rolled his eyes. "As if being at the Embassy wouldn't be the same security level as right here?"

"Sorry, can't allow it. ETD rules." Chuckie was good—he had a poker face and sounded like he was going to start quoting the rulebook any second.

Tim sighed. "Alicia's parents are still getting used to things. I don't think she and I can, in good conscience, leave them alone here." He grinned. "Much as I, personally, would like to go to one of those huge penthouse suites at the Embassy. To guard Kitty, of course. No selfish reasons meant to be implied or intended."

Reader got control of himself. "Paul and I can't go, Kitty, because he and Richard need to sort out Pontifex things. Richard probably needs to stay, too. Sorry. Understand why you would want someone else along who makes you feel safer."

Jeff gave him a dirty look. "Since when don't I make her feel safe?"

White cleared his throat. "Perhaps Miss Gaultier could go along, to help with the baby?"

Christopher gave his father a betrayed look. "I guess."

"Wow, what a good idea. But, gosh, Amy can't defend herself against a stiff breeze. Maybe someone else could come, too, who might be able to help Jeff protect me, Jamie, and Amy."

Jeff and Christopher both stared at me. "Baby, why are you talking so slowly?"

"Maybe my husband's cousin and best friend, who is also my baby's A-C godfather, could come along to help me feel safer and more secure in the creepy Embassy of many empty rooms."

"Kitty, I have a name."

I gave up. "Yeah, and it's Tweedle-Dum. Don't get too hurt, I apparently married Tweedle-Dee." Got hurt looks from both Jeff and Christopher.

"I don't think that was called for," Jeff said quietly.

"Geez, you two. Jeff, I truly don't want to spend one moment in that building without someone else there in addition to you and Jamie—I've seen too many horror movies. However, I've never met two guys who are slower on the uptake than you and Christopher. I mean, good lord, Christopher, your own *dad* is trying to tell you to grab your girl and go off and have a good time alone, and you're standing here arguing about how I should be setting the bravery example. I've got an overactive imagination, but I'm, at least, not a total idiot when it comes to getting a free pass to do the nasty all night long." I looked at White. "You're sure he's your son? I mean, really sure?"

White laughed. "Yes, Missus Martini. Some men just seem more worldly than they are."

"Huh." I looked back at Jeff and Christopher, both of whom looked really embarrassed. "I think Jamie had it figured out faster than you two."

"This reminds me of when the rest of us figured out how to kill Mephistopheles, even though the two of you had, realistically, held the clues for a decade." Lorraine was back to laughing her head off. "Do you two work at being this dense or does it come naturally for you?"

"Kitty can't even say that human guys are this dense," Claudia added. "Since all our human guys caught on a long time ago."

"Or that it's just an A-C thing, since everyone other than Jeff and Christopher was clear on where Amy was going with it from the beginning." Reader laughed. "But, you know, I'll bet if the four of you, accompanied by Doctor Hernandez and the baby, rushed on over to the Embassy, the rest of us would only spend the next hour or so laughing at you behind your backs."

"What a great suggestion," Jeff muttered. "Are there diapers over there now?"

"Yes, Commander Martini," Gladys' voice came over the com. "Security and Operations had plenty of time to equip the Embassy seventh and third floors with appropriate necessities. Thank you and Commander White for playing stupid to give us more time."

"Hey, Gladys, can you please see if Walter, who's on gate duty, is open to coming with us to handle Security?" I wasn't pretending—the suite in the Embassy was larger than my parents' house. And empty buildings creeped me out, for a variety of reasons. The idea that Tito would be alone on the third floor was enough to make me want to have him sleep in one of the many rooms in our penthouse. If I could have taken the entire team with us, I would have.

"Of course, Commander Martini. Walter isn't seeing anyone currently, however, so I can ask him straight out with no risk of innuendo confusion."

"Good, good."

Kevin and Denise Lewis came up to us. "Glad we caught you," Denise said. Kevin was carrying a big box of diapers on which boxes of other things, like wipes, were perched, and she had a big plastic bag in her hand. "Your friend Sheila said you'd need this, too." She unswung an awesome diaper bag from her shoulder and handed it to me.

Christopher took the boxes from Kevin. "I'll just carry this over for them. Jeff has the bassinet." Might take a while, but apparently he could be taught.

Amy took the plastic bag. "That looks heavy, Kitty. Let me."

"Electric pump's in there," Denise told Amy. "Be careful with it."

"Thanks, you guys are the best."

Kevin grinned. "Some of us remember what new parents need better than others."

Everyone said goodnight, Tito said he'd be over once he gathered his medical equipment and so forth, and the four and a half of us took the elevator to the launch level. It was remarkably silent. Amy and I were looking at each other. I couldn't speak for her, but if I looked at Jeff and Christopher I was either going to laugh my head off or ask them again how it was they were so remarkably dense.

"You're dense, too," Jeff muttered.

"Not about getting to have sex."

"Good point."

More silence.

"So, think the bed sheets are changed?" Amy asked finally.

"Yeah. The A-C Elves are pretty efficient. And, per Gladys, they had plenty of time."

"Elves?" Amy sounded as though she'd believe it.

Christopher sighed. "It's a subatomic, spatiotemporal warp process, filtered through black hole technology causing a space-time shift with both a controlled event horizon and ergosphere that allows safe transference of any and all materials. Similar to gate technology."

I looked at Amy. "I've waited almost two years for that explanation. Not, I must admit, that I have any idea of what Christopher just said."

Jeff sighed. "I knew you'd be happier not knowing."

I shrugged. "I don't care how the Elves do it, I just care that they can."

Christopher opened his mouth, to do a fuller explanation, I was sure, but Amy beat him to it. "Do the A-C Elves cover the housekeeping, too?"

"Yeah, they're great. Supposedly the Embassy has a full staff of Elves."

"Cool!"

Jeff cleared his throat. "You know, for two women who just spent time making fun of us for being a little slow, you're not clear at all on this particular scientific theory, are you?"

I looked up at him as the doors opened. "You can spend a lot of time explaining it to me, or we could just, you know, put the baby to sleep in her bassinet."

"I'm not *that* dense."

CHAPTER 75

WALTER WAS PACKED and waiting for us at the launch area. He wasn't alone. William was with him.

It was clear from their expressions that they'd been catching up on all the horror. I didn't know what to say. "Sorry we weren't in time to save your brother" just didn't seem anything like enough.

William gave us a weak smile. "Good to see you again, Commanders."

"Good to see you, too." I had a lump in my throat.

Jeff shook William's hand. "Glad to have you back. Good work."

William swallowed. "Wayne did more on this than I did." He looked down. "A lot more."

"He and the others gave the ultimate sacrifice," Jeff said quietly. "But surviving doesn't mean you didn't do your job well."

"It should have been me," William said. "Captain Crawford only sent me to Florida because—"

"Because he made a command decision," Jeff said sternly. "Are you questioning our chain of command?"

William looked up. "No, sir, Commander." He looked and sounded shocked. A-Cs really didn't question authority. Unless they were Jeff.

"Good. Choices are made every day that have ramifications we're not happy about. But you don't get to take the blame for someone else's decision."

Christopher cleared his throat. "I'd like you to ensure

that the people Captain Crawford assigned you to protect are still protected and are dealing with their indoctrination well. Advise me if there's anything out of the ordinary going on."

"Yes, sir, Commander," William said. He sounded more normal. He nodded to all of us, hugged Walter tightly, then zipped off, presumably to find Alicia and her family.

I hoped Tim wasn't beating himself up over the loss of the agents with him, but reality said that he was. Our team didn't like to lose—it cost us a lot more than we wanted to part with. Every battle was a chess game, but we hated to lose a pawn as much as we did a power piece. A fact our enemies enjoyed using against us.

Jamie fussed again, and I shoved Commander-level worries aside for a moment. "You clear on what's going on?" I asked Walter.

"Yes, Commanders. Gladys told me I was assigned to Security duty for the duration of your stay at the Embassy." He was practically vibrating with what looked to be a combination of pride and shock.

"Welcome aboard, Walt. Let's do the spatio-time warp to the Embassy now, shall we?"

Amy put her hand over Christopher's mouth when he attempted another explanation.

"Yes, ma'am." Walter did the spin the dial thing, and then we walked through. Landed in the basement again. It was still a nauseating experience and, sadly, it was also still dark and creepy down there. I found myself wondering about A-C mentalities for a bit while my stomach settled.

I insisted on checking in on the third floor first, just in case there was something lurking there, waiting to attack Walter or Tito. Walter hypersped through and pronounced it monster-free. Third floor rooms were a lot like the ones at the Science Center—nicely done hotel suite style.

We all went up to the seventh floor, and Walter did a check there. Amazingly, no monsters. He explained that, as the Acting Head of Security, he would be the one on the com, should we need to contact him at any hour of the day or night. Walter was clearly determined to do a great job. I resisted patting him on the head, but it took effort.

We went into what I figured I'd better start thinking of as our home and loaded everything into the nursery, other than the bassinet, which went by my side of the bed, per earlier instructions from Tito.

I checked the closet—our clothes were in it. Same with the drawers—A-C nightwear, underwear, and the like were there. I explained how it worked to Amy, told her to get used to wearing a white Armani Oxford and a black Armani slim skirt for the rest of her life, and then gave an example of how to drive the Elves crazy by requesting different sodas every three seconds. She was as awed with this as I was, Christopher's attempts to explain away the magic with even more incomprehensible magic notwithstanding.

Amazingly enough, now that we were over here, the four of us were not anxious to separate. Christopher and Amy unwillingly went to their half of the floor, changed into the A-C nightclothes, and came right back. Jeff and I didn't object.

"Okay, let's all admit it. It's freaking creepy here for some reason." I was feeding Jamie while sitting on the bed, awesome new receiving blanket decorated with fluffy lambs and pink clouds providing privacy. Between Uncle Mort, Sheila, the Lewises, and the rest of the P.T.C.U., who had provided everything we'd brought over to the Embassy, we could actually take normal care of our baby.

"You want me to have Tito and Walter come up here?" Jeff asked. He didn't sound like he'd object overmuch.

"Sort of. Sort of not."

"It wasn't creepy here before," Amy said.

"Ames, you were gettin' busy with Christopher. There could have been a freaking stampede of buffalo in the ballroom and you wouldn't have noticed."

Amy blushed. "True." Christopher looked pleased with himself.

Jeff wandered out and came back. "Okay, I'm going to test something. Nothing's wrong, just let me know if you can hear me."

The rest of us exchanged looks. "Okay. Jeff, you feeling all right?"

He rolled his eyes and left again, closing the bedroom door behind him. A few moments later I heard something that might have been him howling on the top of his lungs but could have just been the wind. His voice came over the intercom. "Could you hear that?"

"Not so very much. Were you howling?"

Christopher started to laugh. "Okay, I'm taking the position."

Jeff returned. "Yeah, the soundproofing here is so much better than at the Science Center. No idea of why."

"Oh. Well, no complaints from me, then."

"More goes on that you wouldn't want anyone to know about in Washington." Amy said it as though it was both no big deal and not exactly news. True in both cases, but I knew that it was sort of a wake-up call for the rest of us.

"So, Tito with us, Walter with Christopher and Amy, okay, baby?"

"Yeah. Just for tonight. Or however long it takes to get this place inhabited to where I'm not expecting a Jason or Freddy to jump out at me from every corner."

Jeff called down to Walter, and in a few minutes, he and Tito were at our door. Tito heaved a sigh. "I hate to admit it, but I'm with the rest of you. This place is giving me the creeps."

Walter looked relieved. "I thought it was just me."

"Okay, something's wrong." I dug my cell out of my purse. "James, need to have a serious conversation."

"Sure, girlfriend. Is the baby still awake? I mean, that's the only thing I can come up with for why you're not shaking the rafters."

"James, all six of us are freaked out here. Something's off. Me and Amy, okay, I can get it. But the guys? We just pulled Tito and Walter up here with us, and we're still not willing to leave each other's company."

He was quiet. "Let me talk to Richard and Paul about this. I'll call you right back."

Switched torpedoes and finished feeding Jamie. Jeff was doing her diaper and putting her into a pink Minnie Mouse sleeper when Reader called back. "What took you so long?"

"Had to determine who was going where. We're keeping the three pregnant couples here, but the rest of us are coming over there—Reynolds, Abigail, and Naomi, too. What? No, seriously, I want you two staying here, just in case we need you."

"Who are you talking to?"

"Melanie and Emily. Anyway, we'll all be there shortly. Keep everyone together."

"James, what do you think is going on?"

"No idea, but we're going to find out."

CHAPTER 76

WE HUNG UP. "The majority of the team is coming."

"I'd love to say we don't need them, but I'd also like to get some sleep." Jeff put Jamie into the bassinet while I covered her with the pretty pink blanket decorated with Winnie the Pooh and Tigger.

I knew I'd have hated opening these things in front of an army of people, but I loved them now that I was getting to use them with Jamie. Found myself looking forward to doing the thank you notes and wondered if I had a fever.

I had a thought. "Poofikins, Harlie, come to Kitty." The two Poofs mewled and bounded over, purring up a storm. "Stay with Jamie and protect her, okay?" More purrs, then they cuddled up on either side of her.

"Is that safe? I mean, you're not supposed to leave animals with babies." Amy sounded unsure.

"Let's see . . . do I want to leave the Poofs in charge, so they eat anything trying to hurt my baby, or do I want to buy the incorrect old wives' tale that cats and other cuddly things steal the breath from babies?"

"Oh, fine, just thought I should mention it. How did you get six of them?"

"Long story, but only Poofikins is mine. Harlie is Jeff's."

"Yeah, yeah. Through my father." Jeff tried to hide that he was petting Harlie and Poofikins from me. I decided to be nice and not point it out.

"Fluffy is Chuckie's, Fuzzball is Michael's, Gatita is

James', and Toby is Christopher's. Speaking of which, Toby, go to Christopher and take care of him and Amy."

Toby bounded onto Christopher's shoulder, purring like mad. He looked embarrassed. Until Amy cooed. "I only really saw them large and, uh, toothy. This one is so cute. And what an adorable name." Toby hopped onto Amy's shoulder, purred, and stayed there.

"It was the name of Christopher's stuffed toy when he was little." This earned me patented Glare #2.

"Oh, that's so sweet, naming it after your stuffed animal." She said this with absolutely no irony.

Christopher perked up a bit. "Yeah, well, they make great pets."

Heard a knocking at the main door. Walter went to get it. Tito went with him. They were back shortly with everyone else in tow, former and current Pontifexes, too.

"Wow, it's a party. Everyone talk quietly, the baby just fell asleep. In her own bed."

"Not that it matters," Jeff said. "Because if we don't figure out why we're all feeling uncomfortable, we're all sleeping in this room together."

"Does everyone else feel icked or creeped out?" I still did, even though our whole gang was here.

Most of the others nodded. "I didn't feel anything wrong when we were here before," Chuckie said.

"The place has been swept for bombs and similar things at least five times now, maybe more," Tim added.

"I know you guys searched physically, but how are the other searches done?"

"Radar, sonar, infrared, a variety of other scientific ways, some human, some A-C." Gower looked uncomfortable. "Something's wrong, though. ACE is nervous."

"How does a superconsciousness get nervous?"

Gower sighed. "ACE wants us to figure out what's wrong, but when we don't do that quickly, he gets anxious. Not all of him, I mean, it's not like if we take our time the PPB net will collapse, but the longer we take to determine the threat, the more upset he gets."

"Christopher, I'm sorry I have to ask this, okay? Not trying to make you feel bad. But Paul, was ACE upset when Christopher was being drugged and shooting up?"

"No, Kitty, that doesn't make me feel bad at all." Christopher's snark was on full. Amy stroked his hair and the back of his neck in that "my poor put upon brave and beleaguered warrior" way. As near as I could tell, he loved it. Jeff caught my eye and winked.

"No," Gower said, thoughtfully. "There are so many things going on in the world at any one time. ACE observes them, but like Jeff or our other empaths, he blocks most of them out. The closer a threat gets to us, or the more devastating it can be to the most people, the more distressed ACE gets. He still has a hard time with what we call Acts of God and he calls dangerous weather patterns, as an example. He can't save everyone, and he knows it, but he doesn't necessarily like it."

Reader shook his head. "Let's be honest. ACE has two people who he cares about more than any others—Kitty and Paul. Add Abigail, Naomi, and Serene, and, I'd guess, Jamie, and you have the main humans ACE is attached to. Radiating out, Michael and Brian have been in space, so ACE cares about them and all the other astronauts, past, present, and future. The rest of us, the closer we are to those sets of people, the more ACE cares. Ergo, if ACE is nervous, the threat is centered somewhere around those spheres of influence." He grinned. "Not saying ACE doesn't love all his penguins, but he has his favorites."

"When did ACE get nervous, Paul?"

"Been growing steadily for the past hour or so."

"About the time Jeffrey and Kitty decided to come to the Embassy." White looked thoughtful.

"Gladys said the security checks were run and the Elves had put all the stuff in we'd need. From what little we looked at, that seems done."

Michael pulled out his phone. "Gladys, odd question. Yeah, I know, shocker, right? Did anyone who did the Security or Operations set up at the Embassy mention any feelings of dread or fear? Yes, I'm serious. Yeah, actually. I think all of us who are here. Twenty or so. Huddled in Jeff and Kitty's bedroom. Yeah, true, huddled is probably an exaggeration. Okay, thanks." He looked at me. "She's checking with the agents who were here and running another scan."

Jeff came and sat on the bed with me. I snuggled up against him. "You think it's like with my delivery?" I asked him quietly. "Where Jamie's making it happen because I was scared?"

"Maybe, but . . . I don't think so." Jeff looked uncomfortable. "I'm picking something up—not from anyone in here, but something else. I don't know what it is."

Michael started talking again. "Really? Huh, interesting. No, I think there're enough of us over here. Yes, good idea. Yes, please. Thanks." He hung up. "No one felt anything. Routine personnel transfer. It was pointed out that there were no personal belongings to remove, but we already knew that. Gladys offered to send over more Security, but I don't see the point. She's going to keep active scans going on the Embassy."

"So what do we do? I ask because I'm both tired as hell and freaked out of my mind."

"I don't want anyone going off alone." Chuckie didn't sound frightened, but I could pick up that he was as uncomfortable as the rest of us. He settled down on the floor and leaned his back against the wall. "So, what do we know?"

"Not much. You know, since everyone's here, want to discuss how Amy's stepmom was at our wedding with, I'm pretty sure, Ronaldo Al Dejahl?"

"I'd rather figure out what's going on right now," Jeff said.

Tim cocked his head at me. "You thinking it's related?"

"Not sure." I looked at Walter and took a deep breath. "Walt, we're going to be discussing what . . . happened to Wayne. One of his older brothers," I explained for the others. I saw Chuckie tense and realized he hadn't known—either that Walter was related to Wayne and William or that Wayne had been one of the agents murdered.

Walter nodded. "I'm guessing from your expression it wasn't pleasant."

"No," Tim said quietly. "It wasn't. If you don't want to be here while we discuss it, I know everyone will understand."

Walter shook his head. "I think I need to know. And," he added with a weak smile, "I don't really want to be somewhere else in this building right now."

"Yeah, ain't it the truth?" I took another deep breath. "Tim, Amy, Michael—you want to share the horrific things that were done to our four agents? And by whom? And, possibly most importantly, where?"

"I'll do it," Tim said. "You two chime in with anything I miss." Amy and Michael nodded. They didn't look eager to join in, not that I could blame them. "The only saving grace was the agents died fast. But they weren't killed in a conventional manner—no guns, knives, or blunt instruments. They were . . . tortured. But it didn't kill them. They were all alive after it. It seemed over, like they were going to stop and either move on to torture the rest of us or go play with something else. But then, one by one, they dropped."

"Lethal injection?"

"No. I'm not sure how they died, just that they did. Mister Gaultier was by each one of them, then they went down. One minute alive, the next dead."

"Christopher, I know you saw this, what was it like inside their bodies, did you check?"

He shook his head. "I was watching, but not for internal changes."

"Then they dissected them, in front of us." Tim kept his tone very level. Walter's fists and jaw clenched, but he didn't react otherwise. "We weren't in a medical facility. I think we were in one of Gaultier's warehouses."

"Why in the world would they do that?" Chuckie sounded like the wheels were turning but getting nothing. "It makes no sense whatsoever. As we discovered during our vacation to the French prison, Cooper and his gang have been doing tests on A-C hybrids certainly longer than I've been in the C.I.A., and possibly longer than Kitty's mother's been in antiterrorism."

"Cooper wasn't much older than us, midthirties, maybe. My mom's been in antiterrorism a lot longer than that."

Chuckie shrugged. "I'm sure Cooper wasn't the ultimate brains behind this."

"Reynolds is right," Jeff said quietly. "From what they were saying, this has been going on for decades."

Chuckie nodded. "But regardless, there's not a logical reason to do it where they did, and less to do it in front of the three of you. None of you have A-C talents; none of you have been injected with Surcenthumain. Even if they believed Martini or White was trying to track the hybrids and so using horror as the draw, what was the damn point? Torturing one of you physically would draw any empath faster than performing a vivisection."

"We know they were dead, right?"

Everyone looked at me. "They dropped down on the floor and stopped breathing and moving," Tim said.

Christopher nodded. "I saw them die."

I hated where I was going with this, particularly since Walter was right here. I realized I couldn't say what I needed to in front of him. Then I looked around and realized I couldn't say it in front of anyone. Well, almost anyone. I got off the bed. "I want most everyone to stay up here. Chuckie and I are going to go look for something." Jeff started to protest. "Stop. Really, stop." I said. "I want you to stay with Jamie. I want everyone else to stay here for a wide variety of reasons."

"Put some clothes on," Jeff growled.

I shook my head. "No. It won't matter, okay? We need to go now."

Chuckie stood up. "Yeah. But, Kitty? Take your purse." I could tell by his expression he was making the same assumptions I was.

I managed a chuckle. "Good idea." I kissed Jeff. "Stay here, I mean it. You'll know if I need you. And I need you to keep the others away from us." I kissed Jamie. "I want you blocking her, Jeff, you and Christopher both. I don't know what you'll have to do, but I don't want her seeing anything Chuckie and I are doing, seeing, or experiencing."

Jeff nodded, his face pale. "Why only Reynolds?"

"Because I'm too chicken to go alone."

CHAPTER 77

I CHECKED THE CLOSET. The Elves had provided slippers. They thought of everything. Put them on, went out, even though I didn't want to. Chuckie closed the bedroom door behind us, took my hand, and we went into the hallway.

"You know your husband's wondering if this is just an elaborate ruse for us to have sex under his nose."

I managed a laugh. "Yeah, but I think he's more freaked out than anything else."

"You want to tell me why you don't want the others, any of them, to know? I'm clear on why you don't want your newest recruit involved." He sighed. "Wayne was the empathic brother from the other day, right?"

"Yes. William's still alive—he's married with a baby on the way, and Tim sent him to Florida."

"Thank God. Wish he'd sent Wayne, too." Chuckie cleared his throat. Yeah, there was a lot of that going around. "Why don't you want the others clued in?"

"The agents are trying to reach me. Honestly, I think Wayne, specifically, is trying to reach me. And while I knew him, I didn't know him too long. And I didn't know the others—they won't be my brother, my second cousin twice removed, someone I christened or married, someone I counseled, someone I may have done medical on or trained with, someone I've known my whole life, or someone I led into their horrific not-quite-death."

"Why, do you think? I mean, I know you think they're still alive."

"When Paul was in that airless chamber, he wasn't moving and his hearts were barely beating. And Al Dejahl told me he could make me brain dead but still impregnate me, and I could have plenty of babies that way because of the medical advances Gaultier had made. I'm betting they did the vivisection right then because they needed to, due to the process or whatever it is the new Doctor Mengele created."

We were in the elevator. "What floor?"

"Basement."

"Why there? Everyone goes in and out of there. And there's no elevator stop for the basement."

"So we go to the first floor and walk down." I sighed. "A-Cs are weird, Chuckie. Martini Manor has the gate entry in the basement, too. I assume it's somewhat for camouflage. But the few other gate areas I've landed at were all empty, just the gate and the room. No idea why, but potentially to make room if a lot of folks had to fling themselves through quickly."

"The basement here looks like a human basement. It's packed with junk."

"Yeah, I'll bet it is." The doors opened, and I took Chuckie's hand again as we stepped out. "I know I'm going to be sick. I just want you prepared." We walked down the hall and toward the stairs.

"I've seen it."

"Yeah, and I don't need the drinking to excess rant. I don't drink anything now." Flipped on the lights, started downstairs.

"I'd have thought after barfing your guts out, doing a variation of the Dance of a Thousand Veils on the bar, and then passing out, you'd have never wanted to drink again."

"Dude, it was one freaking frat party, okay?"

"You'd have been gang-raped if I hadn't been there."

"Which was why I took you with me, if you'd care to recall." We reached the bottom and stepped into the basement.

"Yeah. As I recall, we got into a huge fight about me going with you, and I was only along because I threatened to call your mother. Are there lights in here, do you think?"

I squinted. "I can see in the dark now. But all A-Cs can,

so maybe not. I forgot what a narc you were when we were younger."

"Wonderful. I'm not enhanced, so I can't see a thing. And I did it for your own protection." He sounded hurt.

I squeezed his hand. "I know, I'm just teasing you. Sort of. You did end up in the appropriate line of work, I guess."

"Yeah, tell me that later, once you see what they did to my apartment."

Squeezed his hand harder. "I'm just so thankful you were with us, not there."

"Me too. Let's find a light switch or a flashlight. I don't want to see what we're going to find, but I'd rather see it than feel it, if you catch my drift."

My cell rang. I dug around in my purse. "Jeff, what's up?"

"Lights are behind the gate." He sounded annoyed.

"Thanks. You're supposed to be blocking this from Jamie."

"Wow, news flash, I can do that and talk to you at the same time. Realize I'm not as awesome as Reynolds is, but I sometimes make do."

"You know, did we not *just* have the jealousy chat? Again?"

He sighed. "Yes. You're holding his hand."

"Because I'm freaked out and would like not only Jamie, but you and all the others to not know what we're doing. Not, I obviously must add, because Chuckie and I are going to have sex in the icky, creepy basement just so we can earn the title of World's Stupidest Clandestine Lovers but so, in fact, we can discover the horror and keep it from the rest of you. Feel free to continue to piss me off, however, and I may consider kissing him just to prove your ridiculous jealousy concerns are valid. I mean, you so clearly want to be right and all."

"I'm willing," Chuckie said, loudly enough that I knew Jeff could hear it.

He was quiet for a moment. "You're really expecting this to be beyond God-awful, aren't you?" His voice was very gentle and also low.

"Yes. Well beyond."

"Okay, baby, I'll do my best. Tell Reynolds to keep his paws off you."

"Yeah, he and I have that one memorized, Jeff."

"Be careful."

"We will." Hung up and looked around behind the gate. "Good grief, they're not all tall. Chuckie, I'm going to lead you to the light switch. I can't reach it." I put his hand on the wall, but the lights didn't go on. "Um, dude? Why are we still in total darkness?"

"I haven't flipped the switch yet. Who would put a light switch up this high?" he asked slowly.

I looked around some more. Found another switch, at a normal height, but had to let go of Chuckie to get to it. "Um . . . you know, this is why I brought you with me. Don't turn that on yet." Flipped the switch I could reach, lights came on, just like magic.

We took a look. Boxes and crates. Lots of them. Chuckie still hadn't flipped the switch his hand was by. We both looked at it. "I don't see anything. I feel it, but I don't see it."

"It's cloaked. I can see it because I'm enhanced. Dude, this is going to suck in a really bad way, I think."

He reached out and grabbed my hand again. "Okay, I want you to see if I've tripped something."

I looked. "Can't see anything. But I can't tell, either. You're Mister Covert Ops. I'm Megalomaniac Girl. Different skills."

"Okay. If I die from turning this thing on, I just want to go on record that if you wanted to be stupid enough to go for it here just to prove your husband right, I'd honestly be willing." He grinned. "Of course, I'm also willing to just pretend we did and torture him that way."

"You're as evil as my mom."

"I did pick up some tips from her, yeah." He took a deep breath. "You ready?"

"Born ready or some such. Flip it, big guy."

He did. And the last thing I was expecting happened.

CHAPTER 78

OKAY, PERHAPS NOT the last thing. But it was up there on the list.

The floor moved down.

I managed not to scream, though I had Chuckie's hand in a death grip.

He stepped away from the wall and looked around. "Interesting. Whole floor's an elevator. But the gate's stationary." He didn't sound freaked out at all. "This normal?"

"Not for A-Cs, at least, not that I've ever seen."

He nodded. "Wonder how long it's been here."

"Uh, don't these sorts of things have to be created as the building's being built?"

"Not always. I mean, it's easier, sure. But if you've got plenty of time, tons of money, and the will, there's always a way."

The floor was still moving. "Think there's anything in the boxes?"

"Yeah, but not what we're after. Assume it's supplies. They have the boxes and crates in here so you can't see the floor and wall aren't butted up together. No one looks around behind the gate, and if they do, it's for the light switch, which everyone other than us would know about."

"This couldn't have been here when Jeff and Christopher were kids. They'd have found it. They were here alone a lot and were inquisitive little boys with a healthy distrust of authority."

"Huh, explains Martini's attitude toward authority

other than his own now. However, doesn't mean they couldn't have missed this."

I dug my phone out. "No service. Hope we don't run into trouble."

"I'm taking trouble as a given. You have a gun?"

"Nope, Jeff took it away. Do you?"

"Yeah, he can't take mine away."

We stopped moving. I estimated we were three stories down. "Um, now what?" I was expecting a door or something, but it looked like we were still in a basement, just one for storing the Jolly Green Giant. The lighting was dim since the lights were a long way away.

"Look for another switch or set of switches."

"Here's one."

"Don't!" Chuckie said at the exact moment I flipped it. We started moving up. He gave me a dirty look.

"Sorry."

"Do you do things like that all the time?"

Considered lying, figured he'd know. "Yeah, pretty much."

"And Martini somehow thinks it's cute and doesn't try to strangle you or just lock you up in your room where you can't do any damage?"

"Yeah, pretty much."

Chuckie nodded. "I think you married the right guy."

"Thanks, I think."

Took time to think as we took the boring trip to the surface. If we were going to go exploring, which was a possibility, I didn't want it to be just me and Chuckie, for a variety of reasons, all of them connected with keeping us alive. Considered who'd handle the horror the best. Probably the guy who'd been handling it for decades. "I think I want Richard to come with us. So it won't be a waste that we're going back upstairs."

Chuckie gave me a long look. "I'm not buying that as a good enough excuse for, ah, your impetuous decision to flip a random switch in a danger situation."

"But it works for me. Oooh, look, reception." I dialed. "Mister White. Changed our minds. Would like you, and only you, to come along."

"I'm ecstatic, Missus Martini. Jeffrey looks very pleased for some reason."

"Yeah, Chuckie's had the realization of how I roll thrust upon him."

There was a pause. "Are you both uninjured?"

"So far."

"So, you just did something typical for you that Mister Reynolds viewed as foolhardy, dangerous, and unthinking?"

"Sarcasm is really one of your fortés, isn't it? Yes. Please meet us in the basement."

"On my way."

He arrived as we came to a full stop. Chuckie sighed. "Since we're all the way back up, you want to tell us if you knew about the elevator?"

"We have two elevators in the building. Neither one goes down to the basement."

"No, I mean the hidden one." Chuckie was watching White carefully.

"What hidden one?" He wasn't trying to lie or be evasive—he didn't know. We pointed out the switch. White shook his head. "It wasn't here when my wife was our head diplomat."

"Okay, so it was put in after. The Colemans had two decades to do the work, after all."

White looked angry. "I wonder how many problems they caused for us, over the years. I find it difficult to believe they ever had our best interests at heart."

Chuckie flipped the switch and we started back down. "No idea. After this is over, however, I promise you I'm going to find out."

"Mister White, why were the Colemans picked after Terry died? Lucinda told me that they were aware Yates was alive, but I don't know if they were also in on his world domination plan."

He looked thoughtful. "All our original Diplomatic Corps knew, the ones who were . . ."

"Loyal to you and Terry?"

"Yes. However, while neither Theresa nor I told them, and neither did Alfred or Lucinda, the Colemans and the rest who became part of their Diplomatic Corps confronted us about it while she was still alive."

"So, safe bet they were on Beverly's side, so to speak. I know most of the older generation of A-Cs didn't know

Yates was your father or still alive. Of those who did know, how many are still alive?"

"Myself, Lucinda and Alfred Martini, Stanley and Ericka Gower. Yes, she's human, but she figured it out. Gladys and Harold Gower."

"That's our Intercom Queen Gladys, right? And she's married to Stanley's brother?" He nodded. "That's why Michael calls her at the drop of a hat, she's his closest aunt."

"And he's her favorite," White added with a chuckle. "I believe Gladys is the only one who considers Michael's dating exploits to be adorable."

"Someone should. Anyone else alive who knew about Yates? I'm asking so we can kind of get a heads-up for who's going to try to destroy us next under the guise of purity of the race." We came to a stop. I pointed to the switch. "Don't flip that one until we want to go up."

White looked over at Chuckie. "She flipped it, didn't she?"

Chuckie nodded. "I'd tie her up, but Martini would probably object."

"Humph! Mister White, while we look for other switches we won't flip until Chuckie says okay, any other A-Cs in the know about Yates?"

"Possibly. Can't come up with them right now, other than the ones your mother questioned in regard to having helped Beverly with, as you call it, Operation Fugly. They implicated neither the Diplomatic Corps nor themselves. I'm sure I can retrieve a full listing at a time when we're not once again heading into life-threatening danger. Have you noticed the dread is decreasing?"

"Just because they didn't implicate anyone doesn't mean they're innocent," Chuckie said.

"Dude, you made your point prebirth. I've dealt with and talked to Camilla, I'm a believer. As my partner pointed out, this is probably not the right time. And as for the dread, Mister White, it was a signal for me. Now that I'm moving, I think they know they can relax a bit. So to speak."

"They?" White sounded guarded.

"I don't see anything but that one switch."

Chuckie looked around. "Then the boxes are in place to hide the door or switch." We started to move them carefully.

"They?" White asked again as he helped move boxes. I saw him jolt. "Oh. Oh, dear. No wonder you wanted the others to stay as far away as possible."

"Yeah. I think they moved Jamie to the highest point away they could. They were trying to reach me, but I'm sure she was integral to whatever horror Gaultier and company thought up, and the agents would know it. They're protectors, after all."

"And you and Wayne had a connection," Chuckie added quietly.

"Yes." Now wasn't the time for the lump in the throat. Grief was really trying to shove in and ride shotgun with Guilt, but under the circumstances, Rage felt it had the floor. I noted that I was getting less tired in direct proportion to the fact that my anger was building. Figured I'd worry about becoming She Hulk after we'd handled this next round of horror.

"Got it," Chuckie said as we moved the last of the boxes that would have been opposite the gate if we were back at the basement level. He pointed to something near the floor—a circle divided into thirds with A, B & C in each section. "He really got around."

"Wow, messed up another twenty-year plan. I feel all tingly."

"Yeah. I knew Amy's mother was the only thing keeping Gaultier in line." Chuckie looked over at me. "I won't tell her."

"Tell her what? She already knows her dad was Mister Evil."

Chuckie sighed. "Kitty, think about it."

I did. "I have no idea what you're talking about."

"Maybe you don't. Amy's mother had an odd illness, right? Something that couldn't be medically cured?"

"Yeah. Can't even remember the name, it was so obscure."

Chuckie nodded. "I'm sure it was obscure." He took my hand. "Hold onto the former Pontifex, if you would." I grabbed White's hand and Chuckie kicked the circle. We lowered again, but this time, I could see an opening immediately. "He murdered his wife. Either from using her as a guinea pig, or because he didn't want the restraint any more."

I knew he wasn't talking about White. "Oh. How long have you known?"

"Figured that's what it was the moment she died. I haven't had a lot of time or ability to research it. But he remarried pretty quickly, and I do know he married his mistress."

My throat felt tight again. "You never said a thing to Amy, did you?"

"No. Couldn't stand her, but saw no reason to be vicious. Still can barely stand her, by the way, in case you were wondering if White was going to have to do the jealousy bit your husband's so fond of."

"Dude, really, I know. But remain civil."

"Oh, I will. I appreciated her trying to defend me." The floor stopped again. Another long corridor. This one was lit, however. "You two ready?"

"Not so much," White said, as he kept me from moving forward. He looked around. "I see no traps or trip wires, Mister Reynolds."

"Me either. Have to admit it's a relief to know you're not as willing to die as Kitty seems to be."

White laughed. "Opposites attract."

CHAPTER 79

WE RAN DOWN THE CORRIDOR. It went on for a long way, but we reached a door in about five minutes of the slow hyperspeed, which meant we were probably far away from the Embassy. The tunnel continued on, but we stopped here. The dread hit me, hard, while Chuckie got his stomach under control. "They're in there."

White and Chuckie examined the door. "I think it's safe," White said. Chuckie nodded and opened it. It wasn't locked.

We walked in to see a textbook mad scientist medical lab. There were the usual vats of fluids of all sizes, tubes and wires, steel tables, usual implements, and plenty of things I couldn't identify.

The room was big, well lit, and temperature controlled, and it had what looked like a full communications area. I examined the console—full phone and intercom set up, similar to what I'd seen at Area 51, though not all that much like the Command Centers in the Science Center and Caliente Base. There were twelve video screens, each showing something different. "They have feeds into what looks like every main Centaurion base."

Chuckie and White joined me. "Yes, Missus Martini, you're correct."

Chuckie pointed to two of the screens. "That's Langley. And that's ETD headquarters. Jesus. What areas are they monitoring? And how did they tap into your system and ours without us knowing?" I could hear Chuckie's wheels turning.

I looked around, at the phone in particular. "They did it right after Terry died. That phone's easily twenty years old. Richard was grieving, the boys were with Alfred and Lucinda, the Embassy was being taken over by Yates loyalists."

"The tunnel would have had to have existed before then," Chuckie said. "No way you could get this low and long in a few weeks."

I looked at White. "Bet you could if you were using hyperspeed, superhuman strength, and a lot of alien technology. Chuckie, you said yourself they could have put in the elevator after Terry died. Why not the entire Underground Complex of Doom?"

White nodded. "We built the Science Center in a matter of months. We only have to move slowly when humans need to see us do so. We stay in practice by moving slowly under most circumstances. Building secret tunnels and labs would not be most circumstances."

"So, was the C.I.A. always working with Yates?" What Jeff called my feminine intuition said yes.

"Probably." White shook his head. "Mister Reynolds is our only ally there."

"Angela's the reason I joined the C.I.A. in the first place," Chuckie said. "She helped me get the appointment into the ETD, too."

I thought about this, while trying not to be offended again that my mother had felt Chuckie was total superspy material but that I wasn't even up to being told the truth about much of anything. "Mom didn't know there were aliens on Earth, and even though Dad's Mister NASA ET Cryptology Guru, he said he didn't know, either."

"Your mother really didn't know?" Chuckie sounded shocked. "I thought she was just testing my ability to keep the secret."

"Near as I can tell, Mom didn't know there were aliens or that Dad worked in NASA's ET division, and Dad didn't know how frequently Mom was doing active fieldwork. I, of course, was clueless about all of it until I met Jeff."

"Killing a superbeing was the wake-up call for the majority of our human agents. At least, until you started hiring, Missus Martini."

"Not my fault I pick well. So, Yates and the C.I.A., best friends forever?"

"Probably. I'd figured out what your parents did." Chuckie smiled at the betrayed look I knew I was giving him. "In high school."

"Dude, sometimes I hate you."

He shrugged. "Couldn't tell you. I promised Angela I wouldn't. Besides, it was for your own protection."

"That why you waited until I was fully hooked into Centaurion to share?"

He got a sad look on his face, but he wiped it away quickly. "Somewhat." I squeezed his hand while I felt like a complete clueless jerk. Guilt waved merrily at me. "I was appointed head of the ETD division about a year or so before you joined up. But I'd been working with Centaurion for my entire ETD career. There are factions within the organization that have the same views Angela and I do about how best to utilize our A-Cs. Thankfully, some of them are much higher up than me."

"But the rest of them want the War Division, right?" I wondered how much higher you could get than the guy in charge of the entire division and then decided I could table that question for another, less creepy time.

Chuckie nodded. "Or the Power Division, if you want. Everyone wants to control the X-Men, remember."

"Good point. Everything I ever needed to know I learned from comic books and my Conspiracy King." Chuckie grinned and squeezed my hand back. Okay, good, we were back to normal for us, which meant Jeff was probably growling again, but oh, well.

"I do remain thankful every day that Mister Reynolds, you, and your mother are ever vigilant." White looked around. "I'm also very glad the Poofs ate our former Diplomatic Corps, though right now having someone to question might be helpful."

"Oh, that's what we're here for. So, back to Chuckie's question. It looks like they're monitoring all the launch areas and main living quarters. The launch areas I can get, but why are they watching the bedrooms? I mean, unless they're just too cheap to buy their own porn over the Internet like everyone else."

Chuckie looked thoughtful. "Let's see what this does." He pulled out the chair and sat down.

The console leaped to life. Images started shifting rapidly, lights were blinking, and a modulated female voice spoke. "Hello, Doctor Gaultier. What would you like VARIS to show you?"

"Varis?" I whispered to White. He pointed. Voice Activated Recovery Information System was in official lettering on the console. In big, obvious letters. Oh, well, that's why I had a partner, right?

"VARIS, show me the most recent activity."

"Yes, Doctor." We all let out the breath we'd been holding. Not using voice recognition software. Images started to come up. Apparently they'd filmed the murder and vivisection of our four agents. I had to turn away. I didn't want to see that, and I wanted to be able to remember Wayne the way I'd met him—alive and smiling.

"Tell me when it's over."

It took a few minutes during which I wandered around some more. The room was a big rectangle, but after the hidden elevator, I looked for the supersecret portion of the secret lab. Rewarded by looking behind things. "I found what looks like a humongous freezer. Ten bucks says they're in here."

"Let it wait for a minute. The gruesome part's over. Need you to pay attention." Chuckie sounded tense, so I trotted. "Note whose bedrooms we're now visiting."

"Well, gosh. That's the Lair, and that's Christopher's room . . . everyone's on Alpha and Airborne. And yours, too."

"Yeah."

"Doctor Gaultier, would you like status on the subjects?"

"Yes, VARIS, thank you."

We all stared at the screen, but the images didn't change. I heard a printer and looked over to my right. Sure enough, there were papers coming out. I picked them up and stared at the title. "Operation Alteration. Why do I doubt this is going to relate to buying suits at wholesale and having them tailored to fit?"

White took the pages out of my hands and did a quick scan. "Hmmm. Three main subjects expected to be operational within two days, remainder within two weeks." He looked up at me. "I don't think we're going to like this, Missus Martini."

"VARIS, I'd like a status report for all other team members," Chuckie said to the console.

"Robert Coleman, dead. Barbara Coleman, dead. Agent John Cooper, dead."

Chuckie interrupted. "I'd like a printout, please."

"Yes, Doctor Gaultier." The printer revved up again. I pulled out the list. "Huh. Shows Clarence as freed on his own recognizance and Ronaldo as being held captive by, and I quote, the enemy."

"Didn't think they were our friends." Chuckie turned back to the console. "VARIS, what stands in the way of our success?"

"Katherine Katt Martini, Jeffrey Stuart Martini, Christopher Terrence White, Charles Martin Reynolds, Angela Fiore Katt, Kevin Sidney Lewis, Richard Trevor White, Paul Stanley Gower."

"Why?"

"They provide the leadership and protective core for Centaurion Division. Their removal will allow free access to all Centaurion resources."

"What do we need to complete Operation Alteration?"

"The progeny of Katherine Katt Martini and Jeffrey Stuart Martini."

White put his arm around my shoulders and hugged me.

"Why?" Chuckie took my hand.

"Due to father's genetic alteration, child possesses enough power to fuel an incalculable number of replicants."

"Replicants?" White asked softly.

Right, A-Cs didn't really watch or read science fiction. They lived it. "Replicants, clones, duplicates. Robots that look and function like humans." My stomach clenched. "Chuckie, I have a really horrible feeling about this."

"I was at horrible feeling in the basement." He squeezed my hand, let go, and took the papers from White. "VARIS, we lost personnel. What do we need to do to recover?" He rifled through the Operation Alteration papers.

"Gain progeny of Katherine Katt Martini and Jeffrey Stuart Martini. Plan is operational as long as progeny is obtained." Discovered I didn't like Jamie being called "progeny" any more than "spawn."

I scanned the status list. "Chuckie, Herbert Gaultier is listed as dead."

"Right. So?"

"So, how is the computer thingy talking to 'you' if it knows 'you're' dead?" White pointed to an entry farther down the page. It said LaRue Demorte Gaultier was alive and at large. "Wow, the trophy wife's the brains of this operation?"

"You're the brains of our operation, Kathy." White managed to make us both chuckle. I treasured it, because I had the feeling I wasn't going to be chuckling for a while. I put the page in front of Chuckie. He looked up and gave me the "duh" look. Fine, so he'd already figured it out. Not my fault.

"Her name means the Street of the Dead. By the way." Got the "so what?" look from Chuckie. I had the feeling he was moving at warp speed in terms of getting over me romantically. I gave it one more, as Christopher called them, "Kittyism," and Jeff might not need to do the jealousy talk with Chuckie, ever.

Chuckie turned back to the computer screen. "VARIS, how close are we to gaining progeny?"

"Operation has been affected by murder of majority of participants. Replicants One through Three are ready without progeny."

"What do you recommend?"

"Activate One through Three, have them remove their counterparts and Katherine Katt Martini, recover progeny."

"Do we have to remove Katherine Katt Martini?"

"Yes. Identified as single point of disruption for all active plans and organizations. Has single-handedly destroyed at least ten major offensives. Considered Enemy Number One. Should be destroyed with extreme prejudice."

"I feel the love."

"Our side loves you," White said.

"Doctor Gaultier, Katherine Katt Martini identified within medical lab."

"Thanks, VARIS. She's my prisoner."

"Recommend immediate termination. Subject has exhibited random abilities."

"Random abilities?" What the heck did that mean? I had the skills.

Chuckie looked over his shoulder and grinned at me. "Means luck."

"Oh." Well, couldn't argue that one.

"Shall I activate One through Three, Doctor Gaultier?"

"No, VARIS, not just yet. I'll let you know."

"Very good. Can I assist with anything else?"

"Not at the moment. Thank you, VARIS." Chuckie stood and the console went quiet. The video feeds were still active. Happily, most of the people who were being spied on were in my room at the Embassy, and, thankfully, the others seemed to still be at the party in the library.

"Now what?"

Chuckie sighed. "Now we go into that freezer and see just what One through Three really are."

CHAPTER 80

"CAN'T WAIT. OH, WAIT. Can wait. Would love to wait." I sighed. "Of course, they're after my baby, so, back to can't wait."

Chuckie nodded. "Ditto. So, where's the hidden freezer?" He took the list of operatives from me, folded up the printouts, and shoved them into his inner jacket pocket.

I led them over, and he pulled the handle. It opened, but nothing fell out. Because there was a big room back there. We all peered in. There were bags of various sizes hung up on meat hooks. I found myself wishing I'd listened to Jeff and changed clothes.

"Wow, it's going to keep on sucking until it just can't suck any more, isn't it?"

"Looks that way." Chuckie took my hand and indicated White should take the other, then we all stepped inside. It was freezing, but I was revved up on fear and horror, and it didn't bother me as much as it could have. Chuckie looked down and jerked his head away. "I wish you'd put on some clothes."

I looked down. Yep, the torpedoes were doing a good imitation of getting ready to be ravaged by Jeff. "I didn't know we'd be in a freaking meat locker."

All of us froze. "Oh, I wish you hadn't said that. Because, as I look around at oddly shaped bags hanging on meat hooks, I'm hearing horror movie music in my head."

"Dude, you too? Thank God it's not just me expecting to see severed limbs and such in the bags. But, you know, you're the top man, so I'm not going to steal your thunder. You get to open them. I'll wait by the door so I can run screaming back down the hall." I pulled my phone out. "How the hell do they get reception down here?"

Chuckie cleared his throat. "The phone system is twenty years old, Kitty. It's run on landlines. Like all the rest of their computer equipment." I was getting a look that said my time with Jeff had caused brain damage.

"I can still beat you at chess."

He and I stared at each other. "Queen." We said it in unison. Too creeped out to care.

"Pardon?" White asked, sounding confused.

"Operation Invasion was one big chess game, Mister White, remember? Realistically, every elaborate ruse is, in its own way. We haven't won yet, because the White Queen is still free, and the King is not dead, merely locked up."

"Why are we black?" White still sounded confused.

"Because white goes first. Our enemies always make the first moves. How you start the game matters, but how you end it is what counts."

Chuckie laughed. "And to think I had to beg you to join the Chess Club."

I shrugged. "Until I realized I was going to be the only girl, and the rest of the guys were all fun and cool like you."

He gave me a very fond look, and I wondered if I'd just put us right back to Jeff having to have the jealousy chat. Oh, well, more important things to worry about. Like what was in the icky bags and what One through Three would turn out to be.

"Okay, Richard and I will look in the bags. Kitty, you look around for whatever else they have hidden here. Stay in sight of us, though, and, seriously, feel free to scream if you need us."

"You got it." I was working to not scream. Screaming would be easy.

The men went to the nearest bag and started to gingerly open it. I busied myself elsewhere. This room was bigger than the lab and seemed to be L-shaped. I examined the part of the room we were in first. Lots and lots of bags. Lots. Moved through them carefully. It was like the Hanging Forest of Horror in here.

Got to the walls—a stainless steel counter ran along

three quarters of the room—only the wall that held the door didn't have any counter. On the metal counters were things that looked like very large, weird metal Crock-Pots. All of them had wiring and other oddities coming out and trailing along the counter, one hooked into the other, to create one long daisy chain of weird. It headed toward the end of the room I hadn't examined yet.

Heard gagging and spun around. Chuckie and White were closer to me. Both of them looked the way I felt after every gate transfer combined. "Okay," Chuckie gagged out as they closed up the bag they were looking in. "We've seen enough."

"More than enough," White agreed.

"I know I'm going to regret asking, but what's in the bags?"

"Exactly what you think is in the bags." Chuckie really looked like he was going to throw up.

"Erm . . . severed body parts from all the two hundred or so male hybrids who died mysteriously as well as a variety of our agents, probably the ones with empathic and imageering talents, including the four who were murdered earlier in Operation Confusion?"

White nodded. "And this is why you're my partner, Missis Martini. You continue to think like the megalomaniacs and psychos above all others."

"Damn. I was so hoping I'd be wrong, and the bags would be filled with candy or fluffy bunnies."

"Might not be all two hundred, but, there's plenty of parts." Chuckie shuddered. "Replicants. Oh, my God."

I pointed to the containers on the metal counter. "Master, Igor has found some lovely brains for you."

CHAPTER 81

WE ALL STARED AT FRANKENSTEIN'S Crock-Pots.

"You think it's just their brains in there?" Chuckie asked hopefully.

"No idea. I hope Jeff and Christopher can figure out how to lock this memory away so Jamie never, ever sees it." Found myself wishing we had a Dazzler along. This all looked extremely scientific. Camilla might have had the stomach for it, but since I had no phone reception, I couldn't call her down here to find out. "Any clue what'll happen if we open things up?"

"None." Chuckie was studying the wires, and he began to follow the trail of vats. As before, each one was hooked into the next all the way down the line, to the far wall, where we turned the corner and moved farther into the Freezer from Hell. I started humming "Whatever Happened to Saturday Night" from *Rocky Horror*.

"I still think you made the best Columbia ever," Chuckie said as we moved along. More stainless steel counter on both sides, more creepy vats, all connected one to the next.

"You're so sweet. You did Brad really well, too."

"Nerd was natural, yeah."

"What are you two talking about, Missus Martini?"

"Shared experiences at the midnight movies, Mister White. Long in the past now. Similarities to our current situation, however." Wondered if a saxophone would be involved, figured it couldn't possibly end up that enjoyable an experience. I didn't luck into Tim Curry in a leather teddy and fishnet stockings. My luck ran to creepy fuglies and insane politicos. I consoled myself that I'd married the hottest alien in the galaxy. Just hoped I'd see him again soon.

"I counted well over a hundred of the containers." White said quietly. "And that was in the other room alone."

We turned again. Counters and vats continued on, but then stopped at another freezer door. "What are the odds?" Chuckie asked.

"Oh, pretty freaking good. Clone army or Gaultier's Monster?"

"No bet. Could be either one, could be both."

"I'm getting a horrible feeling about what the two of you are talking about, Missus Martini. Should we be prepared for attack or merely for unmitigated horror?"

"See, this is why you're my new partner, Mister White. 'Cause you continue to rock above all others. Cover all the bases, assume both."

Chuckie opened the door. Inside was a room lit up like the proverbial Christmas tree. And inside it was something that, even though I was prepared, made me scream.

White hugged me to him and I buried my face in his chest. "Mister Reynolds, your thoughts? About what to do, I mean. I assume we're all sharing the horror."

"The room's rigged. I don't think we can enter it safely." I felt Chuckie's hand on my back. "Kitty, you have to pull it together, right now."

I took a deep breath, pulled away from White, and turned around. Nope, I hadn't imagined it. Sent a memo to the cosmos to clarify that when I'd thought about wanting to see Jeff again soon, I hadn't meant like this.

"Jeff" was standing there. There were tubes and wires going into "him." "Christopher" and "Chuckie" were on either side of "Jeff" just as they'd been in the Paris dungeon. Tubes and wires in them, too. They were naked, and I could confirm that "Jeff" and "Chuckie" were anatomically correct.

There were replicas of every one of the men from Alpha and Airborne in there. I did my best not to check them out. Failed. If the attention to detail on "Jeff" and "Chuckie" was accurately spread across all the others, we had the best-hung guys in the galaxy working for us. "Brian" was the most average, if you could call it that. "He" was in the back, so I'd missed him earlier. Yep, anatomically correct if faded memory served. I was impressed with my taste and selectivity. Oh, sure, I'd married the pick of the litter, but I'd known that already.

"You done checking everyone out?" Chuckie asked, sarcasm knob up to eleven.

"No need to be snide. I'm just trying not to scream again, okay?"

"Out of horror or excitement? I'm not sure from your expression."

"Hilarious." I looked at all of them. "Why isn't there one of Richard in here?"

"I'd make the others seem inadequate."

"Dude, I so love being your partner I can't even find the words. But, I'd also guess the plan was for one of the Ronnies to take your place, either Yates or Al Dejahl. But they would have to get rid of Jeff and Christopher, and Chuckie, in a way that wouldn't cause suspicion."

"Makes sense." Chuckie heaved a sigh. "I'd like to be on record that, as a straight male, this isn't remotely enjoyable for me, on any level."

"Noted, and I never had a doubt." Went back to examining the replicants. "I figure One through Three would be our three main men here." The ones that resembled Jeff, Christopher, and Chuckie all seemed alive. Their eyes were open, at any rate, and it felt as if they were watching us. "Bet we can't shoot them and expect to kill them."

"Doubt it." Chuckie was examining them, too, though none of us had crossed the threshold. "They're not all that accurate. I mean, decent for the shock value, but not for too much longer."

I managed not to mention that they were damned good for fakes. Put them into Armani suits so you couldn't see the very careful stitching, and they'd pass pretty well. "Um, Chuckie? Remember how all of you were hanging like meat in the prison in Paris? I think you all were supposed to, well, be the basis for the more accurate final models. The next level in robotic replacements—replace them with something that feels alive, presumably."

He was quiet for a couple of moments. "Oh."

I went to the doorway. "Chuckie, you said this room is rigged. So, where're the bombs and such?" The one who looked like Jeff raised its hand and pointed. "Oh. Uh. Huh. Erm. Hi. Yeah, guys? Number One is ready for sure. Can you dismantle the bombs?" It shook its head slowly. I couldn't think of it as Jeff, or even real. It was too beyond gross. And even more horrifying, because if they could think and were put together this well, the odds were they could feel.

"Don't go in there," Chuckie said.

"Dude, neither that moronic nor that foolhardy." I looked around at the others. It did seem only the three were alive. But never hurt to check. "Are the others . . . ready to go?" The Christopher one shook its head slowly. "Number Two is ready also, guys. Do you have more than one brain inside you?" The Chuckie one nodded this time. "And, happy day, Number Three's up and running as well."

I didn't want to ask, but I had to. But I sort of crept up on it. "Does one of you have a brother named Walter?" All three nodded. "And another brother named William?" More nods. Dammit.

I swallowed hard. "Um, Wayne, is that you?" All three heads bobbed. "Only you?" I asked almost hopefully. The heads shook. That was a negatory. So much for optimism.

"Wayne, the other three agents who were just killed, they in there, too?" Three heads bobbed. "How about the brains or consciousnesses or whatever from the other hybrids? Are they in there, too?" More head bobbing.

"Okay. Um. Great. Give us a moment to freak out. Be right back."

"How did we miss this? How could Jeffrey and Christopher have missed it?" White asked quietly as I moved away from the doorway.

I was shivering, but it wasn't really from cold. Horror made you shiver, too. "We're four stories underground, in a chamber built with the same stuff your other strongholds are, and undoubtedly reinforced by whatever horrible things the C.I.A. reinforces with. This was why they tried to get Jeff and Christopher and everyone during Operation Fugly."

"Why isn't there a replica of you in here?" I could hear Chuckie's wheels turning.

"Because I showed up less than two years ago, out of the blue, and they have no female hybrids to use for parts.

They have plenty of leftovers or extras to make the guys who increased in importance in the last couple of years. A-Cs come in all the skin tones and body types humans do, after all. I mean, we went through the Parts Department on our way in, remember? If you're cutting and pasting from almost two hundred options, it would make creating new male bodies reasonably simple. Maybe cutting them up while alive provides some horrible helpful oomph for this sort of mad scientist scheme. I really liked Amy's dad better when I thought this whole thing was about money."

"And they want your child to power them." Chuckie sounded furious. I was too horrified to feel all the fear and rage that knowledge gave me, but I felt plenty anyway.

The one that looked like Jeff opened its mouth. "Please." It got a lot of pain, suffering, and horror into that one syllable. I went back to the doorway. "Please."

I knew what they wanted me to do. But I couldn't. They were made out of Wayne, and other guys just like him. They weren't evil. They were our people, cut up and reattached and tortured. But they weren't willingly trying to hurt anyone. "I can't."

It reached both hands to me, in supplication. "Please. Make it stop."

I heard a voice in my mind. *Where's the fight in you when we need it?*

Christopher?

Not really. In a way.

Wayne?

Yes. All. We're all here. Kill us.

I can't. You can't ask me to kill you, kill all of you in cold blood.

You must. We won't be able to fight the programming. Took too much from my, his, our memories.

How?

Drugged, helpless, memory probes. They know what he knows, so all weaknesses, strengths. The torture meant we couldn't hide anything from the probes. Stop it before they condemn us to living hell.

What's above us, do you know or can you tell?

Nothing that will be damaged. Help, please. Getting stronger every minute. Once started, can't be stopped.

Will be worse monsters than any superbeing. Don't let them do this to us, don't let them win.

Wayne, I—

Please! Don't let me, us die in vain, or worse, live like this. Please . . . Commander.

I looked around. "Oh, um, Chuckie? There's a feed of Surcenthumain going into them."

"Wonderful. What are we doing to do?"

I took a deep breath. When it came down to it, I had no choice. "Mister White? Please make sure Chuckie's okay." I leaped into the Room of the Hot Zombies before Chuckie could grab me.

CHAPTER 82

I COULD SEE LIGHTS START flashing. Risked a look over my shoulder—White was dragging Chuckie away. Good. Turned back. Apparently all the zombies were ready to go, just not as ready as the main three, because all the eyes opened and they all started to move toward me.

Wanted out of the horror movie immediately. I ran to where the Jeff zombie had pointed. Yes, big bomb, ticking. I had about one minute from what the timer said. "What needs to be destroyed besides this room?"

Whole thing. Bombs will not do it alone.

"Mister White! You and Chuckie need to destroy the rest of the lab, all of it, and get out! And in less than thirty seconds. I'll meet you elsewhere!"

I looked around. Moved at the really fast hyperspeed and hoped that ACE was recovered, willing, and able to help me, though I couldn't spare the focus to ask. My fast hyperspeed wasn't graceful, but I was able to aim and hit, so to speak. Pulled all the tubes and wires out of the walls. All but the Jeff, Chuckie, and Christopher zombies stopped moving. A couple fell over. It had the potential to be comical, in about fifty years.

Saw a small red lever tagged "Final Solution" in white letters. Figured this was what I was probably going for under the circumstances and hoped I wasn't defusing the bomb somehow.

Something that felt like a dead human hand touched

me. I looked. The Jeff zombie had its arm around my waist. "Betting this isn't good."

Hurry. Pull it.

"I hope you know what you're talking about." I pulled the lever. A horrible sound started, like a car engine grinding but about a thousand times louder.

Thank you for saving us. Take care of our people. Take care of my brothers.

"Good Kitty," the Jeff zombie said as it flung me through the door.

I landed on Chuckie who just managed to catch me. "Can we go now?" he asked as he put me down.

"Is the rest of this house of horrors rigged?"

"We found a red lever that said 'Final Solution' and pulled it."

Grabbed his hand and White's. "I think that's our cue to leave." I looked back at the Zombie Room. They were watching me. The Jeff zombie raised its hand to say goodbye. And then the room exploded.

Ran like crazy for the main exit as the grinding sound got louder. Looked behind again and saw the room slamming in on itself. Decided I'd scream later and sped the hell up. Got outside one second before the door slammed. Didn't stop, figured we could come back later with a whole lot of flamethrowers to see if we'd destroyed everything or not.

The tunnel shook, and I stopped running because I lost my footing. White and Chuckie pulled me back to my feet. "Think it's going to come down?" Chuckie shouted over the noise. He was only gagging a little—from experience, adrenaline highs made the nausea of hyperspeed less.

"No," White shouted back. "It was A-C created, and our fail-safes are self-contained."

Apparently true. After a few minutes the rumbling and shaking stopped, and we were still alive and unburied. "Okay, that was, truly, the most horrible thing I've ever gone through, bar absolutely none."

"What part of 'not that moronic nor foolhardy' did you decide didn't apply to you?" Chuckie sounded as shaken as I felt.

"They needed me. They . . . wanted to die." I wanted to cry but just refused to allow it. "They were being programmed to take over and didn't want to be. They were all decent, normal A-Cs. They didn't deserve anything close to this."

"Why were they talking to you?" Chuckie asked.

I thought about it. "I think . . . some because I actually knew Wayne, some because of who they were being programmed to be. And . . . " I closed my eyes and concentrated. ACE, are you there?

Yes, Kitty, ACE is here.

Are they all dead or destroyed or whatever the right word is?

Yes. Kitty did well. ACE has joined their consciousnesses with Paul's permission. Paul will not tell, not even James.

Good. Tell . . . tell Wayne I'm sorry.

Wayne says what ACE says—Kitty did right.

I decided not to argue. Should we find out where the rest of this tunnel leads, or can it wait for another time?

It leads where Chuckie thinks it leads, Kitty. Kitty and Chuckie and Richard can come back, the others are worried.

Okay, thanks, ACE.

I opened my eyes. "Chuckie, where do you think the tunnel leads?"

"C.I.A. headquarters, probably to a Gaultier facility, perhaps to a couple of other locations."

"Well, figure you're right. Let's get back to the others." We ran back. I had to control myself from going as fast as I was able to—it would probably cause Chuckie to black out, and I couldn't take seeing him crumple right now. I was so thankful his and White's hands felt normal I couldn't even describe it. It was one thing to have looked at the replicants when they seemed like wax figures. It had been another to talk to them and be touched by them.

Reached the elevator, and Chuckie looked around for the Gaultier Circle of Doom. Found it on the side opposite the door; he kicked it, and we went up one level. I flipped the switch, we went the rest of the way up to the basement.

"How do you want to tell the others about this?" Chuckie asked me.

"I don't."

White stroked my back. "We must. It could happen again."

"I won't let it."

He pulled me into his arms and rocked me. "I know, Missus Martini. However, sometimes it takes more than one of us to save the world. And the more information we have, the more likely we are to spot threats, trends, and enemies."

I nodded. "I don't want to tell them tonight."

Chuckie sighed as we reached the top. "Kitty, they'll know. Abby and Mimi will pick it up, so will Martini and White. Frankly, the looks on both your faces, and, I'd guess, mine, will be a giveaway, too."

White let me out of his arms, and we all started up the stairs. "I suppose." I was in the lead, and as we got toward the top, I looked up. There was a man that looked like Jeff standing there, and I gasped and jerked back. Chuckie caught me and kept me moving forward. Got to the top and realized it was really Jeff—at least, the man who picked me up and let me wrap my arms and legs around him while I buried my face in his neck sure felt like the real Jeff.

"You three all right?" he asked as I felt us moving.

"In a way," Chuckie answered. "How much did you see?"

Jeff sighed. "All of it."

"You weren't supposed to," I said against his neck.

"Yeah? You weren't supposed to jump into the room with the bombs, either." I started to shudder, and he held me tighter. "I'm still the head of Field, baby," he said quietly. "And I'm never letting you race into danger without at least keeping an emotional eye on you."

"Are you all right yourself, Jeffrey?" I felt us start to move upward as White asked and figured we were in the elevator.

Jeff heaved a sigh. "Yeah. You did the right thing. They all . . . wanted to die. I could feel them once you were in proximity." He gave a bitter chuckle. "They did a good job, all things considered."

"Where's Jamie?" My head jerked out of Jeff's neck. "You were supposed to keep this from her and stay with her!"

He kissed my forehead. "I did. She's blocked from it, by me and by Christopher. And everyone else is guarding her. Including the Poofs."

"Only three of them."

He coughed. "Actually, several more."

"Come again?" I checked my purse. I still had three Poofs in it, snoozing away.

Jeff managed a grin. "Royal wedding's imminent, baby. Thankfully we don't know how, but we have many new Poofs."

"Poof breeding for fun and profit." Nice to know Christopher and Amy were, apparently, going to work out. Tried to focus on the positive that, from what I'd just learned, he'd keep her very happy in bed. Didn't help much.

"Fun. Not selling them." Jeff kissed me. "They aren't something to be sold."

"Okay, whatever you say." Not selling them meant more Poofs for me.

Elevator stopped, and we got out and into our room. Christopher was holding Jamie, and she seemed to be sleeping. People were milling about, and I couldn't feel any more dread, just an ache in my heart. Everyone looked at me expectantly, and Jeff gave me a little squeeze. "We'll debrief everyone tomorrow or the next day. Right now, I think we're okay to be in here, just the few of us who were planning to stay tonight. But the rest of you are welcome to stay if you want. I just recommend spreading out into the other rooms."

"Third floor has plenty of rooms, and they're all ready," Tito offered. "Walter and I sort of got our pick."

Tim shrugged. "I'm going back over to the Science Center. One of us should probably be there, no matter what, and Alicia's there." Michael, Jerry, Hughes, and Walker indicated they were heading that way as well.

Reader and Gower exchanged a look. "We need to get back over, girlfriend. Pontifex duties for Paul and all that." He gave me a long look. "We'll talk about it later, okay?" I nodded.

Chuckie looked at Naomi and Abigail. "Up to you two where you want to go. I think Kitty's right, it's over for right now."

Abigail shrugged. "Where're you going to stay?"

He shook his head. "No idea."

"Then we'll sleep here on the third floor," Naomi said. "That way, we're around to help out, and you get into bed that much faster."

Chuckie managed a laugh. "What are you, my mother?"

Naomi grinned. "No. Just worried about how you run yourself ragged."

"Mister White?"

"Staying here, Missus Martini. Third floor with the rest of the singles." He chuckled. "Just shout if you need us." With that he ushered everyone else out of the room.

Jeff put me down, and Christopher handed Jamie to me. "She won't be able to access it, any of it, unless her life depends on it."

"Why so?"

"We're big on the fail-safes." He bent and kissed my cheek. "You did the right thing, Kitty, the hard thing. The right thing for the right reason. Don't forget that." He clapped Jeff on the shoulder, took Amy's hand, and they left for their rooms.

Jeff and I went into the bedroom, and I put Jamie back into her bassinet. I noted we had a new, deluxe, extra levels Poof Condo in there. "When did that arrive?"

"I had Gladys send it over once we realized we were having a Poof explosion. You're not allowed to name any of them, by the way. Amy, Naomi, and Abigail already named one each before we could stop them."

"Do I want to know?"

"No worse than the name you came up with. No better, either."

"How many more are there?"

"Not sure. The numbers keep on increasing." He pulled me into his arms. "You okay, baby?"

"Sort of." Not so much. "What did you mean when you said they did a good job?"

He stroked my back. "The one that was supposed to be . . . me . . . it . . . loved you. The other two did, too." I started to sob. "Shhh, baby, shhh. They were thanking God you did what you had to. The only way to save them was to destroy what they'd been tortured and forced into against their wills. They don't hate you for doing it, baby, they love you for it."

Jeff moved us into bed and held me while I cried. I cried for a good long while. "They were innocent." I was winding down and finally able to talk again.

"Yeah, they were. And they were suffering, in a way I

thank God you couldn't pick up. It hurts to put something innocent out of its misery, baby, but doing that's just as brave as killing something evil. Braver, in a way."

"I feel horrible."

"I know. I think I'd worry if you didn't. But, I promise you, you did the right thing, and they appreciated it and always will."

I wanted to say that I couldn't believe people could do things this horrible, but I knew better. People were all too able. It was heartbreaking to discover A-Cs were, too. Somehow, Beverly and Yates aside, Chuckie's warnings notwithstanding, I'd managed to convince myself that all the Earth A-Cs were incapable of this kind of sick and twisted evil.

"Anyone's capable of it, baby," Jeff said as he kissed my head. "You know that. It's sweet that you convinced yourself otherwise."

"Sweet, not stupid or naïve?"

He hugged me tighter up against him. "No. Baby, like I told you the first night I knew you, you're not stupid and never have been. And believing the best in other people doesn't make you naïve, it makes you an optimist."

I managed a laugh. "If you say so."

Jeff shifted us a bit, slid one hand up my body up to my chin, and tilted my head. "I do. Know what else I say?"

"What?"

He gave me a slow smile. "I say the baby's asleep in her bassinet." Then he kissed me, and, happily, like always, I forgot about everything else.

CHAPTER 83

JEFF'S HANDS STARTED TO ROAM as our kiss got deeper. He had great hands, and they knew how to stroke innocuous parts of my body until my pelvis was slamming against his. Sometimes this took a few minutes, sometimes a few seconds.

Since we hadn't had a real chance for anything remotely resembling intimacy for what seemed like months but was, in reality, only a week or so, it only took seconds. He moved his mouth to my neck, and I started to moan. I heard Jamie make baby sounds and I froze.

Jeff stopped, leaned up, and looked over. "She's still fast asleep." He started kissing my neck again.

I gasped. "What if she wakes up?"

"Then we'll stop." He nibbled my ear.

"I hear something."

Jeff smiled against my neck. "It's my breath. The baby's asleep. Soundly. She's having happy little baby dreams, I can feel it." He ran his tongue down to the point where my neck met my shoulder.

"Uh-huh." I wanted to howl. But the baby was right there. I clenched my teeth together.

Jeff started to laugh softly and pulled away from me. "You want to just go to sleep?"

"No." This came out like a whine. "I just don't want to wake the baby up." I'd never been able to make love to Jeff and stay quiet. I could barely make out with him and stay quiet. A life of celibacy loomed ahead of me, and I started to cry.

"Oh, baby." Jeff shifted to a sitting position and picked me up so I was sitting in his lap with my legs around his waist. I was still blubbering. He pulled me against him and rocked me. "Kitty, baby, you're just tired. Couples make love while they have babies . . . how do you think you get more babies?"

"Everyone makes fun of how much noise I make. I'm going to wake and scare the baby. And I want to make love to you." This came out a whine-sob combo. I sounded like a tired little kid.

My phone rang. I didn't want to get it, but Jeff grabbed my purse, and I answered. "Hi, Mom." I sniffled.

"Kitten, James told us all seems to be well."

"I guess." I tried to stop crying but I couldn't.

"You and Jeff fighting?"

"No." This was on the quiet side of wail.

Mom was quiet for a moment. "Is the baby asleep?"

"Yes."

"Huh. And yet, you answered your phone. Tell me, did you get everything from Kevin?"

It had been so long ago, at least in terms of experience. "Um . . . think so."

"They why are you crying?"

"Is this a trick question?" Tears were still rolling down my face.

Mom sighed. "Let me talk to Jeff."

I handed him the phone. "Hi, Angela. No. No. No! Really? Hang on, let me check." Jeff moved me off his lap and raced into the nursery. I could still hear him. "Yes, we never got to it, it was under something that looks like a bizarre shower cap for thirty. Oh? Really. Huh. She seems so small to put out that much wet. Oh, really? Thanks for the heads-up. Yeah, seems easy. Batteries included? Yeah, you are the mother- and father-in-law I always hoped for. Great, talk to you later, thanks again. I think this will end up my favorite gift, right after the bassinet."

Jeff trotted back in the room, put my phone on the nightstand, took the bassinet and moved it carefully into the nursery. "What are you doing? Tito wants her right by me."

"He meant when we were asleep. Besides, your parents sent over something we missed that will solve everything. Just give me a second." I heard him doing something in there, and then he came out with a white plastic thing that resembled a walkie-talkie or a radio.

"What's that?"

"A parent's best friend. Baby monitor. The receptor end is in the bassinet with Jamie and the Poofs." He looked at the new Poof Condo, picked it up and moved it, Poofs and all, into the nursery as well. "With Jamie and all the Poofs. Now, you hold this end and listen." He handed me the radio thing, then trotted into the nursery again and closed the door. I heard him through the radio. "All Poofs, pay attention. Guard the baby and alert Kitty and Jeff if the baby needs anything or is in the slightest danger. Got that?" I heard loud purring. "Good, now hush, the baby's still asleep." The purring quieted and Jeff came out of the room, closed the door quietly, then hypersped into bed.

I put the baby monitor on the nightstand next to the phone. "You sure it works?"

"Uh-huh. Now, where were we?" He pulled my T-shirt off. "My God, they really are more magnificent right now." He buried his face in my breasts. I hoped I wouldn't leak. I listened—I could hear Jamie breathing normally and making sleeping baby sounds. Jeff kissed and stroked my breasts and I started to relax.

Jeff slid my pajama bottoms off and his mouth trailed after. He nibbled my inner thighs and I moaned. Loudly. I froze and listened. Jamie was still asleep, and I could hear quiet Poof purring.

I felt Jeff smile against me. "Told you." Him talking down there made me gasp. His tongue trailed all over me, and I went from nervous to howling orgasm in about ten seconds. Jeff moved up my body again and kissed me deeply. I clawed at his shirt and pants, and he got out of them quickly.

It was wonderful to feel his naked body against mine and even better to feel him inside me. Normally we'd have spent a lot more time on foreplay, because he liked to have me out of my mind, but in deference to how long the baby might or might not sleep, he didn't wait. I didn't mind in the least.

He was being careful, though, which, if I'd still been completely human, would have been necessary. As things had turned out, not an issue. I wrapped my legs around his butt and shoved. "I'm fully recovered. And I do mean fully."

Jeff grinned. "Just wanted to be sure." He kissed me. "I never want to hurt you, baby, you know that." He was still being extremely gentle.

"Jeff, please." I tried not to sound like I was begging while I slammed my pelvis against his, but didn't succeed, if the jungle cat look he got on his face was any indication. "She could wake up any second."

"What do you want, baby?" he asked, his voice a low purr.

"I want *you*. I don't want gentle, I want you; take me, please, now." I thrust against him wildly. "Please, Jeff, please."

He was on his forearms, his hands in my hair and on my head. "Mmmm, I don't know. I'm not sure you want it badly enough." He bent and ran his teeth and tongue against my neck. My body went crazy, and I started my standard cat in heat yowling.

Jeff moved up onto his hands, flipping my thighs up against his arms. He grabbed my wrists in each hand and held them under my thighs, effectively holding me captive. His eyelids were half-closed and the jungle cat look was in full snarl on his face. "You have no choice now," he growled.

He started to pound into me, and my orgasm hit. It was deep and powerful, and I wailed. He kept the speed and intensity going, and another orgasm crashed. Then another. My fingers dug into the bed—I couldn't move in this position, I could only let him do whatever he wanted. Another orgasm hit, and my eyes rolled back. He was going faster, and it was incredible. Fireworks went off in my head while my body shook from climax after climax, and I wailed from pleasure overload.

Jeff changed the rhythm of his thrusts, still strong and deep, but slower now, more deliberate. He was building me up again, I could feel it, but couldn't do anything to affect the outcome. He was in complete control of my body and playing me as if I was a Fender guitar and he was Joe Perry, Carlos Santana, and Eddie Van Halen all rolled into one.

I managed to look at him, and I could tell he was close.

He gave me the jungle cat smile again and said one word. "Mine." Then he slammed into me, still deliberately, but faster and faster with each thrust. My orgasm started, and he flung his head back and roared as he erupted inside me, and my body shuddered and shook in time with his, while I sobbed from the intensity.

Jeff let go of my wrists and let my legs down gently. He slid his arms around my back, and I managed to follow suit as he kissed me deeply and rolled us onto our sides. I was still trembling, and he stroked my back while he wrapped his leg over and around mine, pulling me even closer against him.

He finally ended our kiss and tucked my head under his chin. "Go to sleep, baby."

I nuzzled into his chest. I was almost asleep when I remembered something. "Have to get Jamie." Couldn't believe I'd forgotten about her and figured I was the winner of today's Bad Mother Lottery.

Jeff kissed my head. "I'll get her, baby. And, you didn't forget about her any more than I did. Even at the newborn stage, you're allowed to think about someone else now and then, including yourself." He unwrapped from me slowly, rolled off the bed, and went into the nursery. I heard an increase in purring in the baby monitor. "Not now," Jeff whispered. "No pets now. No, I mean it. Later." He sighed. "There, happy?" The purring increased. Jeff moved the bassinet back beside the bed, then went and got the Poof Condo and brought it back out. "Figure you want them out here, right?"

I managed to keep a straight face. "Yeah, great, thanks. Are Harlie and Poofikins still in with Jamie?" At the mention of their names, two Poof heads popped up from the bassinet. They mewled at me and then went back down, I assumed to snuggle next to Jamie. Figured I'd better get up to look, just in case.

"No, you stay lying down." Jeff came over and looked in the bassinet. "Yes, she's fine, and the Poofs are with her. You need to trust sometimes that everything is as fine as it seems."

"I suppose." Jeff got back in bed, pulled the covers over us and me into his arms. I snuggled back into his chest. "I've never lived outside the desert."

He held me closer. "I know. It'll be fine. We can go back any time you want, you know."

"Just want to be with you. As long as I'm with you and Jamie, don't care where we are. I mean as long as we're safe and secure and all that." Didn't figure it was safe to leave that open to interpretation.

Jeff chuckled. "Me too. Go to sleep, baby. Plenty to do tomorrow. Including test the range on the baby monitor."

I smiled and rubbed my face against his chest hair. "Yeah. This place has a lot of rooms."

"And we're going to test out every one of them."

"I love being married to you."

CHAPTER 84

WE WOKE UP LATE the next day. Well, that's not quite accurate. We woke up to feed the baby an hour after we'd made love. Then four hours later. Then another four. To make the waking up fully worthwhile, we made love each time after Jamie was back to sleep. On the next feeding arousal we decided we could get up and function outside the bedroom, which was something of a sacrifice on my part.

We didn't have a baby bath, but Jamie was small enough that we could give her a sponge bath in the sink. She seemed to enjoy it, and I knew Jeff and I did. Opened the drawers to find clothes for Jamie in there. They had to have been from the shower—none of them were black, and there wasn't that much white, either. Apparently Armani didn't go for baby wear, or Reader had managed to ensure one of us would be in an actual color, at least for a while. I put my money on Reader.

Called over, apparently all was quiet on our western front. So we made good on the plan to test the baby monitor. That thing was a godsend, and by the evening, I was feeling pretty good about the new penthouse. After all, we'd made love in almost every room, other than the nursery, which just seemed wrong to both of us, or the isolation chamber, which seemed unromantic to both of us and, homey room or not, decidedly creepy to me. The baby was basically angelic, and I was feeling pretty darned good about the way things were turning out, as long as I didn't allow myself to think about what I'd seen and done in the now-destroyed secret lab.

Dinnertime was upon us. The full-sized fridge worked just like the mini ones, and there had been plenty to eat and drink in it during the day. However, we figured it might be a good idea to see how the others were doing.

Intercommed over to Christopher first. "WHAT?"

"Oh, sorry, guess you two are still having sex."

"That was the idea, right, Kitty? I mean, why you had us come over last night?"

"Somewhat. We want to get dinner."

"There's food in our fridge. Bet there's some in yours, too. Go ahead, eat up." Boy, his snark was on full. Must have caught them at a really inopportune moment. Resisted the urge to keep them on the line. Barely.

"Okay, fine. We'll let you know if something's going on, but otherwise, have at it. Enjoy yourselves. And all that."

"Great, thanks." The com went dead.

"Boy, he was pissy."

Jeff laughed. "Can't imagine why."

Com came back on. Amy this time. "Kitty, I know it's New Year's Eve, but are you okay with us just staying in? Christopher and I really don't want to go out."

New Year's Eve already? How had this happened? "Sure, Ames, no problem. Enjoy yourselves. Ring in the new by ringing each other's bells and all that."

"Great, thanks, you're the best." Com went dead again.

Checked with Tito and Walter. Walter insisted he'd already had dinner and was not deserting his post, regardless of day or time. The kid was dedicated, I had to give him that.

Tito was working out and then had plans to go over to Dulce and hang with Michael and the single flyboys and, as near as I could tell, hit on my cousins and any Dazzlers whose resolve they hadn't managed to break down yet. Apparently Uncle Mort had left some Marines to keep an eye on things, and the Centaurion boys felt they needed to represent. From what I gathered, my grandparents had also had Uncle Mort bring in New Year's Eve party supplies—Dulce was going to be party central, to the point where the other A-C bases were going to be running on skeleton crews.

Jeff called Gladys and made sure continuous scans were running for all bases and strongholds, and he also tripled the security around Al Dejahl's chamber. Felt sorry for the Security A-Cs, but then again, most of them seemed a lot like Walter, extremely keen and more interested in doing their jobs slavishly than partying.

This left Chuckie, White, and the Gower girls. We decided to check on them in person, which was simple because they were all in the group dining area on the first floor. Shockingly, they were all having an early dinner and heading over to Dulce, too.

"Why don't you come with us?" Naomi asked. "It'll be fun."

"It'll be loud. Jamie isn't thrilled with loud."

"There's going to be a kid's party, a young singles party, a young marrieds party, and a wild old folks' party," Abigail supplied. "Your grandmothers set it all up. On two levels—kids and young marrieds on one, singles and wild oldsters on the other. It's going to be great; your Nana Sadie said she might have your Uncle Mort bring in more Marines."

"Oh, my God. Who put my grandmothers in charge?"

"James," Naomi said with a laugh. "He said he wanted to enjoy a party for once."

Figured. The King of Planning would know his counterparts, wherever they might be. "Well, have fun."

"You sure you don't want to come with us?" Chuckie sounded mildly concerned. "It's just going to be the three of you here by yourselves."

"Christopher and Amy are here. Sure, they're screwing like it's nineteen-ninety-nine, but they're here. And Walter's on duty."

"That kid needs to come over to the party. Talk about tightly wound."

"This coming from you?"

"I'm not now, nor have I ever been, tightly wound." This was true, I had to admit.

"Yeah, but you're Mister On Duty."

"It's New Year's Eve, and we've taken care of the threats. Sure, it's a perfect time for the last ditch attempt at a successful end to the elaborate ruse and plans of world domination, and yeah, okay, the Queen's out and potentially doing something we won't like. And, yes, the King may be captured, but in our brand of chess, he's still alive, so that means we haven't won. But we can't find her. I already have every agent searching for her. Wherever LaRue Demorte Gaultier's gone, it's not out in the open."

"You know, it's no wonder she's screwed up, being named The Street of Death."

"You sure you can trust the agents you sent, Reynolds? I mean, it was pretty clear you're unpopular." Jeff didn't sound like he was trying to start a fight; he sounded worried.

Chuckie shrugged. "I think the Poofs ate all the problems. But who knows? I don't." He didn't sound right. "I have the files we took from the lab, copied and in various secured locations. I'll get to them later and hopefully figure out what else we've missed, or at least who was knowingly involved, as well as who else in the C.I.A. wants to get rid of me." The words were sensible, but the way he said them made it sound like he wasn't really paying attention to what he was saying.

"Chuckie, are you okay?"

He gave me a long look. "As okay as you are, I'd guess."

"Oh. Yeah." I realized he wanted to stop talking about real life and all the things trying to destroy us and just go to the party to avoid thinking about what we'd seen in the Lab of Horror.

White cocked his head. "Perhaps you should join us."

I heaved a sigh. "No. Jamie really doesn't want to go." I didn't either, for a variety of reasons.

"Well, if you change your minds, come on over. I'm sure you guys will be allowed to drop in on the singles and wild oldsters floor." Naomi grinned. "We'll vouch for you, anyway."

I laughed. "Thanks, you're the best."

The four of them finished up, Tito joined them, and they all left for Dulce.

"Entertainment level?" Jeff asked. He didn't sound like he was interested, he sounded like he was worried about me.

"I just don't want to go to the party."

"I know. Totally out of character, but understandable." We went into the elevator, but since Jamie was with us, Jeff just put his arm around me and held me close. "So, you really feel I'm the pick of the litter, huh?"

"Yeah, of course. Why do you ask?"

"You checked out every naked replicant in that lab."

"Well, they were all naked. And it was a shock. Besides, I needed to see how well made they were. Not my fault they appeared anatomically correct."

"Just your fault that you did a detailed visual check. And then complained that you couldn't see my uncle naked."

"Hey, every one of them's seen my crotch, most of them during the most unattractive time *to* see my crotch. I think it was only fair, turnabout and all that jazz. They stared at me when I didn't know; I stared at them when they didn't know. See? Totally fair."

Jeff laughed. "And here I was worried for a minute there."

"You're always worried. Jealousy is your watchword."

"True." Reached our floor, went into our rooms. Jeff hypersped through and verified all was well, just in case. Then we went to the living room, turned on the fireplace, and cuddled onto the sofa together, Jamie still snuggled in her Snugli, one little hand on each torpedo, presumably to keep the food nice and accessible.

I leaned my head against Jeff's shoulder. "Why did they clear out all their belongings?"

He kissed my head. "You know, you're allowed to take the night off, baby."

"She won't. She has to get to Al Dejahl. Or destroy all of us. Or both. So she's not taking a break."

"Okay. No idea why nothing's here."

I stared at the flames. "They had the place rigged to go up, so maybe they moved all their things so that, should they blow the place, they'd still have their belongings."

Jeff nuzzled my head. "Maybe the building was supposed to go up, no matter what, not just as a fail-safe."

"Why? Secret labs and underground elevators are hard to come by."

"I know you think they were planning to go to Alpha Four. Gaultier sure seemed to think so, too."

I sat up. "Does the 'com on' thing work here?"

"Yeah, I had Gladys make adjustments."

"I need Christopher on the com!"

"WHAT?" Amazing. He sounded as pissy as the last time.

"Stop having sex, or at least pause. I need you to tell me if Leonidas, Victoria, and Alexander, over on Alpha Four, are all right or not."

"Come again?"

"Just do it!"

"Geez, fine." He was quiet. "They're healthy."

"When I was in isolation with you, you said Alexander and Leonidas were having some troubles but not with each other. What kind of troubles?"

"They don't like the people Reynolds sent over to help with interworld politics." There was a pause. "I don't think Leonidas trusts them, either."

I looked at Jeff. "Chuckie didn't send anyone."

Jeff pulled out his phone and dialed.

"Christopher, you remember what Amy's stepmom looked like?"

"Vaguely." I heard some talking in the background. "Okay, Amy has a picture of her and her father."

"Can you look at the picture and find her?"

"I'll try. Why?"

"Because she's the White Queen, and Chuckie's people can't find her. And I think they maybe can't find her because she's not on Earth."

CHAPTER 85

JEFF WAS STILL ON THE PHONE, but he nudged me. "You're right, Reynolds didn't send anyone over to Alpha Four."

"Get him back here, Naomi and Abigail, too. Alexander and possibly Leonidas will need to hear that from Chuckie himself."

"Ten to one they think they already did. Al Dejahl probably imaged himself to look like Reynolds."

"That would make sense. Alexander trusts Chuckie, and Leonidas respects him." Councillor Leonidas probably didn't trust Chuckie because I doubted Leonidas trusted anyone completely. He was too smart a man and too good a politician to give anyone full benefit of the doubt.

There was a pounding at the door. Jeff got up, and Chuckie and the Gower girls came in. I was happy to see that White was with them as well. "Heard you tell Martini you wanted us back here."

Brought them quickly up to speed. "Christopher, what have you got?"

"Nothing, but I think we need to contact Alexander."

"How?"

Jeff answered. "ACE. That's how I asked Alexander to be in our wedding."

"ACE isn't the phone company."

Jeff gave me a long look. "No. However, he's capable and normally willing." His eyes narrowed. "Why . . . oh.

Baby, ACE handles things like last night better than humans, at least from what Paul's told me."

"It was really horrible."

"Baby, we're trying to stop the ones who did it, right?"

I sighed. "Right." Shut my eyes and concentrated. ACE?

Yes, Kitty, ACE is here.

I'm sorry to ask this, but can you connect me to Alexander, over on Alpha Four?

Yes, Kitty. Alexander will be relieved. Alexander has wanted to come here for several days.

Decided not to question why ACE hadn't shared earlier. Because it fell under the rule of us having to do most things ourselves. I felt another mind, at the edge of my consciousness. Alexander? It's Kitty.

Kitty, I'm so glad. Councillor Leonidas and I are quite concerned. There's something wrong with the people Charles sent over.

Starting with the fact that he didn't. Don't know what they showed you or told you, or even if someone who looked and sounded just like him was there, it wasn't the real him. The usual take-over-our-world-and-the-galaxy plans are in place, and we're foiling them, but you're involved.

I'm not working against you!

No, dude, seriously, no kidding. And I don't think Leonidas is, either. I mean the bad guys are trying to take over Alpha Four, too. Who's there now?

Only one of them. We were told you were moving in an entire diplomatic crew in order to help us maintain good relations with Earth, because the heads of the governments were ready to come attack us.

Untrue. Is it a woman with you?

Yes. I can't stand her, there's something about her that makes me uneasy. And I know Councillor Leonidas feels the same way—he won't let her near my mother, and he hasn't allowed her to tour the other planets. She's been demanding it for some time.

I can only imagine. Okay, here's the thing—she and one other are the only conspirators left. If we can lock her up, we have them both in custody and can get information. If she's out, we're all still in danger.

I'll see what I can do.

Felt the connection break. Christopher and Amy were in the room with us now, fully dressed. "It's the usual for Operation Confusion. Alexander and Leonidas thought Chuckie had sent the Diplomatic Corps to help them. They couldn't stand any of these people, meaning they've been stressed and so perhaps not doing everything the conspirators wanted. But it explains why none of their stuff is here."

Jeff nodded. "Blow up the Embassy, make everyone think the Diplomatic Corps were all dead, they're on Alpha Four, able to do their dirty work with none of us on Earth any the wiser."

"Al Dejahl impersonated me?" Chuckie asked. He sounded thoughtful.

"I'd assume so. Alexander knows you too well for Amy's dad to have been able to pull it off, or for them to send an actor, and Leonidas is too smart for them to risk someone giving an off answer. And, since LaRue and Al Dejahl were at our wedding, they got to see us all interacting with Alexander and Victoria, you in particular." It was a creepy feeling in a boatload of creepy feelings, to know they'd been watching us, our every move, for years. Wondered if they'd made sex tapes of me and Jeff and, if so, if they'd been destroyed with the lab or not.

He laughed. "God, I love how you focus, baby." Jeff rubbed the back of my neck. "What's our next step?"

"No freaking idea. Chuckie? Christopher?"

Before they could answer, more knocking. Christopher got the door, and Gower and Reader came in. "ACE told me we have a problem," Gower said by way of hello.

"Two problems." Reader looked stressed.

"James, are you okay?"

He shook his head. "Al Dejahl's gone."

Let that sit on the air for a moment. "Anyone hurt? Or worse?"

"No one. It's just like when they removed the prisoners during the invasion—Security had no idea, nothing was disturbed, looked into the room, gone."

I looked at Jeff. "Where's Clarence? And the rest of his family?" Jeff dialed. I looked back to Reader. "The Lilith-PPB net did that last time. Any guess what did it this time?"

"Wasn't ACE," Gower said dryly. "But I'll let him talk to

you, because I haven't felt palsied for at least an hour and I miss it." Wow, even Gower had a sarcasm knob. He twitched, and the ACE voice started. "Kitty, Alexander is upset."

"Yes, thanks, big guy, I know that. Who got Ronaldo Al Dejahl out of his prison?"

"Alexander provided a small interstellar ship, because Alexander believed Chuckie had told Alexander to do so."

We all exchanged the "this so sucks" look. "So, um, just guessing here, but that ship has the ability to beam someone up, and LaRue's in it, and we can assume Al Dejahl's beamed?"

"No."

"Oh. Good news."

"The ship is capable of interstellar flight. It is also protected by a small version of what ACE is and Lilith was. It is that which rescued the prisoner. However, Councillor Leonidas has deactivated it. The PPB portion. They are unable to deactivate the ship, though Councillor Leonidas tried."

"So, good news is, they can't beam my baby up. Bad news is, we have two evil, enhanced megalomaniacs out there, racing around in space."

"Yes. Councillor Leonidas had tracking devices put onto the ship. All have been deactivated now, but Alexander says before the last one was deactivated, Alexander could tell the ship went to Earth, then left our solar system. It is not headed for Alpha Centauri, however."

We all looked at each other again. "Live to fight another day. So . . . these two are actually smarter than the rest. Or at least LaRue is."

"She's a total fucking bitch. But, yeah, she's smart." Amy's expression was as furious as her voice. She looked at Chuckie. "They killed my mom, didn't they? LaRue and my dad."

"Ah . . ." He shot me a desperate look.

Amy made the exasperation sound. "Chuck, for God's sake. Kitty said you were always right. Just tell me, yes or no—did they kill my mother?"

I shrugged. "Go for it, dude. What choice do we have, really?"

Chuckie sighed and looked back to Amy. "Yes."

Amy turned to Christopher. "Can we take a spaceship and go after them?"

Lots of coughing from the men. "Ah, Ames? We here on Earth don't exactly have a spaceship capable of following them, or anyone else, really."

"Why not? I mean, just borrow one from that Alexander guy. He's handing them out like party favors!"

"We'll go along," Naomi offered.

Abigail nodded enthusiastically. "We'll be able to track them, I'm sure."

Other mouths were opening, but Gower's opened first. "Kitty? ACE would like Amy to know that Alexander has offered to follow them."

"ACE, please tell him no, thank you."

CHAPTER 86

"WHAT?" THIS WASN'T JUST from Amy. Everyone other than Gower shouted that out.

Jamie fussed, and I got up and did the "in the Snugli" version of the Mommy Dance. "Guys, really. While I agree that the idea of pursuing the evildoers to the ends of the universe sounds all cool and whatnot, I'd like to point out a couple of things. One would be that Amy, Naomi, and Abigail are currently untrained in anything remotely resembling self-defense, weapons, or tactics."

"Never stopped you, girlfriend," Reader said with a grin.

"Per our latest set of megalomaniacs, I'm special. Two would be that we have just a tonnage of work that has to be done here, on Earth, to counter the latest decades-in-the-making elaborate ruse. Chuckie's got a list of all their operatives—we have to make sure they're hunted down, nullified, and give us their information. Three—we have a destroyed secret lab down under and a long tunnel going who knows where. Let's get what we can out of both. Four would be that Richard already told us what our new jobs were to be, and, news flash, unless or until we're actually assigned to another planet, this is the one we're supposed to protect and serve."

"They'll come back." Chuckie stated this as solid fact.

"Dude, no kidding. And in greater numbers, blah, blah, blah, seen that movie, too. Here's my final news flash—we freaking need the rest to have a chance to regroup, adjust, assimilate, and all that jazz. What's wrong with you people?

I have a freaking newborn here who's the target for our fave power couple. I want to be ready when they come back, not go running off like a moron so they can have a chance of success."

Everyone was staring at me, in shock, as near as I could tell. Gower nodded. "Councillor Leonidas agrees with Kitty. ACE agrees with Kitty, too." Gower did the twitch. "Fun as always."

"Why are all of you staring at me?"

"Because we're so used to you running off like a moron," Christopher supplied.

"Yeah? Well, I'm always right when I do it. Unlike some of you I could name."

Jeff nodded. "Yeah, you are, actually. Speaking of Clarence, Sylvia and the kids are with my parents, no idea where my great brother-in-law is. Richard, what do you want to do?"

White shrugged. "Missus Martini, sitting as she does at the top of our enemies' Most Wanted list, has the floor, so to speak. If she doesn't want to race off, I'd assume it means we shouldn't."

"See?"

Jeff shook his head. "You're proud you're number one on the hit list?"

"Yeah. The bad guys' evil computer said I'd single-handedly destroyed at least ten operations, and I only know about four. I'm pretty proud of myself. Destroyed without knowledge of. Totally cool." Jeff didn't look like he thought it was cool. "Steven Tyler and Joe Perry would think it was cool," I muttered under my breath.

Jeff rolled his eyes. "Yeah, yeah. Aerosmith is off limits to you, still and forever."

"You're high if you think I'm never going to an Aerosmith concert again."

"Oh, that I know. You're just going with me, and I'll have a restraint on you." Jeff heaved a sigh. "Okay. So, I guess that's it. We need to get something over to Alexander and Leonidas so they can confirm it's one of us dealing with them."

Chuckie nodded. "Sign, countersign, password, counter-password, individualized to each of them, and so forth. Standard. I'll run it by you before we finalize it."

Jeff sighed again. "Run it by James, Tim, and Serene."

Reader laughed. "Uh, Jeff? We're honored and all, and Serene is, I think, still jumping up and down because of her promotion from Ditz-in-Residence to Head of Imageering, but none of us expect to start tomorrow without your advice and guidance. Yeah, we've been paying attention, but, it's sort of sudden, and none of us saw it coming. None of us have takeover plans in place."

"Not even you, Mister Organizer?"

He grinned at me. "No, girlfriend, not even me. I never thought I'd see the day Jeff would retire from active Field duty."

"Hey, I'm a father now. Have two girls to watch over. I'm sure Jamie-Kat's going to be just like her mother . . . genetics seem to work that way. Need all my focus to keep up with them." He grinned at me, and I went over and sat on his lap.

"We don't have anyone to learn from," I reminded the others. "Diplomacy is sort of challenging."

"Especially for some of us," Gower said dryly.

White smiled. "I'm sure we'll all adjust. Everyone who works with us is adaptable, Missus Martini, or else they wouldn't be here. I'm sure Mister Reynolds and your mother can come up with some suggestions for who might be able to assist us with the learning of diplomacy. Sooner than all of you think, we'll be through the transition period and onto the next threat to our safety and security."

"My partner. I'm so proud. 'Cause, yeah, we know something else will show up."

"And return," Amy said darkly.

I shrugged. "We'll be ready. Might be tough, might be scary, will for sure have some freaking fugly, lunatic politician, or power-mad megalomaniac involved, but we'll have what they don't and they won't."

"What's that?" Chuckie asked. Everyone else looked like they didn't know, either. Amazing. Then again, maybe they were just being modest.

"Um, guys? Us. As long as we're together never torn apart sort of thing."

"Oh." Chuckie nodded. "Great. Yeah. I was hoping you had some weapon you hadn't told me about."

"Yeah, or knew some weakness of Al Dejahl's," Reader added.

"Or had a bomb strapped to my stepmother's ass," Amy snarled.

"I thought she meant our alliance with Alpha Four," Naomi admitted.

Abigail shook her head. "Me, I thought it was going to be that ACE was going to go kick butt or something."

Christopher sighed. "I was hoping you knew where they were headed. They're past whatever range I have, so, no clue now."

"Geez, last time I try to give you guys a 'go team' talk. Fine, get out and go back to the party. I think we actually can, now, relax and take the rest of the night off."

CHAPTER 87

GOT THE ENCOURAGEMENT to come over to the party again. Declined. Christopher and Amy decided that, since they were up, they'd go to the party, too. White ushered the gang out, and we were alone, back to just the three of us.

Jeff whipped up dinner. He was a great cook, the kitchen had everything you could want or need, and the Elves provided all the fixings. There was a breakfast bar with stools, so I perched and watched while he cooked. The Elves took care of cleanup. I loved the Elves, whoever they were. I didn't believe Christopher's weird scientific explanation, and even if it made sense, someone was doing all the housekeeping work. Wondered if, now that we were here, I was supposed to leave milk in shoes or silver dollars or something.

Jeff laughed. "No. The Operations team's jobs are to do all forms of maintenance. We're not big on being tipped for doing our jobs, baby." He'd gone for simple on the meal—steak, potatoes, and vegetable primavera.

"Dinner smells great."

"Thanks. Where do you want to eat, at the bar, in the nook, in the informal dining room, or in the formal dining room?" He was serious.

"Um . . ."

He grinned as he picked up the filled plates. "We'll go for the nook." Which was in the kitchen, table for four.

Cozy. More my speed. "This way I get to sit across from you and watch you and Jamie."

Dinner was nice. Just us, talking about things that didn't matter to the whole world. I felt more normal after eating and being with Jeff this way. I didn't feel celebratory, but my heart wasn't aching so much, and I wasn't too homesick for either Arizona and New Mexico in general or the Lair in particular.

We finished up, and Jamie wanted her next meal, so we took care of that. Jeff gave me a funny look as he changed her diaper. "Put on some warm clothes and boots."

"I'm from freaking Arizona, Jeff. I don't own those items."

He rolled his eyes. "This from the girl who talks about Elves."

Oh. Duh. Well, it'd been a busy week. Got up and went to the closet. "Wow. Black pants and a white sweater, black hooded coat, black boots. Thank God. I was so afraid I'd be seen out in like red or blue or something."

"I understand the diplomats have to wear colors. And," he added as if he were eating a lemon, "they have to dress casually frequently, to fit in."

"Wow. So I'll see your amazing butt in jeans again sooner than in a year? I can get excited about the new job after all."

I got dressed while Jeff put Jamie into another pink Baby Minnie sleeper and then into a pink Baby Piglet snowsuit, complete with fleece-lined hood. It was a little big on her, but not a problem.

Someone knocked, so I took Jamie and went to the door. Reader was there. Got the cover-boy grin. "Figured you'd need this sooner than whenever." He pushed a stroller in. Top of the line, greatest thing ever. I'd drooled over it for three months, but Jeff had felt it was too much. Reader, apparently, hadn't agreed.

"Oh, James." Gave him the around the neck with one arm squeeze.

He laughed. "I had it modified." He pointed to the handle, where I could see a variety of A-C buttons there, including "Laser Shield" and "Invisibility Cloak." "They'll protect you and Jeff, too, anyone, really, as long as you're touching the stroller."

"James, you're so awesome. I love you so much."

He kissed my cheek. "I love you, too. Enjoy. Looks like you're going out. Good. I was hoping this would move you along." He put his arm around me. "Christopher showed us all what went on down in the lab, Kitty. Jeff felt we needed to know. He was right—we did need to see. And we needed to see what you did, too. You did the right thing, the hard thing, and the thing the evil people would never have done. And now you have to get past it. Start by doing something you and your husband haven't been able to—go enjoy being the new parents of a beautiful baby girl."

Jeff came out. He was, shockingly, dressed in the suit. However, in deference to the snow and the cold, he was in a white sweater over his white shirt. Impressively, no tie. It was New Year's Eve, so we were going *casual*. He also had a long, heavy coat, no hood. Guess hoods were only for girls and babies, per the Elves.

He had the diaper bag, and he gave Reader a beaming smile. "You're the best, James."

"I thought you were going to complain about this model. You said you didn't want it. Not that I mind."

"Nah. The moment I realized just how much stuff we have to cart along was the moment I decided the one with all the stuff on it was the way to go."

"When was that?"

"Five minutes ago."

Reader laughed. "I'm going back to the party. I'll tell you what your family's up to later. But don't worry, I'm having it videotaped."

"Can't wait. Say hello to Mister Joel Oliver for me."

"Will do. He said to tell you the Gucci Baby Book is from him. I already sent it to be checked for bugs and hidden cameras." Reader gave us both the cover-boy grin, then sauntered off.

Jeff took Jamie from me and settled her in the stroller. "Get your purse."

I trotted in, grabbed my purse. "All Poofies who want to stay warm, stay here. All Poofies who want an adventure in Kitty's purse, hop in." There was much mewling and purring. I checked. Wow. I had a lot of concentrated cuteness in there. Cool. Made sure everything was off and closed or whatever it was supposed to be and joined Jeff in the hallway. "Where're we going?"

He just smiled as we walked to the elevator. "You'll see."

CHAPTER 88

"OH, JEFF, IT'S BEAUTIFUL."

"Yeah. Aunt Terry took us here every year when we were kids. I think the last night to see it is tomorrow . . . if you want to come back."

We were at the National Christmas Tree, by the White House. The tree was huge and patriotically decorated. There weren't a lot of other people here tonight. Most were at parties or already in bed. A light snow was falling. Jamie was out of the stroller and in my arms, the Poofs and my purse were in it. All of us were watching the lights.

"I do."

"Still love hearing you say those words to me." He kissed me as I cuddled Jamie between us. He ended our kiss slowly. "Still love doing that, too."

"I still love doing everything with you, Jeff."

He grinned. "Good to know. Oh! Almost forgot." He reached into his pocket. "I have something for you." He handed me a small package wrapped in festive paper.

Oh, great. I had nothing for him. "Oh, thank you."

Jeff took Jamie from me. "Open it."

"Jeff, I don't have anything for you."

He gave me a blank look. "Why should you?"

"Uh, Christmas, Hanukkah, New Year's, whatever reason you're giving me this."

"Just had my child. I'd have given it to you a week ago, but for some reason, things were a little tense."

"Oh." Felt stupid. "I should still have something for

you." Jeff was incredibly thoughtful, and I was incredibly not-so-thoughtful.

He laughed. "Open it, baby. I like giving you presents a lot more than I like getting them. You are my present, remember? And you gave me the next best present in the world a week ago." He kissed Jamie, who cooed at him and the lights.

I opened. The light from the Christmas tree showed a beautiful scarf—in red. "Oh, wow, Jeff. Color! And it's gorgeous, too."

"Unroll it."

As I did, I felt something smaller inside. Decided it would be smart to finish unrolling carefully. A diamond tennis bracelet landed in my palm. "Oh, Jeff. Oh, my God." There was one charm hanging on it, a single diamond encircled in platinum, with December 25th etched on it.

"We can add more, if . . . you still want more." He sounded hesitant. I looked up at him. I could tell what he hoped I'd say, but also that if I didn't, he'd still love me.

I leaned up and kissed him. "Jeff, I want as many of your children as we're given. Whether that's one, two, or many."

"Really?"

I laughed. "Yes. Really. And I want to practice all the time, too. Just so we never miss a chance and all that."

He grinned. "Like I've said since the moment I met you, I love how you think."

Jeff kissed me again, our usual wonderful kiss. Then he gave me Jamie, put the bracelet on my wrist, wrapped the red scarf around my neck, and put his arm around my shoulders. We stood there, watching the tree that represented, in its way, everything we worked and sacrificed for every day, while the snow fell softly on our little family and the rest of our lives stretched ahead of us.

It was the best New Year's Eve of my life.

Coming in April 2012.
The fifth novel in the *Alien* series
from Gini Koch

ALIEN DIPLOMACY

Read on for a sneak preview

"WHO'S THAT?" LEN ASKED.

"Someone from my Washington Wife class."

"Why's he here?" Kyle asked.

"No idea."

I pondered this weirdness for about half a block, when a familiar figure with black hair and beard stepped out of a doorway. He was dressed as I was used to, in casual, baggy, well worn but clean clothes, big camera around his neck. I still couldn't tell if the clothes were hiding muscles or pudginess. He was under six feet and much smaller than Len and Kyle all the way around.

He beamed at me, blue eyes twinkling. "Here you are, my favorite alien lover."

"Mister Joel Oliver, always a pleasure. Meet Len and Kyle, my friends who, like me, don't believe in aliens."

Oliver snorted. His snort was a lot more like mine than Mrs. Darcy Lockwood's. I wondered for a moment what her opinion was of Mister Joel Oliver, then figured it had to be poor. He was the main investigative reporter for the *World Weekly News* after all, and I didn't have to ask to know what Lockwood thought of those kinds of newspapers.

Len and Kyle nodded at him. "Nice to meet you, Mister Oliver," Len said, in a tone indicating he was lying.

Oliver smiled wider. "Mister Joel Oliver, please. As Missus Martini is well aware, a man in my position needs to ensure whatever shreds of respect he can garner. How are you, my dear?"

"I'm good. Why are we having this conversation?"

Kyle shoved past Oliver, gently, as Len took my arm and kept me and the stroller moving along.

Oliver wasn't fazed, of course. He trotted along with us. "I have more information," he said quietly.

"This is you barking. This is me being the wrong tree."

"I can't risk going to your oldest friend right now," Oliver said as he tried to get a couple of snaps of Jamie, which Kyle quite effectively blocked. Football players as paparazzi protection was rather brilliant. Not a surprise Chuckie had come up with it.

"And why is that?"

"I'm being followed." He said it calmly.

"Turn about being fair play and all that?" Hey, I had a sarcasm knob, too.

Oliver sighed. "I'm not your enemy. But I believe the people following me are."

We turned a corner and kept on walking. We weren't rushing; in fact, we were going quite slowly. I was used to having big guys around, but Len and Kyle were clearly adjusting to their new protection detail, and having Oliver along was causing some issues on the sidewalk. I considered if we should just run for it. It was a safe bet that Len and Kyle would have no problem beating Oliver over a short distance, and circumstances constantly ensured that my sprinting skills remained topnotch.

Jamie started to cry, loudly. We all stopped while I did a fast diaper check. Oliver poked his head around as I was doing this. "Oh, what a beautiful baby!" He sounded sincere, and the camera wasn't snapping.

Jamie looked right at him, gurgled and smiled. He bent closer; she reached up and tugged on his beard. Oliver laughed and tickled her tummy, earning giggles. I cleared my throat and Oliver backed off. Jamie looked back at me. I decided to take the hint.

"Fine. Why don't you come along with us and share the latest?"

Len and Kyle gave me looks that said I was crazy. I was used to looks like that. Since meeting the boys from A-C, I got those looks on a very regular basis. "Jamie likes him."

Which, because she had both empathic and imageering blocks implanted, courtesy of Jeff and Christopher, likely meant that ACE was giving me a hint.

Since ACE tended to leave us alone so it didn't interfere with our free will, I'd learned to pay close attention to whatever hints Jamie seemed to be giving me. I was all over getting an assist from the superconsciousness whenever possible. I liked being alive and keeping my nearest and dearest alive, too.

Len shook his head. "You're the boss."

We started off again, Len on one side of the stroller, Kyle on the other, Mister Joel Oliver walking next to me while I pushed. If we went at a leisurely pace, this wasn't too bad. The limo appeared to be several blocks away, but even though it was cold, it was a pretty day, so I decided to enjoy our impromptu constitutional. "So, MJO, how did you find out about the assassination attempt?"

"MJO?"

"I like to save the breath when I can."

He gave me a look that said he didn't believe me. I glared at him. He sighed. "I have a network of informants. All of them agree that something big is going down, and the President's Ball came up as the likely location more often than not."

"That's it? Something big?" We had our entire network panicked over this? I began to wonder if Chuckie needed a vacation or something.

He sighed again. "Missus Martini, there's more to it than that. I have informants all over the world. When, worldwide, the same things start popping, you have to pay attention."

This I knew to be true. "So, why are we assuming assassination?"

"Every major political player will be there, foreign dignitaries, high-ranking military..."

"Got it. It's essentially like shooting fish in a barrel, right?"

"So it seems. Thank you for listening to me," Oliver said quietly. "I appreciate you and Mister Reynolds occasionally treating me as more than an idiot annoyance."

I broke down and shot him a smile. However, I neither confirmed nor denied. No reason to let Oliver feel like he was a trusted member of our team, though he certainly seemed to want to be. "You said you had more news."

"I do. I haven't shared it yet because I still feel I'm being followed."

I faked a trip, stopped and checked my shoelace, taking the opportunity to do a quick scan around me. I saw no one and nothing suspicious, however, if they were good, I wouldn't be likely to spot them anyway. "So, now whoever's following you knows you're with me," I said as we started up again. "How is this a good plan? If you have a plan, I mean."

"You have a beautiful little princess there, and I mean that quite literally. I'm negotiating for another *World Weekly News* exclusive. After all, we got all the pictures from your wedding. It makes sense that we'd want to gain the exclusive baby pictures. And, of course, I'm approaching you while your husband isn't around because he'd object and you might not."

It was a good story, actually. I figured it was even one Chuckie would approve of, though Oliver was right—there was no way Jeff would okay pics of Jamie being published anywhere, let alone in the tabloid with the worst reputation around. "So, you spend time on that or are you just winging it?"

"Unlike you, I tend to think things out beforehand. However, a good investigative journalist has to be instantly adaptable."

I decided to let the comment about my ability to plan pass. After all, in some ways, he was right. "Who's following you?"

"I'm not sure." We finally reached the limo. Against all odds, Len had found a street without any cars on it. "Please check the car before we get into it," Oliver said to Len.

"Why?" Len asked.

"You shouldn't have left it out of your control."

I coughed. "They're special cars."

"Yes, but even the most advanced car can be tampered with if it's left unattended."

Len looked like he felt he was flunking his first assignment. "Len, it's fine."

Kyle looked worried. "Not if there's something wrong. Mister Reynolds will be furious."

"Dudes, seriously, we leave the limos unattended all the time. But, if you have some special way of checking for car bombs, let's be paranoid. Chuckie will be happy if we find a bomb, in that sense, and pleased with your precautionary instincts if we don't. Win-win all the way around."

The SUV we'd been in for a big battle during Operation Fugly had been tampered with—by an A-C. I'd learned early on that we couldn't really trust anyone and were probably not safe when we thought we were. While Len and Kyle made a couple of phone calls, I did what Reader wanted. I thought. The first thought that came to mind was that ACE had clearly allowed Jamie to share that she liked Oliver. Meaning, there was a reason ACE felt Oliver should be with us, right now.

I looked up and down the street. "Why are we the only car on this street?"

"A good question," Oliver said. He sounded like he thought it was not only good, but that it had occurred to him, too, and he didn't like his conclusion. I was with him.

"We weren't when I parked it," Len said. "Two cars pulled out while I was cruising around, so I took advantage of the opportunity." He and Kyle exchanged a look. "I think we might want to move away from the limo."

I did a fast inventory. I had Jamie, my purse, the stroller, and her diaper bag. I didn't think we had anything of importance in the trunk, and the boys hadn't brought any paraphernalia with them that wasn't on their persons. "What about Jamie's car seat?"

"If I were planting a bomb that wasn't set to go off when the car started," Oliver said quickly, as Kyle moved to open the door, "I'd absolutely figure the new mother would want her baby's car seat."

Kyle's hand froze. "That makes sense to me. You think Kitty's the target? Or the baby?" He growled this last question. I liked overprotectiveness toward my child from our new bodyguard.

"As I already told your superior, I don't know who the target is. However, Missus Martini is on the guest list for the President's Ball, ergo, she's a potential target." I realized we weren't even pretending that Chuckie was just a globetrotting millionaire playboy, nor we were pretending that Len and Kyle were merely along for the ride. Under the circumstances, I decided to table my worry about our lack of good security procedures and just accept that Oliver clearly knew all about us. No one believed him other than us, so really, it was back to the bigger issues for me, like getting away from a potentially rigged limousine.

We quickly moved our little group across the street and back down the block. "I'm not that new a mother anymore," I mentioned to Oliver as I took Jamie out of the stroller and held her tightly.

"Three months is still new," he said with a smile. "How long for the bomb squad?"

"Not too much longer," Kyle said shortly. He and Len were busy looking all around. We weren't exactly being subtle, but no one really seemed to be around to notice.

I dug my phone out of my purse. Jeff answered immediately. "What's going on? Reynolds has been making urgent calls for the past few minutes and his stress is off the charts."

"There's been a lot of that today. Your blocks okay?"

"I'm fine. I'm concerned about my wife and child."

"We're fine, as far as we know. We're with our personal paparazzo. Len found a too-convenient parking place and we're all waiting for some folks to come and let us know if our limo's been rigged or not."

"Reynolds says his people will be there in another minute. How far from the limo are you all?"

"We can still see it."

"Get farther away."

"Jeff, really—"

I was going to tell him he was overreacting. Only the limo exploded before I could finish my sentence.

Gini Koch lives in the American Southwest, works her butt off (sadly, not literally) by day, and writes by night with the rest of the beautiful people. She lives with her husband and daughter, 3 dogs (aka The Canine Death Squad), and 3 cats (aka The Killer Kitties). When she's not writing, Gini spends her time going to rock concerts with her daughter, teaching her pets to "bring it," and driving her husband insane asking, "Have I told you about this story idea yet?" You can reach her via her website (www.ginikoch.com), email (gini@ginikoch.com), Twitter (@GiniKoch), or FaceBook (facebook.com/Gini.Koch).

Gini Koch

The Alien *Novels*

"This delightful romp has many interesting twists and turns as it glances at racism, politics, and religion en route. Darned amusing." —*Booklist* (starred review)

"Amusing and interesting...a hilarious romp in the vein of 'Men in Black' or 'Ghostbusters'."—*Voya*

TOUCHED BY AN ALIEN
978-0-7564-0600-4

ALIEN TANGO
978-0-7564-0632-5

ALIEN IN THE FAMILY
978-0-7564-0668-4

ALIEN PROLIFERATION
978-0-7564-0697-4

ALIEN DIPLOMACY
978-0-7564-0716-2
(Available April 2012)

To Order Call: 1-800-788-6262
www.dawbooks.com

DAW 160

Celia Jerome

The Willow Tate *Novels*

"Readers will love the first Willow Tate book. Willow is funny, brave and open to possibilities most people would not have even considered as she meets her perfect foil in Thaddeus Grant, a British agent assigned to look over the strange occurrences following Willow like a shadow. Together they make a wonderful pair and readers will love their unconventional courtship." —*RT Book Review*

TROLLS IN THE HAMPTONS

978-0-7564-0630-1

NIGHT MARES IN THE HAMPTONS

978-0-7564-0663-9

FIRE WORKS IN THE HAMPTONS

978-0-7564-0688-2

And don't miss:
LIFE GUARDS IN THE HAMPTONS
(Available May 2012)

To Order Call: 1-800-788-6262
www.dawbooks.com

DAW 170

Katharine Kerr

The Nola O'Grady *Novels*

"Breakneck plotting, punning, and romance make for a mostly fast, fun read." —*Publishers Weekly*

"This is an entertaining investigative urban fantasy that sub-genre readers will enjoy...fans will enjoy the streets of San Francisco as seen through an otherworldly lens."
—*Midwest Book Review*

LICENSE TO ENSORCELL

978-0-7564-0656-1

WATER TO BURN

978-0-7564-0691-2

DAW 180